THE
SHOP
BEFORE
LIFE

THE SHOP BEFORE LIFE

NEIL HUGHES

ENTHUSIASTIC WHIM PRESS

Published by Enthusiastic Whim
www.enthusiasticwhim.com
Paperback ISBN: 978-0-9931668-4-6
Hardback ISBN: 978-0-9931668-5-3

Cover art by Tom Humberstone
www.tomhumberstone.com
Book design by Sienna Tristen
www.siennatristen.com

The author gratefully acknowledges the creators of the following typefaces, which
were used for the text of the book and in the production of some artwork: 'Radley',
'Jost*' and 'Gentium', all available under the SIL Open Font Licence, and 'Colus',
available under the Fontfabric Licence v2.00.

For everyone still choosing who to become.

 *zero*

TO FULLY UNDERSTAND Faythe's story—or, truly, anybody's—you must first understand the entire history of the universe. Luckily, provided you're willing to skip a detail or two, that won't take long.

Before anything, there was nothing. But now, there's plenty of stuff. Bacteria. Geese. Tables. More kinds of cheese than anybody could count. Trees. Cathedrals. Even *goats*.

Some consider it strange that each of these 'goats' appears with an individual personality. Why do those in charge consider *that* necessary? Surely nobody would object if all goats were exactly the same.

Perhaps Management simply appreciate the personal touch. After all, they don't reserve this luxury solely for goats. Virtually anything more complex than a worm comes with unique personal characteristics.

In *most* cases, it is unclear how this individuality comes about. How does, say, any given potato know to be one shape and not another? Frustratingly, no matter how forcefully they are begged or threatened, no potato has ever answered even this simplest of questions.

Fortunately there is one species that is simpler than potatoes: humans.

This unusual bunch spend most of their time on Earth, but new humans don't simply appear there out of nowhere. That would be *ridiculous*. Instead, they appear out of nowhere in the prelife. From there, they travel to Earth as quickly as they can, pausing at the very end to visit the Shop Before Life, the magical emporium where they choose who they will become.

It's a shame that no other species handles their affairs in such a straight-forward and easily understandable manner. Certainly, whatever the goats are doing, it doesn't involve the Shop. In fact, during the entire history of the universe, only one goat has ever been seen in the Shop Before Life—and the Security officer involved was fired shortly afterwards.

Faythe was mostly unaware of all this. She knew about the Shop, of course. Everyone did. But it had been decades since she'd given the place much of a thought. And she knew nothing at all about goats.

Her prelife had been derailed long ago by a particularly vicious case of curiosity. Most people rush to Earth, but she had succumbed to the opposite impulse and simply stayed put. Time was plentiful, so why hurry? The Shop Before Life would always be there, and Earth always beyond it.

And so, centuries ago, she had abandoned the well-worn Road to the Shop, diverted by nothing more than the intriguing sight of a tall tree atop a faraway hill. From this peak, she had been drawn into a valley filled with interesting-looking plants, after which she'd followed a deep blue stream up another hill, and from there she'd seen a towering rock jutting high above a plain, far beyond the Beginning of the Road.

That rock—*the* Rock—turned out to contain deep caves, and, even more thrillingly, a small community of others who'd also been distracted from the natural human impulse to migrate towards the Shop. She had been welcomed with open arms and so she'd stayed . . . just for a short while.

An instant later, two centuries had passed, and the instinctive itch saying 'go to Earth' was barely even a memory.

# *one*

IT WAS SEVENTY-FOUR THOUSAND and twenty-one days since Faythe had first awoken at the Beginning. A day of no significance whatsoever.

Then again, no day had been significant for a long, long time. She hadn't even noticed the passing of her two hundredth pre-birthday until weeks afterwards—which was, honestly, a mercy. Some decades ago her friends had discovered the Earth tradition of blowing out one candle for each year of existence, and ever since, pre-birthdays had become a devastating test of endurance.

On this particular unremarkable day, she was atop the towering Rock which had been her home for almost her whole existence.

She sat cross-legged in the sunshine, enjoying the heat of the rough stone on her legs, and concentrated as she piled stones into a pleasing shape. This was partly what passed for fun after two centuries living inside a hollowed-out rock in the middle of nowhere, but mostly she was waiting for an opportunity to try one of her *ideas*.

Just as she was about to give up on making these particular stones into a perfect pyramid, a flicker of motion from below drew her attention. She peered over the smooth edge of the Rock with a thrill of anticipation as she saw what she'd been waiting for. Jahu was approaching his customary sunbathing spot.

She held her breath and ducked as her friend paused to peer around suspiciously. It was fine, though—he didn't even attempt to look up.

3

She'd been counting on this neglect of the third dimension ever since she'd heard that on Earth people consider it plausible for someone to be surprised by a stationary banana skin on a floor.

Apparently satisfied, Jahu lay down and closed his eyes. She grinned. It was time for today's experiment in creative annoyance.

Moving quietly, she released a rock onto the steep slope beneath her. In accordance with the ancient principles of gravity, it dropped *exactly* like a stone, tumbling down a narrow gap and out of view.

Perfect.

She counted. *One two thr-* CUCLRNCH. The sound of a falling rock hitting a sturdy homemade seesaw was one of her favourites.

Her eyes darted back and forth, scanning the space between Jahu and the Rock. If the seesaw worked as expected then . . . there!

A tiny cluster of blurs whizzed towards her unsuspecting friend from the base of cliff, below the overhang. Quickly, she whistled for his attention, and—yes!—he sat up to wave, just in time for the battalion of flying eggs to smash into his happy, smiling face.

Furious cursing mingled with her gleeful laughter, loudly filling the space between the Rock and the nearby woods.

Today's prank had definitely been a success.

"You are the *worst* person." Jahu was wearing a fresh shirt and a furious expression as Faythe entered the cave system beneath the Rock.

After thousands of years of human occupation, the Rock was surprisingly spacious and comfortable, at least by rock standards. A long, straight shaft in the ceiling brought evening sunlight into the cosy living room, where it illuminated both the hand-made furniture and Jahu's righteous indignation for her to enjoy.

"You've always been the worst," he continued. "One day Management will hear about you, and you'll suffer some sort of eternal punishment. And you know what? You'll deserve it!"

This was too much. She cackled, which only irritated him further.

The final remaining occupant of the Rock, Tapak, didn't look up. He was at the far end of the room, chopping vegetables and dumping them into a pot. Nearby, the fire crackled and belched smoke up a narrow chimney.

"Eternal punishment!" She made a mock-terrified face as she pulled up a chair next to Jahu. "Management famously hate eggs, pranks and fun, don't they?"

He narrowed his eyes. "It's not the prank, it's the cruelty. I was sure I was safe this time."

"That's right," she said, with pride. "I waited for *ages*." She nudged him under the table. "You have to admit it was funny though."

"No."

Tapak coughed from across the room. "In fairness to Faythe, it's definitely funny." He returned his attention to the vegetables.

Jahu gave the back of Tapak's head a long look, and then sighed. "This is why we have no other friends."

She stuck out her tongue. "Lucky for me you'd never be so immature."

This post-prank teasing was always her favourite part. No doubt he would already be planning tomorrow's revenge, just as she was planning for the day after.

"Well, lucky for me I don't need to be so immature." Jahu leaned back and slid his feet up onto the table. It didn't look very comfortable, but he grinned nevertheless. "The universe is going to punish you for me. Isn't that right, Tapak?"

She raised an eyebrow. "Oh yeah? Management themselves said so, did they?"

"Even better." He rocked his chair back on two legs. "The storyteller told tales of all of our futures. And yours is . . ." He let out a slow whistle.

Faythe's mouth dropped open. "Uh . . . a storyteller? When? Don't lie to me!"

"Do I ever lie? He came last night, while you were clunking around above. We shouted for you but you never heard."

"I did hear," she said, through gritted teeth. She'd spent the previous evening experimenting with her seesaw. "I thought you just wanted me to clean up in here."

"That's *exactly* what we wanted," said Tapak, still not looking up from

5

his work. "But we also thought you'd want to meet the storyteller."

"Of course I'd want to! I can't believe you didn't physically come get me."

She aimed a swipe across the table at Jahu's feet. He scrambled to get out of the way, narrowly avoiding tipping his chair backwards.

"You missed!" he gloated. "Just like last night!"

"But what did I miss?" She glared at Jahu. *No.* She wouldn't give him the satisfaction of asking again. "Tapak?!"

The rhythmic chopping noise halted for a moment. "Do you have to drag me into it? It was just the usual stories."

"Pleeaase! It'll annoy Jahu . . ."

Tapak sighed. "Fine. It was mostly tales of the Shop. He told the one about the Shopkeeper and the magic cat."

Faythe cursed. She loved that story.

"And he told us all the news from Ostholme—they've voted to expand again, in case you care."

"I think you're forgetting the best bit . . ." prompted Jahu, his eyes glinting.

"And then he told all of our futures."

Her mouth dropped open. "What? No! What did he say?!"

Jahu rocked his chair again with a satisfied grin. "He said you'd have to wait to find out. Or be very nice to me."

She scowled. "Did he happen to predict you would suffer painful injuries in about thirty seconds?"

He laughed and let his front chair-legs crash to the ground so he could lean over the table. "Fine! I wanted to tell you anyway. Me and Tapak are going to have great lives on Earth!"

She looked at him sceptically. "*Earth?!* For a moment I was scared I'd missed something good. Planning to go there, are you?"

Jahu shrugged. "No. But it's nice to know the universe has grand plans for when I do." He gave her a sly smile. "But don't you want to know your future?"

"Yes . . . but I don't like that look you're giving me. Is it bad?"

"Not bad, exactly. He said—what was it, Tapak?"

"The end of everything is within its beginning." The sound of vegetables being scraped into a pot echoed off the rocky ceiling.

She frowned. "What does that mean?"

"No idea," said Jahu. "That wasn't the bit I meant. He said that you, Faythe . . ." He paused, relishing her impatience. "—yes, you . . . are going to experience trials."

"Trials?!"

He wiggled his fingers and exaggerated his voice. "Threeeeeee triiiiaals. And you will suffer in the process!"

"Suffer *greatly*," added Tapak.

"Oh, come on." She scowled. "How could he know that? He's never even met me!"

"You shouldn't question the man's powers!" Jahu raised a finger in mock warning. "Maybe he stole a jar of SEES THE FUTURE from the Shop."

"Not this again! That would never work as a trait. Management wouldn't allow it."

"How do you know? You've never even seen a trait in person."

She rolled her eyes with a theatrical sigh. "Yes, yes, we *know*, someone once showed you a trait from the Shop Before Life. And it 'glowed'. But it doesn't make you an expert in how the traits work! And there's no way that Management would let people mess with *time* when—"

"Anyway!" Tapak interjected before the old argument could build up momentum. "The story was about you facing all these trials. It was a good one—the world turned black and you raced around painting it full of colour again. Though the end was a bit disappointing. It turned out you had what you needed all along. Still, your future was way more interesting than ours. Mine is probably just endless lonely vegetables." He waved the knife dramatically. "Like my present."

That was clearly a hint to help, but she ignored it. "Hold on," she said, frowning. "If I know I'll experience great suffering, why would I go to Earth in the first place?"

"That's the best bit!" Jahu thumped his palm on the table as he prepared to deliver the final twist. "Your terrible suffering—"

"*Great* suffering," corrected Tapak.

"Yes, great suffering, whatever. It wasn't on Earth—it happens here, in the prelife!"

Faythe snorted. "Hilarious," she said drily.

7

Nevertheless, her scalp prickled with discomfort and there was an odd, anxious twisting in her chest. She squashed the feelings down. It wasn't as if she *actually* believed travelling storytellers could tell the future. They just wanted to entertain their audience and earn a good meal. But still . . .

"I'm serious," said Jahu, rocking his chair again. "That's what he said."

"Well." She stood and moved past the table. "The universe needn't bother punishing me further. I'm already suffering living with *you*." She jabbed Jahu playfully on the back of the head, and ducked out of the way as he leapt out of his seat. The pair began chasing each other around the table.

"Let's start your first Trial of Suffering now!" yelled Jahu.

Tapak rolled his eyes. "Food's nearly ready," he announced, resignedly. He watched them run around for a moment. "With no thanks to you two idiots. Fetch some plates, you fools!"

It was an ordinary evening in the Rock.

That night was a long one. After dinner Faythe felt oddly unsettled. Her mind was buzzing uncomfortably, but not in a way she could express. She quickly made excuses and retired to her bedroom.

But after hours of restless failure to sleep, she gave up. She picked up her blanket and slipped out through the living room and along the wide passage leading outside.

It was a warm night and the sky glittered with stars. She climbed the winding path to the top of the Rock and gazed out towards the horizon. If nothing else, she would punish her brain for the unscheduled insomnia by forcing it to think. She strongly suspected human brains hated thinking—why else would they avoid it at all costs?

She and Jahu had spent many hours up here, often arguing about whether it was possible they could see the faint glow of the Beginning of the Road. He claimed that it was too far away for anybody to see, and, more importantly, that there were actual physical hills in the way. Her counterpoint was that it *wasn't* too far, and that he wasn't trying hard enough if he let a few mere hills stop him. Neither of them particularly cared who was actually right, but it was fun to debate.

She stretched and yawned. Being tired but unable to sleep was so unfair. She had often wondered why Management allowed it. Or why you could be thirsty while also needing the bathroom. The prelife was full of such mysteries, but presumably Management knew what they were doing.

There was no mystery about what was keeping her up, however. Missing the storyteller had been needling at her since dinner. It had been such a long time since any visitors had passed by and even longer since she'd seen a proper storyteller. She would have loved to have heard all their futures.

She became aware of a pain in her leg, and shifted awkwardly as she sought a comfortable position on the stone. Thinking of the future always made her uneasy. She preferred to give it as little attention as possible, but the nonsensical prophecy of 'trials' was an uncomfortable reminder that she *had* a future, whether it truly contained terrible—no, great— suffering, or not.

She sighed, trying to dislodge a tightness in her chest. Perhaps she wasn't destined to spend eternity finding creative ways to splatter loved ones with eggs?

Aimlessly, she threw a stone off the top of the Rock. She waited, but the sound of the landing was drowned out by the wind.

An unfamiliar feeling settled over her, not one she could name. Her shoulders were tense, and her foot jiggled of its own accord. In the back of her mind, a quiet voice piped up. *What if the storyteller is right about the future?*

She frowned. Only Management knew the future.

I mean, he ISN'T right, obviously, continued the voice. *But what if great suffering IS awaiting here in the prelife?*

She chewed the idea over. There was a simple answer: if she knew staying would cause misery, then obviously she would accelerate her plans to go to Earth.

Wait . . . accelerate?! What plans?

She suddenly felt defensive against her own thoughts—always an unsettling sensation. Her plans had always involved Earth, hadn't they? Just . . . not yet.

9

Why not yet?

This thought echoed into an abrupt silence in her mind. The wind picked up further, and she hugged her knees. That uncomfortable, nameless feeling scratched at her once more, a restless, agitating sensation which made her want to get up and move and . . .

In an instant, it dawned on her what she was feeling. What she'd been feeling all night. And perhaps for even longer than that.

Faythe was *bored.*

Boredom is dangerous to humans. It makes them *do* things.

Perhaps that had been Management's intention, but—as with all higher beings—it's impossible to be certain.

Some of their design choices were certainly strange. Humans could have been devised to be rational, to calmly weigh up pros and cons and to sensibly calculate the best option in every situation. But there must have been a rushed design meeting, or tight production deadline, because humans *actually* operate via an unholy mix of borderline irrationality and random impulse.

Once boredom is added to this mix, humans are not immune to recklessness. They're very, very mune to it.

A crack appeared in Faythe's centuries-old repression of her hunger to live, and, quite accidentally, she came to a decision.

A new life on Earth beckoned. A *first* life, even.

As she considered the possibility of leaving, it seemed as if the future physically morphed before her eyes, the comforting certainty of constant routine transforming into a vast swell of endless potential.

Suddenly overwhelmed, she summoned all her powers of emotional control and ran down the path in a blind panic. When she reached the bottom of the Rock, she kept charging onwards, up and over the small wooded hill where Tapak liked to take his walks.

A few minutes later, she leaned against a tree, gasping for breath. Now that the nervous adrenaline had burned off she felt a little silly. She took a slow, deep breath. It wasn't as if she had to go to Earth just because the idea had suddenly appeared in her head. She should sleep. This itch would be gone by morning.

But just as she turned back towards the Rock, a muffled shout drifted between the trees.

She frowned. The others would never be awake at this hour, never mind alert enough to be shouting. Curiosity engaged, she made her way towards the noise, carefully picking her way over criss-crossing roots in the bright starlight. High above, the sky was developing the faintest hint of deep blue, suggesting the sun was considering showing up to work today—but not quite yet.

Soon, the sound resolved into two unfamiliar voices.

"—complete waste of time! And I'll tell him it's your fault."

Two strange men were facing one another in a clearing. She couldn't make out their faces in the dim, greyish light under the trees. The speaker—the shorter one—had a nasally voice, a drawl of vowels punctuated by unclear consonants. The man was waving his arms forcefully as he yelled.

She couldn't believe her luck. Strangers were exciting, but getting to eavesdrop on a public argument was a real treat.

The taller man appeared unmoved by the apparent threat. "Pah! What will you tell him, exactly? He won't care."

"Nonsense! Why send us out at all, if he doesn't care?"

She ducked behind a tree as the taller man glanced around the clearing. "You don't get politics," he replied, sounding bored. "Look, I've noted your opinion. Now can you help me find that cursed Road?"

"What does politics have to do with anything?"

"Come on! It's all politics. You'd think after all this time you'd get that." He sighed. "Listen, both of us know precisely how important this is, so can we work together and get it done, already?"

"Exactly! We have to do it *right*," said the shorter man, pleadingly. "Otherwise, any old—"

She leaned around the tree to get a better view, but as she shifted her weight, she tripped and stumbled into the clearing. The pair whirled around to face her.

"Oh, hello!" she said, thinking hurriedly. "I was just, um ... not eavesdropping."

Her brain had no muscles, but it still managed to cringe.

The men exchanged glances. Now that she was closer, she could see that they appeared unlike anybody she'd ever met. She squinted in the subdued light, staring at the patches in their hair where the colour was all washed-out—almost grey, even—and at the curious wrinkles around their eyes and across their foreheads. *How did they get those?*

She decided to keep talking before they picked holes in her expertly crafted cover story. "I'm from nearby!" she said, with all the cheeriness she could force. "Anyway ... did I hear you say you were looking for the Road?"

They could hardly be blamed for getting lost. The nearest part of the Road was barely more than an overgrown path, and, anyway, every single road in the prelife was called "The Road". The residents of the prelife either didn't care enough to change this, or had forgotten they were allowed to.

The tall stranger eyed her curiously. "So you *were* eavesdropping?"

Admittedly, that cover story hadn't been her finest work. "Only a bit," she admitted.

"Very well. And you live nearby?"

The shorter man clicked his tongue in frustration. "Now who's wasting our time?" he said.

"I'm just doing due diligence."

The shorter man rolled his eyes. "Seriously? On her? She's already lied to us once!"

"Better a bad liar than a good one," replied the taller man, winking at her.

Faythe laughed politely, suppressing her usual quip about lies being more fun versions of the truth, at least until she had more of an idea what was going on.

"I disagree." The shorter man huffed.

"Well, do you have a better idea? It's your fault we're in the middle of nowhere, remember."

"Not that again! Look, I was saying we need to do this right, and—"

"I'm saying that when Management provide us with a perfect opportunity, it ought to be explored!"

"Oh, a perfect opportunity is, what, a girl who *exists in a clearing*, is it? Our standards fell faster than I expected."

The tall man smiled at her. "Please, forgive my colleague's rudeness. It's been a long trip."

She had no clue what to make of any of this, but it was all so interesting that any rudeness was quite irrelevant. In place of the restless boredom of earlier, she was filled with energy. Questions tumbled through her mind faster than she could grasp onto them. "A long trip from where?" she asked. "And a perfect opportunity for *what?*"

The tall man opened his arms wide, and answered neither question. "My name is Aaron, and this is Gabriel." His teeth sparkled brightly, even in the early morning twilight. "We're looking for someone."

Disappointment flooded through her. "Oh. I don't know many people. I probably can't help you."

"No, no," Aaron waved his hands dismissively. "We're not looking for anyone specific—"

Behind him, Gabriel coughed.

"Well, okay, we are, but not *specifically* specific, as it were."

Gabriel's cough became a sigh, and then an interruption. "What my extremely intelligent partner is attempting to say is that we need a person with certain qualities. I think we're unlikely to succeed here, so if you could point us towards the Road, then—"

Aaron stepped forward and put a friendly hand on her shoulder. "Isn't Gabriel funny? I do enjoy his hilarious cynicism. But *enough,*" he said, shooting his partner an intense look. "Let's have a chat. I have a good feeling about you, er . . . ?"

"Faythe."

"Faythe! How perfect. Tell me, where exactly are you from?"

"I lived—" she caught her incorrect use of the past tense with surprise, and corrected it immediately "—I *live* in the Rock. It's a big, um, rock. Where I live."

Aaron nodded. His expression was disconcertingly sincere. "And how long have you lived there?"

It felt oddly embarrassing to admit it. "About two hundred years."

Aaron shot a told-you-so look at Gabriel, who looked up with sudden interest.

"Two hundred, you say?" said Gabriel.

"Yes?"

Aaron's grin—impossibly—got wider still. "What did I tell you! Management always provide. We're searching for someone who will stick around, and you"—he jabbed a victorious finger towards her—"are showing the kind of dedication to the prelife we need. What did you do with that time, precisely?"

Her eyes darted around while she thought. "I played with friends. Explored, a little. Some art, sometimes." She tensed uncomfortably. These men appeared well-travelled, and she'd basically only ever lived in a cave. "I suppose I haven't done much," she admitted.

He clapped. "That's wonderful, really wonderful."

"I have been considering going to Earth," she said, hoping that sounded impressive.

"Earth!" He laughed. "I think we can do better than that."

She frowned. "Better . . . how?"

But no answer came. The wind picked up, rippling the grass around their ankles.

Aaron nodded smugly to his partner. "I think we may have found who we're looking for."

Gabriel rubbed his chin as he studied her. "Let's see about that. Tell us more about 'considering' going to Earth."

She bristled irritably. "I just decided to go tonight."

Aaron smiled. "Sounds like you're not particularly committed to the idea?"

She shook her head uncertainly.

Gabriel pulled a faintly disgusted expression. "So you just suddenly felt like being born as a *baby*, did you?"

He might be very irritating, but she didn't blame him for this disgust. Apparently people didn't just appear on Earth, nice and cleanly, like they did in the prelife. It was customary to emerge in a smaller form, or something. She even had the vague sense other people were involved. Probably wasn't a big deal, though.

"Maybe being born is the price you pay for an interesting existence," she said.

"And that's what you want? An interesting existence?"

"Yes! Doesn't everyone?"

Gabriel turned to his partner with a smug smirk. "You see? It's no good. She's seeking adventure."

She frowned. She still had no idea what this was about, but she refused to be sneered at. "Maybe not adventure, exactly. I just needed some change."

Aaron's toothy grin returned in full force. "Precisely! The right amount of change. Not enough to rock the boat, but sufficient to change course."

She knew exactly nothing about boats. "That's right," she said, nodding wisely. "I change the direction of boats, but I don't rock them."

He clapped. "Perfect."

"Perfect for *what*?"

The tall man's teeth dazzled further. "We work for the Shop Before Life." He left a suitably dramatic pause. "Or, rather, we represent their Management."

Her eyes widened twice—first at the mention of the Shop, and then nearly falling out of her head altogether at his second statement. "You're *Management?!*" Tingles of excitement shot through her whole body. Management were in charge of life, death, creation *and* a highly successful retail enterprise. "What are they like? Do they know everyone, like the stories say? Are they watching us right now?"

"Oh, we'd love to answer all your questions," said Aaron, "but I'm afraid we don't have much time. We're searching for a new Apprentice to work at the Shop Before Life. If that's not you, we need to move on quickly."

Her eyes had already run out of room to widen into so her jaw dropped open instead. "Why does the Shopkeeper need an Apprentice?"

Gabriel gave a snort so disparaging that she winced. "You think she runs the entire Shop Before Life? Alone?"

That did sound silly, but she'd never questioned it until now. "I, uh, always thought the Shopkeeper, um . . ." She trailed off, unsure how to finish.

"That was an excellent question, Faythe," said Aaron, perhaps too kindly. "Along with the Children, the Shopkeeper often has an Apprentice to assist her. And I'm hoping we've found a new candidate."

Children! Wasn't that the smaller form people used on Earth until they became normal-sized? "The Shopkeeper has children?!"

"Never mind that," snapped Gabriel. "We truly don't have time to educate you about everything in the whole prelife. My partner might have given the mistaken impression that this search for an Apprentice is trivial, but we require dedication, loyalty, willingness to listen, and more. The new Apprentice can't just be anyone. They must be *perfect*. And—"

"So." Aaron's interruption made Gabriel's eyes bulge with fury. "Does any of this sound like anybody you know?"

She had to admit it did sound like her. She was dedicated and loyal. Mostly. But . . . "I'm not sure about 'perfect'", she said, biting her lip.

"And that's what makes you perfect!" said Aaron, punching the air triumphantly. "A perfect candidate would be aware of her own flaws. Of course, in an ideal world you'd already have experience running a magical shop, but since that would disqualify everybody except the Shopkeeper herself, we'll let that one go, shall we?"

Her mind was reeling. *Apprentice at the Shop Before Life!* Was this really happening? And, more importantly, did she want it? "If I applied for this job—" she said, to Aaron's visible delight, "—which I'm not saying I'm going to, you understand? *If I did*, then I'd get to learn all about how the Shop works?"

He nodded. "Naturally. Comprehensive training will be provided."

"And you'd have to learn quickly," warned Gabriel. "All human life depends on the successful running of the Shop."

Aaron bobbed his head. "You'll have many duties. Everything from assisting customers with their choices to restocking the traits."

The traits! She'd always been fascinated by them. What could be more magical than jars of pure human characteristics? The chance to work with them, to learn about them, to understand them . . . it was irresistible.

Gabriel took a deep breath. "And more duties would be revealed in due course. In the meantime, everybody's life would literally depend on your work." He looked at Aaron. "Which is why we need to ensure we don't rush this decision."

"It's fine," his partner said. "Remember who's in charge here. And I'm certainly impressed by Faythe's eagerness to learn. I believe she's an excellent choice."

Gabriel looked extremely unhappy, but he stayed quiet.

She bit her lip. Already she knew she couldn't turn this chance down. "And I can always go to Earth afterwards, right?" she asked.

For the first time, Aaron hesitated. "Management require a certain amount of loyalty from Apprentices, so your contract will ensure you remain in place for a minimum period."

"Which is . . . ?"

"A thousand years."

Her stomach churned. A thousand years was a long time. But then, two centuries had passed at the Rock without any effort at all. And she'd still get to go to Earth eventually.

Gabriel wagged a finger at her. "Let me warn you. This is an immense privilege. The Shopkeeper understands the sacrifice required for this job, and she expects the same from her Apprentices. And Management will expect even more, as your contract progresses."

Aaron gave him a be-quiet look, but this seemed fair.

Only a few hours ago, this would have been a harder decision. She loved her prelife. But after mentally uprooting herself once, it seemed much easier to replant herself again. Particularly if that meant living in the most important place in the universe, and delving into all of its mysteries.

"I want to apply for the job," she said.

"You've got it," said Aaron immediately.

"Wait, what?" It couldn't be that easy. She looked from one man to the other. "Isn't there an application, or interview, or something?"

Gabriel glared at his partner, mouthing words she didn't catch.

Aaron shook his head. "You just passed your interview. As *Senior Talent Executive*, I have the authority to appoint new Apprentices on behalf of Management as soon as I deem them worthy. And I could tell immediately that you were the person for the job. Our conversation only confirmed your qualities."

"Really?" She couldn't help prodding further. "Your partner doesn't seem so sure."

Aaron didn't give Gabriel a chance to speak. "We are great judges of character."

"And wise," added Gabriel, sourly. "For example, we would never make hasty decisions we may come to regret."

Meanwhile, Aaron was already crouching to pull paperwork from a document case. "Never mind that old grouch. I always know when we're doing the will of Management. Now, sign your name here, please."

She bent down to sign, using his case as a makeshift writing surface as Aaron produced paper after paper.

"Sign here, and here, and here. Now, please take this letter, which explains that you've been hired on behalf of Management as the Apprentice at the Shop Before Life for a period not less than a thousand years. Please remember that Management reserve the right to terminate or amend your contract for any reason—"

"Do *I* have that right?"

Too late, she realised hasty decisions worked two ways.

Aaron gave her a pitying look, one appropriate for those who haven't yet discovered the fundamental unfairness of the universe in general, and of contracts in particular. "No. But that's the deal. Luckily, Management are extremely fair."

Gabriel stifled a laugh.

She took the letter, frowning.

"Very good," said Aaron, who was zipping up his document case with solemn formality. "It's been a pleasure. You are expected at the Shop immediately."

He held out his hand and she shook it, dazed. "Immediately? I need to get my stuff . . . and say goodbye to my friends."

The pair exchanged glances once more.

"I warned you . . ." said Gabriel, softly.

"Sssh," hissed Aaron. He turned to her. "One more thing: there's a 'secrecy' clause in your contract. So you mustn't mention your new role to anybody until you've reported to the Shop. Once you're there, you won't hear from us."

"At least, not for a while," Gabriel interjected.

"Exactly, yes, we'll be in touch eventually. But in the meantime, your training will be provided by the Shopkeeper. Show her the letter."

Faythe reeled at this onslaught of information. "What?! A secrecy clause? Can I see it?"

Aaron held the document case away from her. "The secrecy clause is also a secret, of course," he said.

"It wouldn't be much good otherwise." Gabriel suddenly seemed to be enjoying himself.

"And Management will know if you break any of these terms," warned Aaron. "So . . . promise us."

She rubbed her forehead. "Okay," she said, finally. What choice did she have?

Gabriel offered his own stiff handshake. "Best of luck," he said. "We'll all need it."

Quickly, the pair strode away, leaving Faythe stunned and alone. As soon as they were a short distance away they launched into a heated conversation, involving much gesticulating.

Sunlight was starting to creep over the horizon, and the birds were greeting it with their unchanging daily enthusiasm.

She looked down at the still-drying ink on the letter which named her "Apprentice at the Shop Before Life". That had all happened extremely fast. But perhaps that was normal? She'd never been hired at a magical shop before.

Excitement coiled in her chest and immediately tightened around her heart. It would be hard to leave without explaining everything that had just happened to her friends.

But then, it would be hard to leave at all.

As she walked back to the Rock, she suddenly laughed giddily at the thought of Jahu's face when he showed up at the Shop and she was the one serving him.

This might be her best prank yet.

two

FAYTHE WAS UNUSUALLY AWARE of her heartbeat as she entered the cave beneath the Rock. She couldn't remember the last time she'd been this nervous.

It was oddly thrilling. She felt alive.

Or, as she often liked to joke, she felt *pre-alive*, to be *pre-cise*. For some reason, the others pretended not to find this observation funny.

Her friends were sitting blearily around the breakfast table. Tapak noticed her first. "Morning! Been out for a walk?" When she didn't respond, he tried again. "Planning to get Jahu again today?"

At the mention of his name, Jahu looked up from his food like a startled animal, but she was too absorbed to play along. "Yeah," she murmured. *How do I do this? Do I just come out and say it?*

Tapak gave her a funny look and turned to Jahu. "What about you? Plotting anything fun today?"

"Maybe," said Jahu, who had stopped chewing. He was looking thoughtfully at her too.

Perhaps later would be better. Yes, that was a good idea. She should calm down before she accidentally committed some drama.

Tapak looked at the other two. "You're no fun today. Did something happen? Besides the usual, I mean."

She shook her head. "Nothing's happened," she squeaked. Just yesterday, this comfortable breakfast scene would have been the most natural thing in the world, but right now she felt like an outsider in her own home.

Jahu narrowed his eyes. "Where did you come from just now?"

She tensed. After two hundred years of shared company, of course the tiniest change would be easily detectable. The little bored voice in the back of her mind used this moment to give her a powerful nudge into action.

"I think I might have made a decision," she said, her voice wavering.

"Oh?" Tapak put down his fork. Amongst the trio, this was a sign of the deepest possible respect.

She glanced at Jahu, who looked apprehensive. He knew her best, after all.

Silence.

"I'm leaving." She took another breath. She hated being forced to lie, but perhaps partial truth would be enough. "For the Shop."

Somehow the silence changed tone while still remaining completely silent. The air around Faythe became denser, closer, oddly charged. She held her breath.

Tapak broke the tension, barking a laugh. But when nobody else reacted, he looked around, searching for clues. "You're joking, right?" he asked.

She shook her head. "No, it's real. After we talked last night I couldn't sleep. I got thinking, and—"

Jahu didn't wait for her to finish. He stood and left the room without a word, and without looking back.

"Jahu! Please!"

He was already gone.

"Wow," said Tapak, to himself. Next to his plate, his fork remained untouched.

If you dropped a human from Earth back into the prelife, they'd probably say something like: "Where am I?!"

But even after accepting the answer, they would find the prelife rather strange.

On the surface, much seems similar. People still look like people. They have four limbs, they speak using their mouths, and they live and laugh and fight and play—just as they do once they make it to Earth.

However, there are significant differences. Not least that what they call 'dying' in the prelife is mostly just an inconvenience. One moment you're hurtling towards the ground, then, after a confusing instant, you're back at the Beginning. Those who've experienced this say that it isn't pleasant, so most avoid it. (Although, humans being human, there are groups who pass time in the prelife by creatively murdering one another over-and-over, just for fun.)

Eventually, the displaced Earth human might also notice the curious absence of other aspects of life they previously considered crucial, such as family, ageing and sex. Instead of the genetic system they're used to, everybody simply appears at the Beginning as an adult without parents. After that they remain youthful for—at least—centuries. And while they *could* technically have sex if they wanted to, they just aren't as interested in the idea as people supposedly are on Earth.

Unfortunately, nobody has ever studied what difference—if any—this makes to human psychology. Earth-based scholars have largely forgotten about their prelife, and everyone in the prelife with a fascination for Earth tends to go straight there.

As a result, anyone who claims a deep understanding of humans is likely just making it up as they go along.

Fortunately, making it up as you go along is *precisely* the experience needed to become an expert in human behaviour for real.

Over the centuries Faythe had picked up a little knowledge of Earth through gossip and hearsay, but exactly how the fabled world compared to its grand reputation remained a mystery. She couldn't wait to finally see it—even if only from a distance for the next thousand years.

In the meantime, she was discovering a whole new source of suffering and pain: *packing*.

She stared at the pile of clothes spread over her bed, perplexed. She had no idea what to take—not even for the long journey to the Shop, never mind for being mysteriously born on an entirely different world a thousand years later.

Something warm, probably.

As she sifted through the heap, she wondered at how calm she felt, although perhaps 'calm' wasn't quite the right word. 'Total emotional chaos wrapped in a mysterious layer of detachment' was more like it. All her feelings were puzzlingly remote, as if her life were happening to somebody else.

Most confusingly of all, she couldn't detect any doubt within that maelstrom. It was as if an internal switch had flipped in an instant from *STAY* to *GO*.

She frowned. Surely uprooting herself so suddenly couldn't be so easy? For a second, she doubted her lack of doubt, but she quickly shushed that thought before everything got too confusing.

Instead, she concentrated on laying out her shoes in a row. Shoes, she could handle.

She would wear her favourite pair, naturally, but what about the second-most comfortable set? Her frown deepened. Were you allowed to take spare shoes to Earth? It might be a thousand years before she would actually be born, but in the face of such terrifying, vertiginous change she wanted to be as prepared as possible, and she couldn't remember whether people got born wearing shoes or not.

After some thought, she decided she'd feel like a right idiot if every other baby on Earth had shoes and she didn't, so into the bag they went.

Someone coughed at the entrance to her bedroom. She looked up to see Jahu, arms folded. He looked so completely calm and collected that it was obvious he'd been crying.

"Tell me Tapak was right," he said. "This is a bad joke, and you're not really leaving."

She gestured towards the clothes strewn all over her bed, and her half-packed bag. "Have I ever done any work I didn't absolutely need to do? Even for a joke?" She forced a smile.

Jahu didn't return it. "You must have been thinking about this for ages. Why didn't you talk to me about it?"

"How could I have hidden it? You knew before I'd even opened my mouth. I honestly only decided today."

He stared at her incredulously. "You *just* thought of this?"

"I know it's a bit spontaneous—"

"A bit!" he spat.

"Well, okay, a *lot* spontaneous."

He searched her face as he leaned against the doorframe. "Won't leaving us make you sad?"

Frustration twisted deep in her stomach. She wished she could beam all of her thoughts and emotions directly into his brain so he'd understand. *Or at least tell him about the job at the Shop.*

She sought for words that might bridge the gap between them. "I'm sad already!" That didn't begin to cover it. A huge part of the chaotic emotional whirl was the deep weight of impending loss. "But maybe that's why it had to be spontaneous. If I thought about it, I'd never leave."

"Isn't that a sign you shouldn't?" he fired back.

That heavy sensation churned within her. Jahu was always so much fun to debate with, about anything. Even this.

"Maybe. But let me tell you how it happened. Please, come in. It's weird talking with you half in another room."

At last, he entered. She made room for him to perch on the edge of the bed.

"Last night I couldn't sleep. And I got thinking. About Earth and life and the prelife and everything. And this idea to go arrived in my head from nowhere, and it instantly felt right. You ever get that?"

He stared at her blankly. "No, I've never thought that maybe ripping my whole life up is a good idea."

She tensed her hands in frustration. "I can't explain it to myself, never mind you. It's just time."

It was all true. Even before meeting Aaron and Gabriel—and signing a binding contract with the actual gods—this feeling had been insistent, and she couldn't have ignored it forever. A day like this would have come eventually.

"No." His look was intense. "Nobody abandons their whole prelife, their home, their friends, on a whim!"

"Maybe I do."

"But why? What's wrong with here? With us?"

"Nothing!" She searched again for words which would help, though she was unsure any existed. "Maybe that's the problem."

He screwed up his face in incomprehension. "How could nothing being wrong be a problem?"

"Because it means I could have stayed here forever!"

"And what's wrong with that?" He was clearly struggling not to shout.

She glanced away, unable to bear his expression any longer. "I could spend my whole prelife here," she said softly. "Maybe even the whole of eternity. But if I did, then . . . well, I'd have spent the whole of eternity here." She caught sight of a pinecone on her bedside table. It had been a gift from him, long ago. Maybe she could demonstrate. "Look. This has been on this same table for years, Jahu. It hasn't changed."

"Why would it change? It's a pinecone."

"Okay . . . sure, it wouldn't. But maybe it wants to change."

"Why would a pinecone want to change?" He looked more hurt and confused than before.

She put the pinecone back down. That hadn't been a good idea. "All I mean is . . . if I stay, I'll never know anything else. And if I stop to think too much about leaving, I'll feel too much, and . . ."

He appeared emotionless once more, which was worse.

"I don't want to leave you," she said, almost a whisper.

"Then don't!" His eyes burned, even as they glazed with the tears he was—just—holding in.

She shook her head. "I can't stay." For an instant she longed to tell him the truth about the Shop. "I . . ." She faltered. She'd made a promise to *Management*. "It's just . . . if I don't go after making the decision, then I'll never leave—"

"Good!"

"— which would mean giving up Earth forever. It's now or never."

"But going to Earth means giving up here." His voice cracked, pleading. "It works both ways. And look what you've got. Me, you, Tapak. It's a good life."

"Prelife." The distinction suddenly mattered. "It's a good prelife.

Neither of us knows what life is, yet."

They stared at each other in thick, gathering frustration. She reached out to touch his arm, but he shrank away.

Suddenly, she had an idea. "We always said we'd all go to Earth eventually! Why don't you come with me?" She held her breath, excited. It could work! She could confess about the contract when they reached the Shop, and then . . . maybe . . . Jahu and Tapak could leave for Earth? Or stay at the Shop with her? They'd figure something out. Probably.

But he sprang up, his face blanketed with dread. "No!" he yelled. "I . . . I can't." As he reached the door, he spun and pointed at her. "I know you don't really mean this. This is one of your jokes. And it's not funny!"

The door slammed shut.

Her emotions suddenly all spilled out at once, and she yelled at the thick wooden planks, "AT LEAST ON EARTH EVERYONE WILL RESPECT MY DECISIONS!"

That *had* to be true. Surely a whole planet full of people must have figured out how to get along by now.

But if any hint of doubt about leaving had remained, it would have burned away after that conversation. After brushing away a stray teardrop, she packed a third pair of shoes, just for luck.

Faythe's biggest struggle was choosing which mementos to keep. She left most in a neat pile by her bed, but found room for three: an incredibly round stone from a memorable day competing to skip stones across a pond, a terrible drawing by Tapak of the trio standing in front of the Rock, and a tiny four-legged creature she'd carved with Jahu when they'd wrongly assumed they'd have a natural talent for sculpture.

She hoped that eventually she'd be allowed to bring the carving through to Earth. It was only small.

The string on her bag had just been tied and she was collapsing wearily onto her bed when there was another knock at the door.

"Come in!" she muttered, reluctantly.

The door creaked open and Tapak gingerly leaned inside.

She took a deep breath and steeled herself for another unpleasant conversation. Tapak was easily the most routine-driven member of their little community. Every day was the same for him: breakfast, a morning walk along his favourite—and only—route, lunch, and then an afternoon of play, chores and home improvement before coming together for stories in the evening. He wasn't going to be happy about her leaving.

"I'm not in the mood for another argument," she said, holding up a hand. "Jahu's already tried talking me out of it. I'm going, and that's that."

He tilted his head to the side. "I think you're right to go," he replied.

"I'm serious, Tapak, I'm—" His words sunk in. "Oh."

Her friend smiled ruefully. "I always knew this wouldn't last. To be honest, I never expected everything to stay as it was for this long. One of us was going to leave eventually, and it was always going to be you."

She struggled to catch up. "It was?"

"Come on, Faythe, you're supposed to be the smart one. May I?" He indicated the corner of the bed and she shuffled up to make room. "If nothing else, Jahu would never leave without you, and, well, I like it here."

"So do I! And you both used to talk about leaving someday, too."

He shrugged. "You never noticed that nobody else ever brought up leaving? It was always you."

Was that right? Now that he mentioned it, she couldn't remember anyone else actually saying it. Perhaps her decision wasn't quite the instantaneous switch-flip it seemed.

He smiled to himself as he watched her think. "Remember the other day? When Jahu fell off that mountain?"

She furrowed her brow. "That was fifteen years ago! And it wasn't a mountain, don't exaggerate. And he wasn't *really* stuck."

"Was it fifteen? Whatever. You were so determined to carry on exploring."

She held her hands up. "I was going to pick him up on the way back! He would have been fine." *He would have too*, she told herself. He just didn't like straying far from home.

"And then you sulked for days after he made us come back here when we pulled him out."

"I only wanted to see what was over the next hill."

Even as the memories returned, frustration roared within. She'd been stifling her boredom for her friends' happiness for years.

She looked at Tapak. "That was the last time we went on a trip."

He nodded. "So I always knew you'd go eventually." He snorted, a laugh tinged with sadness. "It's still a shock you're actually doing it though."

"I'm shocked too, if it helps. More than I can say." *Literally*. Once more, she suppressed a flash of irritation at her own willingness to sign contracts without reading them. She glanced towards the door, through which they could clearly hear Jahu stomping around. "Is he okay?"

Tapak followed her gaze. "He's pretty upset."

"People have left before."

Her friend looked unconvinced. "A long time ago." He paused. "And none of them were you."

There was a thumping sound from the living room. Her heart was abruptly full of the doubt she'd been denying all day. "Be honest. Do you think I should stay?"

"Aren't you listening?" He opened his arms wide and looked around for support from an imaginary audience. "I already said you should go!"

"But what about Jahu? He's upset."

He fixed her with a steady gaze. "You shouldn't stay for him, if you're leaving for yourself."

"I agree!"

"Then what are we talking about, exactly?"

She paused. "I don't know."

Silence.

She rested her head back against the wall. "I'm just scared."

"I know," he said. "It's hard. And I don't want to lose you."

"I don't want to lose you. Either of you." She drew a deep breath. She had to ask, even if she knew what the answer would be. "Do you want to come with me? It'd be fun to journey together."

And less scary.

He nodded sadly, as if he'd expected the question. "Thanks, but no. This is the right place for me now."

"But how do you know that? If you never try anywhere else?"

"I just do," he replied.

28

She couldn't argue with that. For a long time, that would have been her answer too.

His eyes met hers. "How do you know leaving is right?"

She hugged her knees. "I guess I don't."

"So both of us are guessing." He reached out for a hug, which she gratefully accepted. "You okay?" he asked.

"Not really."

"That's probably the right reaction. No matter when you went, it would always feel like this." He looked at her bag, packed to nearly bursting. "When are you going? Tonight?"

She scrunched up her face. She should probably go sooner, but . . .

"In the morning. I want to sleep first."

Tapak nodded. "He'll have calmed down by then. We can have a proper goodbye."

He got up, but as he reached the door, he turned back with a thoughtful expression. "You know, it doesn't matter what you choose to do, Faythe."

She furrowed her brow. That made no sense at all. "What do you mean? Choices are important!"

"I mean, yeah, choices matter. But how do I put this? Whatever you choose, you still find what you need. You could be happy if you passed through the Shop to Earth, or if you explored the rest of the prelife, or even if you stayed here at the Rock. *That* you choose is more important than *what* you choose."

She looked at him suspiciously. "Sounds like you're trying to get me to stay."

"Maybe I am. But if I was, why would I have already told you to go? Twice!"

"Mind games?"

He smiled. "Nah. You're too smart for my mind games."

She flung her pillow at him. It hit the closing door and slid to the ground.

It was lovely that Tapak had tried to make her feel better about going. And, in a way, it was good that Jahu was upset. It meant they both cared.

But . . . Tapak was right. Leaving was always going to be hard. And if she stayed, whether for Tapak's kindness or Jahu's passion, then she'd never leave. Whatever he said about choices not mattering, living forever under a rock in the prelife—no matter how much she loved it—could never compete with the entire rest of the universe.

Or the chance to learn about those magical jars of human characteristics at the Shop Before Life.

The next morning, Faythe awoke before the sun was up—a time of day she'd always believed didn't morally count as "part of the day" at all. Such an early hour surely had to be a mistake of Management's; a wholly unnatural moment when nobody and nothing should be moving at all.

Nevertheless, some ancient human instinct insisted that grand journeys require early starts, so she dressed by candlelight at this un-Management-ly hour.

Finally, she picked up her bag and padded towards the cave entrance, where for a long minute she stared silently at the distant horizon. The morning stars were fading, but still plentiful. Was that dim light an early sign of the sunrise? Or a trick of her tired brain?

She swallowed, with difficulty. A lump in her throat had been slowly forming since she'd awoken. All night, her sleep had been punctuated with fitful dreams, each filled with painful goodbyes—and lizards, for some reason.

She'd planned to wake the others, but the temptation to slip away painlessly was quite insistent.

"Faythe?" Tapak's voice echoed from inside the cave. "I couldn't sleep. You're not going to leave without saying goodbye, are you?"

She gulped. The lump disappeared, but only for an instant.

Jahu appeared at the door to his bedroom, his hair even messier than usual, and his face unreadable. "I want to say," he mumbled. "If this is a joke, you've taken it too far."

Dread settled in her chest, and reached up to bolster her still-growing throat lump.

But he grinned. "It's still dark! And the sun is nowhere. This is an inhuman time to wake us up!"

Relief washed through her at the weak joke. Things felt momentarily normal, given the circumstances. "I'm sorry, I'm a bad person," she said, hanging her head in false shame.

Jahu nodded. "I knew that. This early morning just proves it."

She swivelled her head up. "Hey! You're not meant to agree!"

He grinned, but his eyes were sad. Gratitude and loss both swelled at once. She didn't want this to last longer than it had to.

Tapak was nearest, so she hugged him first. "Have a happy life on Earth, and make good choices in the Shop," he murmured. "And stay safe. Don't try dying, not even here."

"Believe me," she replied, drily. "I have no intention of seeing what dying feels like."

"I never know what you'll do next," he said, eyes sparkling. "But you know what the storytellers say. It's a big world out there."

"I'll be careful," she promised.

"No, you won't." He hugged her a final time. "See you on Earth."

Her heart lurched. Tapak thought they'd never see each other again, and it was breaking her heart. Hopefully he'd leave for Earth before her thousand years were up, so they'd have a chance to meet again.

The goodbye was stirring up emotions she wanted to pretend didn't exist. She turned quickly to Jahu, who was standing unnaturally still, radiating waves of tension so tangible that perhaps the staff of the Shop would be able to scoop it into one of their famous jars.

"I'm sorry for all the eggs," she began. Being unsure what to say to Jahu, of all people, was an alien experience. "But at least I won't be around to annoy you anymore."

His lip trembled. She tried to ignore it.

She ought to say something deep and wise. Perhaps if she kept talking it would happen automatically.

"Look, I don't know what I'm doing—and, before you say it, yes, I never know what I'm doing—but I *really* have no idea now. And it's possible that this is a really bad idea, but I have to try it, and I want to say that living with you has been—"

His emotional wall cracked, and he pulled her in for a hug. She stopped talking and closed her eyes.

At last, he spoke. "I still don't believe you're going," he murmured, his face pressed to the side of hers. She squeezed him tight, and then they both let go.

She stared into his eyes for a moment, trying not to cry, until, finally, she turned her back and began to plod along the path leading away from the Rock.

From behind, she heard a loud sniff. She looked back. The cave entrance was already empty.

With her heart full of emotion—which one, she honestly couldn't tell anymore—Faythe stumbled over the hills towards the Road, at the end of which lay the Shop Before Life.

 *three*

FOR THE MOST PART, the universe seemed quite sensibly designed. However, even Management's staunchest defenders would admit they'd missed out features which would have been *cool*. For example, any decent Management would surely have considered giving humans the ability to summon a stirring fanfare at suitably dramatic moments in their lives.

If they had, Faythe would have used that ability as she got her first view of the magical place which was going to be her home for the next thousand years.

Over the last few days, the dirt path 'Road' had become increasingly wide and well-worn, before transforming entirely as she reached the parts which had been paved for countless millennia. She'd passed houses, villages, and the fork where people chose between visiting Ostholme or going directly to the Shop. All the while, the Road became busier and busier as travellers converged from all over the prelife, drawn inexorably to the Shop by powerful instincts.

At first, the unfamiliar sensation of novelty had played with her perception of time. Her brain noticed every little detail, from the subtle changes in birdsong to the new landscapes around her. Nothing remarkable had happened, but it was all *new* nothing and therefore thrilling. After a few days, the constant novelty had itself become normal, and the whole journey had merged into a single smudge in her memory.

And now she was cresting the final hill to see the Shop Before Life for the first time.

The stirring fanfare conspicuously failed to play, but she halted regardless, shocked at the sudden appearance of the Earth in the sky. She'd heard rumours that the planet came into view this close to the Shop, but the sudden appearance of an entire planet was still astonishing.

"Incredible, isn't it?" Another bystander smiled knowingly.

He was right. The Earth was beyond beautiful. The world shimmered as it hung in the sky, a roiling kaleidoscope of blue, green and white, an intricate patchwork of continents and oceans and islands and clouds, so vast that her attention was drawn in every direction at once. Her eyes roved over it hungrily until she gave up trying to take it all in, and simply marvelled. All around her, many others had stopped to admire the world that would soon be their home. With a shiver, she realised that everybody who ever lived would someday pause on this hill.

The bystander was still waiting for a response.

"It's . . . big," she said, unable to think of any other words. She felt immediately silly—of course a whole world must be pretty big—but she'd never imagined it might appear larger in the sky than the sun.

The man raised an eyebrow and turned away to share the moment with another traveller, presumably somebody more able to speak.

Faythe tore her gaze away from the Earth and drank in the equally spectacular vista beneath. From here, the Road wound downhill before opening into a large field in front of the Shop Before Life. To one side of the Shop, a broad river approached from a distant mountain range, slowly widening as it crossed the plains before curving around the Shop grounds.

On the far side of the river was a field, deep green and covered in wildflowers, while on the near side, grand gardens sloped uphill to meet the Shop building. The gardens contrasted colourfully with the grassy field, like an emerald part-dipped in rainbow paint.

Then there was the Shop itself. If it were possible to breed vast wooden warehouses with cosy stone cottages then the result might resemble the Shop Before Life: many storeys tall, yet without being forbidding; simply constructed, yet ornately decorated; at once overwhelmingly large and comfortingly homely.

Overall, it looked as if separate teams of builders using conflicting blueprints had spent centuries constructing on top of one another, each using whatever materials happened to be close to hand. Presumably they'd eventually given up on their endless war of construction and wedged a huge domed warehouse atop the whole muddle, and this—somehow—had worked.

It was dominated by a huge wooden building, a rectangle with the long side facing towards the field. This building was itself topped, improbably, by a giant glass dome. A tangle of vestigial buildings writhed alongside and underneath this central edifice, a series of annexes, wings, extensions and blocks, all made from a mess of stone, brick and wood.

Around her, the crowd on the hill chattered excitably. The mood on the Road had shifted over these last few miles. With the Earth in sight—and now she had seen it, it was impossible not to be aware of it, spinning slowly in the sky above—the people on the Road felt more like pilgrims than travellers. There was a tangible thrill in the air.

She herself rippled with nervous energy. For most, this hill marked the end of a brief prelife, but—after a mere two centuries—hers was just getting interesting.

The large field in front of the Shop acted partly as a gathering place, but mainly as a queue.

She had never seen so many people in one place, and never realised such a gathering had its own noise—an unintelligible hubbub of conversation, laughter and shouting. The body language of the arrivals was fascinating, too. Some were clearly excited, running to claim their place in line, while others trudged more reluctantly, or clung to one another nervously.

She began to pick her way through the crowd towards the Shop building, but she didn't get far before she was halted by an impossibly loud shout—high-pitched, but not shrill. "You there! No queue jumping!"

She leapt in the air, startled. "Me?!"

A tiny girl wearing a blue uniform was waving a clipboard and brandishing a megaphone. Faythe gaped. She'd never seen anybody who looked like this, but some instinct told her that this was the youngest person she had ever seen.

"Yes, you! Please pay attention to the staff! New arrivals must go to the far corner of the waiting area."

The child pointed to a roped-off pen, where customers joined the back of the queue.

"Ah, I think you've mistaken me for—" began Faythe.

The girl blasted another instruction through the megaphone. "Ma'am, I'm going to have to ask you to start moving."

"You're *going* to ask me? So you're not asking me yet?"

The girl looked unimpressed. "Move."

Faythe glowered at the child—Jahu would have loved that joke, and it was annoying to waste it—and fumbled for her letter from Management, but the girl had already moved onto another hapless arrival who was taking too long to join the queue.

She tapped her foot and looked around the busy field. Surely the new Apprentice wouldn't actually have to wait? After a quick backward glance, she resumed weaving towards the corner of the Shop nearest the Gardens, where the front of the line climbed the steps leading up to the main entrance.

But as she neared the front, the voice of the tiny traffic director boomed once more into her ear.

"Ma'am," she said, in a voice which subtly hinted at unspecified—but excruciating—punishment. "As you can see we are very busy today, and we take queue jumping extremely seriously." The crowd around Faythe muttered with disapproval. She shifted uneasily. "If you do not move to the back of the queue, I'm going to insist that you leave the grounds entirely."

She rooted in her pocket. "I have a letter," she announced, holding the paper out triumphantly.

"Very good, ma'am, that'll be something to read while you wait," replied the child, whose roving eye had already detected another miscreant some distance away. She raised her megaphone. "Please do NOT attempt to duck under the ropes or Security will escort you from the grounds. May I please remind you that much of humanity passes through here every day, and we are doing our best to get each of you into the Shop as quickly and smoothly as possible. Please. Follow. Directions. Thank you!" The target of her ire slipped away abashed, and the child returned her attention to Faythe. "Are you still here?"

"Like I said, I have a letter—" she began, but she got no further.

"Ma'am, I will call Security if you don't co-operate immediately."

"But I'm the new Apprentice!" Faythe waved the letter in desperation.

The child aimed the megaphone directly into Faythe's face. "*Get in the queue!*"

Faythe yelped and scurried away in defeat.

Her brain was already scrambling for positives. Perhaps this outcome was for the best. It might even be fun to queue—she could meet the customers and soak up the atmosphere. And there was a chance that another staff member would be more amenable to reading her letter.

Around her, customers chattered excitedly. She settled in for a potentially long wait.

Unbelievably—and Faythe would surely have to talk to someone about this!—the back of the queue was *not* staffed by anybody who wanted to discuss the possibility of her skipping ahead.

Like the tiny girl, the staff here were children too. Perhaps they all were. "The Children", Aaron had called them, with an audible capital C.

Either way, they were all too busy for her protestations, so she waited with hundreds of other potential customers in a series of pens surrounded by ropes. Periodically, a Child would lift a rope and everyone would obediently trot into the next pen.

She tried not to fantasise about slipping under any ropes. She had a strong sense that her megaphone-wielding friend would detect any such trickery immediately. There was nothing to do but wait.

Thankfully, there was plenty to look at. She and her fellow customers gazed up at the Earth and speculated about where they might be born and what they planned to do there. She pitied the new arrivals to the prelife, who knew hardly anything of Earth compared to the facts that she had gathered over the years.

"They all own animals, like dogs and camels, and are totally obsessed with ageing," she confidently told an open-mouthed group.

Some of her fellow customers chatted with anyone in earshot, bragging about the traits they planned to take.

"Extroverts have it best, let me tell you," said one guy standing nearby, who had been talking eagerly with—or, maybe, at—a bored-looking woman for a while. "I know a lot of people are planning to take INTRO-VERT, but I think the clue is in the name. Extra, right? So you get more." He tapped his nose, as if he was imparting secret wisdom.

The woman harrumphed vaguely in response.

"I've been thinking about the physical sorts of jars, too," he continued. "Lots of people forget about the physical. It's easy to get distracted by personality. But being able to build muscles, now that's useful. I see the pros and cons like this—"

Faythe moved to a different corner of the pen, so he wouldn't start talking to her.

Eventually they reached the front of the queue. The crowd cheered as another Child toddled over to unhook the rope at the bottom of the steps. "Welcome, one and all," he said. "First, let me remind you there's no need to rush. We close around sundown, so there's plenty of time for you to select your traits. Once you have filled your basket, please bring it to the checkouts, where you will be informed how to pass through to Earth with your selection."

How many times had this Child given this speech? Hundreds of times just today, presumably. Yet he sounded genuinely enthusiastic.

"Do ask any of the Children if you require assistance," he said, beaming.

Unless you're the new Apprentice and you want to skip the queue to present yourself, she thought, with a hint of bitterness.

The Child lifted the rope and allowed the first customers through. "Good luck everybody, and best wishes for your life on Earth."

Her anticipation grew as the crowd shifted forward. She had to keep reminding herself she wasn't about to choose traits and pass through to Earth. Although as the entrance drew nearer, escape seemed more and more tempting.

What if she wasn't cut out to be the Apprentice?

The burden was suddenly immense. Could she truly have responsibility over all these lives?

She danced nervously from foot to foot as the group slowly shuffled forwards; up the steps, onto the verandah, and up to the large front door.

Finally, she reached the threshold.

"Welcome, ma'am," said a small girl handing out baskets. She wore a badge saying "ASK ME QUESTIONS".

Faythe held up a hand to refuse the basket. "Excuse me, but where can I find the Shopkeeper?"

The Child pressed the basket towards her. "I'm sure you'll need this, ma'am," she said.

Faythe stared at the basket. It would be so easy to take it and slip through to Earth, unnoticed. This would be her last chance to remain anonymous.

But then . . . breaking a contract with Management probably wasn't the easy option it seemed right now.

"No, thank you," she replied, eventually. "And the Shopkeeper?"

"If you insist, ma'am," said the girl, with a shrug. "And I'm afraid not everybody gets to see the Shopkeeper." She caught Faythe's expression and added: "Though she occasionally works on the checkouts, so perhaps you'll be lucky."

Faythe thanked her again and, finally, entered the Shop Before Life.

It is said—at least, it is said right here—that after the first truly great cathedral was built on Earth, the builders captured an enemy, and dragged him, blindfolded, inside. When they removed his blindfold, he was so struck with awe that he renounced his old tribe and their clearly inferior ways, and became a great warrior for his new people.

Perhaps those builders remembered something of their first entry to the Shop Before Life.

When Faythe crossed the threshold, she didn't renounce her old friends at the Rock or rend and tear at her clothes, but she *did* halt suddenly and cause a minor jam just inside the entryway.

The Shop was delightfully overwhelming.

Before her, an open concourse swarmed with people brandishing baskets and bee-lining for one of the tall aisles stacked with jars to her left. Along those aisles, far above the shelves, multiple floors criss-crossed confusingly, all the way up to the enormous glass dome ceiling.

On her right were the checkouts, long wooden desks obscured by a lengthy queue which snaked back and forth. Opposite the entrance, across the narrower width of the main building, was an enormous window inset with a glass door, through which a wooden platform hung high above the Gardens.

"Ma'am, please keep moving!" Another uniformed Child waved her forward. She was supposed to report to the Shopkeeper, but having made it inside, the urge to explore was irresistible.

She neared a display on the concourse, a tall stack of jars arranged in a pyramid with the labels facing outward: WELL-INTENTIONED. Inside each jar, a thick liquid glowed deep red. Her stomach fluttered, and she fought an overpowering desire to snatch a jar and place it in her basket.

How were the other customers keeping so calm?! They were surrounded by every possible human trait, available for the taking! She wanted to shake somebody and scream about how impossibly thrilling everything was.

She glanced down an aisle to her left and her jaw dropped open. Shelves stretched into the distance as far as she could see, all along the length of the Shop—which was, as lengths go, a lengthy length. Each shelf towered over the customers, colossally tall and filled with jars of traits. Her eyes darted around, drinking in a jumble of human attributes which went on, and on, and on.

And this was just *one* aisle.

"Excuse me, ma'am!" A Child darted past, deftly pushing a tall ladder on wheels as they led a customer down the aisle. "It's down here, sir," said the Child. "It's no wonder you missed it—this one is pretty hard to spot even with a ladder! Now, I always think a touch of INTROSPECTION goes well with . . ."

Their conversation was lost in the noise of the crowd. On a whim, she followed the pair, taking the opportunity to peer at the nearest traits. Her blood was on fire with exhilaration. Not literally, of course, although . . . perhaps that was possible? Could she light a jar of EXHIL-ARATION on fire? Management would presumably disapprove, so she wouldn't try, but right now the possibilities seemed endless.

She wanted to run and laugh and dance. Even on this one shelf, on this one aisle, the variety was incredible. PAINSTAKING, BREEZY, INCOR-RUPTIBLE, HEROIC, in jars which were tall, small, fat, thin, made of colourful glass and clear. Some had brilliant white labels, while others were older, yellowing and cracked. The contents were more diverse still. A few crackled, while others oozed, swirled, sparkled or even remained still, silent and inert. She gazed deeply into the jars, noticing that each glowed, so gently that you might not notice at first, but together they all added up to bathe the aisle in a medley of colour.

She glanced back towards the checkouts. There was no obvious sign of the Shopkeeper. Surely it wouldn't hurt to look around just a little more?

It didn't matter—her legs were already moving. No-one even knew she was here yet, so surely exploring must be fine. Elated, she practically skipped deeper into the Shop.

In contrast to the open space of the concourse, between the high shelves everything felt cosy and secluded. The sunlight from the giant glass dome over the concourse didn't reach this far down the aisle, so the further she went, the more she had to rely on the eerie, soothing luminescence from the assorted jars, or on light from the dribbly candles which were scattered apparently at random, on shelves or on the floor, sputtering with flame and dripping with wax.

Occasionally she had to step out of the way of Children carrying totter-ing, physics-defying stacks of jars.

Along the way she greedily read labels on any jar which grabbed her attention. One marked CURIOUS was filled with a pink and fluffy substance, unlike anything she recognised. NIMBLE was white and gaseous, while TINKERS WITH MACHINERY was—strangely—also pink and fluffy. Each shelf contained many copies of its traits, which was strange to imagine. Could multiple people really take the same INAP-PROPRIATE HUMOUR?

Too soon, she reached the end of the aisle, but—delightfully—it turned out only to be a dividing wall peppered with entryways which led deeper into the main building. Inside the first door was a passageway lined with yet more shelves, these made of darker red wood. Unable to resist entering, she read more labels as she walked past. GENEROUS HEART, THOUGHTFUL, WILL TALK TO ANYONE. At the end of this passageway she found some stairs, and at the top, a mezzanine which overlooked the aisle she'd walked along.

The distant concourse was bright with sunlight from the glass dome, while the aisle beneath was dark but for the glow of the jars and occasional pockets of light bobbing along the ground where Children were carrying candles. The chatter of customers drifted upwards, punctuated by a strange sound which she eventually realised was the creak of a nearby ladder. A sphere of candlelight was climbing slowly higher and higher against the muted glimmer of the shelves. She wondered which trait the Child was retrieving, and who might have requested it.

Once she had committed the scene to memory, she turned around, looked up, and gasped. The intertwining maze of floors above was even more overwhelming from this end of the building. She lost count of the number of storeys as they crossed back and forth all the way up to the ceiling far above.

By now, she had completely abandoned the idea of reporting quickly to the Shopkeeper. Getting thoroughly, delightfully lost was too enjoyable.

She headed deeper inside this vertical maze, following twists and turns through aisles and archways, up and down stairs, along squat passages and through rooms of varying sizes, until she had no idea what storey this was, or even in which direction the entrance now lay. And this was still only the main building! She hadn't even seen the tangle of older buildings at the far end of the Shop.

Compared to the earlier busyness of the concourse, it was eerily quiet here. The jars glowed through a thin layer of dust, and the candles were extra dribbly.

She laughed aloud. The Shop was already every bit as magical as she'd hoped. Why had she resisted coming here for so long?

But now, it was finally time to head back to the checkouts and report to the Shopkeeper.

"Reporting for duty," she said, with a giggle which echoed off the low ceiling.

She did her best to retrace her steps, and gradually found the Shop's entrance getting closer. As the checkouts were coming into view, she was interrupted by a small boy clutching a basket brimming with jars.

"Excuse me miss," he called. "Can you help me?"

Faythe smiled, proud to be recognised. She must be a natural Apprentice. "I don't exactly work here, but of course."

He gave her a funny look. "I know. I'm not stupid. I just need help reaching." He pointed to a shelf that was slightly too high for his outstretched arm.

She flushed. Obviously, he wouldn't have known she worked here. Still, it was his lucky day. He had unwittingly requested the assistance of the new Apprentice, and helping customers was her job!

At least, she assumed it was.

She peered up at the trait he was indicating, a row of squat jars filled with what appeared to be yellow pebbles.

"TALLER THAN AVERAGE," she read aloud. She grinned. "Someone here has a sense of humour."

"Ha-ha," said the boy, with an edge to his voice. "Want me to help you find MAKES OBVIOUS JOKES?"

She opened her mouth to argue back, but thought better of it. "Very good, sir," she said, receiving another funny look in return. She stretched upward, pursing her lips. The jar was just out of her grasp.

After watching her scrabble unsuccessfully, the boy looked disappointed. "I'll go get help," he muttered, looking around for any nearby Children.

"No, I've got it." She strained determinedly on her tip-toes, just managing to nudge the jar with a fingertip. "I'm really close."

"Seriously, I'll get a ladder."

"I'm happy . . . to . . . help." She held her breath and thrust higher. The jar shifted as she practically tickled it sideways against its neighbour. "There!"

She pressed against the glass, and it slid on the smooth wood of the shelf. Instinctively, she tried to snatch at it, but she slipped as her tiptoes gave out beneath her. She missed the jar and brought her hand down on the shelf, which bent and buckled under her weight, and came crashing down. Dozens of jars of TALLER THAN AVERAGE smashed to the ground, showering her ankles in glass and yellow pebbles. The pebbles evaporated into nothing in an instant—unlike the noise of the glass cascade, which went on seemingly forever.

Then, silence.

The boy stared at her, horrified, then sprinted away without a word, leaving her paralysed amongst the mess she'd made.

A Child appeared nearby. "Tsk. Tsk. Quite the shambles you've left here." He was a touch plump, and wearing blue stretchy dungarees. A lump of wood was sticking out of his front pocket.

"I was trying to help!"

"Oh, were you?" He chortled to himself. "Thanks so much! Normally we have to smash up our own shelves so we have something to clean up, so it's really appreciated." He turned to inspect the broken shelf.

"I'm sorry. There was a boy—" She trailed off. This was an unimpressive introduction to the Shop. *But nobody else knew who she was.* Perhaps she could still run away, and report to the Shopkeeper tomorrow, after this incident was forgotten. Or find a whole heap of EXTRA CAREFUL and sneak through to Earth, contract with Management or not.

Either way, remaining here was a bad idea. She began creeping backwards over the broken glass, towards the darker end of the aisle.

Moments later, the Child turned back over his shoulder. "Tell me, what were you saying about a—hey! Where are you going?"

She was already sprinting deeper into the Shop.

From behind, she heard a loud, shrill whistle, and then shouts. "Security! Suspicious runner on Aisle Twenty-Four!"

She cursed as she skidded at the end of the aisle. Quickly, she took the door on her left, and ran up the stairs. Maybe she could lose them in the mezzanine area ...

Faythe ran, choosing doors and stairs and passages at random, hoping it would make her behaviour more difficult to predict.

Too late, she realised how awful this plan was. It's very, very hard to escape a co-ordinated team of people in a maze, especially when they know the maze intimately and you barely know it at all.

Seconds later, she ran straight into a group of Children who were lying in wait, camouflaged in the gloom by their dark blue uniforms. Exhausted, she gave up and allowed herself to be led back to the plump Child at the ill-fated shelf.

As they approached, her heart sank further. The Child was talking to an elderly lady with bright, sharp eyes. It could only be the Shopkeeper.

"So we've caught one of our vandals, at last?" the Shopkeeper was saying.

"It seems so," said the Child. "I assumed it was an accident, but she ran away as soon as I turned my back."

Faythe closed her eyes. Her past self, of several minutes ago, had been *such* an idiot. To her considerably more enlightened present self, it was obvious that running away had been an extremely bad idea. "It *was* an accident," she insisted, as the Shopkeeper turned to look at her. "A boy asked me to help him, and—"

"Just so you know, Shopkeeper," interrupted the Child. "I didn't see a boy."

"Thank you, Omaro." The Shopkeeper nodded thoughtfully, and squinted at Faythe. "You're not what I expected."

As well as being a figure straight out of genuine legends, the Shopkeeper was the oldest person Faythe had ever seen. She fought the urge to stare. It was fascinating what a difference wrinkles made to a face . . . *Not now, brain!* "I'm really sorry for running away." That was an understatement. "But I'm not whoever you think I am."

"I think you're whoever has been smashing parts of my Shop recently. Are you saying you're not?"

"That's right. I only just got here and I haven't been smashing anything." Faythe glanced at the mess around them. "Well, except this one shelf."

"I'm afraid I still don't follow," said the Shopkeeper. "Why did you vandalise my Shop?"

A team of Children bustled around them, sweeping up the broken glass and repairing the shelf. Already, there was no trace of any TALLER THAN AVERAGE to be seen.

"It was an accident. But the more important thing is . . ." Faythe drew a breath. "I'm the new Apprentice you're expecting."

The pair exchanged a stupefied look.

The Shopkeeper tightened her mouth. "I can't imagine why you think lying to me would help your cause. We're not expecting any new Apprentice."

Faythe's chest tightened. That couldn't be right. "Please!" she said. "I'm telling the truth."

At least, she thought she was telling the truth. Had those men lied to her about the job? She was beginning to wish she'd taken the cowardly way out and anonymously filled up a basket to take to Earth. Next time she had to make a decision she was *definitely* going to take the easiest possible option.

The Shopkeeper rubbed her forehead. "I think I would know if there was a new Apprentice, dear."

Omaro tugged at her arm, lightly but insistently. "Shall I take her outside?" he offered. "We'll keep her off the premises for a few years, let her cool down."

Panic swelled, tightening in Faythe's throat. "Please! I have a letter!" she spluttered. "They told me it was from Management." She sucked in a deep breath, trying to calm down and soften her voice. "Please. It's signed by men called Aaron and Gabriel. Check my pocket. At least tell me if they were lying."

The Shopkeeper frowned and signalled to the guard, who reached into Faythe's coat pocket, carefully withdrew the letter, and passed it over.

Omaro hopped from foot to foot, staring at the Shopkeeper as she unfolded the paper to read. By the time she finished, her lips were so tight they were virtually invisible.

She gave her would-be Apprentice a long, searching look. Faythe had heard legends of this wise old lady her entire prelife. Now she could see why. There was an intensity to the Shopkeeper, an almost tangible weight of personality which commanded the whole Shop—or all of reality, perhaps—to flow around her. It was terrifying. The stories also spoke of the Shopkeeper's kindness. Faythe hoped those stories were true.

By now the mess in the aisle had been completely cleared, and the shelf repaired. The Children disappeared as quickly as they had arrived, leaving her alone with Omaro, the security guard, and the Shopkeeper.

"It's real," said the Shopkeeper, holding out the letter for Omaro.

The Child waved it away. "If you say so." He let out a slow whistle. "Weeee-ooo. Another Apprentice."

"Another Apprentice, indeed. I do wish they'd informed me that those two would be out recruiting." The Shopkeeper spoke out of the side of her mouth, without looking away from Faythe. "And as for you, my dear, I do not understand why your first actions here were to cause all this damage."

Faythe heard the question mark loud and clear. "Let me explain, ma'am." The 'ma'am' slipped out automatically, as if her mouth couldn't comprehend addressing the Shopkeeper any less formally. "I was honestly trying to help a boy reach a jar, and . . . I slipped and knocked over the shelf, and then I was scared I'd get in trouble so I ran away. Or tried to." She gulped for breath. It was taking tremendous effort to withstand the Shopkeeper's fierce gaze. "It was a bad decision," she admitted. "I'm sorry."

The old woman's expression softened a little. "I'm pleased to hear it. Although I do hope this sort of behaviour isn't a habit of yours." She drummed her fingers absently on a shelf and then shook her head. "No, no. Forget I said that. I know when I'm being unfair. Let's get you settled"—she glanced down at the letter—"Faythe. Come with me."

Faythe's heart still pounded as she fell into step alongside the Shop-keeper. The silence between them crackled as they walked briskly down the aisle. She didn't feel relieved, exactly—after all, receiving the benefit of the doubt was only possible if there *was* doubt—but at least she hadn't been humiliatingly ejected from the Shop Before Life. Yet.

As they emerged onto the busy concourse, a ripple of excitable whispers arose at the sight of the Shopkeeper, whose unreadable mask instantly transformed into smiles. She waved around benevolently as the pair weaved towards the long checkout desk.

Faythe anxiously shrunk away amidst all the attention and point-ing fingers, but she still couldn't help grinning at a surprised look of recognition from the man she'd met earlier in the queue. He clung tightly onto his five bright jars of EXTROVERT and sniffed loudly as they passed.

Moments later, she pushed against the door marked PRIVATE, tingling with excitement. What wonders would be kept where only the Shopkeeper and her staff could go?

Inside was a vast administrative area, filled with Children bustling around with arms full of files and the occasional stapler. It was no less wondrous than Faythe had hoped. After decades of hearing tales like 'The Shopkeeper & the Missing Stapler', seeing the mythical device in person was itself a surprisingly magical experience.

Their eventual destination turned out to be the Shopkeeper's private office, a room which was theoretically large enough to be spacious, but was practically so full up that it could only truly be described as 'cosy'. Yet more files bulged out of half-closed cabinets, stacks of well-thumbed books teetered haphazardly on high shelves, and binders were heaped on every available surface. This complex muddle looked more lived-in than Faythe's old bedroom. Clearly not all of the Shopkeeper's time was spent handing out magical traits.

Her new boss sat in a comfortable-looking chair, brushing papers aside to make space for her elbows. Naturally, most of her desk was buried under a thick layer of papers and semi-submerged coloured wooden trays. Archaeologists could probably spend years piecing together a history of abandoned attempts at desk organisation. The orderly chaos reminded Faythe of the Shop building itself.

"Can I fetch you a drink?" asked the Shopkeeper, after a pause.

She shook her head.

"Well, Faythe . . . as you can tell, this has come as quite a surprise."

"To me too, honestly," she muttered, before realising she had spoken. She bit her lip.

The Shopkeeper only smiled. "Truly, I wasn't aware we were being sent a new Apprentice. It's been a little time since we've had one at all. Perhaps you could inform me how this came about?"

Faythe told the story of her meeting with Aaron and Gabriel.

When she'd finished, the Shopkeeper glanced down again at the letter. "I wonder what they're planning," she said, half to herself.

"Management work in mysterious ways," said Faythe. She knew that was the kind of thing people said in such situations, though it wasn't clear why anybody expected to understand gods at all.

"Indeed, they do," sighed the Shopkeeper. "As ever, in the meantime, we must make the best of it. I'll have Beris take you to your room. Beris!"

A Child entered the office, wearing a bright lime-green suit and a serious expression. He waved stiffly at Faythe.

"Beris, this is Faythe. She's our new Apprentice."

The Child gaped like a shocked fish and his officious manner dissolved in an instant. "App-uh-buh-buh?"

"Never fear. I'm sure Management wouldn't have chosen her if she weren't going to do a spectacular job."

The pointed comment wasn't lost on her.

"I'll be the best Apprentice there is." She blushed. She'd spoken without thinking again, and with a level of confidence she didn't truly feel.

"Let's hope you achieve more than that," said the Shopkeeper, with a quick glance at Beris.

Faythe wanted to ask what that strange comment meant, but neither speech nor action had worked well for her since she'd arrived. She resolved to stay quiet.

In the meantime, Beris had recovered his composure. He bowed to Faythe. "Pleased to meet you." His voice was gentle, and oddly shy despite his formality.

"Show her to the Apprentice's chambers, if you don't mind." The Shopkeeper scrawled something on a scrap of paper and handed it to Beris. "And have her report to you tomorrow for introductory training. I trust you to cover everything she needs to know." Beris nodded. "And I will check on how you're doing in due course, Faythe."

"Thank you, ma'am," she said, grateful to be excused. Her head was full of everything that had happened. Had it really been only hours since she'd arrived?

"Please, call me Shopkeeper," said the Shopkeeper.

Was that a joke? Or was 'Shopkeeper' actually her real name? Either way, with a final nervous smile to her new employer, Faythe followed Beris out of the office.

Beris appeared lost in thought as he led her back through the administrative area and into the living quarters, where he abruptly appeared to realise that perhaps a tour might be helpful to the new arrival.

"The Shopkeeper lives above, and the Children live in this section"—he gestured at a spiral staircase and then at a series of doors scattered seemingly at random around the hallway—"but you will have the Apprentice's quarters to yourself." He opened a door to reveal a corridor of bare stone, brightly lit through large glass windows. "There's a bedroom, a bathroom, and a spare room you can use as you wish. Do you need anyone to fetch you anything?"

She shook her head. Right now, she needed time alone. "No," she said. "I mean . . . no, thank you."

The Child nodded. "Very well. Ask anyone in the administrative team if you need anything this evening. I have training to prepare."

Was that a pointed comment? Had she disrupted his evening? She felt a pang of guilt at the chaos she was causing. She waved a weak goodbye at Beris and closed the door.

Once alone, she flopped onto her new bed and stared at the ceiling. It felt wrong. Instead of the familiar stony surface of the inside of the Rock, above her was a window, and above that, a starry sky. Apparently she'd missed the sun going down while she'd been almost getting banished from the Shop.

For a time, she emptily gazed at the stars. Her initial elation had ebbed away, leaving behind a tight, cold apprehension. Everything felt so strange, like she was wearing a different skin. But she was the same. The whole universe had changed around her.

She thought of Jahu and Tapak. What would they say now? It wasn't difficult to guess. They'd be unable to stop laughing at her spectacularly embarrassing arrival.

She stifled a sudden urge to cry. She'd been trying to avoid thinking about her friends in case she was tempted to go back. Although, after signing a thousand-year contract with Management, returning home had never been a realistic option.

She felt simultaneously heavy with responsibility and light with disbelief that any of this was real. The Shop was too small—she was trapped and claustrophobic. But it was also too vast—she was tiny, overwhelmed by her insignificance in this new, unknown world.

The room spun dizzyingly.

A quietly reasonable voice in the back of her brain spoke up: *You've not even been here a day yet. This is merely an awkward start, and you're missing your friends. Give it time.*

Of course, like all humans, she ignored such quietly reasonable voices whenever possible. She cried until the tears ran out, and then stared upwards at nothing in particular.

The Earth drifted into view, vast and beautiful. The room shone with cold, blue-green earthlight. If she hadn't signed that contract, she might have been being born over there right now.

She shivered.

Tomorrow was the first day of what might be a long thousand years.

four

A NEW START is a rare moment of purity. For the briefest instant, the present is free of baggage and the future explodes into uncountable alternatives, each brimming with infinite possibility. In these pregnant moments, *anything* could happen.

Unfortunately, 'anything' also includes introductory training on retail management systems.

On the way to the classroom, the morning stars still twinkled brightly above. Had the stars sparkled so much back at the Rock? All that twinkling felt vaguely patronising. Faythe sincerely hoped her life wasn't going to be twee now that she lived in a magical shop.

As she passed the checkouts, she received a lukewarm smile from the Shopkeeper, who was surrounded by a gaggle of excitable customers. She glanced back and saw somebody ask for—and receive—a hug from the Shopkeeper.

Suppressing a brief pang of envy, she entered the classroom, where Beris was paging through a truly massive stack of notes. Today he wore another bright green suit, of a slightly different shade, along with tiny spectacles with matching green rims and a neon yellow tie over a grey shirt. Somehow, this suited him perfectly.

Without greeting her, Beris cleared his throat and began to teach, as if he were delivering a lecture to a packed hall.

"The Shop Before Life is an ancient institution which plays a crucial part in enabling humanity to live their lives on Earth. Naturally, we take this responsibility seriously. And today, we will enable you to play an important role in this enterprise, as we empower people to choose who they want to be . . ."

Faythe selected a pen—blue, with a red one on hand to underline anything important—and scribbled notes as swiftly as she could.

Beris was an excellent teacher, and his grand formality was oddly endearing. First, he drew a complicated series of maps to demonstrate the baffling geography of the Shop. Afterwards, they discussed the daily tasks which the Shop required to function, from controlling the physical flow of customers to the nightly restock of the shelves. After that came paperwork, customer service, checkout operation, proper jar handling, and a confusing diagram called a Staff Organisation Spider, which showed the Shopkeeper at the centre, surrounded by a colourful mess of teams and people's names. Her name was already pencilled in, just next to the Shopkeeper's, although Beris appeared to find the use of pencil embarrassing, as he apologised several times and promised an official reprint of the chart as soon as possible.

The day was long and unmagical, but her natural fascination kept her going. It helped that Beris was affable company, provided the topic didn't stray too far from logistical systems. Throughout the day, the pair instinctively colluded to create unnecessary educational theatre, as Faythe held up her hand to ask questions and Beris pretended to select a student to speak.

As the day came to a close, she held up her hand for a final time.

"I have a question!"

The Child pointed to indicate permission. She was brimming with questions about the history of the Shop and the magic of the traits, but something important had been bugging her all day. "May I ask where you got the idea for your suit?"

His eyes sparkled. "You like it?"

"I do!" she replied, genuinely. It suited him, anyway.

"I read a book on popular Earth fashions," he said, proudly. "And after I saw these suits I had to get a colleague to make one for me."

She raised an eyebrow. So they wore this on Earth? Interesting. She made a mental note to read more about life there as soon as possible.

"Of course," he continued, "the picture was in black-and-white so I had to guess the colours."

Immediately, everything made sense. "I think you did a great job."

"Thank you." He beamed. "Now, I know it's been a long day, but how about we finish with a test?"

She grinned and held up her sheaf of notes. "Do your worst."

"Very well." Beris thought for a moment. "Imagine I'm a customer looking for DOGGED DETERMINATION. Where do you take me?"

She chewed the end of her pen. "DETERMINATION, but not the standard variation, a dogged variety. So, not in the main aisles, or even the mezzanine maze"—Beris frowned in confusion—"sorry, that's what I call the vertical bit at the far end, you know? Anyway, it must be in one of the wings behind the maze. Probably . . ." She squinted down at her hastily drawn map. "GRIT? Do I look in the GRIT wing?"

He clapped in delight. "Very good! I don't expect you to have learned the location of every jar in only one day. But if you remember which wings exist, that's a fantastic start."

She tried not to look smug, which made her look very smug indeed.

"Oh, and the mezzanine maze? We call it the Stacks."

She shrugged. "I like my name. But okay."

"Next question! Where do we store excess stock overnight?"

She glanced down at her diagram. "Easy! The Warehouse."

"Fantastic!"

He fired several more questions at her, all of which she batted away with ease. Afterwards, her tutor was extremely satisfied. "You've done splendidly, Faythe. I'm confident you'll pick up everything rapidly."

She shone with pride.

"I think that's enough for today," he said, already packing away his notes, "unless you have any final questions?"

It had been a long day, but one question in particular still needled her. "I've wondered about the traits forever. How do they work? I mean . . . how do people use them?"

His eyes sparkled. "Aren't they wonderful? They raise so many fascinating questions. Of course, I've never actually witnessed any individual passing through to Earth, for safety reasons." Seeing her puzzled expression, he continued. "We can't allow anyone to get too close, lest they end up being born accidentally." He straightened a stack of papers against the desk before sliding them into his binder. "Myself, I've always been more fascinated by how the traits are made."

She frowned. "Why?"

"It's always seemed to me that consuming is trivial, and it's creation that's the real magic."

Faythe paused. "I thought Management just sent them?" Insofar as she'd thought about it at all, anyway. "Where *do* they come from?"

"Remember what I told you? We restock nightly from the Warehouse."

She should have expected this response from the logistically minded Child. She tried again.

"Yes, but before that. Where do they come from?"

"All of our stock comes from the Supplier."

Well, that was useless. She tried one final time.

"And the Supplier gets them from . . . ?"

"Through manufacture, naturally." He twiddled his tie. "Well, manufacture isn't a natural process, technically, but I mean—"

"Don't worry, I knew what you meant," she said, before Beris could tie himself in knots.

"I can't tell you more about the process, I'm afraid." He sounded genuinely regretful.

Interesting. 'Manufacture' wasn't very different from 'magic', as far as explanations went. Both were less of an answer and more of a polite way of saying 'don't know', or worse, 'stop asking'. She would learn the truth behind all these mysteries, eventually.

Beris paused on his way out of the classroom. "One last thing," he said. "I heard about your incident with the shelf." He smiled. "You ought to remain within the private quarters until you're ready."

Ouch. Apparently the Shopkeeper bore grudges.

It didn't matter. She would prove herself soon enough.

Training resumed the next day . . . and the next, and the day after that.

In fact, several weeks passed during which Faythe did nothing but eat, sleep and receive information from Beris. Each day, on her way to lessons, she looked longingly at the door to the concourse, desperate to roam the Shop once more.

Her days were filled with relentless education on customer service techniques and paperwork procedures, and endless memorisation of the locations of particular traits. Even for a student as enthusiastic as Faythe, this was too much. As the end of her first month neared, she was lonely—she tried hard not to think about Jahu and Tapak—and bored. Everything was beginning to chafe.

"When can I *do* something?" she wailed, as yet another session of memorising jar handling procedures came to an end.

Beris clasped his hands and attempted to look enthusiastic. "You are doing something! Learning is a thing too."

"I meant other than learning, though. I'm bored. When can I start work?"

"I know you're keen, but the Shopkeeper did insist that you be thoroughly prepared before you begin."

"But when will that be?"

The Child blinked. "I can't say. But I'm sure she'll discuss it with you in the near future." He looked guiltily down at his papers. "I believe we've reached a satisfactory place to pause. Shall we take a break before the evening session?"

She sighed as Beris packed his things up and left her alone in the training room. She'd barely seen the Shopkeeper since the day she'd arrived. Sure, her employer was the busiest person in the whole prelife, but surely she could find a few minutes for her new Apprentice? Every time she brought it up, Beris acted sheepish. She was sure the Shopkeeper was deliberately keeping her contained.

Perhaps she would do the same, in the Shopkeeper's position. But right now, she was bored.

In an instant, she made a decision. She left her notes on the desk, and made straight for the Shopkeeper's office. She knocked before her nerves could talk her out of it.

"Come in!" called the Shopkeeper.

Inside, Beris was standing in front of the Shopkeeper's desk. Both looked surprised to see her, but the Shopkeeper smiled and waved her inside. She joined the Child on the plush carpet in front of the desk.

"Greetings, Faythe," said the Shopkeeper. "Beris was in the middle of his weekly report."

"Actually," he coughed. "I'm nearly at the end. I've been so busy with training that several sections are yet to be compiled."

Faythe couldn't help smiling. From anyone but Beris that might have been a barbed complaint about how much time she was taking up, but she knew him better than that by now.

"I'm sorry about that," she said. "And I'm sorry for interrupting you both, too."

The Shopkeeper held up a hand. "There's no need to apologise, I didn't mean to imply you weren't welcome. I just didn't want you to worry that Beris had run straight here to tattle on you after training."

He frowned. "Why would I do that?"

"You wouldn't," said the Shopkeeper, warmly. She winked at Faythe. "Anyway, it's me that should be apologising to you. I know I've been unavailable lately. I'm afraid there's a lot happening, and I was hoping you would be using your time to settle in. After all, we will have plenty of time together to get to know one another."

Her heart accelerated a little at the reminder of how long, exactly, she had committed to stay here.

"I have been settling, a bit. Although I've not really been anywhere, or done anything. Besides training, of course." She glanced at Beris. "Which has been very good," she added, hurriedly.

He beamed. "She's been an excellent student too. One of the best I've seen."

"So you've told me," said the Shopkeeper.

Warmth spread through Faythe's chest. "I'm not sure I'd go that far," she said, laying on the bashfulness as thick as she could.

"Well, quite," said the Shopkeeper. "I suppose the proof will be in your eventual performance as Apprentice."

She nearly bit her tongue. People aren't supposed to *believe* you when you're pretending to be modest. "That's actually what I wanted to talk about," she said. "I'm wondering when you think I'll be ready to start?"

The Shopkeeper looked thoughtful. "You think you're prepared, already?"

"I do!"

The Shopkeeper clucked her tongue. "I do like your enthusiasm. And I do imagine you must be getting a little bored—no offence, Beris."

"None taken," said the Child, with a confused look.

"But I have to be absolutely sure I can trust you," she continued. "Our work is important."

Faythe nodded vigorously. "I know that."

"Do you realise how important? Every interaction with a customer is literally life and death. And you'll have many thousands of interactions every single day. Mistakes cannot be tolerated."

"I know that, too." She shifted on her feet. The Shopkeeper was gazing at her as if to prise her open and see what was inside.

"So you can surely tell me where to find a jar of ARGUMENTATIVE?"

"Yes!" She leapt at the chance to show off. "Aisle Fourteen."

"And which stacking layouts are optimal for different types of jars?"

She nodded, hoping the Shopkeeper wouldn't press further. Beris had spent a remarkable amount of time explaining the multi-dimensional tessellation algebra which described how to stack the occasionally misshapen jars sold at the Shop, but she doubted her brain had retained all of it.

"And how to fill in the end-of-day paperwork?" More nods. "And what to do if the Shop is on fire?"

She drew a deep breath to cover the sudden blankness in her mind where the answer should be. "Run . . . ?" she hazarded.

The Shopkeeper laughed, a genuine, warm chortle. "That would do, I suppose! And how to handle an angry customer?"

"De-escalate the situation if possible, first," she said, on cue. "And if that fails, whistle for Security."

"A sound I believe you're already familiar with, correct?" The Shopkeeper's eyes sparkled.

Faythe blushed at the reminder of her chaotic arrival. "I'm sorry about that," she muttered.

"Oh, I'm only teasing you!" The Shopkeeper drummed her fingers on the desk. "Enough testing. I'm sure Beris has drilled you with enough knowledge. But I have been wanting to learn more about you. I don't even know how old you are!"

She eagerly leapt to answer. "A couple of centuries, more or less." She smiled, remembering how this had impressed Aaron and Gabriel.

"Ah! Still so young!"

She blinked, taken aback. Her eyes drifted over the Shopkeeper's wrinkles. What length of time could make two centuries seem so little? "I suppose so," she mumbled.

"And what did you spend your time on during those centuries? Did you travel?"

"Not a lot," she admitted.

"You never explored the prelife? Visited Ostholme, or the other great cities?"

She shook her head. Ever since she'd left the Rock, her prelife had felt much smaller. "I mostly stayed in one place," she said.

"Nothing wrong with that," said the Shopkeeper, not unkindly. Her expression became intent. "And you never met Aaron or Gabriel before that day?"

"No." Faythe frowned. *How could she have? What a strange question.* "Why do you ask?"

"No reason." The Shopkeeper drummed her fingers once more. "I'm sure two hundred years seems like a long time to you, but believe me, it is very short indeed. And a few weeks of training is shorter still." She drew a deep breath. "I'm not sure what would be best. All of this came as such a surprise. I planned to ease us both into your time at the Shop."

"To wait until you can trust me, I get it." She smiled to indicate that she understood her boss's predicament.

The Shopkeeper's eyes narrowed. "Trust. That's it, precisely." Her face softened just as quickly. "I was planning for you to take several months of theoretical training before we let you loose on any customers."

Faythe's stomach bubbled with thwarted hope and frustration. "Months!" she whined. That was basically *forever.*

But Beris stepped in on her behalf. "May I interject? Faythe has been a superb student. Keen to learn, and quick. I wonder if she might benefit from practical experience, rather than additional theory."

The Shopkeeper blinked. "*You* think no more theory is required?"

"More theory is always required, Shopkeeper," he said, adjusting his glasses. "But, in this case, I think practice might be better still."

The old lady chuckled. "There really is a first time for everything."

She looked at Faythe with a sudden frown. "You weren't prepared in advance, were you?"

Faythe screwed up her brow. *How could she possibly have been prepared? And why would that matter?*

"No," she said, uncertainly. "I guess I'm a quick learner."

The Shopkeeper nodded thoughtfully. "So Beris tells me. But remember, my first responsibility is to my customers—and that means everyone. I have to consider what might happen if you make a serious mistake."

"I promise I won't make a mistake!" Faythe's eyes widened as she realised she'd replied without thinking again. That was becoming a dangerous habit. She'd have to watch out for it in future.

The Shopkeeper smiled. "Ah, the arrogance of youth."

"I'm not!" she blurted.

She bit her tongue. *So much for keeping her mouth shut.*

"Not arrogant? Or not young?" The Shopkeeper still seemed amused. "Either way, we shall see. If Beris thinks you're sufficiently prepared, then that's good enough for me. We will put you on duty tomorrow. Begin at the checkouts, and afterwards you can help customers find what they need."

Faythe trembled with excitement. At last she would get to see the Shop again. She'd gone to sleep every night remembering the magic of that first day of exploring. "Thank you!" she said. "You won't regret it!"

Behind her, Beris was scribbling notes. "I will reprint the rota immediately," he said, his eyes twinkling with pride. "You'll have a good day, Apprentice." Suddenly, his face became sad. "I suppose this means our class tonight is cancelled."

"I think having the evening off is a good idea," agreed the Shopkeeper. "Besides, Faythe can perhaps use the time to re-familiarise herself with the grounds."

"I can leave the quarters?" She nearly danced on the spot.

The Shopkeeper frowned. "Of course! Did you think you could not?"

Her eyes widened. "I was told not to!"

They both looked at a puzzled Beris. "I didn't say that," he said. His eyes widened. "Although I did make a joke about you staying in your quarters until you were ready!"

"That was a joke?" Even as Faythe spoke, she remembered Beris's grin as he'd delivered the line.

The Shopkeeper breathed sharply through her teeth. "We did think it was odd that you spent so much time inside your room," she said. "I assumed you wanted more time to adapt."

"I thought you didn't trust me to go outside!"

A flicker passed over the Shopkeeper's eyes, but it was gone before Faythe could interpret it.

"I'm so, so, so sorry," said Beris, crestfallen.

"It's not your fault," she said, hurriedly. "I should have asked."

"And I should have checked on you, instead of assuming you would come to me," said the Shopkeeper. "Let this be a lesson in communication for all of us."

Beris still looked devastated.

Faythe had an idea. "Could we continue our lessons even after I start work?" she asked. "I'm sure I still have lots to learn."

The Child brightened up.

"That's an excellent idea," said the Shopkeeper. "And I'm sure Beris will agree. Now, I must get on with my work. Thank you for coming to see me, and do get some rest before tomorrow—remember, you promised no mistakes!"

Faythe laughed, but moments later—the very instant the office door swung shut—her excitement transmuted into anxiety.

"'I promise I won't make a mistake!'" she muttered sarcastically, as she walked through the bustling administrative area. "Very smart, Faythe."

She made for her quarters, intending to take the Shopkeeper's advice and stifle her growing nervousness with an early sleep.

Typically, she got distracted first.

five

FAYTHE'S FIRST INSTINCT had been to collapse onto her bed and ruminate nervously about tomorrow, but the instant she arrived in her room a second instinct suggested she leave and explore the Gardens instead. Her third instinct said to eat on the way, but she ignored it for now. She didn't want her instincts getting overconfident.

As she crossed the administrative area towards the back exit, her mind fizzed with apprehension. Several distinct worries were competing for her attention. The possibility of failure, the weight of a thousand-year contract, the sheer necessity of impressing the Shopkeeper, her responsibility over people's lives . . .

A weighty sigh escaped her as she crossed the Viewing Platform, swerving to avoid groups of customers who were admiring the Earth above. 'Life and death', the Shopkeeper had said. The words chafed against her like a stone under her whole skin. The more she considered her new role, the heavier and more impossible it felt. There was no way she was ready.

Admittedly, she had positively demanded to start after *insisting* she was ready. But as soon as she'd got what she wanted, her confidence had drained away. This seemed like an unfair way for the universe to behave.

The tide of fear rose further as she descended the steps into the Gardens. The busy noise of the Shop was fading away, but somehow the sound grated against her more and more until she paused on the path and closed her eyes, swallowing an abrupt urge to scream.

Stop overreacting, said a sensible voice somewhere in the back of her mind. She ignored it. If anything, overreacting felt like the correct reaction to her swirling feelings.

How can OVER-reacting be the right reaction? By definition, it—

SHUT UP! She squished the sensible voice, wishing desperately she had somebody to talk to. Beris would never understand, and the Shopkeeper was an actual legendary figure. Worse, she was directly in charge of Faythe for a thousand years and making a good impression was crucial. Crying to her the second she'd been given the slightest responsibility didn't seem wise.

But Beris believes you can do it, nudged the sensible voice, insistently.

That didn't help either. In fact, it made everything worse. Now she was responsible for Beris' reputation too. And there were infinitely many ways to fail.

As if on cue, her imagination helpfully began listing possibilities: not knowing how to help a customer, arguing with another, breakages, accidents, fights, tripping and falling and looking silly in front of everybody, getting lost, making administrative mistakes . . . it was *endless*. What if she forgot how to speak overnight?! Anything could happen!

Anxiety gripped her ribcage tighter and tighter. She stared into the distance. The faraway mountains had never looked more inviting, even during all these weeks of gazing at them longingly from indoors. How long would it take to reach them if she crossed the river right now and just kept going?

A bird landed on the path nearby, momentarily distracting her back into reality. She took in the sight vacantly, without truly seeing the beauty around her. Here, about halfway down the main path into the Gardens, she was surrounded by more colour than she'd ever imagined possible. The sun was low, and the light had an ethereal quality as it reflected off the blooming flowers, bushes and trees.

Eventually, Faythe stirred from her trance. She breathed out. It was good to be outside. Still, she couldn't quite relax—

Behind her, someone coughed. She yelped and nearly leapt into the bushes in terror.

The intruder was wearing a broad-brimmed hat, and appeared as old as the Shopkeeper. "Sorry," he said, tipping his hat. "Didn't mean to startle you."

She put a hand to her hair and attempted to look unruffled. "You didn't." A pause. "I was just thinking, that's all."

"Glad you're enjoying the Gardens," he said, amiably ignoring her obvious lie. "People tell me they're very verdant."

"Verdant?" She frowned.

"It means 'green, but impressive'." His eyes twinkled, and he held out a hand. "I'm the Gardener."

He said it more like a name than a title. The Gardener. Like the Shopkeeper.

"I'm Faythe. So you made all this?" She pulled what she hoped was an impressed face.

"Well, not made, exactly. I like to think I encourage it into being."

"That sounds a lot easier."

"You'd think so. But you'd be surprised."

She didn't doubt it. "It's beautiful," she said. Honestly, that was an understatement. She'd loved the view from the Rock, but the Gardens were a controlled explosion of colour and pattern and contrast and chaos. They were nothing short of stunning. "But why does the Shop need a garden?"

"Why wouldn't a shop have a garden?"

That was a fair point, although perhaps somebody called The Gardener was slightly biased.

"It's just not what I expected," she said, with a shrug. The breeze picked up, and they both stared down the slope towards the river. "I guess I'd never thought of the Shop as an actual place. It was this thing that everyone did." She remembered the irregular visitors who'd passed by the Rock over the years. "Everyone except me, anyway."

"And now you're here it's not like you imagined?"

"It's not only that." She hesitated, unsure of how open she should be. She allowed her mouth to keep talking, hoping it would find the words to explain by itself. "I expected a big room full of jars. But it's so much more than that. It's incredible. It's so old, you can feel the history. I keep imagining how many people must have found parts of themselves here. And it's so big, you could get lost in there for months . . ." She glanced at the Gardener to see if he was still listening. He nodded encouragement. "But it's also a place with Gardens, and a Warehouse, and a stock replenishment system, and Children. It's like a whole world of its own. I never imagined any of it. I never expected *gardens*."

They stood in silence for a while.

"I didn't mean they shouldn't exist," she said, suddenly anxious she'd insulted his life's work. "I like them."

He looked at her carefully. "Easily worried, aren't you?" He pointed down the path. "Come on then, let me show you around."

That sounded better than an evening worrying about her first day working with customers. After all this time, it was a relief to talk to someone who didn't know she was the Apprentice. They zigzagged back and forth down a narrow cobbled path. As they went, the Gardener pointed out his favourite plants—one which opened up at night, another which reflected earthlight and a particular bush which honestly didn't look that special, but which he was apparently very fond of. After a while, they reached the bottom of the slope and stood together by the river bank.

"Is this the same river I saw from the Road?" she asked.

He nodded. "That's the one. It flows all the way to Ostholme. Gets pretty close to the Road in parts."

"Where does it come from?"

"See those mountains over there? It comes this way, then turns before it reaches the Shop." She squinted towards the horizon, but was distracted by a bright blur zooming across the landscape. It was moving faster than anything she'd ever seen.

"What's THAT?" she squealed.

He grinned. "That'd be the train to the Supplier. He's over in the mountains."

"Ohhh." Beris had mentioned something about a direct connection to the Supplier. "It's so fast."

He nodded. "I thought you'd have heard of it, Apprentice." He paused as he saw her expression. "Yeah, I know who you are."

Faythe's stomach lurched. So he had known all along. A paranoid part of her brain wondered if he was being so friendly *because* she was the new Apprentice, but another look at him quietened that particular concern. He didn't seem the type to pretend.

She didn't know what to say, but luckily she didn't have to, as they fell naturally into a companionable silence. She leaned on a wooden rail and watched the river go by. The evening sun was peeking over the horizon, and the water reflected a deep shade of orange from the darkening sky.

After a minute or two, she relaxed, like a tight net had been unwound from around her brain. She breathed out, slowly.

"Better?" asked the Gardener.

"Did I look bad before?" *Was she truly that transparent?*

"Not exactly," he said. "But I figure a spot of relaxation always helps when you're in a new place. I've replanted many plants in my time and you get to know how it goes." He gave her a warm smile. "Come back here whenever. I'll be off now—got a couple of things to finish before the sun really goes down. See you—oh, wait . . . here's trouble."

Faythe followed his gaze up the path. The plump Child with the perpetually mirthful expression—the one who had called Security after she'd smashed up that shelf—was puffing his way towards them. *Omaro,* she remembered.

"Trouble?" She frowned at the Gardener.

"You'll see," he said, darkly.

Omaro reached out a hand to Faythe. "Hi!" he said, cheerfully. She went to shake his hand, but he snatched it away and wiggled his fingers at her with his thumb on his nose.

"Don't say I didn't warn you," said the Gardener, rolling his eyes. "I'm afraid he's always like this."

"I'm sure I don't know what you mean," said Omaro, although his grin suggested he knew precisely. "I wanted to introduce myself to the new boss. We had a complicated meeting a few weeks ago."

"*Boss?!*" She had heard storytellers use the word 'boggling' before, but this was the first time she had ever personally boggled.

The Gardener snorted as he walked away, shaking his head. "Good luck!" he called.

The Child's eyes sparkled with amusement. "Well, perhaps someday I'll be calling you boss."

She looked at him helplessly. "I doubt it," she said. "Listen, I'm sorry about the other day."

"Accidents happen. You probably gathered we've been having trouble, lately. The Shopkeeper's on edge." He shrugged. "I guess when you ran away I jumped to conclusions. Thought you were part of the trouble."

She flushed. "You were right to jump. I was an idiot."

"Was?" He laughed. "If that's all it takes to stop you being an idiot then you're better at learning than I am. Anyway . . ." He reached into his pocket. "I heard a rumour you were coming out of the private quarters to play tonight, so I brought something to do while we get to know each other. Let's make yoyos."

She twisted her face in confusion. "Yoyos?" From the way he said it, they sounded important. Perhaps they were a kind of magical artifact?

"It's my current project." The Child strode to a nearby bench, where he handed her a lump of wood and a knife. "That's for you."

She watched in bewilderment as he began carving away at his own lump.

After a moment, he looked up. "You won't make any yoyos that way, you know." He sighed. "You look worried."

"I guess I am worried," she replied, truthfully. "But mainly I have absolutely no idea what's going on. Or what a yoyos is."

Omaro pondered this. "I can't explain the mystery of the yoyo to you, since I haven't yet discovered it myself. But perhaps I can help with everything else. What's worrying you?"

Faythe had no idea where to start. She picked at random from her list. "I still feel stupid for running away when we first met."

"Not a good look," he agreed.

"I'm not suited to a life of crime."

He grinned. "That's good to know. How're you finding everything else? Beris didn't bore you to death?"

"No, he was great! I love learning how things work."

The Child raised his eyebrows, but when he saw she was being genuine, he laughed in delight. "I can see it'll be interesting having you around."

Faythe smiled, toying with the lump of wood on her lap. "What do you do here, exactly?"

"I'm the Chief Assistant." The Child puffed out his chest and preened. "Or something like that. I don't actually remember my title."

She tried to remember the Staff Organisation Spider from a half-forgotten lecture weeks before. "Does that mean you outrank me?"

He gave her a sly look. "Why? Planning to issue orders?"

"No!" She laughed. "I just want to know where I stand."

"Technically, I think the Apprentice outranks everybody except the Shopkeeper herself. Though I suppose while you're new you're probably better off keeping a low profile."

That made sense. "Trust me, I'm trying."

"Apart from the whole shelf-smashing thing, you're doing great."

"Am I ever going to live that down?"

He giggled. "Eventually, I'm sure you will."

For a fleeting moment, she missed Jahu and Tapak terribly. They would *never* let her live it down. But she smiled. It felt good to be teased about it.

"I'm nervous about tomorrow," she admitted. "I don't know what to do." Instinctively, she braced herself for a rebuke. It was silly to be nervous.

"That sounds natural," he said. "I would be too."

"Oh." Her anxiety immediately seemed completely rational and not silly at all.

"You'll do great," he said.

"I hope you're right."

A customer wandered down the path, and Omaro gave them a friendly nod as they passed the bench. He turned to Faythe. "Are you happy here?"

The question took her by surprise. She blinked, and the Child waited patiently while she figured out her response.

"It's incredible here," she said, after a pause. "I loved the afternoon I spent seeing the jars, and exploring the place, but it's been . . ." She hesitated, still unsure how honest she should be. "It's been difficult. Lonely. And I don't know what to make of the Shopkeeper. She seems aloof."

"Aloof?" Omaro looked amazed.

"You don't think so?"

"I've just never heard anyone use the word 'aloof' before," he said. A bee buzzed around his head and he waved it away. "Also, no . . . I don't think she's aloof at all. She's not been friendly to you?"

"Not exactly." She hesitated again. "You saw how our first meeting went. She didn't seem to want me here at all. And then she ignored me for weeks, and today I sought her out and she was friendly, but towards the end she did call me arrogant."

"She did?!" The Child's mouth was a perfectly round circle of surprise.

"She said I showed the 'arrogance of youth'."

"Ah. That's an expression. It's about how young people often think they know more than they do."

"Oh. I didn't know that."

"Indeed."

They watched the water for a minute before he spoke again.

"I'm sure she'll warm to you. She's been reluctant to get a new Apprentice. We had trouble with the last one, so I think she's worried about how it might go with you. And you know already we weren't expecting you."

Faythe's eyes widened. "So it's not about me?"

"Most things aren't," he said. He thought for a moment. "Though, you try explaining that to anybody. No-one ever listens."

"What happened with the old Apprentice?" she asked, suddenly curious.

He hesitated before responding guardedly. "It's not for me to say."

"They didn't get on well?"

"That's very much an understatement." Omaro sighed. "I wish I could tell you. But a tiny part of it—and trust me, there was a lot—was him arguing that she was too controlling, so maybe that's why she's been giving you more space."

"Oh." She watched the breeze ripple through the flowers in front of them. "Is there anything else I should know?"

The Child's expression hardened. "I really can't talk about it." He looked around cautiously before leaning closer. "Management were unhappy with the whole situation, especially how it ended."

Management were unhappy! She shuddered involuntarily.

"You really knew nothing about this?" He watched her carefully.

She shook her head. "Why would I? I lived in a rock."

"Nobody said anything about it when you got the job? You're sure?"

"No. Management's people didn't say much at all. It was all quite hurried."

"Hm. Sounds like them. Listen, there's only one thing you need to know about the Shopkeeper: her only priority is the Shop. Be good for the Shop, and she'll be good for you. Why are you pulling that face?"

She swallowed. Her anxiety was back as if it had never left. "The

Shopkeeper's letting me work on the shop floor tomorrow, and I'm scared I'll mess it up."

"So she's allowing you to work even before you've finished training, and you think she doesn't like you?"

"I didn't say that."

But she had thought it. Perhaps there were jars of MIND READING somewhere and the rest of the staff knew how to use the traits. It would certainly explain a lot.

"Well, whatever you actually said, it looks to me like she's putting a lot of trust in you."

She nodded silently and gritted her teeth. If she felt any pride in that, it was buried under a thick layer of anxiety.

"You had one more question," he prompted.

"Did I?"

He held up the piece of wood and wiggled it. She couldn't help smiling. "Okay . . ." she said. "What's a yoyo?"

Omaro shrugged. "I have no idea," he replied. "They're an Earth thing. But I'm pretty sure I'll know one when I see it."

She laughed. Well, that explained everything. This Child was silly. She liked him a lot. "Any clues for me?" she asked, holding up her lump of wood.

"I know two things: it's a source of great joy, and it goes up and down," he said, solemnly.

That was a start. They resumed working on their yoyos together, commenting on each other's efforts and giggling, until it got too dark. It wasn't long before they had successfully reduced their lumps to piles of misshapen shavings.

Omaro looked at the ex-wood sadly. "Not today, then, I suppose."

"You've done this before," she guessed.

He nodded. "Once or twice. I'll make one eventually." He leaned back on the bench and stretched. Around them, the Gardens were changing colour as pale earthlight began to dominate over the weakening sunlight. The distant hubbub of the Shop had died down, leaving only the gentle splashing of the river.

"Oh!" he said, out of nowhere, reaching down to scrabble on the floor underneath the bench. "I nearly forgot! I brought you a present."

He held out a brown woven bag.

"A present!" She quivered with delight as she took it. "Really?"

"Absolutely! I've been saving it for days. Everyone should get a present, especially when they're new. Go on, have a look."

She opened the bag. Inside were . . . "Jars?"

"I picked some that you might like."

She took the first out of the bag. It was tall and filled with rainbow sparkles which glittered and dazzled. "It's beautiful," she said, her voice catching in her throat.

His face lit up with joy. "I'm so happy you like them! I like to give our Apprentices a few jars to hold onto while they work here, as a reminder that life still awaits. When your time is up here, you can take them to Earth and actually use them, or swap them for others, as you wish."

"What are they? Did you pick them specially for me?"

His grin widened. "That's the best bit. I don't know!"

"How can you not know?"

"I got someone to cover the labels for me and then I picked the ones I liked the look of the best."

She spun the jar around to examine it closer. Sure enough, a blank label had been placed over the original label.

"If you do want to know what they are—say, if you want to actually use them in a thousand years and don't want to gamble—then you can pick off the label. But I think the mystery is quite fun."

What sort of person would actually gamble with the traits they took for their life on Earth? Someone like Omaro, she supposed.

Part of her itched to know which aspects of human personality were trapped inside these containers. But he was right: there was something strangely enjoyable about not knowing. For now.

She smiled. "It *is* fun. Thank you. I'll treasure them."

She felt like a wholly different person than the tense, stressed girl who had wandered into the Gardens earlier that evening.

Omaro stood to leave. "Good work this evening, Apprentice. I'm sure we'll figure out the yoyo in no time."

"Maybe there's a book in the library that would have a picture of one?"

He looked horrified. "Books? That'd be *cheating*." He winked. "See you tomorrow. And don't worry, I'll help you out."

She stayed to watch the Earth drift slowly across the sky. It had been forever—well, weeks—since she'd simply had fun. For an hour or two she'd even stopped missing everything she'd left behind.

A visiting alien might have found it unbelievable that shredding a piece of wood with a stranger could make such a difference to someone's mood.

But, to a human like Faythe, it made perfect sense.

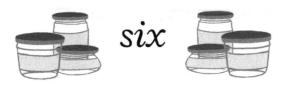# *six*

THE NEXT DAY Faythe awoke to a chamber bathed in pale, comforting jarlight.

On Earth, they reportedly went to great lengths to make work satisfying and rewarding for everybody, but here in the prelife it was often viewed as a chore. However, she had fallen in love with the Shop already. Simply being here made her happy, and it was exhilarating that today she would truly be part of it.

The morning passed in a blur of jars and customers and queries. Eventually she would take on more of the Shopkeeper's duties, but for now she simply helped the Children with the day-to-day running of the Shop.

She was busy with a customer when Omaro came to see her. He gave her an encouraging thumbs-up and she grinned back so widely that it nearly hurt. This had been her favourite morning . . . perhaps ever. If only there was a word for how good it felt to hold jars of pure JOY.

The work was humbling, too. Helping customers make such intimate choices was like looking through a window straight into their hearts. One customer favoured ATHLETICISM, another longed to be GENEROUS. A third refused to go to Earth without SLIGHTLY MODEST, and yet another preferred a TENDENCY TO OVERANALYSE. It was fascinating, and endlessly surprising.

As the end of her first shift approached, her earlier nerves seemed ridiculous. A thousand years suddenly seemed absurdly short.

She was filing away a receipt from another happy customer when the Shopkeeper came by. "I hear you've had a good day," she said.

Faythe jigged with excitement. Perhaps it was unprofessional to dance in front of your boss, but she was delighted enough not to care. "It's been wonderful!"

The Shopkeeper smiled. "All the Children have spoken highly of your work today."

She couldn't hold back the question. "Does that mean I can work again tomorrow?!" She held her breath.

But her boss nodded towards a boy waiting at the checkout. "Let's see. Looks like you've got one last customer to tend to."

Faythe recognised the boy. He'd been hanging around all day with a perpetually empty basket. Occasionally she'd seen him take a jar and study it, but each time he'd rejected it with a shake of his head.

"Can you help me find my traits?" he asked in a small voice. His eyes were slightly watery.

"I certainly can!" She spoke with a confidence that was partly directed at the watching Shopkeeper. "Let's go."

She picked a direction at random and led him into the Stacks. "So you don't know what you want?" The boy shook his head and sniffed. "It's okay. I'll help you!"

They went deeper into the Shop. She tried to interest him in various traits, but he rejected each without articulating a reason. She was about to give up when—finally—he noticed a jar he liked. His eyes lit up, and he thrust it eagerly into his basket.

She craned her neck, curious to see what it was. Inside was a reddish grainy powder, and the label read BAD WITH NUMBERS. Without thinking, she groaned aloud. "Whyyyy?"

The boy looked up, shocked.

She covered her mouth in embarrassment before realising she would need it to explain herself. "Sorry," she said, sheepishly. "It's just . . . why did you choose that one after all this time? It doesn't seem useful."

"Useful?" The boy frowned. "What do you mean?"

"You know, up there." She pointed towards the Earth, somewhere beyond the ceiling. "What do you want that one for?"

"I liked the way it looked," he said.

She stared at him blankly. "You liked the way it *looked?*"

"What else is there?"

She opened her mouth but had nothing to say. His thinking was too alien.

"Do you have any more like this?" he asked.

"What do you mean by 'like this', exactly? More, um, anti-numeracy jars?"

"I dunno," said the boy. "Ones that feel the same. I just want to like them."

She could practically hear Beris' voice inside her head. One fundamental theme of her training had been 'the customer is always right.' She had playfully argued back: what if the customer was lying? Or misinformed? Or, most shockingly, *wrong?* But Beris had been clear that this was a logical impossibility, and she'd agreed to pretend it was true.

She clicked back into professional mode. "Follow me," she said. "We'll get you what you want."

It made no sense to choose jars based on feel alone, but who was she to judge? Following her instinct, she headed beyond the end of the Stacks to a little-used aisle in an obscure wing. The boy, with apparent glee, chose a heavy jar labelled POOR DIGESTION. She bit her tongue and led him onward.

As the tour continued, her resolve to respect his choices dwindled as he picked up BAD BREATH, CAN'T CONTROL VOLUME OF VOICE, and CONFLICT MAGNET. *The customer is always right*, she reminded herself.

Unfortunately, as they approached the checkouts, the boy picked up ALWAYS LATE and she cracked.

"Always late?" She placed her hands on her hips and grinned the false grin of someone hiding their real beliefs behind a joke. "Are you planning a life of great evil?"

"What?" The boy looked up wide-eyed from his basket. "Evil?!"

"Yeah, you know." She tried to look playful. "Being late all the time. The worst of all evils!"

He didn't look amused. "You think I'm picking *evil* things?"

"No, no, of course not! Well, maybe a bit." The boy's face collapsed and his lip trembled. "I mean . . . not *evil!* I was just playing! What I'm saying is, um, your choices . . ." He stared at her mournfully as she sought for the right words. "Perhaps these jars might not help as much as you think."

"Help . . . me?" He sniffed. "I was just picking the jars I liked. Are you saying I'm going to have a bad life?"

She groped for solid conversational ground. "I just wonder if the jars you like are necessarily the best ones for having a good life?"

If anything, he looked more distressed. "But I looked at the other ones and I didn't want them!" He wiped at his eyes. His hand came away glistening. "It took *all day* to get these and now you say I'm bad."

"I didn't say that!" She stepped towards him reassuringly, but he cringed away.

"Leave me alone! I . . . I don't want to do this anymore. I'm not going to Earth!"

He dropped his basket and ran, leaving her alone in the aisle. He nearly knocked over one of the Children as he charged through the front door, yelling something she couldn't make out.

Faythe sighed. *That could definitely have gone better.*

She rooted through his basket. She should figure out a route to return all these jars before the end of the day. But barely a moment had passed before the Shopkeeper came storming down the aisle with a face as cold as an avalanche, and nearly as dangerous.

"Faythe!" she yelled. The distance between them closed in record time. "Please explain why you talked that poor boy out of passing through to Earth. What were you thinking?"

"That's not what happened!" she protested. "He decided himself that he didn't want to go anymore."

The Shopkeeper's eyes drilled into her. "The Child who managed to catch him told me that you called the boy *evil* and said he shouldn't go to Earth."

"No, that's not . . . that's not right." She didn't understand why the Shopkeeper was so angry. "I was only trying to help."

The old lady tutted. "Isn't that exactly what you said when you broke my shelf immediately after you arrived? I do hope this isn't a pattern."

"No, it's not a pattern . . . well, okay, it *is* a pattern, but only because both times I was genuinely helping and it went wrong. So it's not a *bad* pattern!" She swallowed. This argument had seemed more convincing before she'd voiced it aloud.

A passing customer who was pretending not to listen in on the argument accidentally made eye contact with her. Both looked away, embarrassed.

The Shopkeeper appeared unimpressed by Faythe's defence. "I don't understand why you believe telling a customer that their choices are 'evil' is helping them."

"I didn't mean evil, exactly, that bit was supposed to be a joke." She struggled for breath through a tight throat. "But this boy was picking jars just because he liked them! I mean . . . why would he . . ." The last of her confidence drained away as she trailed off.

The Shopkeeper's gaze skewered her. "*Why* is a question with no end of answers, but in this case he told you himself: he *liked* those jars."

She gulped. This was the terrifying Shopkeeper she remembered from the day she'd arrived. Her obvious disapproval made her seem taller.

Faythe summoned the will to explain herself for a final time. "But aren't I supposed to help customers pick better jars?"

"Was that ever part of your training?"

She shook her head.

"And even if it was part of the mission of the Shop Before Life, what does 'better' mean? What do you know about life on Earth?" She never gave Faythe a chance to answer. "It's not for us to choose people's lives for them. We help them discover which traits they already want."

That didn't seem right. "But doesn't that mean some people will have harder lives than others? Isn't it unfair?"

"Do you think it's fair that that boy is not going to Earth at all, thanks to you?"

She winced. So that was why the Shopkeeper was so angry. "No," she said, miserably. "But . . ."

"But nothing! No matter what happens in this prelife, some will have harder lives than others. The Shop is merely a beginning—everyone on Earth can always grow beyond any choices they make here, I promise."

She opened her mouth, but the Shopkeeper wasn't finished.

"I've watched countless people pass through to Earth, and you can never predict how their lives will go. Some take every positive jar they can carry, only to find other circumstances bring them great misery. Others, perhaps like your boy today, take what appear to be disadvantages, but they turn out to be greatly useful."

Faythe knew she ought to keep quiet and nod. But a surge of annoyance, confusion and curiosity outweighed her good sense. "What's the point of all this then?" she said, gesturing at the countless jars along the aisle. "If nothing here matters, then why bother?"

"Oh, it matters," said the Shopkeeper. "But it doesn't matter in the way you expect."

"So I just let customers take whatever they want, then?" She realised too late how foolish that must sound.

The Shopkeeper pursed her lips. "Faythe, it sounds like—even after all that training—you don't understand the purpose of your job at all. I fear you are not truly ready to work here."

This was so unfair. "But I was only trying to help!" She tried, unsuccessfully, not to yell. "You said I did a good job earlier!"

The Shopkeeper sighed. "I'm not sure you understand how serious this is. You stopped that boy from beginning his *life* today. You don't get credit just because you didn't stop anybody else."

Another couple of customers passed by, whispering to one another as they gawked. Faythe flushed hot with shame and frustration. She hung her head, defeated. "I didn't mean to."

Her boss narrowed her eyes. "I certainly hope not." She sighed. "I'm not sure what to do with you."

"Do with me?"

"On the very first day I put my trust in you, you prevented a boy from beginning his life. As I told you, every time you talk to a customer, you hold their life in your hands. And do you remember your promise? No mistakes." She tapped the side of her head irritably. "I'll certainly have to raise questions with Management about their hiring procedures."

"Management?" Fear rippled through Faythe, mixing and reacting with the frustration and burning sense of injustice which were already swirling inside.

"Of course. Contracts can be broken, even ones with Management. But I'm reluctant to do that unless I must."

The potential humiliation of losing her job after a single day added another toxic ingredient to Faythe's churning emotions. Her anger cooled and coalesced into pure stubborn petulance. "If you fire me I'll just pass straight through to Earth," she said. "It's what I was planning originally anyway."

The Shopkeeper raised an eyebrow. "Is that so? You're so sure that I'd allow that?"

She blinked. "You can stop people going to Earth?"

"It would be a pretty ironic punishment in this particular case, but *yes*, I could prevent somebody from passing through to Earth, if I chose." Her eyes flicked away sadly, as if recalling a painful memory. "Though I assure you I would take no pleasure in it."

"Not until the contract is finished?" said Faythe. Anxiety rippled through her, halting her breath. "Not for a thousand years?"

"If I were to banish someone, it could mean not *ever*."

The babble of conversation from the nearby aisles faded and all she could hear was a high-pitched whine. The Shop around her blurred. *An eternity confined to the prelife. Never visiting Earth.* During her time at the Rock that might have seemed an acceptable, even desirable, fate, but now it seemed a claustrophobic and small existence. She held out a hand to steady herself on a shelf, and blinked slowly until her vision steadied and her hearing returned.

"I'm sorry," she said in a small voice.

The Shopkeeper pressed her lips together. "Thank you. You might have said sorry earlier, instead of being so desperate to defend yourself."

Frustration welled once more at the unfairness of it all—she had only been trying to help!—but she bit it back. She swallowed with a dry mouth.

"I'm not trying to upset you," continued the Shopkeeper. "But I need you to understand that this work is important. Today, your actions prevented one life from beginning. And who knows what repercussions that might have?"

She fought to hold back tears. She didn't want the Shopkeeper to see her cry. "I'm sorry," she said, again.

"I understand. I'm not going to do anything extreme. But I'm afraid we'll have to have a disciplinary meeting."

She blinked. The aisle now appeared extremely blurry. The Shopkeeper handed her a handkerchief—how *did* everyone read her so easily?—and a warm tear streaked down her cheek to splatter on the floorboards.

"It won't happen again," she said, without looking up. She wanted this to be over.

"I hope you're right. The Committee will meet about this tomorrow evening. I shall see you there."

The Shopkeeper left Faythe alone with the boy's basket. Around her, the sounds of the Shop persisted as usual. She leaned on the shelf and stared down at the basket, where a red gas swirled and popped in the jar labelled CONFLICT MAGNET.

It was a while before she moved.

Later that evening, the sound of Omaro's carving was getting on her nerves.

They sat opposite one another, leaning back against thick shelves of dark wood, deep inside an old wing beyond the Stacks. The stone roof was low and the windows were few, so no sunlight, earthlight, or even twinkly starlight made it here. Only gentle jarlight washed the cramped aisle in a muted, eerie glow.

Omaro had suggested she might enjoy an evening of exploring and making yoyos, but Faythe preferred to sulk.

It felt right to sulk. Everything was so unfair. She'd been blamed—twice!—for things that weren't her fault. And the threat of this Committee Meeting was hanging over her head. Her imagination was constantly filled with terrible, detailed fantasies of public recrimination which ended with her being banished permanently from Earth.

In between anxieties, she moodily watched Omaro's latest attempts to discover the yoyo. Occasionally, she sighed loudly, or made an acerbic comment about how stupid his hobby was, but, annoyingly, the Child just found her insults hilarious. He hummed to himself as he concentrated.

"Having fun?" he asked, without looking up.

She aimed her best withering gaze at the top of his head. "Does it look like I'm having fun?"

"I'm having a good time," he said, easily. After a long moment, he spoke again. "How are you feeling?"

The question annoyed her.

Being so easily annoyed made her even more annoyed. "Frustrated," she said.

"Understandable."

As she leaned her head back against the shelf, a newly paranoid instinct made her check there was no irreplaceable ancient jar in the way. That would be precisely her luck.

"She threatened me!" She thumped the floor in sudden resentment. "She said she'd stop me from ever going to Earth!"

Omaro lowered his knife and looked straight at her. "That doesn't sound like the Shopkeeper."

"It was!"

The Child furrowed his brow. "She actually said 'I will stop you going to Earth'?"

She paused. "Well . . . she said she *could.*"

"I'm sure she only wanted to warn you. She doesn't want a repeat of what happened with the last Apprentice."

She threw her arms up in frustration. "How am I supposed to avoid repeating things if I don't even know what they are?"

Omaro hesitated. "That's fair," he said. "But the Shopkeeper doesn't want you to know too much about him."

"Why not?"

"I think she thinks you might follow his example."

She furrowed her brow. "What example?"

"That's the problem. I'm not meant to tell you." He sighed. "He had weird ideas. He got really obsessed with the traits."

"Obsessed how?"

"I can't talk about it. I'm not meant to mention him at all."

"I won't tell." She definitely wouldn't. If she could avoid talking to the Shopkeeper entirely, that would be ideal.

"You won't tell anyone because I won't tell you." Omaro looked pained. "At least, not everything. He was rude to customers. Always thought he knew best." The Child flashed a meaningful look. "He talked a few out of going to Earth."

Ah. That explained the Shopkeeper's reaction.

"That wasn't the worst of it, though. He started stealing traits. And more. By the end, Security had to follow him all the time."

She tried to imagine it. "How humiliating."

"Maybe to you and me! But I'm pretty sure he enjoyed it. It made him feel important." Omaro's cheeks flushed with anger. The emotion looked strange on his normally cheerful face. "And then things got really nasty . . ." He hesitated. "No, I can't talk about that. Management got involved. Afterwards, the Shopkeeper fought with them, demanding to be left alone—no replacement Apprentice, not ever. And then they sent you anyway."

She screwed up her face. The Shopkeeper's behaviour since she had arrived made much more sense now. "I get it . . . but none of this is my fault. It's not like I'm going to start stealing things."

He smiled sympathetically. "I'm sorry. You've been caught in the middle of a real mess."

"I still don't get why she'd be suspicious of me, just because a past Apprentice behaved badly."

Omaro shrugged. "People can get funny about past experiences. They start seeing them everywhere. But remember she doesn't know you—for all she knows, you could be part of a shadowy conspiracy to destroy the Shop."

She furrowed her brow. "I was recruited by Management."

"Well, then, as long as Management aren't plotting against us, we'll be fine!" He resumed his carving with a wink.

She laughed. "I guess this explains why she took this so badly."

"It did look like something the last Apprentice might have done. She probably overreacted out of habit." He hacked at the wood, seemingly at random. "I don't know . . . maybe somebody should have told you all this history straight away. I guess this is what happens when Beris is in charge of training."

That made her laugh, too. Beris was wonderful, but subtle political currents weren't his strong point. "Could have been worse," she said, playing along. "Imagine if it was the Gardener!"

"You'd have been the universe's leading expert on worms, at least."

They fell into a comfortable silence. She watched him carve for a time. But there was a question still nagging at her. "Omaro?" she said.

"Yes?"

"Do you think I'm part of a plot?"

She felt pathetic asking, but she would wonder later if she didn't.

The Child lowered his misshapen lump of wood. "How do I put this? You remind me of me. By which I mean, we're both fools. So, if there was a plot, it'd be too stupid to be worth worrying about." He gave her an overly stern look, and then winked, as if to say *don't ask ridiculous questions*, and then resumed his artistic endeavours.

Faythe smiled. At least somebody here trusted her. And it was comforting to be insulted by a friend. Everything had changed so much, but at least that was normal.

She picked up the knife and a fresh lump of wood, and resumed the search for the mystical yoyo hidden somewhere inside.

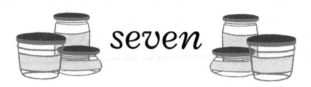

seven

FAYTHE AWOKE with an anxious jolt. For an instant, she couldn't place why . . . but then she remembered the Committee Meeting that evening. A deep heaviness settled within her chest. It was still there when she arrived at the checkouts to serve her first customer of the day.

Searching for a distraction, she stole a glance into their basket. CONFIDENT was a popular choice despite its unattractive appearance—a jar barely one-tenth full with an ugly, greyish substance. Next to CONFIDENT lay OUTRAGEOUS, a fierce orange gas which fizzed as the jar moved. Then WILDLY IMPATIENT, a stringy and tangled—

"Are we going to be here all day?" The customer tapped the desk irately.

She forced a smile and began running jars through the checkout.

Her shift passed by in a whirl of activity. In contrast to the exuberant joy of the day before, most of her time was lost in apprehensive fantasies of Management punishing her. Several times, she noticed the chief of Security—a Child named Risk—passing by. Each time he wore an increasingly worried expression.

As the day wore on she became steadily more agitated. Finally, hoping to escape her growing anxiety, she volunteered to take the discarded-at-the-last-minute jars from the checkouts back to the shelves. It was a simple, relaxing job, far away from all the busyness of the concourse.

Deep in the Stacks, she came across a jar of COOL, CALM & COLLECTED lying in the middle of an otherwise empty aisle. It had been abandoned annoyingly close to its proper spot.

"Tsk," she said as she bent down to pick it up. She smiled in satisfaction. *Tsk*ing seemed like the kind of habit which an Apprentice Shopkeeper ought to adopt.

As she approached the trait's proper home, a face appeared in the gap between jars. "Psssst!" it hissed.

She nearly flung the jar into the air as her hand instinctively flew to protect her chest. Her heart beat like a drummer in an earthquake. "What are you *doing?!*" she yelled at the man, who seemed deeply amused by her reaction.

He grinned. "I just wanted to talk to you, obviously."

She shook her head violently. "This is not the way to get my attention. Please can you move so I can put this jar back?"

"Oh believe me, this is the only way we can talk," he said, ignoring her request. "Unless you want to be seen with me, which I rather suspect you don't."

"What do you mean by that?"

"I'll tell you. But I want us to talk properly afterwards. I've waited all day for this chance."

His intense gaze would be disconcerting in normal circumstances, but being studied by his disembodied head at waist height was even more unnerving. "Fine, we'll talk. But can you come out? It's too weird talking to you like this."

He nodded. "That way." He raised a single eyebrow to point deeper into the Stacks—a precise motion, with zero wasted effort.

She followed the stranger into one of the many neglected wings which intertwined at this end of the Shop. Inside, everything felt older; all dark wood and crumbling stone. Around them, the jars glimmered with a yellowy tinge, giving the stranger an eerie tint.

Now that he was standing up properly she had to crane her neck upwards to look him in the eye. "So," she said. "What's this about?"

"As I said, I want to talk to you." He enunciated each sound with unusual, crisp precision.

Oh, great. Was he an admirer? Faythe rolled her eyes. She'd never been in this situation before. Not many people remained in the prelife long enough to strike up intimate relationships, and those that stayed mostly didn't experience physical attraction. At least, not compared to how things were on Earth, where she had heard bodies were considered more important. It all sounded quite exhausting.

The stranger caught her expression and held up a hand. "No, it's nothing like that. I want a private chat."

"What for?"

He tilted his head. "To get to know the new Apprentice, of course."

"By sticking your head through a shelf? I've been at the checkouts all day! You could have talked to me there."

He smirked. "I've spent enough of my prelife at checkouts."

Whatever his private joke was supposed to be, she wasn't amused. She folded her arms. "You said you'd tell me who you are."

"Ah, my apologies." To her surprise, the stranger bowed, apparently sincerely. "My name is Zariel." He looked up, and snorted at her lack of reaction. "I see they never told you about me."

"Should they have?"

"I would think they might. After all, not so long ago I was the Apprentice here."

She opened her mouth wide while every other part of her face tried to escape from her head.

Zariel laughed. "I see they said something, then. I'm pleased I haven't been entirely forgotten."

So many thoughts flooded her mind at once that she could hardly keep track. She forced her mouth closed. "They never told me your name," she stammered.

He snorted again. "Naturally. We must never speak the name of The Forbidden One!" He held up his hands in mock fear, and, despite herself, she suppressed a smile.

"Zariel," she repeated. "Doesn't sound that scary to me." She looked him up and down. "You don't look that scary either."

His eyes glinted with amusement. "Appearances can be deceiving. I hope you understand why it was necessary to surprise you. I must say I'm pleased you didn't run away crying as soon as you found out who I am."

She kept her face still. Weirdly, this was the least frightened she'd been all day. "Actually, this is exciting," she said. She blushed, immediately regretting it. It felt pathetic, too desperate to impress.

He looked at her thoughtfully. "I suppose it must be. Not every day you get to meet somebody so important."

She searched his face for hints that he was joking, but he appeared to be sincere. She had no idea what to say. Not only was his manner disconcerting, but Zariel was the last person she should be talking to today. She was yet to be punished for yesterday's incident, and secretly meeting with an outlaw presumably wouldn't be popular with the Committee.

She laughed. At this rate they wouldn't be able to punish her fast enough. It'd be an administrative nightmare.

He picked up a jar from a half-empty shelf behind him and spun it around. "Something funny?"

She glanced back towards the Stacks. "I shouldn't be talking to you."

He idly teased at the lid of the jar. Her eyes widened in horror—was he going to open it? He saw her reaction and put it back, laughing. "Afraid of the Shopkeeper?" he teased. "For a moment I thought she'd replaced me with somebody with a spine."

She glared at him. "My spine exists, thank you. But I have a Committee meeting any moment now."

He frowned. "They invited you onto the Committee already?"

Embarrassment flooded her. She shook her head. "They're discussing my punishment." He leaned forward, his eyes hungry for more. "For talking a boy out of going to Earth."

"Ohoho! That's perfect!" He clapped, just once, like an unambitious sea lion. "On your first day?"

Faythe tingled with delight at the unexpected approval. In the back of her mind a lone sensible voice yelled that she shouldn't be here, that even *Omaro* got angry whenever Zariel was brought up, and that talking to him could only lead to bad things. It screamed desperately that she should stop trying to impress him.

On the other hand, this *was* exciting. She shushed the sensible voice. "I called a boy's choice of traits 'evil'," she said, modestly.

He threw his head back and laughed. "Oh, wonderful! I wish I'd seen her face."

"And then I told him not to go to Earth!" The sensible part of Faythe's brain gave up in disgust.

The ex-Apprentice appraised her carefully, as if seeing her for the first time. Then he smiled. "Well, you're much more interesting than I expected. Perhaps this was worth the trip after all."

She studied him in return. "I want to know what happened. Why did you leave the Shop?"

"You sure you've got time for a long story before your oh-so-important Shop Committee meeting?"

She flinched at the reminder.

He snorted. "You shouldn't be so afraid of them. The worst they can do is report you to Management."

If he intended that to be soothing, it didn't work. She trembled. "Management?!"

"... are nothing to be afraid of. They've certainly been good to me, no matter how hard the Committee tried."

She couldn't quite process his indifference. "You got reported to *Management*?"

"Many, many times." He managed to give off the impression of preening without actually moving. "Fortunately for me, Management know potential when they see it. They took my side against ... her."

She stared, excited and nervous and impressed all at once. *The actual gods had supported him.* But she didn't want him to think she was easily awed, just because it happened to be true. "Wouldn't this story be more impressive if you'd never been banished?"

"Ha!" he barked—actually saying the word, rather than laughing. Nevertheless his eyes sparkled with amusement. "You know ... when I heard she'd picked a new Apprentice I assumed they must be the polar opposite of me. Somebody easy to control, who wouldn't cause trouble, or ask questions. A non-entity. But you ... you might live up to my legacy after all."

Legacy? He certainly thought a lot of himself. She didn't think he was joking this time either, although his unusually clipped manner of speaking made it difficult to be sure. He had a disconcerting habit of stressing all the wrong parts of words. She found it oddly intriguing.

Not that she wanted him to know that. She stared him right in the eye. "I don't need to live up to anyone's 'legacy'. I've got nothing to prove to you."

He looked down at her with a smile. "Which only proves there *is* something to you."

Her cheeks flushed red, in pleasure and annoyance. *I don't need to impress him!* Although . . . it was nice that he was impressed.

She glanced away, and then back. "So, aside from advice about the Committee, what did you want to talk about?"

"I just wanted to satisfy my own curiosity. And to encourage you to ask awkward questions. They certainly need it around here."

She frowned. "What kind of awkward questions?"

He gestured at the jars which glowed softly around them. "Don't you think this place raises questions? Wherever you look, you find secrets. The deepest workings of all humanity are displayed in public for all to see."

She peered at a nearby jar. "LIKES WEDNESDAYS," she read aloud.

He waved a finger. "Perhaps not that one."

"I know what you meant. I came here because I wanted to know more about the traits."

"Precisely! If you understand the traits, you understand people. But . . ." He beckoned her closer, and almost whispered into her ear. "What doesn't she want you to know?"

She screwed up her face. "You mean the Shopkeeper? She's hiding something?"

"She's hiding everything. The whole prelife has been fooled." His mouth turned down in disgust. "A kindly old lady who helps everybody live the life they want. It's *lies*. All of it."

She shivered. "Then . . . what's the truth?" she whispered.

"It all comes back to the traits. Think about it. Imagine you could control who people become. What would you do?"

"I, um—"

They were interrupted by a distant shout which echoed into the cosy space. "Faythe!" It was Omaro's voice. "Faythe! Are you here?"

He was getting closer. *He would find them together.* She panicked, suddenly swamped by visions of punishment and banishment and other, possibly worse, *-ishments.*

"I can't be seen with you!" she hissed.

Zariel stood and gave an exaggerated, leisurely stretch. "Very well," he said. "It was a pleasure to meet you, Faythe." Before she could reply, he disappeared deeper into the darkness.

Omaro was just outside the archway. Her heart hammering, she darted out to meet him.

His face lit up as he saw her. "There you are!" He nodded towards the archway with a puzzled expression. "What were you in there for? A tryst with a customer?"

She thought fast. "Just one?! I've got *hundreds* of admirers fighting over me in there!"

He grinned. "They're being very quiet . . ."

"I attract very respectful admirers." Adrenaline was gushing through her veins. She felt incredibly alive.

"Ha! Well, I came to tell you I'm planning dinner in the Gardens before the Committee meeting. Want to join?"

She was delighted to. As they ate, she thought about Zariel. Omaro had made him sound dangerous, but he seemed so normal. Moreover, Management had sided with him over the Shopkeeper. That had to mean something. *Perhaps the Shopkeeper wasn't all she seemed?*

She smouldered with frustration at all the unanswered questions. What had Zariel been about to say? She burned to ask Omaro about the traits, but she didn't want him to think she shared Zariel's obsession.

The Child was chattering happily about his day and how he was convinced that tonight would be the night he successfully made his first yoyo, but she was only part-listening.

Most of her was wondering when, exactly, she'd get to see Zariel again.

An Extraordinary Meeting
of the Shop Before Life Committee

ATTENDANCE
   Voting: The Shopkeeper, Omaro (Sub-Management), Beris (Clerical),
   Risk (Security)
   Non-Voting: The Apprentice; Others

AGENDA
   A recent incident in which the Apprentice discouraged a customer
   from passing through to Earth.

AFFAIRS
   1. It was mutually agreed that it is bad for business when staff members encourage customers to abandon their lives on Earth.
   2. A suggestion was made that "being 'bad for business' wasn't really
   the point, was it"?
   2a. After brief discussion, it was mutually agreed that the incident was
   better described as regrettable.
   2b. After *extended* discussion, it was mutually agreed that "regrettable" is an excellent word, and congratulations are due to those who
   came up with it.
   3. At this point, the Apprentice was asked to explain her actions to
   the Committee.
   4. There followed a spirited debate about whether good intentions
   can ever justify bad outcomes.

5. After a *considerable* time, all abstract philosophy was banned at both this meeting, and all future Committee meetings.

5a. An important question was raised about what, precisely, counted as abstract philosophy.

5b. Another ~~spirited~~ prolonged debate followed.

5c. After a second considerable time, it was agreed that debating 'what counts as philosophy' *also counts as philosophy* and that the current discussion was therefore already banned under the new rule.

5d. A potential issue was raised that even mentioning that a subject was banned could be considered taking a philosophical position, and that therefore the Committee might have accidentally banned *all* discussion at *all* meetings.

5e. By a vote of 3-1 (and 0 abstentions) the Committee agreed to a joint resolution that stated they "no longer care and would move on to the votes."

6. The Committee agreed, by a vote of 3-1 (and 0 abstentions) that the effect of the Apprentice's actions were severe enough to warrant a formal report to Management, regardless of intention.

7. In response to an emergency question, it was further agreed, by a vote of 2-0 (and 2 abstentions), that 'prolonged' is a better word than 'spirited' to describe the earlier philosophical debates. (The minutes on file have been amended accordingly.)

8. At this point, a final emergency resolution was introduced, in which it was agreed, by a vote of 3-1 (and 0 abstentions), that trivial debates about words are also banned from both meetings and minutes.

9. The Apprentice interrupted to make it known that she was extremely upset with the outcome of this meeting.

9a. After a follow-up question, it was clarified that the Apprentice was upset about being reported to Management, and that she didn't want to challenge the vote about which word to use in the minutes.

9b. The Apprentice was thanked for saving both paper and clerical time. She responded by remaining silent and withdrawn.

ACTIONS

1. A report will be filed with Management regarding this incident.

2. For some reason, a further meeting will be scheduled to discuss finding a replacement to take minutes in future.

(Note to self: does this alleged requirement for a replacement minute-taker include the further meeting itself? Or is it further-further meetings only? Who will take minutes during this further meeting? Perhaps a meeting will be required to plan.)

 *eight*

IT TURNED OUT that being formally rebuked in the eyes of the gods was kind of upsetting.

Faythe had always assumed she was naturally capable, reliable, and trustworthy. But this failure had made her question her whole self-image. What else was she wrong about? *Was she even a good person?*

Thoughts like these wounded her, over and over.

Several weeks had passed since the awkward, lengthy Committee meeting. She'd been told not to expect any further consequences from the report, but she nevertheless remained constantly on edge, half-expecting divine retribution to smite her at any moment.

She and the Shopkeeper hadn't spoken at all during that time. At first, a mixture of embarrassment and mistrust kept her away, but the longer the silence persisted, the harder it was to break.

A cloud of self-recrimination followed her everywhere. Luckily, her days were always busy, so at least they went by quickly. She'd asked Beris about this, and he'd shifted his glasses around and muttered something about differential time and experiential paradoxes. She'd nodded politely and resumed her work. But perhaps there was a simple explanation: she genuinely enjoyed her job.

There were even times when she enjoyed it enough to forget the shame she carried. The customers were just too fascinating. After centuries living in a tiny community, she'd been surprised to discover that she loved meeting people. There was plenty of choice; chatty, quiet, obnoxious, warm, reserved, confident, afraid—she met them all.

She found that the easiest customers to deal with were the scared ones. Often, they were intimidated by the scale of their potential choices. All she had to do was act reassuringly, pretend to have answers, and point them at various traits until they picked those they liked, while—and this was important, she had learned—constantly encouraging them and *not* calling their choices 'evil'.

She also liked the independent-minded customers. They mostly left her alone. She found it oddly endearing as they struggled to carry their—always oversized—heaps of jars around, while refusing all assistance.

The worst customers were the aggressive ones. She simply couldn't understand them. They had all the time in the world, and every possible option open to them. There was no pressure, no competition, no cost they couldn't afford. And yet they shouted at her and the Children, treating them like personal servants whilst being abrasive and unpleasant. She occasionally imagined keeping a stash behind the counter and swapping one of their jars for POWERFULLY FLATULENT or AGGRESSIVE DIARRHOEA, but had so far decided against it. Just.

On this particular day, she had met several strange customers.

"I want to be a Sexy Woodelf Rogue," announced one boy, earnestly.

"A what?!" Faythe narrowed her eyes. Her shift was nearly finished, and she was excited to spending an evening relaxing in the Gardens. She didn't have time for any nonsense.

"Sexy. Woodelf. Rogue."

She grimaced. She had heard correctly. "We don't really do 'Woodelf' here, I'm afraid. It's human or nothing." The boy didn't try to hide his obvious disappointment. "But you can find rogueish tendencies all along Aisle Eighteen, and there's a wing devoted to varying kinds of 'sexiness' at the end of that aisle there. But be warned that—"

He was already gone, so she didn't have to explain the perils of sexiness, which, honestly, was a relief. Mysteriously, some jars came with mandatory warnings to read to customers. Apparently, long ago, a jar which was never meant to be released had made its way to Earth. Faythe was unclear on the details, but it seemed too much concentrated sexiness led to problems with wooden horses. Yet another thing she'd have to worry about later.

Her next customer was an older man, one of those rare few that appeared aged even in the prelife. He requested a wheeled basket to transport his chosen traits to the passing-through area.

"Have you been here long?" she asked as she scooped QUESTIONABLE DECISION MAKING and REASONABLE METABOLISM into the basket.

"Me?" His voice was slightly raspy. "Oh, no, I just got here a few hours ago."

"No, I meant . . . you know, in the, um, prelife." She laughed, embarrassed by her real question. *How come you look old and I don't?*

If the man was offended, he didn't show it. "Oh, who keeps count? I never have!" He chuckled. "What about you?"

"I guess I've not kept count either." She picked up the next jar: RESISTANT TO SOULMATES. "Whoa! Won't this limit your options on Earth?"

She'd spoken before thinking, but he seemed amiable enough to cope. Indeed, he chuckled again. "I've met two soulmates already, and let me tell you—" he lowered his voice—"I hope I never meet a third."

She laughed, astonished by his vehemence. "I thought meeting a soulmate was supposed to be a powerful, healing experience? Like getting your soul cleansed by another person, I'd heard."

He beckoned her closer, as if to impart a secret. "You know what else is a powerful and cleansing healing experience?" He paused. "Getting sandpaper blasted up your bum."

She wrinkled her nose. "I'll have to take your word for it."

"About the sandpaper? Or the soulmates?" His eyes twinkled with amusement.

"Both!"

The old man grinned. "A little experience goes a long way, trust me."

She didn't ask which experience he meant. Instead, she handed over his final jar without a word. SECRETLY ROMANTIC.

He winked. "Got to keep it interesting, though, don't you?" He grabbed the loaded basket and made for the passing-through area, brandishing his receipt like a weapon. "See you next time!"

She waved him goodbye. *Next time?*

She shook her head and turned back to the desk, where a girl was waiting for her. The clock next to the checkout said it was ten minutes past the end of her shift, but one final customer wouldn't hurt.

The girl pointed at the empty wheeled baskets. "Can I get one of those too?"

Faythe handed one over, distracted. The conversation with the old man had made her think of Jahu. She felt suddenly raw, as if a plaster had been ripped off a not-yet-healed wound.

For some reason, Zariel's sly smile drifted through her imagination. She shivered. Why couldn't she handle this Management humiliation as coolly as he would have?

The girl twirled her hair and gawked. "How come you don't look like the other staff?" she asked.

"Other staff?" Faythe blinked. "Oh, you mean the Children. I'm not sure. I'm new."

The girl looked confused. "*You're* new? They look much younger."

She sighed. She didn't feel like conversing. "They've always been children. And I've always been like this." She pointed at herself, somewhat unnecessarily. "They've been here since the Shop opened, I think."

She actually didn't know much more than that. Both Beris and Omaro had seemed to think it was rude to ask. Perhaps she'd find out one day.

The girl still looked confused. "How come you're here, then?"

She started scanning the girl's jars. INQUISITIVE. No surprise there. "I was travelling to the Shop to pass through, but they offered me a job instead. I couldn't exactly turn that down."

"Wow!" The girl's mouth hung open. "It must be hard not passing through."

Faythe glanced through the glass dome to the Earth, far above. Her spine tingled with an uncomfortable mix of dread and longing. Even after all these weeks, she still wasn't used to the sight. Sometimes Earth looked so vast and uncaring, and she feared she'd vanish without trace if she went there. At other times a desire for life throbbed within her and she dreamed obsessively of what might be.

She reflexively buried all of that complexity and shrugged. "I've got more to do here first. And how many people get to work at the Shop Before Life?"

The girl pursed her lips. "You're really lucky." She glanced around and lowered her voice. "You know, I never wanted to pass through. Not ever. I loved it here. Had a really good prelife, great friends, happy times."

97

Another jar zipped through the checkout. PUTS DOWN DEEP ROOTS, which—thanks to the Management of the universe, no doubt—was pleasingly appropriate. She thought of Jahu again, and her reservoir of emotion sprang another leak. "I know how you feel," she stammered, swallowing.

The girl smiled sadly. "It was good while it lasted. But I guess everything ends. My home—Ostholme, you know it?"

She shook her head, desperately trying not to think about the Rock, and picked up the next jar for scanning.

"No?" said the girl. "It changed a lot since I first lived there. Long ago." Her lip quivered. "Recently I realised everyone that mattered had left and everything had changed. I accepted it was time to go. To pass through."

The girl was scared, Faythe realised. She should probably comfort her, but all she could think about was her old friends and her old life. She sniffed. These last two customers had really knocked her off balance. All this stupid talk of soulmates and homes . . .

Do NOT cry, she thought, forcefully. Unfortunately, the idea of crying in public upset her further, which made it harder not to cry. "I guess . . . everything ends," she replied, between gulps. She scanned another jar: EMOTIONAL CONTROL.

Both women remained quiet as Faythe scanned the final few jars. Her vision was blurry and her thoughts were loud. *I gave up my home. I gave up my friends. Only to disappoint Management. And the Shopkeeper. And me.* She blinked away a tear, hoping the girl wouldn't notice.

The girl's eyes shone with tears of her own. "Thanks for the help," she said.

She wheeled her basket towards the mysterious passing-through area. Faythe watched in silence as Security nodded her through.

What a shift. Thank Management it's over. She couldn't wait to sit in the Gardens and recuperate.

She picked up the girl's bag, but, to her horror, it wasn't empty. A single jar remained inside.

Instantly she charged towards the passing-through area. A guard waited at the start of the long corridor leading to the door to Earth. He held out his arm. "Ma'am, I'm afraid you can't go in there."

She brandished the missing jar. "That customer left this behind!"

He sucked air through his teeth. "I'm sorry, but you know the corridor beyond this line is strictly for people passing through to Earth. I can't let you through."

"But she needs this!"

She waved her arms desperately. In a way, this was worse than when she'd talked that boy out of going. He could always come back another time, but this girl would miss out on one of her traits *forever*.

The guard was implacable. "Ma'am, she's gone the moment she steps over this line. You know that."

She stared at the door at the far end of the corridor. Perhaps if she ran, she could make it.

The Child watched her closely. His face said *please-don't-do-this* as clearly as if it were tattooed on his forehead.

She closed her eyes. His face's unspoken message was correct: this was a bad idea. Besides, the girl might be on Earth already.

Despondently, she trudged back to the checkout, dreading Omaro's disappointment when she reported this.

Although . . . she didn't HAVE to tell him.

She gulped. That thought had arrived out of nowhere, enticing and unwelcome all at once. Of course, she was supposed to report things like this. But wouldn't admitting it only get her into trouble again? The humiliation of the Committee Meeting was still fresh in her memory.

Her gaze landed on the girl's receipt. That could be a problem, too.

She skimmed the list, slightly ashamed that she was already more concerned for the correctness of the paperwork than for the poor girl whose entire life would lack this trait. Maybe she *was* a bad person.

There it was, listed at the bottom of the receipt: SCIENTIFIC DEDUCTION. She'd scanned it and mistakenly put it back in the bag after. So stupid! If only she hadn't been distracted by trying not to cry.

But this did mean that the trait was accounted for. Nobody would know it was missing.

She stared at the jar for a moment. It sparkled, a deep sky-blue. After a quick glance around, she slid it into her pocket and walked as quickly as she dared to her chambers.

Once inside, she searched for a good place to hide a stolen jar of human personality. After it was safely stashed away, she would simply never think about it again. That *couldn't* fail.

 *nine*

THE DAYS AFTER stealing the jar were more difficult still.

It was amazing how lonely it was possible to be whilst constantly surrounded by people. Even spending time with Omaro was torture. She longed to talk to him about Zariel, or the stolen jar, or to ask the questions Zariel had put in her mind, but doing so could only make everything much, much worse.

The Shopkeeper remained distant and uncertain—to Faythe, anyway. To the customers she was always attentive and friendly.

On a whim, she'd asked the Gardener if he knew any good secrets. After some thought he had pronounced that most people significantly underrated the usefulness of worms. But this didn't seem likely to solve any of her problems.

Loneliness, shame and self-doubt came and went, and through it all, Zariel's words kept echoing: 'ask awkward questions'.

Finally, Faythe snapped. *Surely curiosity was no crime.* She approached the Shopkeeper on the busy concourse.

"Excuse me. Can I ask a question?"

The Shopkeeper waved goodbye to a customer. "Of course," she said, looking surprised. "I'm glad you want to." There was a brief pause while Faythe wondered what to say. Eventually, the Shopkeeper broke the silence. "Can we walk together? How are you finding things at the moment?"

She thought as they crossed the concourse together. *I'm constantly afraid of messing up again and being seriously punished by Management. I desperately want to talk to the ex-Apprentice you banished and who I'm not supposed to even know exists. I'm fairly sure you're hiding deep, dark secrets . . . oh, and I stole a jar by mistake but I don't intend to give it back even though I feel incredibly guilty about it.*

"I'm really good," she said.

"That's good. I've heard you've been working hard." A pause. "What can I help you with?"

She hesitated. "I'm not sure if now is a good time."

The Shopkeeper, sensing it was important, stopped walking. Children and customers were milling around nearby. "It's fine. Go on."

She twirled her hair between two fingers. "I've been wondering about the traits. How they work, and how they're made, and things like that." The Shopkeeper's face went blank. "And how do people pass through to Earth with them? We never really talked about all this in training. Will Beris explain eventually?"

It was a long moment before the Shopkeeper replied. "I am glad you're talking to me again." The Apprentice blushed. "I know I'm not your favourite person after what happened with the Committee. I was hoping that, after some space, we'd find it easier to start afresh. And I do appreciate your curiosity. But I'm afraid these particular questions aren't appropriate."

She stared right into the Shopkeeper's eyes. "Can you at least tell me why not?"

When the old lady spoke again, there was a discernible edge to her voice. "For business reasons, these matters are highly confidential."

"Okay," muttered Faythe. She regretted asking already.

"However," continued the Shopkeeper. "Why don't we use this opportunity to build a better friendship? I like to take tea in the afternoons—perhaps you might join me one of these days?"

Faythe stared down at her feet. Her old self would have been thrilled by such an invite—from the actual Shopkeeper, no less!—but a boring old tea couldn't compare to the answers she'd wanted.

At least she'd learned one thing. Zariel was right: there were questions she wasn't even permitted to ask. *Perhaps this invite was part of the Shopkeeper's friendly act.*

"Maybe," she said, without looking up.

"It's up to you. The invite will remain open. And, in the meantime, I'd prefer if you stopped this line of inquiry. Confidentiality must be respected, for the good of all."

Faythe boiled with frustration, but nodded her assent.

"Good." The Shopkeeper sighed. "I'm sorry, but you have to trust that I have the best interests of the Shop at heart, and they won't always coincide with what you want." With that, the old lady left.

Faythe stood alone among the busyness of the Shop. *She should never have opened her mouth.* The Shopkeeper would be even more suspicious of her after this.

And she was still lonelier than ever. *Unless...*

Perhaps there was someone. She yearned for a confidante to talk to, and a teacher to provide answers.

One other person could be both.

Zariel.

How do you contact a mysterious stranger who you know very little about? In the stories Faythe had heard, lovestruck teenagers wandered around, hoping for an intervention from fate. Wiser adults narrowed the possibilities using the few clues they had.

Faythe, being much older than a teenager and yet infinitely less experienced than any adult, quickly came to the conclusion that crime was the answer.

The plan was simple. She couldn't openly ask how to contact Zariel. But the information must be somewhere—most likely, in the Shopkeeper's office. All she needed to do was break in and borrow it.

As usual, the sensible voice in her brain wasn't convinced of the wisdom of this plan, but since she needed a friend, and it wasn't directly forbidden to talk to Zariel, by twisty logic—that made sense *as long as she definitely didn't think about it*—stealing his contact details must be morally fine.

Dark deeds are best performed in darkness, and mildly dark deeds are best performed under twinkly starlight. She waited until after sundown before creeping out of her room and padding quietly through the private quarters and into the administrative area.

At night, the shop floor felt intimate and secret, but this deserted office was eerie. There was no scritching of ink or clacking of equipment, and the empty desks were near invisible in the deep blue earthlight. The complete absence of activity made the space feel strangely inhuman, and the quiet made her jumpy. Quickly, she shuffled into the Shopkeeper's personal office, her eyes still adjusting to the gloom.

And there, in the corner: a figure, watching her.

Her heart beat so hard it hurt, and she leapt in terror, her knees thrusting her instinctively high into the air.

The figure didn't move.

A moment later, her brain sheepishly realised its mistake. The 'figure' was only the Shopkeeper's coat hanging from a hook on the wall. Her overactive imagination had done the rest.

She relaxed and stepped further inside. Beneath her feet, the floorboard creaked loudly. She froze, tense and frightened, before slowly forcing herself to relax once more.

Perhaps this isn't actually a good idea, suggested the quiet voice in her mind. The voice had a point; this plan had seemed much more reasonable in daylight. But she was already here. No point going inside the office without getting what she needed.

She lit a candle. As the room brightened, and the shadows in her imagination burned away, she relaxed.

Opposite the office were the private quarters. She watched as a light flickered in a remote window before going out. On a night this still, noise would easily carry into the bedrooms. She tiptoed over to the Shopkeeper's desk, the carpet scratching at her bare feet, not unpleasantly.

As usual, the desk was a mess of books and papers and toys and trinkets. Zariel's details would surely be filed away somewhere. She tried a drawer and sifted as quickly as she could through paperwork, copies of delivery manifests, invoices from the Supplier, discarded scraps of hastily written to-do lists, and a truly impressive pile of pens. Nothing useful.

The rest of the drawers appeared to be much of the same, so she turned her attention to the tall cabinet behind the desk. The largest drawer was locked, but the next opened. It too, was full of papers, organised in sheaves and labelled with a mix of dates and mysterious titles like 'PMI Inspection Preparation'.

She rifled through as fast as she could. Again, nothing.

In the third drawer there was a binder marked 'Apprentices'. Her heart paused for dramatic effect before resuming its habitual pumping.

Inside the binder were several folders, a thin file marked 'FAYTHE', and, underneath, a much, much thicker file labelled 'ZARIEL'. There were also two more files, dog-eared and tattered, with names so faded they were unreadable.

She gazed hungrily at the file with her name on it, but her blazing curiosity would have to wait for now. She flicked through Zariel's folder. It seemed to be a chronological description of his time at the Shop. She read a page at random.

He attempted to get in again today, must talk to K or P about it.

Immediately curious, she flicked back to the beginning and skimmed through as fast as she could. *He shows satisfactory progress, but refuses to accept the need for patience . . . his usual politeness failed him in this instance . . . this is the third such customer complaint this year . . . Beris is sceptical that he will ever understand . . . I believe these questions are primarily rooted in boredom, and the others agree . . .*

These observations were interspersed with written complaints from customers who'd been irritated by his poor service. It seemed he regularly skirted the edge of real trouble . . . although, here was a copy of a report made to Management for a major transgression: stealing jars.

Faythe paused to stare out of the window. The ill-gotten jar under her mattress burned brightly in her imagination.

If the Shopkeeper ever discovered it . . .

She shook her head and resumed reading. The following pages appeared to be increasingly frustrated disciplinary statements from the Shopkeeper. Her attempts to keep Zariel in line continually backfired for years. Everything she tried just made him more determined to disobey her. And over-and-over again, she wrote that he kept asking about the traits: first how they worked, then how he could make them, and how he could use them, and where they came from . . .

No wonder the Shopkeeper had reacted so flatly to her similar questions.

A sudden, distant thump brought Faythe back to the present. She waited with bated breath, but no other noise followed.

She didn't have time to read the whole story. But she had to know. Her nerves twanged as she turned to the final pages.

The situation has become unsustainable. P agrees Z isn't ready, which means, for the good of the Shop, he must go. I'm concerned that the others will disagree. My preferred solution would be for him to pass through to Earth. However, they appear to have a plan of their own. I suppose we ought to discuss in person.

A slip of paper was attached to the final page. It had 'Current Address' printed in neat, intricate handwriting. *Thank Management for Beris.*

She tore off a scrap from the Shopkeeper's pad and quickly copied the address: Zariel, The Complex, Near Valley.

Just then, the unmistakable sound of conversation echoed from the office outside. Every muscle in Faythe's body attempted to tense at once. *Did some of the Children work this late? Cleaning perhaps?*

She couldn't wait to find out. She stuffed the folder back into the drawer and slid it shut.

The speakers were close now, just outside the door.

Without pausing, Faythe blew out the candle and dived under the desk. She lay as still as she could in the darkness.

Silence. Had it been her imagination again, like the coat hook? Maybe it had been—

Suddenly, the door opened.

"—really think you should wait until morning, Shopkeeper."

That was Beris' voice . . . although Faythe was far more concerned that the Shopkeeper was with him. *Was she normally in her office at this hour?!* Too late, she realised that this was precisely the sort of information which ought to be acquired *before* breaking into your boss's office.

She scrunched her eyes tight, irrationally hoping that if she couldn't see, then nobody could see her either.

"I agree. No good ever comes of rushing to action." That was Omaro! As ever, he was dispensing wise advice. She wished she'd considered the wisdom of patience earlier on.

The trio were inside now, the timbre of their footsteps altering as they stepped onto the carpet. The Shopkeeper walked to her desk and sat down. Her long skirt practically brushed against Faythe's bare feet.

The terrified Apprentice tried not to breathe, before realising that she definitely would be better off if she carried on breathing ... as long as it was very, very gently.

"I'm sorry," sighed the Shopkeeper, noisily lighting a candle above. Faythe's eyes widened—*will she notice it's already melted and hot?* "You're both correct. I know it would be sensible to sleep on it, but I simply won't be able to relax until I've replied. This is a tremendous threat to us all."

Faythe frowned. The Shopkeeper sounded upset. *Who was threatening her, and with what?*

The Shopkeeper dragged her chair forward an inch. Faythe shuffled backwards as quickly as she dared, pressing deep into the blackness where the back of the desk met the floor.

"If you're sure," said Beris, doubtfully. His voice sounded odd as it filtered through the thick wood. Inches above Faythe's head, the scratching of a pen began to vibrate through the desk.

"I'm rarely sure," said the Shopkeeper. "But this reply will be brief, and I'd like you both to check it before we send it."

"I trust your instincts," said Omaro. He sounded uncharacteristically worried.

Faythe stared at the Shopkeeper's foot as it gently tapped up and down. If she got caught, this would surely be the end—certainly of her time at the Shop, and potentially even of her hopes of life on Earth. A litany of self-recrimination echoed through her mind—*you idiot you idiot you idiot you idiot.*

It wasn't a particularly creative litany, but she focused on the words, hoping desperately that distracting herself intensely enough would prevent her from accidentally sneezing, or getting cramp, or itching, or ...

As if summoned by these thoughts, her stomach rumbled. Loudly.

The noise echoed off the underside of the desk, sounding as if the Earth itself had plummeted into the Shop and was destroying everything in its path.

Her body was already motionless but her heart stopped too.

Nothing happened. The Shopkeeper hummed quietly as she scribbled.

After several long, tortuous eternities—which lasted perhaps another forty seconds—the Shopkeeper put down her pen and stood. The total blackness receded slightly as candlelight weakly reflected to illuminate the underside of the desk.

"Can you take this?" said the Shopkeeper, crossing to the other side of the room.

Faythe still didn't dare move.

"I'll send it first thing in the morning," replied Beris.

"Thank you," said the Shopkeeper. She sighed. "I still don't know if I'll be able to sleep. Perhaps I ought to stay here and catch up on paperwork."

Faythe's stomach tumbled. *Please, no!* she wanted to scream.

"I think you should rest," said Omaro.

She closed her eyes. Her heart pounded in her ears.

"You're right," said the Shopkeeper, finally. "Thank you both for your advice. It's appreciated."

Faythe closed her eyes in relief. She held her breath as they left, ignoring complaints from her contorted muscles which were begging her to stretch.

Footsteps padded across the carpet, the door swung open, there was a huff as the candle went out, and she was plunged into complete darkness once more.

She waited until she was definitely alone before rolling out from under the desk and stretching her agonised muscles.

There was a piece of paper on the previously empty part of the Shopkeeper's desk. She squinted, but in the starlight all she could make out was the seal of Management at the top. Was that the letter the Shopkeeper had replied to?

But there was no time to investigate. She opened the door as quietly as she could. The administrative area was deserted. Once more, she let out a breath and paced rapidly back to her bedroom.

The instant the door closed behind her, she covered her head with her hands. Her whole body trembled with residual terror as the enormity of the near miss sunk in. Her whole future existence on Earth had been put at risk—for nothing except a crumpled piece of paper.

She reached into her pocket and unfolded the paper. Her desire to contact Zariel had completely evaporated. Perhaps it was reading parts of his story, or maybe it was the fright of so nearly being caught. Whatever it was, she didn't want to travel the same path he had.

She would be here for a thousand years. A contract with the gods ensured it was so. And *nothing* was worth getting on the wrong side of Management.

If the Shopkeeper said Faythe was seeking knowledge she shouldn't have, then she would simply have to believe her. No matter what Zariel had said.

She scrumpled up Zariel's address, and lifted her mattress to reveal the stolen jar of SCIENTIFIC DEDUCTION glittering in a hollow of the bed frame. She threw the paper inside and let the mattress drop.

Enough risk, betrayal, rashness and trouble. From now on, Faythe was determined to be a model employee. Forever.

Or for a thousand years at least.

ten

TIME PASSED.

This *always* happens. Nothing is more predictable than time—or more selfish. The instant it seems to be under control, it squirms away without consideration for anybody else's wishes. It ticks away in an endless succession of instants, each precisely as fleeting as the last. There's no slowing it down and no speeding it up. One second per second—that's all anyone ever gets.

Fortunately, time gives equal regard to each and every moment, so tedious hours dribble away with the same crushing inevitability as joyous ones.

That is, unless you're travelling very fast, which—for reasons known only to Management—slows the speed of time itself. Some philosophers argue that this is a necessary limitation for the universe to physically function, but it is also possible that Management simply wanted their groceries to remain fresh while being delivered.

For Faythe, this particular passage of time was pleasant, arguably even good. As months passed into years, she felt ever more at home and fell increasingly in love with the Shop.

As ever, she didn't bother keeping track of time. It could have been two years since she'd arrived, or perhaps five. Maybe more. Who kept count, in the prelife?

Everything wasn't perfect, especially between her and the Shopkeeper.

Over the years they'd developing an understanding—not a relationship, exactly, but a civil approximation of one. Each thought they might grow into a true friendship eventually.

After all, there would always be more time.

Everything is connected. It seemed to Faythe that people said this a lot. Customers said it, the Children said it—even she said it, whenever she wanted to give the impression of being wise.

It had always appeared to be a wishy-washy sentiment, but recently Beris had explained that everything was literally connected. Apparently even the motion of a single ant in one tiny corner of the universe would bend all of spacetime at the speed of gravity across the whole rest of the cosmos.

She'd asked if this made any difference, and he'd said "not really".

This seemed a shame. It would be better if everything were meaningfully connected—especially during those moments of loneliness which surfaced periodically. If a single ant could affect the whole universe, why couldn't she summon people back into her prelife merely by thinking about them?

At this precise instant, she was physically kneeling down to rearrange the display on a low shelf, but in her imagination she was back at the Rock. This was a common occurrence lately. Her old friends were frequently on her mind. She kept wondering whether they were happy, and she was curious to know whether she'd been replaced . . . or even forgotten.

A voice rang out behind her. "Hello, Faythe."

She was so wrapped up in her thoughts that she assumed the voice was just her imagination. She shuffled forward to adjust the placement of another jar.

Wait. That had sounded like—

Tapak coughed. "Faythe?"

It WAS him! She leapt up and shrieked and hugged him all at once. "What are you doing here?!"

"Same as you, I guess. This is the Shop Before Life, right?" He scratched his head and looked around in pretend confusion. "Everybody comes here! Although I didn't dare hope to catch you here. You must have taken a long route." He craned his head to peer curiously at the display she'd been fiddling with. "What's that you're planning to take? It looks pretty."

She smiled with professional pride. Beris had recently been inspired by a training day (which, naturally, he himself had organised) on creating displays which would induce 'optimal customer engagement'. She'd only vaguely paid attention, but he seemed happy whenever she simply made the shelves look beautiful.

"Thanks! I'm glad you like it." She grinned at her friend's bewildered expression and took his arm. "Let me show you around. We have a lot to catch up on."

◆ ◆

Much later that day, the pair were sitting in Faythe's favourite spot in the Gardens, an enclave underneath the Viewing Platform, just off the path. From here the view was uninterrupted all the way to the distant mountains. At this time in the evening, sunlight glittered orange on the river, so it appeared more light than water. A few insects buzzed around quietly, while snippets of indistinguishable chatter drifted down from above.

She fiddled with a piece of grass, patiently tying it into ever bigger knots while Tapak gaped at the view.

Eventually, he turned back with a disbelieving shake of the head. "It's amazing that you work here!"

"It's still weird to me, if it helps."

He snorted. "What's really weird is that I'm not really surprised."

She raised an eyebrow. "What do you mean?"

"If anyone were going to stumble into a job at the actual Shop Before Life, it'd be you. You attract ridiculous situations."

"I do not! I lived in a *rock* for two hundred years, Tapak."

"Yeah—and think about everything that happened just while you were there! Remember that guy who decided he was in love with you after visiting for a day? He basically moved in until you pretended to leave and he went on a quest to find you."

"Oh yeah." She had forgotten about that. "But that was just one strange person getting over-excited."

"Maybe. But you're like a magnet for weird happenings. I mean, you ran into those guys in the middle of nowhere to get this job in the first place." She shifted uncomfortably. Tapak hadn't cared when she'd confessed the truth about why she'd left, but she felt guilty regardless. "What strange things do you think will happen here before you're finished?"

Memories of breaking into offices and being reported to Management leapt around in Faythe's imagination. "Nothing, probably," she said.

But the pair shared a lot of history. He gave her a knowing look. "Something happened, then?"

She pulled a face. "Maybe." His eyes shone, and she sighed. It was so good to see him. "Okay, fine—I'll tell you! When I first got here—years ago now! Those days are behind me, alright?—there was, um, a little chaos." She laughed in embarrassment. "I got reported to Management. In my first week."

Tapak roared with laughter. "Management! Getting reported to the gods is so you, Faythe."

"That was ages ago, though. It's all quiet now, except for the odd thief."
"Thieves! Here?"

"Yeah, just idiots. The Shopkeeper thinks they're all one group, but I'm not sure."

Her friend looked impressed. "You talk about her like she's a regular person."

"She is, kind of." Faythe frowned. "We have a complicated relation-ship." Suddenly, talking about the Shop felt boring. "How's Jahu?"

Her heart skipped even as she asked. A large part of her didn't want to know. If he was unhappy, she'd be unhappy to hear about it, and if he was happy *without* her, well . . .

She fiddled with the knot of grass she'd created.

"He's not great," said Tapak. "After you left, he was miserable, and that lasted a long time. Then, after I decided to leave . . ."

"Let me guess—he blamed me?" She'd always been able to read Jahu's thoughts.

"He didn't say so, but I think he did, a bit." Tapak shrugged. "You know what he's like."

She smiled weakly. It hurt to picture her old friend, alone and dejected at the Rock.

"Last I heard," continued Tapak, "he was thinking of heading to Ostholme."

Ostholme! That was a jolt. Weirdly, the thought of him travelling was nearly as painful as him being alone. "I've heard it's nice there," she said, abruptly regretting the change of subject. Apparently she hadn't wanted to know what Jahu was doing after all. "What about you? Tell me what made you leave!"

"Destiny!" he said, grandly. But before she could ask what he meant, Omaro strolled into their enclave.

"Greeting, mighty Apprentice!" he yelled with a bow and a flourish. "I heard you have brought a friend, oh great one?"

Tapak's eyebrows joined in puzzlement. "Is this how everyone speaks to you?" he muttered to Faythe.

She rolled her eyes. "Definitely not," she said. "Omaro, this is Tapak. We used to live together."

"Ah, indeed," said the Child. "And now *I* have that incredible honour. Surely we have both been blessed mightily in this prelife."

She threw a grass clump at him. "Omaro is always an idiot, though he's particularly showing off today because you're here."

Tapak grinned. "Hi! We were just talking about how Faythe tends to attract chaos. You got any good stories about her time here?"

"Yee- nooo," said Omaro, noticing Faythe's warning glare. A sly grin appeared on his cherub-like face. "But maybe you have good stories from your time together?"

Oh Management, no! She coughed. "Hey, Tapak, have you heard about yoyos?"

"Yoyos?" He frowned. "What's that?"

To her relief, Omaro took the bait. "I can show you!" He pulled out a wooden circle which dangled from a string. "It took a long time, but I figured out the ancient secrets of the yoyo, all by myself."

Tapak looked uncertainly from the yoyo to Faythe.

"It's an Earth toy," she explained. "He plays a game where he has to make them from just vague descriptions. And he claims he didn't look up how to make this one."

"Why would I do that?" Omaro opened his arms in feigned offence. "It simply took persistence." He turned to Tapak and wiggled the yoyo vigorously so that waves travelled along the string while the wooden circle remained completely still at the bottom. "And soon I'll figure out what it actually does, and then I'm sure she'll be suitably impressed." He swung it from side to side like a pendulum. "Check that out!"

"Can I have a go?" asked Tapak.

Faythe smiled, happy the topic had moved away from swapping embarrassing stories. "What were you saying about destiny?" she asked Tapak, as the Child handed him the toy.

"Oh, nothing." Tapak frowned and bounced the yoyo on the palm of his hand. "I was just being dramatic."

Omaro stuck out his lower lip. "I don't have much time for destiny, myself."

"You don't believe in it?"

"Nah, I'm just busy. I don't have time for anything." The Child laughed at his own joke.

Faythe threw another clump of grass at him. "Idiot."

"Seriously, though," said Omaro. "How would we even tell if destiny was real? Everything could be planned to look like an accident. Either way, it doesn't make much difference."

She pulled a face. "That's even more idiotic. How could it not make much difference? You don't think it matters if nobody ever makes real choices?"

"How would I act differently even if I knew the answer for sure?"

She opened her mouth, and then closed it, stumped.

He stuck out his tongue. "Who's the idiot now?"

Tapak laughed. "He's got you there." He handed the yoyo back to Omaro, who jiggled it about in his hand. As always, it did nothing.

She sighed. "How are you so smart, but you can't figure out a children's toy?"

The Child threw his arms in the air. "Some things take more work.

Speaking of which, how did the label switch go?"

"Label . . . switch?" She furrowed her brow, but the words weren't out of her mouth before she realised what he meant. Nearly a thousand jars had arrived overnight from the Supplier with a note apologising that they'd been mislabelled. Thanks to one of her irregular attempts to impress the Shopkeeper, she had volunteered to relabel them. But Tapak's arrival had completely put it out of her mind.

Her stomach churned and her breath quickened. If the universe truly were full of mysterious connections, then at that exact moment a lot of people would be squirming as their partners asked if they'd done That Thing They Promised They'd Do yet.

"I, um, have to go." She stood up, her mind racing to calculate how long it would take to relabel and replace a thousand jars. It was only evening. There was still time before tomorrow, wasn't there?

Tapak lumbered to his feet, looking concerned. "I'm sorry! Did I distract you from something important? Can I help?"

"No, no, it's alright."

But he knew her better than that. "Seriously, I'll help."

"You sure? It'd be really boring."

"It's not like I'm doing anything else. Besides, it'd be cool to work at the Shop Before Life, just once."

Omaro looked uncertain. "Technically, your friend isn't trained," he said.

She gave him a sceptical look. "Trained? It's only labels."

The Child shrugged. "It's up to you. Just doing my due diligence. But don't let Beris find out!"

"It'll be fine. Come on, Tapak."

Omaro waved as they left. "Have fun, O Princess of the Shop!" he called out.

She shook her fist at him, and his giggles followed them back up the slope to the Shop.

◆ ▭ ◆

Faythe flipped a pile of fresh labels onto the storeroom table and gestured towards the boxes which were stacked up nearby. "Here we go. All these labels need to go onto all those jars."

"Is your life always this thrilling?" asked Tapak.

"Told you this wouldn't be fun. Is magical retail not as glamorous as you thought?"

"I guess I never pictured the boring bits."

"You haven't even seen the properly boring bits. Compared to paperwork, this is sheer joy."

It didn't take them long to set up a rudimentary production line. Tapak peeled off the incorrect labels as fast as he could, and Faythe applied fresh ones over the gaps. They entertained each other by swapping stories of old times. When he reminded her of the time Jahu got stuck in a bog and had to run home without his trousers, she laughed until her face hurt.

"It's so good to see you," she said, once she'd recovered. "I didn't think I would. I never thought you'd pass through the Shop."

"Me neither," he said, picking up the next jar. "But after you left, the idea kept going around in my head. And suddenly I realised it was time."

"Sounds familiar." Her tongue protruded slightly as she concentrated on straightening a label.

"I guess that's what happened to you, too."

"That's it. Sometimes you've just got to move on, even if nothing's wrong with where you are. And afterwards, the new place is where you're supposed to be."

"Destiny again!" He gave a nervous smile. "I hope I feel that way about Earth. But I'm happy that you found somewhere. The Shop Before Life, even! You're so lucky."

She grinned. Despite her complaints, she still wasn't bored of handling containers of pure human traits. She gestured at the jar she was holding. "Isn't it amazing?"

"It is! Remember when we used to wonder about these things? You must know loads about them by now."

Her smile faded. She didn't want to tell her friend that the Shopkeeper didn't trust her with that information. "Not as much as you'd think."

Tapak looked thoughtfully at the jar he was holding. "Does anyone ever take all of the traits? I mean literally *all* of them. They could make themselves a super-human!"

This had been another regular debate back at the Rock. But no matter how often the group pooled their collective ignorance they'd never been able to figure out whether this plan would work.

However, this was one answer she did have. "It turns out you can't do that," she said, eager to show off.

"Oh! They stop you? How?"

"It's so simple," she said. "It surprised me when I found out. Guess!"

"Yeah?" He frowned. "Is it . . . a wizard that controls what you can take?"

"No wizards. No magic." She paused. "At least, none that I've seen. I think you'll figure it out, though. It's a very human solution."

His frown deepened. "Rules? Inspections? Permission slips?"

She shook her head at each guess.

"I give up."

"It's so easy!" She clapped gleefully. "It's this . . . you can only carry so much!"

His jaw hung open. "That's it?! Just *what you can carry?* Isn't that unfair?"

"That's right. But prelife is unfair." She crinkled her eyes, remembering her argument with the Shopkeeper about fairness soon after she'd arrived. Her beliefs hadn't consciously changed in the meantime, but now the system seemed reasonable. People picked differently—that was just how it was.

"So nobody smuggles extra jars through?"

"They'd be allowed to take them, so it wouldn't really be smuggling. They can even use a basket, if they want." She shrugged. "But I don't have much to do with the passing-through process, so maybe I don't know?"

"You'd never guess the universe actually worked like this, would you?" He shook his head and held up a jar. "Tell me about these now!"

"What about them?"

"How do they work? What makes this blue gunk GOOD WITH WORDS?"

The truth wasn't impressive, but she didn't want to lie to him again. "I don't know," she admitted. "I've been trying to find out, but they won't tell me."

"How come?"

"They won't tell me that, either," she said ruefully.

"I guess they're allowed to have secrets."

She narrowed her eyes. It was jarring that he shrugged the question off so easily. He genuinely didn't seem to mind not knowing the answer. To her, these questions were an itch that never went away.

Her friend interrupted her thoughts. "I can't get this label off," he complained.

"I'll get it," she said, rising. "In fact, why don't we change over? This crate's full now, so we're about halfway through." As they swapped stools, she flipped the pile of fresh labels over for him and gave him a meaningful nod. "There you go!"

His eyes glinted. "Bet I'm faster than you were."

"Bet you're not!"

They worked into the night.

It took hours, but eventually the final crate was filled with relabelled jars.

Faythe glanced outside towards the stars. It was that unusual time of night which is neither today nor tomorrow.

"Thanks so much," she said, standing and stretching. "This would have taken me ages."

"It's nothing. I can't believe they expected you to do all this on your own. This is days of work."

She shrugged. "I volunteered."

"You're an idiot." He eyed the crates. "You said we have to put them on the shelves now?"

She suppressed a yawn. It was the middle of the night and she wanted to go to bed . . . but technically restocking the shelves was part of the job. "It'd be better if we could do it, but we don't have to. Would you mind?"

"Not at all." He picked up the nearest crate, making it look effortless. "Lead on."

"Thank you! It'll be faster if we split up." She gestured at the smaller pile of crates. "The ones in these boxes go in the nearby aisles, just off the concourse. If you look for the big signs, you'll see where each jar goes easily enough. I'll take the rest."

He nodded, and soon the pair were wandering back and forth under the dome, placing jars onto the shelves as they went.

She was happy that Tapak was getting to see the Shop at night. Few got to experience it like this: quiet and solitary but not at all lonely. At these times, when the air shimmered softly with the flickering jarlight, the traits felt positively alive. She liked to think that they watched protectively over those who were lucky enough to be inside. The jarlight from the shelves mingled with earthlight from above to form a pale kaleidoscope of colour, bathing everything in a beautiful radiance; a glow made from both human individuality and reflections from the world where they would each—eventually—live.

On top of all that, there were no customers around to annoy her, which was *just* as magical.

She weaved up and down the aisles, mugging and waving to Tapak each time they passed one another. By the time she finished emptying her crates, the sun was beginning to rise. She called to him across the concourse.

"I'm finished with mine. How're you doing?"

"I have one or two jars left."

"You're fast!"

"I'm *amazing*." He held up a jar. "Where does this one go?"

"Follow me!" Despite her exhaustion, Faythe nearly skipped with joy down the aisle. Perhaps it was the thrill of finishing a long job, the manic energy of a night without sleep, or the surprise of unexpected time with an old friend. Whatever the cause, she felt fantastic.

But when they found the shelf where GREEN FINGERS should sit, she stopped and stared at the jar in her hands, turning it over with a puzzled expression.

"Everything alright?" Tapak leaned closer.

"It's not the right colour. Look at the rest."

The other GREEN FINGERS were—perhaps unusually consistently for the Shop, but as one might naively expect—green, while the jar in her hand was an unfortunate shade of bright blue.

"Oh," he said. "They were all like different like that. I figured there were just multiple varieties, or something."

Her insides dropped and she whirled to face him. "What?! They were *all* the wrong colour?"

"Yeah." He fiddled nervously with his fingers. "Is that bad?"

She slammed her eyes shut and thought fast. *What had happened? And how?*

"When we swapped jobs," she began, opening her eyes slowly, "and I gave you the labels . . . did you apply from the bottom of the pile?"

"No." His face radiated anxiety. "Though I did notice the pile was upside-down. So I turned it around."

She put her hands to her face and moaned.

"Did I do something wrong?"

She shook her head in frustration. "No. *I* did. I flipped them so the sticky side was up for you. I thought you saw me, but I should have made sure. I'm an idiot!"

He couldn't have looked more upset if he'd swallowed a mouthful of wasps. "I'm sorry. I should have said something earlier."

She jiggled nervously and tried to figure out a plan. Maybe . . . maybe this wasn't that bad? They'd scattered a few mislabelled jars around the Shop—well, *hundreds* of mislabelled jars. Just as the sun was rising and the Shop was about to open.

It was not at all clear what to do. She gulped. "We'd better find Beris."

eleven

BERIS WAS HAPPY to start work early, but extremely unhappy to hear what had happened. Despite Faythe's protestations, he insisted on informing the Shopkeeper as soon as possible. This couldn't be a good sign. She had never heard of anybody interrupting the old lady's breakfast for any reason. It simply didn't happen.

Their boss listened calmly—albeit with an increasingly grave expression—as they explained. Once they were finished, she put down her fork, leaving a whole waffle untouched, and directed her gaze at Faythe. "And I presume you know where these mislabelled jars are?" she asked.

It was *worse* that the Shopkeeper was so calm.

"Er, well, some of them," stammered Faythe. "It wasn't actually me that put those ones on the shelves."

The Shopkeeper raised an eyebrow. Tapak, who was hanging around behind them in a nigh-tangible cloud of terror and awe, waved awkwardly. "Hello!" he said.

If not for the situation, it might have been comforting to witness somebody else having a disastrous first meeting with the Shopkeeper. Perhaps if Jahu showed up, they could collect the full set.

"We have records of the delivery," interjected Beris. "Apparently it was the bottom half of the fresh labels which were wrongly applied, so we can compare the manifest, and—"

"We have to check everything," said the Shopkeeper, with a shake of her head.

"All one thousand?" said Faythe, shocked. *That would take forever!* "It was only the bottom half which—"

"She means all of the stock," interrupted Beris.

She looked around, confused. "What do you mean?"

The Shopkeeper sighed. "We have no choice. We can't risk customers taking the wrong traits to Earth. They only get one chance, so we must be wholly free of mistakes. There's no option but to close the Shop and audit the entire stock."

"*Close the Shop?*" She looked open-mouthed from Beris to the Shopkeeper. "How does that work?"

"It will be difficult." The Shopkeeper managed to appear solemn even as she resumed slicing her waffle. "We will face a tremendous amount of problems. Unfortunately, temporary closure is still the best option."

"But why?"

"Would you like to explain to a pair of customers why their identical traits look so different? What would you tell them—that that particular one was wrong, but every other trait was fine? After that, why would anybody trust us again?"

Faythe didn't reply. This was bigger than she'd imagined.

"I'm afraid this is what happens," continued the Shopkeeper, "when an untrained customer is allowed to move mislabelled stock around without supervision."

Tapak looked like he was about to be sick.

"I was supervising him," offered Faythe, lamely.

The Shopkeeper didn't respond. "How long will it take to audit the main building, Beris?"

He took off his glasses. "If we ask everybody to take on a double shift then perhaps we can finish within one day."

"As soon as that?"

"I hope so." Beris had never sounded so uncertain. It was disconcerting.

"Please begin," said the Shopkeeper. The Child strode away as fast as he could.

Faythe waited while the old lady finished her breakfast, unsure what to do. She caught her eye and made an exaggeratedly mortified face to signal that she recognised her mistake.

But perhaps that looks too frivolous? She altered her expression, making it more serious. *But what if she didn't look sorry enough?* She reverted to a guilty half-smile.

These facial shenanigans weren't helping anyone.

"Should I go help Beris?" she asked, unable to bear it any longer.

The Shopkeeper drummed her fingers on the table. "No," she said. She sounded tired. "I want you to experience the consequences of your carelessness. You and I are going to inform the customers that there will be a temporary closure, and that we are all doing our best to resolve it. After that, you will spend the day updating them on our progress. Your first task is to advise Risk that we will require Security to accompany us outside."

That didn't sound too bad.

Behind her, Tapak coughed. "Excuse me," he said. "I'm really sorry about all this."

The sharpness in the Shopkeeper's eyes disappeared as she looked at him. "Please don't worry. This is not your responsibility." She returned her gaze to Faythe. "And it never should have been."

A bitter dread settled heavily in her stomach.

"Please don't punish Faythe for my mistake," said Tapak.

The Shopkeeper tightened her lips. "Let's just focus on surviving today, shall we?"

Faythe leaned over the verandah rail and gazed around the field, shielding her eyes from the bright morning sunshine with her hand. The opening of the Shop had been delayed by less than an hour and already a sizable throng had gathered. A thick crowd waited at the bottom of the steps leading up to the entrance, held back by a thin line of Children wearing the blue uniforms of Security. Further out, the crowd became sparser, but the constant stream of travellers trickling in from the Road would soon change that.

She shuffled nervously from foot to foot. Customers were much easier to deal with one at a time.

With a look that was almost sympathetic, the Shopkeeper handed her a megaphone. Faythe looked at it like it might explode. "Can't you do it?" she said quietly.

"I'm afraid not. You need to experience the consequences of your actions, so you get to deliver the bad news."

There was no arguing with that. She gulped, and raised the megaphone. "People of the prelife," she stammered. Her voice sounded alien, much higher-pitched and reedier than she'd expected. "I'm, uh—is this thing on? Okay, thanks—I'm sorry to tell you that the Shop Before Life will be . . . is . . . temporarily closed."

The crowd made several sounds at once: confused murmurs, loud groans, and an angry buzz of heated conversation.

"You'd better explain why," muttered the Shopkeeper into her ear. "But please don't be overly specific—I don't want people worrying about the traits once they enter. Perhaps you could say—"

Faythe was already raising the megaphone again. She wanted this finished as soon as possible. "It's because we are dealing with an issue," she yelled.

More angry rumbles. Perhaps that was *too* unspecific.

She strained to make out the frustrated questions which were flying at her from all directions. "How long till we get in?"

"Did you say the Shop was closing forever?"

"Is something wrong with Earth?!"

"Why won't you tell us what happened?"

"What are you hiding?"

This was *awful*. Now she understood why the Shopkeeper was making her do it.

The crowd beneath the verandah was thickening rapidly as people jostled to get closer. She held up the megaphone once more and attempted to answer as many questions as possible. "It is temporary! We will be quick! We hope to open again later today! Rest assured that there's nothing wrong with Earth!" Her voice was simultaneously loud in her ears and pathetically weak in this huge, noisy space.

"How long do we have to wait?" shouted a tall man. The crowd around him buzzed in agreement.

"We don't know when we will open!" she yelled back, truthfully. Her reward for this honesty was an inflamed angry groan from the whole field and a sudden outbreak of shoving. Further down the verandah, Security rushed to reinforce the line as the crowd surged towards the front door.

The Shopkeeper tapped her on the shoulder and took the megaphone. "Good morning. This is the Shopkeeper."

To Faythe's mild annoyance, the noise abated immediately.

"I know all of you have travelled a very long way, for a very important purpose. And I understand that you're upset to hear about this short delay. Let me assure you that we will reopen as soon as possible, and that all of you will get to Earth very soon. We will update you throughout the morning. Thank you for all remaining calm."

Even more annoyingly, falsely thanking the crowd for being calm appeared to genuinely calm them.

The Shopkeeper handed her the megaphone. "I believe you can take it from here. Update them again within the hour, please."

She nodded, her heart pounding with a hot mix of dread and humiliation. Once the Shopkeeper was gone, she fled inside and slumped near the checkouts with her head in her hands. She thought she might faint.

Unbidden, an image of Zariel floated into her mind. Despite their brief meeting, she was certain he would laugh himself sick at this morning's events, if he ever heard the story.

Someone coughed politely. She opened her eyes to find Beris waiting patiently in his lime-green suit. "Apprentice," he said, matter-of-factly. "As instructed, I am updating you on our status. Currently, the team have begun the audit. I'm afraid it's too soon for me to estimate when we will finish."

Across the concourse, scores of Children armed with clipboards were skittering between the aisles.

"What's your best current estimate?" She swallowed nervously. Part of her didn't want to know, but she wouldn't like to face that crowd again without concrete information.

The Child tilted his head back and forth. He hated guessing. "Perhaps by this evening," he said, eventually.

She brightened up. "That's not too bad!"

"Unfortunately, even after reopening, it'll take us days to work through the backlog. I fear the repercussions may last all week."

Oh. She gritted her teeth, seeing immediately what he meant. With no outlet, and a constant flow of new arrivals, the crowd would continue to grow. "What happens if the field gets full?"

"I hope it won't come to that. We would have to activate emergency measures and extend Security along the Road."

"Do we have enough Security for that?"

"Risk has already assured me his team are ready to put in extra hours, if necessary."

Her heart squeezed with guilt.

But the Child wasn't done. He sighed. "And the consequences on Earth, well ..."

She gave a start. "Earth? What happens on Earth?"

"What do you think? If nobody passes through, then *nobody can be born.*"

Her face froze in place. It hadn't occurred to her that Earth might be affected. She forced down the pressure which was gradually building behind her eyes. She didn't want to cry in front of Beris. "Will ... will they notice?"

"Even a single day without births would be a tremendously large deal for Earth. I am sure they will notice."

Her brain fizzed. She wanted to curl up and hide. This was considerably worse than talking a single customer out of passing through. How many lives would be altered by her mistake?

Beris was still talking. "I suppose you also hadn't realised that if nobody passes through for long enough, then the humans down there will die out entirely, and nobody will ever be born again. This is just how the system works. I thought we'd covered this in our training, but perhaps not."

She felt dizzy. *All of humanity could be in jeopardy because of one stupid mistake?* "I'm sorry," she managed.

"We told you it was important," finished Beris, sadly.

She hid in her hands until the Child left.

Time has a cruel tendency to slow down whenever anything unpleasant is happening. The day contained the usual number of minutes, but it was—by far—the longest Faythe could remember.

Not only was she forced to give regular updates to an increasingly restless crowd, but she couldn't bear to meet any of the Children's eyes. After all, this was her fault.

Worse still, whenever she looked up, the Earth hovered accusingly in the sky—a constant reminder of the chaos her carelessness had caused. She tried not to imagine what might be happening there.

From time to time Tapak attempted to console her, but his reassurances couldn't penetrate her thick wall of guilt. Eventually he gave up, and she caught sight of him throughout the day standing around remorsefully on the concourse.

Finally, just as the crowd was reaching dangerous levels of impatience, Beris informed her that the audit was complete.

Relieved, she charged outside and announced that the Shop would remain open late into the night. She longed to collapse into bed—it had been such a long time since she'd slept—but her guilt overcame her exhaustion, and she remained on the front door to apologise personally to each customer as they entered.

It was several hours before Omaro was able to persuade her to go to bed.

The next morning she awoke to the news that many people had been forced to sleep on the field. She rushed straight to the checkouts and worked with numb determination until late afternoon.

Tapak interrupted her mid-morning. He was ready to pass through to Earth.

She was too dazed to know what to say, and so he left in a blur of awkward apologies and crying and hugs.

Her heart ached.

Five days later, the crowd still hadn't quite returned to normal size. But by then, Faythe's attention was elsewhere.

The Committee was meeting once more.

An Extraordinary Meeting
of the Shop Before Life Committee

ATTENDANCE

The Shopkeeper, The Apprentice, Omaro (Sub-Management), Beris (Clerical), Risk (Security)

AGENDA

A recent Shop closure due to negligence from the Apprentice.

AFFAIRS

1. As per recent custom, a minute-taker was selected for the remainder of this meeting. The Apprentice was chosen by the drawing of lots. (As usual, I will review and amend the minutes afterwards.)
2. Everybody debated the closure incident and agreed that "causing absolute chaos—both here and on Earth—is bad".
3. Someone wanted to know whether "bad" was the best word for it, but the Shopkeeper prevented the debate from continuing.
4. The Committee condemned ~~me~~ the Apprentice for allowing a customer to perform ~~my~~ her job without adequate supervision.
5. The Committee reminded ~~me~~ the Apprentice of ~~my~~ her previous negative reports, and said that this was the final warning. A third report will lead to severe consequences.
6. There was a ~~long, scary~~ conversation about consequences. They might include termination of contract, banishment from the Shop, and even banishment from Earth.

7. An urgent question was raised regarding why the jars had been incorrectly labelled in the first place. It was agreed that enquires would be made with the Supplier. Temporary measures were discussed in order to avoid a repeat incident.

8. ~~The meeting ended. I'm sorry.~~

ACTIONS

1. A report will be filed with Management to inform them of both the closure and the Apprentice's actions.

2. Labelling will take place at the Shop until the Supplier has confirmed that the error in their procedures has been corrected.

twelve

"BERIS?"

"Yes?"

"Is everything okay?"

"Yes, I'm good, thank you."

"On Earth, I mean. Are they okay?"

"Weren't you listening during the meeting just now? I believe they'll be fine."

"But you don't know that for certain, right? People down there might have fought because of me?"

"It's possible. But you shouldn't torture yourself over it. Try to relax."

After the meeting finished, Faythe turned down an invitation to help Omaro discover yoyo tricks. Instead, she went to bed.

She didn't bother lighting a candle. Her three jars of traits provided enough light—and, besides, darkness suited her mood. This entire week she'd felt exposed, excruciatingly aware of judging eyes which were doubtless watching at all times.

Nobody had actually given her so much as a disapproving glance, but,

130

wherever she'd been, the sensation of incoming damnation had been inescapable. And she *deserved* it. It was her fault the Shop had closed, her fault the Earth had suffered, and her fault that everybody was still working extra shifts to fix the mess.

She rolled onto her side and stared numbly out of the window. Tonight's meeting had reopened a deep, partially forgotten wound. Listening as the Committee discussed precisely how terribly she'd failed had brought back the bygone dread of her struggles to settle. By the time they'd decided to publicly disgrace her in front of Management—*again*—she'd stopped even writhing in mortification.

Now she just felt ... empty.

Above all, she was lonely—an intense, scathing isolation which had been absent for a long while. She couldn't face her friends, and she certainly couldn't face the Shopkeeper. She longed for nothing more than to disappear entirely.

As she lay in bed, sleepless and unable to stop thinking, there was a rustling sound and something slid under her door.

Curiosity forced her, irresistibly, out of her warm bed to pick it up. It was a note.

I can't believe you closed the entire Shop! Even I never managed THAT. Z.

Immediately she flung the door open, but the corridor was empty.

With a sigh, she folded the note, and then, with a pounding heart, she unfolded it to read it again.

She bit her lip. Zariel's handwriting was needlessly crisp, and oddly familiar. During a few short minutes he'd created a sufficiently powerful impression that she recognised his handwriting despite never having seen it before.

Her heart still hammered as she lifted her mattress, painting the chamber with a rich, sky-blue radiance from the hidden jar of SCIENTIFIC DEDUCTION. Next to it, scrumpled up, was Zariel's address.

She stared at the paper. For the first time in a long time, she felt like the same person who had stolen it from the Shopkeeper's office.

After a fleeting hesitation, she made a decision. If Zariel had written to her, the least she could do was reply. She scribbled a note.

Hey, I've got questions for you. Care for another visit? F.

Signing with her initial seemed pretentious, but if he was doing it, she would too. She folded the letter into an envelope, ready to hide at the bottom of the outgoing mailbag tomorrow. One of the eccentric volunteers who carried letters all over the prelife would deliver it soon enough.

Afterwards, as she lay in bed, the walls shimmered with the sky-blue radiance of the ill-gotten trait. Loneliness was only part of what had led her to the Shopkeeper's office on that long-ago night. She'd also been overflowing with questions—some about Zariel, but many about the traits.

It still chafed that she'd been forbidden from even asking such questions. But that surely shouldn't prevent her from discovering answers herself.

Nobody would ever notice that this single jar of SCIENTIFIC DEDUCTION was missing. Which meant that, in a very literal sense, she possessed the power of science.

Admittedly, it was a power she didn't know how to use. But perhaps this problem contained its own solution. Why couldn't she use scientific deduction to deduce the secrets of SCIENTIFIC DEDUCTION?

The more she thought about it, the more appealing it seemed—and the more determined she became. For years, she'd tried her best. And now she was being reported to Management *anyway*. If she was going to get into trouble whatever she did, she might as well also get answers.

It was time for some science.

The greatest scientists in history each had their favourite place to work, whether a state-of-the-art laboratory, a garden shed, or somewhere laughably ridiculous like 'under an apple tree'.

Faythe, for her part, chose an abandoned broom cupboard in a faraway wing of the Shop where the floors were more creak than wood. The nearby jars were covered in a thin layer of dust, with grimy labels saying things like "HUMILITY" and "GOOD LISTENER". Deep within this neglected wing was a passage leading to the half-hidden door to her secret cupboard.

Her biggest obstacle was sourcing more jars. She briefly considered using the three Omaro had given her, but she was far too attached to them, especially since she hoped to take them to Earth someday—if she still liked them after finding out what they were, of course.

That left only one alternative: stealing. Now that she had a goal, her moral objections proved weaker than she might have expected. After all, she'd already crossed the line once, and it was alarmingly easy to scan extra jars along with a customer's order and slip them into a separate bag under the counter.

After days of gathering traits, the time came to begin. Once her shift finished, a few hours before the Shop would close for the night, she gathered her collection of jars and made her way to the cupboard.

It seemed appropriate to start with SCIENTIFIC DEDUCTION, since it had generously presented her with the idea in the first place. She cleared the junk from a small table in the corner and carefully placed the jar on the surface. It thinned towards the top, like a cone with its tip sliced off. She gave it a shake and watched as the thick sky-blue liquid swirled slowly before settling back into place.

Her heart quickened as she took the lid into her hand. This would be the first jar she'd ever opened—on purpose, anyway. *This was the point of no return.* Right now, if she wanted, she could put all of these jars back and nobody would ever know.

She took a deep breath and twisted the lid. It resisted before giving way with a loud pop.

Some say the universe acts as a mirror to those brave enough to look into it. Faythe peered inside the jar. Liquid, obviously, can't look accusingly at anybody, but it felt like the substance gazed back with reproach.

Refusing to be tempted into self-examination, she sniffed the trait— gingerly at first, but then boldly. It didn't smell like anything at all. Tiny blue wisps of SCIENTIFIC DEDUCTION ascended to escape the narrow tip of the jar, each fading to nothing in an instant.

Cautiously, she held out a finger and tilted the jar slowly until a single drip of the viscous substance broke off and landed on her fingertip. The tiny blob coalesced and rested on her skin without burning, moving, melting, staining, or reacting visibly at all.

Then, it vanished—not disappearing into her skin, but simply evaporating.

As a true scientist, the total absence of an obvious result didn't dishearten her. No result is still a result, after all.

She opened her notebook and began to scribble notes.

Opening a jar
I opened SCIENTIFIC DEDUCTION. Not much happened.

Senses
There's no scent. I can't hear anything, even with my ear to the open jar. The trait appears to do nothing to the touch. After contact with skin—or air?—it disappears.
I'm not stupid enough to eat any.

Pouring
It flows slowly. On contact with the floor, it fades to nothing.

Eating
I'm running out of ideas. Maybe I AM stupid enough to try eating them? I could try breathing it in, but that wouldn't work with a liquid trait like this.

A Problem!
What am I expecting to happen?! How would I even tell if I suddenly developed the power of scientific deduction?
Except . . . I'm writing this report, so maybe it has worked already? Or would I have done this anyway?
DAMN IT.

How were these things supposed to work? In her imagination, the passing-through process—when people got infused with their chosen traits—had always been a mystery. Sometimes she pictured a medical procedure, in which customers were injected with traits before being thrust into a tunnel to Earth. But for all she knew, it could be *anything*. Maybe an educated horse regurgitated traits into customers' open mouths. Or perhaps they had to be inhaled through a trombone.

At least she could try inhaling one. She paused to inspect her other jars, looking for a vapour with a more obviously measurable effect.

TERRIBLE STOMACH GAS churned around ominously. That certainly ticked both boxes, but perhaps in this tiny cupboard it could be *too* measurable?

Luckily, GRATITUDE was both gaseous and relatively easy to measure. Since she didn't feel especially grateful right now, if she was filled with gratitude after inhaling, then she'd have discovered how to use one trait.

She opened the jar and thrust her mouth close to the opening, sucking in pure essence of GRATITUDE, a concoction of reddish-pink fumes, as hard as she could. Her lungs filled, and she held her breath until her chest tickled and she coughed and spluttered.

Her inner scientist noted with interest that she didn't cough out anything reddish-pink, so the GRATITUDE had either vanished or been absorbed.

She probed her feelings, searching for any extra thankfulness. She certainly felt more silly, as she gazed at a mop and wondered if she were experiencing grateful emotions. Was that a spark of appreciation for the invention of floor cleaning devices? Or was she imagining it?

Suddenly this all felt ridiculous and she collapsed into laughter, before immediately becoming angry at herself for corrupting the experiment. This absurdity was amusing, so she might incorrectly feel gratitude for the amusement!

Maybe GRATITUDE had been a poor choice after all. She didn't even know whether she expected to be grateful right now or to be more open to the idea of it in future. Perhaps TERRIBLE STOMACH GAS would be more quantifiable. At least an utter gassy disaster in this cramped cupboard would be a definite result.

Although . . . presumably the effects of the traits were permanent! It would be unwise to condemn herself to a thousand years of stomach problems.

Instead, she picked up a powdered trait, UNUSUALLY IMPULSIVE, with the intention of eating it.

The sane, sensible voice in the back of her mind spoke up. *Is it wise to eat the contents of a magical jar?*

Clearly, the answer was no—none of this was wise. However, neither of the magical jars she'd opened already had exploded, melted or caused any obvious ill consequences, so it'd be fine. *Probably.*

When she poured the powdered essence of UNUSUALLY IMPULSIVE onto her hand it instantly began to dissipate, fading away exactly like the earlier traits had. Quickly, she flung the remaining contents towards her open mouth—but, in her haste, she misjudged and only succeeded in hitting herself hard in the teeth with the rapidly emptying jar.

She sat on an upturned bucket and held her mouth until the pain dwindled. Science was harder than she'd expected.

She was still choosing her next move when footsteps sounded outside. Immediately, she blew out the candle and remained as still as possible. Her mouth gently throbbed as she strained to listen. The footsteps were quiet—perhaps it was one of the Children? It would be typical of her luck if someone were spontaneously restocking this nigh-abandoned wing.

Her pulse accelerated as the soft sounds neared, bringing with them frightful memories of hiding under the Shopkeeper's desk.

Too late, she remembered why she had decided against this sort of escapade in the first place.

The footsteps slowed, and then stopped. She held her breath. If the door opened, there was no good answer to "why are you in a dark cupboard with a bunch of stolen traits?"

Forbidden science was a mistake.

A muffled sound. The clink of a jar being added to a basket, and then the footsteps moved away.

It had been a customer. She breathed out. *Just a customer.*

Her hands shook as she relit the candle. There were only two traits left: TERRIBLE STOMACH GAS and QUICK READER. She would finish quickly, by performing two experiments at once.

She pressed the lid of QUICK READER, a powder, upside down atop the jar of TERRIBLE STOMACH GAS. Then she opened QUICK READER and slid the lid away carefully, so the powder rested on the lid of TERRIBLE STOMACH GAS beneath. Finally, she unscrewed the lower lid and slipped it aside.

The powder merged with the reddish fumes, and the two traits mixed.

Faythe held her breath, half expecting a bang or spark or tremor or heat or *anything at all*, but the vapour rolled indifferently around inside the container. She waited, just in case, but nothing continued to happen.

Time for the second part of the experiment.

She tipped the contents of the jar into her mouth, swallowing the unholy mix of TERRIBLE STOMACH GAS and QUICK READER as fast as she could.

It was a curious sensation, like eating solid air. Her mouth felt full, but her throat was empty.

After a pause, she prodded her belly. No gas, terrible or otherwise, was evident.

Yet.

What about quick reading? She leafed through the safety information on a cleaning product but it was impossible to tell if she were reading any faster.

And with that inconclusive result, tonight's experiments were over.

As Faythe packed her notebook and the empty jars into her bag, she mused on what, if anything, she had learned. There was only one certainty: the traits vanished on contact. Otherwise, these experiments had been an unqualified failure. Unless she had a sudden outburst of flatulence or speed reading, she hadn't stumbled onto the correct method to infuse them.

Perhaps she should attempt to spy on the passing-through process— although, then again, Beris had warned her that it was possible to get too close and accidentally be born on Earth. She didn't know what would happen if she passed through with no traits, but it couldn't be good.

She slung the sack of empty jars over her shoulder with a loud clink, and ambled towards her bedroom, on the other side of the main area of the Shop. Tomorrow she had an early start, but perhaps there'd be time this evening for a walk in the Gardens.

The voice of the Shopkeeper interrupted her thoughts. "Faythe!" The old lady was standing just inside the main Shop building, near the archway Faythe was emerging from. "What a surprise! Don't you have this evening off?"

She froze. Having never seen a rabbit nor headlights, she had no idea how to describe her predicament. "H-hello," she stammered.

The Shopkeeper appeared not to notice her discomfort. She held up a jar. "I'm just fetching this for a customer. Delighted we've met, though—I was planning to look for you later this evening." She glanced towards the unfashionable, dark wing the Apprentice had emerged from. "What were you doing in there?"

Faythe kept her voice calm. "I, uh, like to explore the Shop sometimes. This seemed like a good place to think."

The Shopkeeper smiled wistfully. "You certainly picked a good spot. That wing was our first extension after we outgrew the original Shop."

"Wow!" Faythe didn't have to pretend to be interested. She'd abandoned trying to understand which of the tangle of vestigial buildings at this end of the Shop had come first. She knew the biggest building—the one which contained the Stacks in one half and the towering aisles in the other—was the newest, but everything else about the history of the Shop was a mystery. She thought back to her hidden cupboard. "*That* was one of the oldest parts? How old is it?"

"I'm afraid I have no idea. You'll have to ask Beris!"

"I will." She glanced at the dark archway leading into the cramped wing. "I can't imagine the Shop fitting in there."

The Shopkeeper was still smiling nostalgically. "You're right. Today's Shop wouldn't come close to fitting inside. Everything is so different now. But it has to be, I suppose."

Some distance along the wall, a Child emerged from the Stacks, holding up a candle to illuminate the area for the group of customers that was following. Faythe loved that this part of the new building didn't *feel* new. She looked curiously at the Shopkeeper. The old lady seemed to be in a good mood. "Do you miss the old days?" she asked.

"Sometimes," said the Shopkeeper, after a moment. "But the trouble with old days is that they belong to someone else. I couldn't go back there, not the way I am now."

Faythe looked at her questioningly.

"You can't avoid change forever," explained the Shopkeeper. "I loved the old Shop, with its tiny corridors and messy dead-ends. But we built all these new buildings for a good reason—we needed them. If I went back, I'd immediately be frustrated with all the same problems which annoyed me back then." She snorted. "Except worse, because now I'm used to the solutions we built."

"I get it," said Faythe. She often imagined going back to the Rock, but in her heart she always knew it would be impossible after her time here. "The past feels small, because we're bigger, I guess."

The Shopkeeper smiled. "That's a lovely way to put it."

She couldn't believe she had stumbled into a friendly conversation with the Shopkeeper. This was the most they'd spoken—beyond pleasantries or work necessities—for years. Unbidden, a comforting warmth slowly burst inside her chest.

The Shopkeeper met her eye, and she was suddenly, sharply aware that she had just been investigating forbidden secrets with stolen traits. Her eyes flicked away instinctively. "Didn't you say you were looking for me?" she asked, to fill the silence.

"That's right. I wanted to see how you were feeling."

She frowned. "How I'm feeling?"

"Beris told me you were upset about what might have happened on Earth after last week. And I saw how upset you were in the meeting. It's been on my mind ever since. I've been thinking about our relationship, and how I've treated you since you arrived."

She couldn't believe what she was hearing. "What do you mean?"

"During the incident last week, my first thought was for the Shop."

"It always is," agreed Faythe, before biting her lip to shut herself up. She made an immediate decision: her next experiments would involve a *pile* of jars of THINKS BEFORE SPEAKING.

But the Shopkeeper nodded. "It always is, indeed. You obviously know me better than I imagined." She paused. "And that's how my priorities should be—the Shop comes first. Except I've realised something important . . . *you* are part of the Shop, too."

The warmth in Faythe's chest erupted in the most delightful manner.

"You arrived at a difficult time. Perhaps you've heard there was trouble with the previous Apprentice."

Faythe kept her face carefully blank.

"And I had reasons to wonder about you—after all, I didn't know you, and, at the time, I wasn't seeing eye-to-eye with the people who chose you without asking. But, as I watched you suffering during the Committee Meeting this week, I admitted to myself that I'd held onto those suspicions for too long. I allowed your mistakes—which, of course, everyone makes!—to excuse my own mistake, of not allowing you even the chance to win my trust." Her voice wavered. "I realised that if my first duty is to protect the Shop, and you are part of that Shop, then my first duty is also to protect you. And so I wanted to see how you are, after what must have been a very difficult week." She reached out to touch Faythe's shoulder. "And *that's* why I planned to find you this evening."

The warmth spread upwards, passing her neck and morphing into tears—hot and quick and freeing. She hadn't realised how badly she needed to hear this.

The Shopkeeper reached out for a hug.

But as Faythe moved in response, her shoulder bag clinked loudly with the unmistakable sound of glass jars. She froze.

The old lady frowned. "What was that?"

"Nothing," said Faythe, too quickly.

The Shopkeeper studied her face and looked down at her bag. "Do you mind showing me?"

She briefly considered running, but past experience suggested this was the *worst possible response.*

Reluctantly, slowly, she opened the bag and revealed the contents.

The Shopkeeper looked at the pile of empty jars, heartbreak and disappointment plain on her face. "I can't think of many good reasons for you to have those," she said. Her voice was flat, and the sparkle in her eye had disappeared. "And your expression suggests that I won't like the true reason very much. Let me guess—you've been researching the traits."

There was no point in denying it. She nodded.

"I remember your curiosity about them. How long has this been going on?"

"This was the first time—honest!" She wiped away a tear. Unlike the freeing, delightful tears of moments ago, this one was pure frustration. "I had a bad week, and I made bad decisions."

An image of the reply she'd sent to Zariel drifted into her mind. *Better not mention that.*

"I don't know what to do, Faythe. I really don't."

She thought she saw the Shopkeeper blink away a teardrop of her own. The row of jars glowing gently purple behind the Shopkeeper's head were labelled LOYALTY. She wished they weren't.

"I'm sorry," she said in a small voice.

"I should report you immediately to the Committee for stealing." The Shopkeeper blinked again. "But we both know this would be your third major offence—and your second within a week. That couldn't be ignored."

"I'm sorry," repeated Faythe. There was nothing else to say.

An eternity passed. It was difficult to breathe. After all this time, she'd finally bonded with the Shopkeeper, and she'd thrown it away *immediately*. For nothing!

Irrationally, a voice in the back of her mind suggested that if she had a sudden outpouring of flatulence then at least she would have learned something. Although that particular knowledge probably wouldn't make an eternity confined to the prelife any more bearable.

"I'm not going to report you," said the Shopkeeper, eventually, her voice laden with sorrow. She shook her head, as if arguing with herself. "No, I'm not. Perhaps I should, but I can't. This might be weakness on my part, but I can't give a speech about trusting you one minute, and potentially banish you the next."

"Not even if . . . I don't deserve that trust?" It was difficult to say aloud.

"I'm not saying this is a wise decision," said the Shopkeeper. "But it is my decision. You will have another chance."

Faythe's heart leapt.

"Although," continued the Shopkeeper. "You won't have my trust."

"I understand."

She understood perfectly. Only minutes ago she had cried with delight at the Shopkeeper's open-hearted welcome, and already she had been cast out once more.

Precisely as she deserved.

The pair walked back to the living quarters in an uneasy, fragile silence, broken only by a rumble from Faythe's stomach. It was such a normal—and not TERRIBLE—amount of gas that she didn't even notice.

thirteen

THE MOST FAMOUS philosopher in the prelife believed that co-operation was the most essential component of a successful society—and he would fight anybody who said otherwise.

Human communities encourage co-operation by advertising the great benefits it brings to all. But since this approach doesn't always work, humans also invented punishment.

True connoisseurs of punishment know that the most effective penalties don't simply make offenders suffer. They prefer to remove the joy from something which wrongdoers previously loved.

Being cruel to be kind is for amateurs; professionals are kind to be cruel.

And if anyone is professional in human nature, it's the Shopkeeper at the Shop Before Life.

Faythe had expected consequences. But when her employer had taken her aside, quietly, to explain what would happen, she hadn't been able to believe her luck. Her 'penance' was to paint labels until further notice—a job which was amongst her favourite duties. This might not be so bad, after all.

How naive she had been.

By now she was convinced she'd been painting labels and sticking them on jars for longer than she'd even existed. An activity which had once been a peaceful, creative respite from the chaotic activity of the Shop had consumed her entire reality.

She rose in the morning. She ate. She went to a tiny workshop. She labelled jars. She slept.

True enjoyment was only a vague memory, but she found hints of amusement wherever she could. Today, she was being gently defiant by making each label as misleading as possible while remaining technically correct. ROMANTIC looked great in sludgy brown robotic lettering, and she was delighted to render LOGICAL in bright rainbow colours and surround it with doodles of tiny hearts. She had just finished a fancy green leaf on DISLIKES NATURE when there was a knock at the window.

"Psst!"

Her breath caught in her throat as she saw Zariel squatting outside the low window into her basement workshop.

A thrill of guilt passed through her. This was very bad. She should definitely send him away. But then, she was very, very bored . . . and still nobody had directly forbidden her from talking to Zariel . . .

. . . *wait!* This was precisely the line of thinking which had caused her current mess.

But that had been months ago . . .

Her desperate desire for entertainment fought against her good sense. Before she could resolve the conflict and figure out what to do, Zariel tapped again on the window, loudly and insistently, gesturing urgently at her through the glass.

He's making too much noise! I should let him in. That didn't sound entirely logical, but there was no time for debate. She gritted her teeth, and moved to open the window. Her hands shook with nerves but she managed it on the second try.

Immediately, he slid through the gap, landing on the floor of the workshop with a graceful bend of the knee. He didn't actually say "ta-da!" but he was surely thinking it.

"What are you doing here?!" she squeaked.

He looked at her incredulously. "You do remember inviting me?"

Her note! Of course. It had slipped her mind. "But I've already been reported to Management. Twice!"

"So I hear. And, trust me, I'm impressed." He leaned down to inspect her handiwork. "Nice leaves."

She jigged anxiously from foot to foot. "I mean . . . I can't get into trouble again. If they find you here, they'll banish me too!"

"You're boring me," he said, irritably. "I don't remember you being so easily scared."

"I'm not, it's just . . ." She waved her arms in frustration. "How did you know I was in here, anyway?"

"I have my ways."

An exasperating answer. She rolled her eyes. "Very impressive and mysterious, Zariel."

The corner of his mouth turned up slightly. "Ah, you do still have a personality. I was beginning to fear I'd misremembered."

His unusually precise voice was just as unsettling as the first time she'd heard it, but in her fun-starved state the prospect of sparring with him was too intoxicating. She exhaled. "Fine, but please don't stay for too long."

"You invited me here!"

"Maybe I changed my mind."

"Oh? Did your latest punishment scare you that much?" He looked around the workshop. "It doesn't seem that bad. Haven't you learnt by now how toothless her threats are?" He took a seat and leaned back with his arms behind his head.

She frowned. "How do you know about this?" As far as she knew, the Shopkeeper hadn't told anyone why she was in here. Most of the Children thought she had volunteered for this work.

"You think the Apprentice can be effectively locked up for months without me hearing about it?"

"Yes! I don't understand how you'd hear."

His face darkened. "This is boring. Didn't you say you had questions?"

"Ye-e-e-es," she said, slowly, wrinkling her nose. Back when she'd written the note, the main question on her mind had been, effectively, "will you be my friend?" But voicing that aloud would surely be fatal to the conversation.

Just then, somebody noisily walked past the closed door, and she half-leapt out of her chair. Zariel folded his arms and looked at her, unamused. "And they are ...?" he prompted.

She took a breath. In the absence of better ideas, perhaps she should try openness and honesty. "There are things I can't talk about with anyone else." He leaned closer, expectantly. "Like, I guess, the Shopkeeper and I don't get on well. So I find that hard."

Zariel's face contorted as if she were trying to feed him live maggots. "And you want *me* to help with that?"

"No ... I just wanted to talk about it."

He exhaled in disgust. "You brought me all the way here to talk about *emotions*?"

She grimaced. Clearly 'openness and honesty' had been a mistake. "Not only that!" she said, hurriedly. She had plenty of questions, of course. How had Zariel become the Apprentice? Why exactly had he left? And could he satisfy her curiosity about the traits?

Perhaps she should start at the beginning. "How did you join the Shop? Was it Aaron and Gabriel for you, too?"

He frowned. "Who?"

"The people from Management who gave me this job."

"Oh. I don't keep track of the priests."

"Priests?"

He looked bored again. "Humans who work for Management."

She floundered for what to say. It was a weird feeling—she knew she didn't have to entertain him, but she nevertheless wanted to seem impressive. "That makes sense. I suppose they're not as intriguing as Management themselves." That gave her an idea. "Do you ever wonder what they actually look like? Management, I mean. Whenever I try to picture them, I just see glowing air. Like traits, but *alive*."

"No," he said. "Not at all."

"Oh."

"I'm more intrigued by what Management can do."

Her scalp tingled. "Like what?"

"Create a whole universe, for one thing." He absently rapped a rhythm on the table. "Is this honestly what you invited me here to talk about? What Management look like?"

She glanced nervously towards the door. It must have been only minutes since he'd entered, but it already felt like an age. "No ... I also wondered ..." She grasped at the first question that came to mind. "If you knew why the Shopkeeper is so defensive about the traits?"

"Isn't it obvious?"

Her face contorted in a way which said *of course it's obvious, I'm very smart ... but also, no?*

He sighed. "She can't stand anybody having authority over her. Apprentices are fine. The Children are fine. Anyone she can order around is fine."

She scratched her head, trying to reconcile this with her image of the Shopkeeper. "Okay. But what's that got to do with the traits?"

"She wants their power for herself."

"Power? What do you mean?" It felt like they were having two completely different conversations.

"Don't you realise what this place is? It's filled with the magic which shapes people. What could be more powerful than that? Even in this tiny room, there are enough traits to mould dozens of lives."

She glanced at a shelf which brimmed with jars. What he was saying made sense, but his perspective was alien. "I guess I never thought of it in terms of power, exactly," she said.

"Then you're missing the point." His eyes blazed. "But I'm sure she isn't. That's why she insists on being in control here. She would challenge Management if she could, and take control everywhere. That's likely why they fought after I left." He delivered this offhandedly, as if being fought over by the gods was nothing. "Still, if this is all you have to talk about, I have things I need to return to. I wish I could say this has been worthwhile." He stood to leave. "Goodbye."

"Wait! I wanted to tell you ..." She thought fast. What would make him stay? One topic stood out. "I've been doing experiments on the traits."

He spun around and thumped the workbench. "Aha! Why keep me waiting?!"

"More dramatic this way," she lied, partly pleased to have his attention, partly irritated at herself for caring.

"Go on."

"I took some jars. And I tried different things, like mixing them and smelling them and eating them." *Did this sound pathetic?* He was unreadable. Or possibly she was too nervous to tell. Something about Zariel made her feel clumsy.

"And what did you learn?"

"Not much," she admitted.

"It's a start," he said, not quite unkindly. "I did much the same myself, a long time ago."

"I know."

He tilted his head in surprise. "She told you?"

She cursed herself. She really needed to stop talking without thinking. "Um . . . I discovered myself. When I found your address . . . in her office drawers." Was this a wise admission to make? Nobody knew she'd broken into the Shopkeeper's office, and now she was telling Zariel, of all people. This whole conversation felt like a precarious walk through a dark cave filled with holes.

"Ha!" He looked delighted, as if he were unwrapping a present. "You stole from her office! I honestly can't believe she picked somebody so similar to me. Wait . . ." He raised a finger. "What were those names you mentioned before? Aaron and—"

"Gabriel?"

"So, she wasn't the one that picked you!"

Faythe shook her head.

"That *is* interesting. And it explains a lot, although, I do wonder . . ." He rubbed his chin for a moment. "Never mind. I'm proud you're following in my footsteps. And don't be disheartened that you didn't learn much from your experiments. I'd have been surprised if you had. The secret of the traits is locked away deeply."

"What secret?" She leaned forward in excitement, but there was another loud thump from the corridor outside and she sprang up nervously.

Zariel laughed. "Next time you ought to just visit me. Perhaps you'll be less nervous there. I'm actually surprised you haven't been already."

"How would I do that?"

He frowned. "They've never even shown you the train? It leaves from behind the Warehouse."

"No, I know the train. It goes to the Supplier. But I don't understand what it's got to do with anything."

He stared for an instant before bursting into laughter. "Oh, this is incredible! So that's why you sent a letter. You don't know!"

Her face went blank. "Know what?" She hated not knowing something, and being mocked for it was intolerable. She tried to piece together what he had said. "Do you live near the Supplier?!"

Zariel had never looked so smug. "My dear, I *am* the Supplier."

There was a pause while Faythe felt the disorienting sensation of her brain rotating ninety degrees, exploding, and instantaneously piecing the fragments of itself back together.

Her first coherent thought was pure annoyance that he had made a prominent position in a retail supply chain sound so *cool*. "What?!" she screeched.

"It's amusing that you didn't know. They certainly did an impeccable job of preventing you from learning about me. What did you think I spent my days doing? Twiddling my thumbs in Ostholme like a fool?"

"I had no idea."

"So you thought I left here without a plan?"

"I thought you got fired," she admitted.

"Pah!" He enunciated the sound with his customary crispness. "No doubt firing me is the story she'd prefer to tell, but no."

Faythe stuck out her lip. Hadn't the Shopkeeper's notes said that he had been fired? She filed this away to ponder later.

"I suppose this explains why you didn't come see me," he continued. "I assumed your invitation was simple laziness. Or perhaps that you enjoyed making me sneak around this wretched place."

She drummed her fingers on the bench. "How *off Earth* did you go from being banish—" She stopped herself just in time. "—from *leaving here* to being the Supplier?"

His smug smile remained in place. "It was the natural destination after reaching the limit of what I could achieve here. And so I convinced the old Supplier that I was the right person for the job."

"The old Supplier? So you're not the actual Supplier? You're an Apprentice?"

Irritation flashed across his face, so quickly she wondered if she'd imagined it.

"No, no," he said, smoothly. "Perhaps at first you could argue I was technically an Apprentice, for a brief moment, though my title was certainly never that, but the old man made way for me. He retired, in a sense. Today I am certainly the Supplier."

"How did you convince him?"

"It was quite simple." He joined his hands behind his back. "People take notice when someone of my talent becomes available. In particular, when I suggested that I was suitable to take over, Management agreed."

"Incredible," she breathed.

He began to pace back and forth. "Perhaps you've realised that not everybody is interested in how the universe works. To me, it always seemed unambitious to simply accept how the world is, without asking questions." She nodded automatically, and he picked up a jar from a worktop and started fiddling with it. "All of humanity passes through this Shop, and most don't wonder. Why is everything like this? Who set it up? And how do they benefit?"

She became aware that her head was nodding. He was putting into words a dissatisfaction she'd never quite been able to articulate.

He toyed with the jar, passing it from hand to hand. "And most importantly—how do these traits work? What magic can trap human essence in a jar? Imagine what could be achieved if you knew!"

"Yes!" she interjected, mostly to feel as if she were contributing— although she also wanted him to know she agreed, passionately.

"I want to go beyond the limits Management have set for us. All of them." He spoke more softly now. "And so, I'm devoted to discovering the secrets of the traits." He rested his hands on the bench and leaned towards her, nearly whispering. "I began here at the Shop. But I soon realised there could be no better place than where the magic is actually created. So I devoted myself to becoming the Supplier."

She gulped. As Zariel leaned closer, she noticed that his eyes were dark, and that they shone as he spoke. "And what have you found?" she squeaked.

He stepped away and placed the jar back onto the worktop, facing out so she could read the label: EQUIVOCAL. She'd been meaning to look that up. "I've learned many things," he said. "But I need help from you before I share."

"Okay," she said. That seemed fair, sort of. "Like a research assistant?"

"We could call it that. Since you and I met, I've been investigating how the machines work."

She blinked. "Machines?"

"Ah, I forget how little they tell you here! The traits haven't been made by hand for a long time. Nowadays, they are created automatically, by machines at the Supplier's Complex. And—after much effort—I now understand how these machines work. But ..." He held up a finger and pointed meaningfully at the closed door. "There's no time for the whole story today. Suffice it to say that even knowledge of the machinery isn't sufficient to understand the traits—deeper answers still elude me."

She nodded, rapt. "I'd love to know everything!"

"Enticing, isn't it? Imagine what you could do with that knowledge!"

She frowned. "Like what?"

"What about creating entirely new traits? Why should we remain within the limits we are given?"

"Oh! We could make new things people need. That sounds good."

He snorted. "Indeed. And that's just the beginning."

"But can't you already do that, if you're the Supplier?"

He shook his head. "My predecessor wasn't as open as I had hoped. Rather than answering my questions, he took pleasure in setting me puzzles, to see if I could figure out for myself how his machines worked. The last thing he told me before he retired was that I was on the path to understanding."

She smiled sympathetically. She knew how it felt to be an Apprentice who wasn't trusted with secrets.

"This is where I need your help," he continued. "I'm sure I could figure everything out much more quickly if I could compare original, hand-made traits with the new, machine-made ones. Studying the differences between them will allow me to see better what they are, so I can understand how they work."

"And you want me to find these traits?"

"Exactly. These aren't any old traits. They must be hand-made. They won't have the same marks as those manufactured at the Supplier."

"Do you have any clue where they might be?"

"They'll be old. Possibly unique. The Shopkeeper always refused to tell me about the truly interesting traits. Or—as you have doubtless experienced—about much at all. Nevertheless, I'm confident that you're more than capable of finding them."

Her heart skipped involuntarily at the praise. "There is one thing. I don't want to get into any more trouble. I'm one mistake away from banishment, and I've already stolen things I shouldn't."

Zariel smiled. "You simply must relax." He indicated her paintbrush. "Think about it. Your big punishment for whatever you did is *painting?* All she has is empty threats. Look at me—I got banished from here, and now I'm the Supplier!"

She rubbed her forehead. *He had a point.* "I don't know . . ."

"Besides, they're not even using these old jars, so it isn't stealing."

Deep down, she knew she'd decided to help the moment he'd asked. Discovering ancient traits and exploring forbidden secrets was just too enticing. She nodded.

Zariel clapped, just once, and beamed. But, before he could speak, there was a knock at the door.

She leapt out of her chair in panic, gesturing wildly at him to get under the bench. "Quick! Hide!"

He gave her a withering look and shook his head. "I told you—relax." He inspected his nails. "And get the door."

"B-but if you're caught—"

He sighed and moved towards the door himself.

"What are you doing?!" she hissed.

As he flung the door open, her heart attempted to flee through her ribs. But behind the door was a man she'd never seen before. He was extremely tall, grave faced, and—most unusually, she couldn't help noticing—there was a giant flaming sword attached to his hip.

"Ready, boss," he said.

"Very good," said Zariel. He bowed to Faythe. "As you can see, my escort has arrived. I shall bother you no longer—until you find those traits." He curled his lip. "You know where to find me."

With a final flourish, he was gone.

She sat back down, staring at the jars as the adrenaline dissipated. That had been intense.

It took time to calm down, but when Omaro eventually checked in on her, her facial expression said only "this has been a perfectly normal day."

Meanwhile, her mind whirred with questions and plans. That evening, she would begin searching for the ancient traits which could unlock the secrets of the Shop Before Life.

fourteen

AT LONG LAST, Faythe's punishment came to an end, and her prelife returned to a blur of normality, or whatever passed for normality at the Shop.

Her days were spent in a flurry of customer questions . . .

"Sorry, I'm completely unable to find MAP-READING ABILITY."

"I'm looking for CONSTANTLY GIVES RUNNING COMMENTARY ON LIFE but on the way here I met somebody who told me something interesting, and . . ."

"Where's ALWAYS CONCISE?"

. . . and her evenings were filled by the search for Zariel's ancient jars.

There was a pleasant mindlessness to wandering the Shop at night, up and down old wooden stairs, following twisty corridors into room after room, each filled with shelves which were themselves stuffed with traits. The jarlight suffused everything with pale colours that shifted subtly as she moved along.

It was easy to get lost, even after all this time—particularly since it had rapidly become obvious that the ancient jars she sought must be buried deep within the warren of older Shops which the modern-day Shop was built upon. Even the oldest jars she'd found in the Stacks, with wonky glass and yellow, peeling labels, were invariably stamped with the *Supplier's Complex* manufacturing mark underneath.

She and Zariel made a game of exchanging letters during this time.

She thrilled at the risk of sneaking an envelope into a boring invoice statement on its way to the Supplier, or hiding a note in an empty crate as it was loaded onto the train.

Each day was enlivened by the anticipatory buzz of a reply finding its way to her. Yesterday's had been particularly pleasing:

Despite the lack of ancient traits, we're making progress. It occurred to me that perhaps, when all this is done, we could open our own Shop? I'm sure SHE wouldn't like the competition, but wouldn't it be fun? With our own hand-made traits. Z.

P.S. Have you tried that little wing—can't remember the name—beyond the Stacks and down a trapdoor located near the Complacency Annex? Just a thought.

That evening, her reply had been hastily scrawled in a moment of fury:

I didn't expect you meant an ACTUAL trapdoor! I got COVERED in spiders. I hate you. Nothing down there. New Shop sounds lovely. F.

So far, all she'd discovered for sure was that the Shop was immense. She kept stumbling on entirely new areas which she was sure didn't have room to exist between the parts she knew—and yet there they were, full of lengthy aisles, each stacked so high with traits that she'd resorted to bringing her own folding ladder almost everywhere she went.

Have you thought of a name for our new Shop yet? Also, how about checking that collapsed building by the corner of the Gardens? There should be a way in from outside. Z.

Maybe the ZAF Emporium? (For Zariel & Faythe! And it's SO fun to say. Zaf!) I got in, but it was only mud. If there's anything there it's buried. Want to come visit again soon? F.

I can't. Busy here with experiments, and making supplies! Keep me updated on the search. Z.

Did you like the name? F.

It's perfect. Z.

After spending an entire week fully exploring one old block which twisted in on itself so many times that it took nearly an hour just to reach the centre, she gave up and asked Beris about the geography of the Shop. He ummed and ahhed before launching into a lecture about how they chose the design for the newer domed area.

She listened politely for several minutes before realising she really, urgently needed to interrupt or she risked losing an entire evening to Beris' well-meaning ramblings.

"But is there a map? Of the area beyond the Stacks, I mean."

The Child gazed over his colourful, thick-rimmed spectacles. "We did once have an artist attempt a map of the old cloisters, but it ended badly."

"Great! Any map would help."

"I mean it ended badly for the artist. The experience broke him, somewhat."

"Oh."

That actually made sense. Faythe felt a little broken already by this search.

He looked at her. "Are you looking for anything in particular?"

She hesitated. Of all the people in the Shop, Beris was the least likely to recognise any potential intrigue in a search for old, handmade jars. But that also made him the most likely person to carelessly mention such a search to the Shopkeeper.

"Not really. Just curious."

As weeks of fruitless failure drifted into months, Faythe became increasingly frustrated with the size of the task. She'd heard there was a game on Earth of hiding needles in haystacks, which sounded simple by comparison. She needed to find a specific needle in a pile of needles.

This morning's note from Zariel hadn't helped her mood. The apparently effortless way he delivered his notes was always slightly irritating—this one had been under her breakfast plate!—but the contents were more annoying still:

No good news? I'm starting to wonder if you're genuinely searching or if you're toying with me. Both of us need to pull our weight if this partnership is going to work. Z.

She tore the note into tiny pieces. Normally, they went in the hollow under her bed so she could re-read them. But she wouldn't miss this one.

Unfortunately, Zariel was partly right: she was making no progress. It could take centuries for a random walk around the Shop to bear fruit. There was only one possibility left. She'd have to question the Shopkeeper, as subtly as possible.

At a certain time of day, it was common to see the Shopkeeper and the Gardener relaxing together on the Viewing Platform. This would be the best time to try.

One afternoon, the Gardener noticed Faythe standing self-consciously nearby. "Looks like you're needed," he said, nodding to the Shopkeeper, who was gazing down into the Gardens.

"Oh?" She looked puzzled to see Faythe. "Is there a problem? Omaro ought to be on duty right now."

Faythe scuffled her feet uneasily on the wooden floor. "No, nothing like that. I just wondered if I could join you? I remember you invited me for tea, a long time ago. Is the invite still open?"

The Shopkeeper exchanged a surprised look with the Gardener, who grinned.

"Yes, you may!" she said, after a moment. "Take a seat. Is there any particular reason?"

"I just . . . I don't spend much time with you two. And I know we've not spoken much since, you know." *You caught me stealing.* "And it looked like you're having a lovely time, and I thought, why not?"

Like all the best cover stories, this had the benefit of being almost entirely true. The Shopkeeper, smiling with delight, poured an extra cup of tea. "Well, the Gardener had been telling me about his ongoing war with herbivorous beasts."

Faythe turned to the Gardener with interest.

He narrowed his eyes. "Butterflies," he intoned, dramatically. "Those beautiful bastards won't stay where I tell them. I've made them the perfect home, exactly where I want them, but they won't stay where's good for them. They leave wiggly spawn everywhere else, which chew up all my lovely plants."

Faythe tried not to laugh, and was successful until she caught sight of the Shopkeeper's own repressed mirth. A giggle escaped. She quickly covered it with a cough. "That sounds like a real problem," she said, sympathetically.

"Oh it is! Everyone wants butterflies to make the place look pretty, but they don't realise how much work that entails. Those little flapsters don't appear out of nothing, you know."

The conversation meandered around as they discussed the Gardens, and gossip, and happenings in the Shop, and it was a while before Faythe realised she was enjoying herself. All around them, customers were chattering contentedly and admiring the Earth. The late afternoon sun was warm, and a light breeze brought the scent of flowers up to the platform. She couldn't remember the last time she'd been so at ease.

The Shopkeeper took a sip from her cup and turned to Faythe. "And what have you been up to?"

It was time for her plan. Ignoring a slight prickle from her conscience, she began talking enthusiastically. "I've been exploring the Shop! I can't believe how vast it is." Once more, her story contained plenty of truth. "I keep getting lost. I don't get how you remember where everything is."

"It helps that I have memories of each part. Most of the old buildings used to *be* the Shop, at one time or another." Her voice softened as she went deeper into her memories. "Each time we expanded we had to remain open—there's no alternative! So it was always easier to add rather than replace." She snorted. "It became a labyrinth, until we built the current Shop on top."

As always, the Shopkeeper loved any excuse to talk about the Shop. Faythe began to prod for anything which might help with her search. "I think I remember you saying that tangle of buildings behind the Stacks used to be the whole thing?"

"Oh yes! And even after we built what's now the main building, the Committee debated how to use it. I wanted to fill it with something interesting."

"Interesting . . . how?"

"How can I put this? We needed the concourse, and the big aisles, but I was concerned that making the Shop more efficient might take away from its character."

"There's still the Stacks."

"Exactly. The Stacks was our compromise. Beris got his tall, straight aisles in the front half of the new building, and I got the Stacks in the back."

The Gardener's attention had apparently drifted away, as he gave a start. "What if I trained worms to do it . . . ?" he muttered to himself.

The Shopkeeper looked at him quizzically before continuing her story. "Beris was right, of course, though part of me misses the old ways."

Faythe tried to imagine the Shop without the long, tall, straight aisles where she spent most of her time. "Customers must have got lost a lot."

"All the time!" The Shopkeeper laughed. "But I used to tell people that getting lost in a maze for a few hours was all part of the charm." She smiled, sadly. "Nowadays we have so many more customers to get through."

Faythe glanced at the Gardener, who was gripping the rail and staring down at the Gardens. "And if they got out of hand . . . maybe birds?"

The Shopkeeper caught her eye and winked.

"When did all the construction stop?" asked Faythe.

Her boss scrunched up her face. "That's a question. Beris would know. But I would guess we haven't built anything in, what, centuries? Gardener?"

"What!" He spun around, blinking, as his attention returned to his surroundings.

"When did we build the dome here?"

The old man scratched his head. "Must be a thousand years old, that dome. I'd barely even started on the vineyard at that point."

Faythe's jaw fell open. "A thousan—wait, we have a *vineyard?!*"

"Sure do," said the Gardener. "Not that we use it properly. Got a whole warehouse full of wine nobody drinks."

"Perhaps we can open a bottle to celebrate if you solve that butterfly problem," said the Shopkeeper.

The Gardener clenched and unclenched his fist. "That sounds good. I'll sort them out."

"You always do."

Faythe smiled absently at the exchange. She was still lost in wonder that the giant Shop building—the *new* building!—was five times older than she was.

"A thousand years!" She whistled. "So the other buildings must be much older."

The Shopkeeper smiled wryly. "Like me."

"I can't even imagine." That was true, as well. In fact, she hadn't lied once during this whole conversation.

A guilty cloud passed across her warm mood. *Why had she needed to plan to deceive the Shopkeeper just to come and talk to her?*

She covered her feelings with a question. "What was it like in the beginning?"

"Oh, it was tiny," said the Gardener. "A few trees, couple of flowerbeds, hardly anything to call a garden!"

She looked at the Gardener. Apparently he hadn't been joking. "And the Shop . . . ?" she prompted.

"The Shop was small, too," said the Shopkeeper. "In the beginning it was no more than a single table. It was years before we even put a room around it. And then the room expanded, again and again and again." She snorted gently. "It's funny to think that when we started, people came to us wherever we happened to be. After a while, we realised a permanent place here, close to Earth, was better."

Faythe frowned. "Who's we?"

"Myself and Management, I suppose."

"You and Management!"

A thrill of electricity shot through Faythe. It was always strange to remember that the Shopkeeper had spoken with the gods.

"I'd been there since the beginning, so they asked me to guard the traits. And here we are."

The Gardener was picking at his fingernails. Either he'd heard the story before or he was thinking about butterflies again.

"Since the beginning? The *very* beginning?" She struggled to comprehend the idea. "Was there a first person?" Her eyes widened. "Were *you* the first—"

The Shopkeeper held up a hand and spoke over her. "No, no, nothing like that! I was there for the beginning of the Shop, but beyond that, I don't know. Many mysteries still remain, even to me."

Every part of Faythe was focused on the Shopkeeper's story. "Why did the Shop start?"

The Shopkeeper sucked a breath in through her teeth. "I'm afraid I can't tell you that." She shook her head regretfully. "I wish I could."

They locked eyes for a few seconds, before Faythe gave a reluctant nod. The old lady smiled in relief.

Faythe wasn't finished, though. "But may I ask . . . did the Supplier start at the same time? How did you get your first traits?"

The Shopkeeper raised an eyebrow. "Oh, Faythe. I've learned there's no point in telling you not to ask questions. I suppose you can ask, as long as you're fine with me not always answering."

She nodded enthusiastically. "That sounds fair."

"We've always had a Supplier, although they were much smaller, too, in those days." She chuckled to herself. "Or their factory was, at any rate."

Was that a dig at Zariel? Even if it were, Faythe didn't understand it. She kept her face straight. "So the Supplier made the traits and you sold them out of a single room?"

"That's right. It's still down there, somewhere."

"Oh?" She suppressed a thrill. That sounded like the perfect place to search for the ancient traits. She almost leaned forward before remembering not to appear overly interested. "I'd like to see that," she said, offhandedly.

"It's not much to look at."

"But it's fascinating. Imagine seeing the original Shop!" she gushed.

Damn it. She was terrible at feigning disinterest.

"Are you two talking about the old Archives?" asked the Gardener, suddenly.

Faythe caught the Shopkeeper's warning look to the old man and realised with a jolt what it meant. *There must be something hidden in these Archives.* She kept her expression plain, as if she hadn't noticed. "You'll have to take me on a tour," she said, casually.

The Shopkeeper nodded, though her reticence was obvious.

"And I could show you the first parts of the Garden, if you like," offered the Gardener.

She grinned. "I'd love that!"

"It's only a worm pit nowadays, but that's actually an interesting story . . ."

She listened politely, but inside she was frothing with excitement. Not only had she enjoyed this conversation, she'd found a new destination for her search, all while avoiding any direct lies.

When the time came to leave, she beamed with delight. "I should get back to work. Thank you both."

The Shopkeeper smiled too. "I'm so glad you joined us," she said. "And I want to add that I'm ashamed that I wasn't the one to make the effort to talk. After our last encounter, I allowed myself to settle into a pattern of avoidance, and I'm glad you broke it."

Faythe's heart squeezed uncomfortably, and she held up her hands. "You really shouldn't thank me," she said. "I don't deserve it."

"No, I insist. Your effort means a lot. And I also noticed how well you responded after what happened. You quietly got on with both your punishment and your work, and I know from experience that not everybody manages so well."

Was that another coded reference to Zariel? She bit her lip, wishing she could ask.

The Shopkeeper hesitated. "Since you've made an effort, I want to make one too. I know you're curious—about the Supplier, the traits, the history of this place. And I know it must be frustrating that I refuse to tell you things. I've not always handled this perfectly in the past."

"I think you've been very fair," offered Faythe. "It's me that keeps screwing up."

"I didn't mean only with you, child. But thank you." She took a deep breath. "I want you to know that, eventually, I would like to tell you everything."

"Everything?" Faythe was stunned. Had she heard correctly?

"Yes. But not immediately. I'm not a fool. It's not so long since the last time I was apologising for not trusting you, and we both know what happened then."

She flushed with embarrassment.

"I don't intend to make the same mistake twice," continued the Shop-keeper. "Trust has to be earned . . . but that requires both a means for you to earn it—and incentive for you to do so. So here's my offer: if I believe that you are trustworthy after five hundred years have passed from your contract, then I will tell you everything you wish to know."

"Oh." *Five hundred years!* She couldn't hide her disappointment.

"I'm sorry," said the Shopkeeper. "But I must take a long view."

"I get it. Even the new building here is a thousand years old. I understand."

"And I understand your frustration. I look forward to the day I can relieve you of it." She looked at Faythe with a hopeful expression which made the Apprentice's heart break a little. "It would be good to have someone else who knows everything about this place."

The Shopkeeper offered her a hug before she left.

"Thank you," said Faythe. "It's been a good afternoon."

That wasn't a lie, either.

That evening, she stared out of her bedroom window.

If these Archives didn't contain the old traits, then Faythe doubted she'd ever find them—assuming they even existed.

She ought to be happy that the end of her search was in sight, but her conscience wouldn't allow her to relax. Clearly, the morally correct action would be to accept the old lady's offer—which was far more than Faythe deserved—and leave Zariel to stew. Eventually she would learn all the Shop's secrets for herself, without any risk. *But could she resist the temptation to explore for another five hundred years?*

She would discover the answers much sooner if she found what Zariel was looking for. And his words about the Shopkeeper still echoed in her mind. What if he was right, and her kindly appearance was just a facade? Management obviously trusted him, or they wouldn't have made him the Supplier . . . so did that mean they mistrusted the Shopkeeper?! He'd said something about her wanting to challenge Management.

Her mind whirled.

Perhaps, as a compromise, she could just *look* in the Archives. If she happened to stumble upon any ancient jars, then she could choose what to do with them afterwards, but if not, it would still be interesting to explore the very first Shop.

And maybe she'd bring along a bag . . . just in case she found anything interesting. *A perfect plan.*

She wrote a note to Zariel.

Made fantastic progress today! There's news you'll be interested in. Following up tomorrow. F.

She re-read her note with a satisfied smile. It would annoy Zariel that she hadn't explained what the news actually was.

Good. He deserved to sweat after his impatient note yesterday.

She slept, and didn't dream.

fifteen

SOMEWHERE BEYOND THE END of Aisle Twenty, past the far side of the Stacks, a narrow passageway led to a stone cloister which jutted out over the Gardens.

Unfortunately, whichever idiot had built it had forgotten to install any windows, so the potentially spectacular view was utterly wasted. Perhaps that was why hardly anybody ever came here.

Faythe was only breaking that trend because she had been informed by an eager Beris that the entrance to the Archives was located in this dull cloister. If so, it wouldn't take long to find, as there was nothing here but a single door.

Like nearly all doors, this one was extremely boring. In this case, it was a small, thick, wooden portal which fitted snugly into its frame, remarkable only for where it supposedly led.

This seemed morally wrong to Faythe. An entrance to somewhere grand should be grand itself. This door suggested strongly that its function was 'cupboard', and not 'gateway to the secrets of a mystical shop'. If it had been Omaro who had given her the directions she might have suspected a prank, but she couldn't imagine Beris playing a joke. And so she pressed on the handle and leaned against the door, which opened— slowly, heavily and with a disappointing lack of atmospheric creaking.

Inside, only darkness. Luckily, Beris had mentioned this. She lit her lantern and edged inside, down a set of ludicrously narrow steps, just

165

about wide enough for one small person. The stairs spiralled down-wards, widening gradually until they opened out into a larger space at the bottom.

Down here the air was noticeably cooler, with a clammy hint of damp. She held up the light and gasped. Before her stood a tremendous stone arch, ornately carved with intricate patterns. In tall, imposing letters, high above the entrance, the word ARCHIVES was engraved.

She looked back up the narrow stairs which led to the tiny, unim-pressive cupboard door. Whoever designed this shop was a fool, or had a twisted sense of humour.

Or, more likely, both.

As Faythe passed under the arch, she was swallowed by darkness. The air around her became colder, and the sound of her footsteps echoed back, distorted by their encounter with a faraway stone wall.

She hadn't been anywhere this dark since her time at the Rock. Up above, in the rest of the Shop, the gleam of the jars and the ever-pres-ent earthlight meant she never really needed a light source, even at night.

Her light flickered, illuminating aisle after aisle of towering wooden shelves which disappeared into the gloom. Immediately, this place felt uncannily familiar, like an imperfect copy of the Shop she knew so well. There was something comforting about the many lines of tall shelves, but the wood looked too rotten, the air was too still, and there was an odd, disquieting smell, like a mix of wet paper and old mud.

Above all, the Archives were too quiet. This wasn't the restful peace of the Shop at night, but a deep, oppressive stillness. It felt as if nobody had disturbed this place for a long, long time.

Faythe turned to the side and immediately screamed, leaping in fright away from a cluster of figures who watched from close by, their shadows cast long and high against the wall.

As she caught her breath, the figures remained completely, utterly still . . . *exactly like a group of statues would*, she realised with a sudden flood of embarrassment.

She closed her eyes and forced herself to take a long, slow breath.

Once she'd calmed down, she crept over to investigate. Each statue was taller than any person she'd ever seen. Most had crumbled, or were covered with moss, but some still had visible features. The biggest statue—far, far taller and much, much broader than any of the others—had a tremendous beard tied up in braids. Another was of a long-haired woman with an ambiguous smile, who stood next to a wiry man with spindly fingers.

Faythe didn't recognise any of them. She peered curiously at each statue in turn, moving quickly past those that were too overgrown or decrepit, until she reached the final statue. Unlike the others, it lay at an angle, apparently having fallen over during the preceding centuries.

Even more notably, this statue lacked a head. From the jagged edges of the neck, Faythe surmised it must have broken off when the statue fell.

Frowning, she cast her light around to look for it, and leapt in alarm once more. A short distance away, a stone head was glaring directly at her from the floor. And it was unmistakably the head of the Shopkeeper. She wore one of her trademark expressions—somewhere between stern and kind—and she looked . . . younger. But it was definitely her.

Feeling extremely perturbed, Faythe turned away from the statues and set off down the nearest aisle. She didn't want to spend longer down here than necessary. The glow of her lantern partially reflected off the nearby shelves before being swallowed by the dark expanse above. Each shelf she passed was empty, which added to her unease—upstairs, an empty shelf meant something had gone wrong.

A sudden distant noise—a crunch, maybe a bump, definitely not a crash—sent her heartbeat racing so hard it thumped in her skull. She held her breath and strained to listen, but no other sound broke the silence. Perhaps she'd imagined it?

Just as she started to relax, she became aware of another sound, a steady, high-pitched hiss. She waited for it to pass, but it continued without variation. Maybe it had always been there, and she'd only just noticed it? She edged anxiously towards the noise, tilting her head back and forth slowly to locate the source in the gloom.

As she neared, it became clear the sound was coming from a jar, alone on an otherwise empty shelf. She picked it up and stared at it, confused. Her ears were telling her that air was gushing out from somewhere, but the jar appeared sealed and there was no motion as she waved her hand over it.

A thought struck her. Could this be one of the ancient jars? Suddenly energised, she examined the neat letters embossed on the base: *Supplier Complex #4.*

She groaned in disappointment. But ... perhaps she ought to take this jar with her, anyway? It was certainly the most interesting jar she'd seen in a while, and—

—on second thought, what would happen if she brought a jar upstairs which was physically hissing?

She felt a slight smug glow as she put the jar back. It felt good to have already made her last ever stupid decision, and she surely wouldn't break that streak today.

With a more optimistic step, she picked her way carefully along the rest of the aisle, clambering occasionally over bits of broken shelf. To her surprise, it didn't take long before she reached the far wall. The darkness made this place seem bigger than it truly was.

Her gaze alighted on a faint glimmer emanating from an old display case nestling against the back wall. She stepped closer and squealed with delight. It was filled with traits!

Even better, they had labels, and they were fascinating. The scrawl on the yellow, peeling papers was mostly words she didn't understand— AUCTORITAS, PRUDENTIA, PIETAS—and on one, under a mess of crossing out and the scribbled word 'discontinued', THE POWER OF WITCHCRAFT. Her curiosity was more than piqued but, sadly, each jar also bore the standard mark of the Supplier.

She sighed and made a mental note to come back and investigate these jars another time. Right now, she just wanted to find what she'd come for—or give up quickly and get back to the surface.

She glanced around. The shelf in the aisle opposite her had apparently rotted through, as the floor beneath was littered with broken glass from its partial collapse. Books lay haphazardly amongst the debris, along with several lumpy, misshapen jars. She stepped gingerly over the broken glass to look more closely at one of the intact traits which were scattered around, glimmering weakly. The faded label was impossible to decipher, but a smaller label underneath proudly proclaimed that this jar contained "Hand-Crafted Human Traits from the Shop Before Life."

Her yelp of joy reverberated for an instant before disappearing into the vast space above.

Closer inspection revealed that several more of the misshapen jars were hand-made. Excitedly, she gathered them into her bag, pausing to wrap them in clothes to avoid any incriminating rattles. She'd definitely learned from her previous failed mischief.

Moments later, she whistled as she made her way up the narrow steps to the surface. After only a short time in the darkness, she was already hungry for natural light.

At the top, she reached to open the door and—

— *there was no handle*. Only a keyhole.

She stared at the door intensely, as if sheer concentration could conjure a handle into existence. She rammed her shoulder against the rough wood, but the door didn't budge. She tried again, pushing and pulling, again and again, harder and harder, until she was kicking and bashing the door with all her might.

Nothing.

And no response from outside.

How long might it be before anybody came along this abandoned cloister? Days? Months? *Years?*

Faythe tried not to panic, which made her notice she was already panicking, which made her panic about panicking even more. Suddenly her skin was tight it was strangling her in her own throat the air no longer felt cool and moist it was hot and clammy and tight in her chest and *she was trapped.*

She felt dizzy, and then she didn't remember anything for a while.

Later, she awoke. Possibly only moments later, possibly hours. She had no way of knowing.

She found herself to be slumped, uncomfortably, a few steps down the narrow twisty staircase, wedged against the wall, atop her bag of clothes and jars. Slowly, she checked her body: no injuries. She checked her mind: no panic. Above her, the door remained closed.

Still trapped.

At least she felt calm. She sat up and rubbed her sore arms.

Perhaps there was a spare key hidden in the Archives. Or maybe something to pick the lock with. Admittedly, she had zero idea how to pick locks even *with* a lockpick . . . but better a bad plan than no plan.

She explored aisle after aisle after aisle, finding many jars, but no escape.

Zariel would doubtless find this funny when he heard. She gritted her teeth. *If he were here, that damnable confidence of his would probably summon an exit into being.*

Eventually, after much searching—and it had certainly been hours, now; many, many hours—Faythe admitted defeat.

There was no key. The door was still resisting all of her efforts.

She slept.

She awoke again. She was hungry.

In a sense, that was a solution of sorts. If she starved to death, she'd awake again at the Beginning.

At least, that's what she thought would happen. She'd heard that people didn't actually starve to death, they just thought they did, and then it happened, or something. Those who'd experienced it weren't very good at explaining. Or maybe the words they knew weren't sufficient.

If she did starve—or whatever it was—there'd be questions to answer, but maybe she could explain?

Her mind wandered. Wouldn't starving be painful? She hated being hungry.

But then, eating the moss down here didn't seem like a particularly fun time either.

Her stomach rumbled. She explored. She got tired.

She slept.

Very hungry now. And tired, and cold, and alone.

Starving to death seemed like the best plan.

It was worrying that her best plan was to . . . sort-of . . . die. Shouldn't she have a better plan than that?

She slept again.

Her bones hurt now, whether from hunger or from sleeping on cold, damp stone, she wasn't sure. How long would it take to starve, exactly? Could she accelerate it by thinking about it harder?

She was thirsty. She licked some moss, and a wall, and other damp-looking things.

Everything tasted disgusting.

It turned out that many things were damp, including her candles, which now wouldn't light properly. It had become *really* dark.

She scrabbled around in the darkness, looking for anything to take her mind away from her stomach.

And then, she realised it wasn't entirely dark. Without the lamplight, she could see other sources of light more easily. High up, above the weak glow of jars from the floor, there was a thin strip of light coming from a wall high up above an empty shelf.

Energy surged through her. She clambered up, and her hand found the strip. A brick came loose and clattered to the floor. The light was brighter now.

The surge of energy multiplied as she felt hope for the first time in . . . she had no idea. Days, probably.

Carefully grasping in the dark, she found something to stand on. Was it a broken bit of shelf? A chair? She didn't care. It seemed sturdy enough. She dragged it in front of the gap and climbed up.

Now she had her face pressed to the hole, she could see the source of the light. In the distance, along a partially collapsed shaft, the deep orange of sunset was dimly visible. A weak draught of air was escaping the hole, bringing with it a fragrant, earthy aroma—in this moment, it was the most beautiful thing Faythe had ever smelled.

She thought fast. This shaft must emerge onto the slope of the Gardens, but it was difficult to tell how far away the end was. Could she make it out?

Did she even have a choice? Without pausing to think any further, she tied her bag to her shoulder and pulled away loose brick after loose brick until the gap was big enough, and then she thrust her arms inside, pushed down with all her might, and lifted herself inside face-first.

Slowly, and painfully, Faythe began to crawl towards the light.

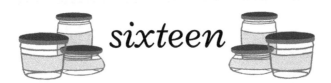

sixteen

MOST CHOICES ARE REVERSIBLE, even on Earth. Beris had once spent an afternoon telling Faythe about various clever human inventions which they used on Earth to overturn seemingly irrevocable decisions, like selling houses, getting divorced, or using literal black magic to get removed from a direct marketing list.

But sometimes there's no going back.

In Faythe's current situation, this was literally true, as the tight channel crumbled behind her as she burrowed her way through. From outside, it had seemed remarkably handy that the bricks surrounding the vent were dislodged by the slightest motion, but the corresponding disadvantages were much more obvious now she was inside a collapsing passage, buried far beneath the Gardens.

It was a *tiny bit* utterly terrifying. Luckily—for now, at least—the passage ahead remained just wide enough to squeeze through.

She concentrated hard on thinking about anything other than her predicament, and especially on not recalling that her earlier claustrophobic anxiety had occurred in a considerably less constrained situation. Strangely, she didn't feel panic. The complete lack of options was oddly freeing. *Wriggle, don't think, try not to panic.* It was a simple existence.

It was also an extremely unpleasant existence. Everything was damp and muddy. And it stank. Her clothes were sticking to her skin, her back was being constantly scratched by something sharp and her neck ached from the strain of holding her face above the muddy surface. But, whatever the discomfort, she had no choice but to keep crawling forward.

Behind her the tunnel gradually collapsed, the centuries-old mixture of bricks and earth finally giving way as she squeezed past. She hoped— she *really, truly hoped*—that it wouldn't start to collapse in front, too. Starving to death had been traumatic to contemplate, but the thought of doing so inside a grave of earth under a hill filled her with a deeper, colder dread.

The tiny window of sky visible ahead was gradually shifting from orange to deep blue. More importantly, it was getting larger as she painstakingly neared the exit. Some of the wetness on her back must be due to bleeding, but by now she was numb to both physical sensation and emotional pain. Exhausted, hungry, petrified, she crawled onward, agonisingly slowly, fighting not to swallow the dirt, hoping that the tunnel would last just a little longer . . . until, after an eternity—seconds? minutes? hours?—she emerged onto a bushy slope in the lower Gardens, thirstily sucking cool air into her lungs, before slumping her face onto the soft earth, too tired even to be grateful that she'd made it.

Moments later, as she attempted to stand, her aching muscles betrayed her and she lost her balance, falling down the slope into a pool beneath the vent exit.

The stagnant, disgusting water felt wonderful. She was free.

She staggered upright, covered in a mixture of green pond algae and horrendous brown tunnel sludge. The bag of ancient jars stung as it pressed against the wounds on her back. She snorted. She'd forgotten about those. It might not seem like it right now, but the trip had, essentially, been a success.

She took a deep breath. First, she needed food. Then, she needed a shower—or possibly many showers. After that, explanations would no doubt be required, although hopefully not until tomorrow.

As she trudged up the hill to the Shop she was relieved to see that the Viewing Platform was deserted. She sneaked inside, over the concourse, and into the living quarters.

But just as she reached the door to her private rooms, a shout came from upstairs. "Is that you, Beris? Can you—"

Faythe closed her eyes. She was too tired to try to hide. "No, it's me," she called back.

There was a moment of silence before the Shopkeeper emerged from her room and ran down the stairs. "Faythe?!" She tightly grasped the exhausted Apprentice, immediately stepping back with a confused look at the sludge which now covered them both. "What . . . what happened? Where have you been? We've been so worried!"

Faythe swallowed. She felt dizzy. As she scrabbled in the empty void of her throbbing skull for something to say, her deepest inner self nudged her. *'Just tell the truth'*, it implored.

"I . . ." She blinked. "I . . . went for a long walk?" The Shopkeeper's disappointed expression matched her own guilty reaction too perfectly. "No . . . that's not right. I got trapped in the Archives."

The Shopkeeper's face flickered with painful realisation. "The Archives!" She sighed, pinching the bridge of her nose. "I should have remembered that dirt-brained Gardener telling you about them!"

"No, no," Faythe swayed as she tried to remain standing. "It's not his fault. It's mine." A flood of repressed terror suddenly hit her all at once. Tears surged to the corners of her eyes and her chest felt as if it might burst with anxiety. "I nearly *died*. I thought—"

The Shopkeeper took her by the arm. "Let's get you—"

But Faythe never heard the end of the sentence. She tilted forward, crumpling towards the ground, and everything went black.

She awoke in an unfamiliar bed. On the table next to her was a bowl of delicious-smelling soup and a hunk of bread, which she consumed ravenously.

After, she slept.

When she next woke up, she felt considerably better. Beris was anxiously fiddling with his glasses beside the bed. On seeing her awake, he gave a start. "I'm so, so sorry!" he wailed.

She frowned, her brain still half-asleep. "Why are *you* sorry?"

"I forgot I told you about the Archives!" The Child looked distraught. "It never occurred to me that you'd actually go there because we emptied most of it centuries ago. If I'd only remembered, we could have found you so much sooner."

She shook her head and patted his arm. "No, this is my fault. I shouldn't have been in there alone."

It took time, but she eventually convinced the upset Child that he wasn't to blame, although he still threw her one last regretful glance as he left.

Shortly afterwards, the Shopkeeper came to see her. Without a word, she handed Faythe a glass of water, which she gratefully guzzled.

"Thank you. Much better than licking moss," said the Apprentice, sitting up with a smile. "Can I ask . . . how long was I gone?"

"Days." The Shopkeeper sounded flat. "Faythe, we have to talk about this." She held up the bag of ancient jars.

"Oh." Faythe had forgotten again.

"Is that all you've got to say?"

She closed her eyes. "I've only just woken up."

"I know." There was a hint of sympathy buried in the Shopkeeper's gaze, but it was veiled by heavy sadness. "Being trapped for so long must have been terrible. But, again, I can't think of a good reason for you to have these." She stared at Faythe. "You were looking for these in particular, weren't you?" Faythe gave a small nod. "Well. That explains all the wandering you've been doing. To think I'd been pleased you were taking more of an interest in the Shop." Faythe's chest squeezed at the obvious pain in the Shopkeeper's voice. "Now, I can't imagine this was entirely your doing. It's too much of a leap, in such a short time, to care about these old things." The Shopkeeper leaned in closer. "Someone else put you up to this, didn't they?"

Her eyes were fraught with worry . . . no, more than that. *Fear.* But fear of what?

"I . . ." Faythe's brain was still foggy. If she lied, would that be to protect Zariel, or herself? She no longer knew.

Either way, she was tired of lying. "Yes," she admitted.

"I knew it." The Shopkeeper visibly deflated with sorrow. "I wanted to be wrong about you." She glanced at the jars with a frown. "I wonder what they want these for . . . but, never mind. You did such a good job of hiding it when you arrived."

Faythe frowned in confusion. "When I arrived? I don't know what you mean. I only found out about these jars a couple of months ago."

"What? They talked to you while you were here?! How could I have missed that?"

"Who's *they*? Do you mean *he*?"

They stared at each other in mutual incomprehension. "Who are you talking about?" asked the Shopkeeper.

"Zariel, obviously! Who are you talking about?"

The Shopkeeper's eyes bulged. "Zariel?!" She blinked. "Are you sure?"

This was not at all the reaction Faythe had expected. Confused, she lowered her guard. "Yes, I'm sure. There's loads of letters from him under my bed. You can look if you like."

"Zariel!" The Shopkeeper laughed. "And all this time I thought . . ." She drifted off, still smiling with visible relief. "How did I miss this? So, Zariel enticed you to steal for him? For experiments, I expect." She snorted at Faythe's nod. "Goodness, I was so wrapped up in my own worries that I missed any other possibilities."

"I'm not sure what you mean." Faythe's mind was brimming with questions, but one was more pressing than the rest. "Am I still in trouble? With the Committee?" *And with Management*, she added silently.

The Shopkeeper held her gaze. Was that pity in her eyes? "Trouble? Perhaps. It seems my instincts were right about you, but for the wrong reasons. You were misled."

"Misled?"

"Let me guess—Zariel talked about discovering the secrets of the traits? Unlocking tremendous power?"

"Something like that." Faythe felt embarrassed without quite understanding why.

"Clever of him. I've been such a fool, ignoring his mischief for this long. I suppose I imagined he'd stop sending all those thieves and vandals if he didn't get any attention in return."

"Thieves and vandals?" She had no idea what the Shopkeeper was talking about.

"Oh, I've long been sure that he's been the one encouraging troublemakers to visit. I assumed it was petty revenge for his many grudges."

Zariel had been sending thieves here?! Faythe reeled. She had always struggled to reconcile her mental image of Zariel with his reputation. Had she simply been ignoring everything she didn't wish to see?

She didn't wish to see that thought, so she ignored it for now.

The Shopkeeper was still talking. "I had hoped he would be content to tinker with his machines, and would eventually leave us alone. Clearly, as in so many things, I was wrong." She looked straight at Faythe. "It's time to put an end to Zariel's games. Tomorrow, you and I will visit the Supplier's Complex." Faythe's heart leapt in surprise. "We'll teach the pair of you a few important truths."

"Truths?"

"About each other. And about the universe, I suppose. Afterwards, you and I will decide—*together*—if you want to go before the Committee."

Faythe blinked. "You want me to choose whether or not to punish myself . . . ?"

"Punishment must serve a purpose. If it doesn't help you become a better Apprentice—or a better person—then what's the point? After tomorrow, I believe you'll see things very differently, and we can decide together what will help us move on. I don't know if you and I will ever repair our trust, but"—she gestured at the bed—"it's apparent that you've already suffered more than any punishment I would ever consider for you." She stood to leave. "For now, get some rest. Tomorrow will be a busy day."

It took a while for Faythe drift off to sleep. As she did, a question floated through her mind, too softly to keep her awake. Who was the Shopkeeper really afraid of?

In the morning they met at the train platform behind the Warehouse. Omaro was waiting, tapping his foot and toying nervously with his yoyo. All around, Children swarmed to prepare the enormous engine for departure. Faythe gazed in awe as a cloud of steam gushed from the chimney with a mighty hiss. After years of helping to unload the train before watching it shoot into the distance, she could hardly believe that today she would finally ride it for herself.

Omaro coughed. "Please be careful, you two," he warned.

The old lady laughed. "Of Zariel?"

"He can be dangerous."

"Dangerously self-absorbed, perhaps. But he's just a boy."

He shook his head. "We've both heard about the army he's building."

"Oh yes, the 'Zeraph', isn't it?" The Shopkeeper sniffed. "A few suggestible fools. Thank you, Omaro, but I'm not concerned."

Faythe blanched. It stung that Zariel had apparently recruited an army—an army!—without telling her. A chill of apprehension passed over her as she recalled the man with the flaming sword. Had he been a Zeraph? Why hadn't she been more curious at the time?

Omaro shrugged. "You're the Shopkeeper."

"Exactly." She tousled his hair. "What can he do?"

"Okay, I trust you." With a smile, the Child turned to Faythe. "It's good to have you back. I knew you hadn't run away."

Her stomach churned with shame. "I'm so embarrassed anybody thought that."

"They were only trying to understand why you'd disappeared. I knew something bad must have happened. I just didn't know what. Sorry I didn't find you."

Not this again. Faythe was fed up of everybody else feeling *her* guilt. "It's not your fault. I appreciate that you tried."

She jumped as a deafening honk sounded from the train.

"Time to leave," said the Shopkeeper, gesturing towards the steps to the driver's compartment.

With a reluctant wave, Omaro made way for the pair to board.

Faythe settled onto a seat by the window, perhaps two storeys above the ground. "It's so high up here. Everything looks so small."

The Foreman, a cheerful Child wearing a delightfully bright hat, grinned. "Glorious, isn't it? Never get tired of this."

She watched in fascination as he pressed buttons and pulled on levers. Moments later, the train pulled away to race through the countryside. Despite her nerves, she couldn't help laughing in delight as trees and fields began to blur in front of her eyes. "This is incredible!" she yelled.

The Foreman twinkled with pride. "I know!"

She looked over to share her joy with the Shopkeeper, but the old lady was staring contemplatively out of the other window. The compartment fell into an uneasy silence, broken only by the rhythmic thumping of the engine, until the Foreman beckoned her over to try the whistle.

A few noisy minutes later, Faythe was banned from the whistle.

She returned to her seat and watched the landscape streak by. They had left the river behind shortly after departing the Shop, but it suddenly reappeared after the track bent around a hill.

If she hadn't known it was the same river, she'd have struggled to believe it. It was much narrower and faster this close to the mountains. The surface was broken by rocks and violent splashes of white foam, all visible for only an instant before being whizzed out of view by the speeding train.

She stared without really seeing for some time. Meeting Zariel again was both thrilling and terrifying, especially as she had no idea what the Shopkeeper intended. What would her employer do when she discovered that Faythe had been an eager participant in his schemes and not some naive girl who had been easily fooled?

Through the window, the scenery continued to speed by. Even if she wanted to, she couldn't stop the train. Once more, there was no going back, and once more her lack of options was oddly freeing. And, if nothing else, at least her relationship with Zariel was no longer secret.

No matter what happened later, she wouldn't have to lie anymore.

Outside, the trees were thinning as the train neared the base of the mountains. She felt peaceful.

Suddenly, everything went black. She yelled in surprise, reaching for the Foreman, but she couldn't hear any reply over the crushing echo of the noisy train. Moments later, the light reappeared and the deafening sound receded.

It had been a tunnel.

She looked around to laugh with the others, but then she caught sight of the valley of the Supplier below, and lost her ability to speak.

seventeen

THE SUPPLIER'S COMPLEX was . . . well, complex.

Faythe stared in wonder. It looked like someone had convinced drunken giant spiders to spin industrial machinery instead of silk for a thousand years. The valley beneath was densely packed with a haphazard mess of structures and motion, all metal and brick and smoke and flame, impossible to tell where one building ended and the next began. Here, a bulky transparent globe rose above a maze of pipes and walkways; over there, a jutting metal skyscraper emitted a tangle of bridges in all directions.

She tried to trace the path of one bridge but her attention kept being drawn by arresting details elsewhere. A sudden flash of light from inside a massive warehouse drew her eye, and then a towering chimney flared with a colourful flame, itself as tall as a house. Everywhere she looked there were knotty snarls of pipes, mostly black, but some shone brightly in all colours of the rainbow.

At the far edge of the valley, a tremendous stone wheel, far taller even than the Shop, was spinning so slowly that it was hard, at first, to be certain it was moving. A thick beam connected its centre to a network of gears and spindles, forming a giant mechanism which distributed the ponderous motion amongst a multitude of dark brick buildings.

With a sudden start, she realised that there were people everywhere; snaking around the complex in orderly lines which reminded her of the ants' nests she used to watch for hours at a time back at the Rock.

Her jaw slackened as she noticed the mountainside opposite. It was completely covered with row after row of identical houses, all the way to the top. This was a whole town, just for the Supplier.

Every day, those first couple of centuries she'd spent at the Rock seemed smaller and smaller.

Soon the train slowed to a stop inside a large stone building which was dwarfed by its giant neighbours. The Foreman gave her a cheery wave as she followed the Shopkeeper onto the platform and outside to a busy concrete-paved street.

She paused to gaze up and around at the buildings around her. Part of her was itching to explore, but the Shopkeeper was already striding away. "Hurry," her employer shouted over her shoulder. "The less time we spend here, the better."

She was torn between disappointment and reluctant agreement. There was something unsettling about this place. It wasn't just the overwhelming scale; after all, the Shop was also enormous. But getting lost in the Shop meant ending up in cosier and more intimate surroundings. Here, the Complex opened up wider and wider until she seemed like nothing—a mote of dust, a blip, a speck—compared to the domineering shapes engulfing her on all sides.

She fought to catch up with the Shopkeeper. The whole way she was irritatingly knocked by crowds of workers who didn't give her as much as a second glance or even a disapproving tut.

She'd never felt so invisible.

"Where are we going?" she asked, as she fell in beside her boss. The old lady, puffing slightly due to exertion, merely pointed up the street towards their destination, an opaque spherical building at the top of a long metal slope. The pair walked the rest of the way in silence, battered by the constant cacophony of the Complex, a mixture of babbling people, deafening flares, and the distant clattering of mechanisms.

Inside the globe they found an airless atrium, with walls painted off-white. A guard nodded to the Shopkeeper in apparent recognition. "That way, ma'am," she said.

The Shopkeeper gestured to Faythe to walk ahead. They climbed a wide staircase and stopped before a double door which was marked, simply, with the word ZARIEL. The sign shone like new, highlighted by the darkness of the wood immediately surrounding it, as if an older, larger sign used to hang in its place.

They knocked and a bored-looking girl opened the door. "I'm sorry," she said. "The Supplier isn't here. Do you have an appointment?"

The old lady shook her head impatiently. "Zariel isn't expecting us, but he certainly will make time to see me. Where is he?"

"He's in his lab." The girl sullenly fidgeted with her cuffs. "Shall I—"

"—show us the way? Yes, you shall."

Faythe was quietly impressed. She made a mental note to use this technique herself in future.

Zariel's laboratory turned out to be underneath the building. As they descended, Faythe couldn't help remembering her trip into the Archives. "Why is everything interesting always in basements?" she wondered aloud.

The Shopkeeper gave her a disbelieving look, but said nothing.

They emerged onto a gantry in the upper half of a large, rocky cavern. The space appeared to have been created by blowing a huge hole in the rock without regard for the shape it would make. Beneath them, the floor was covered with machinery, desks and equipment, scattered haphazardly around a deep crater in the centre of the room. People in uniform swarmed noisily back and forth between the desks and the machines.

With a nervous flutter, Faythe recognised Zariel standing next to an enormous glass box, gesticulating passionately as he explained something to a group of workers. He glanced up, and she waved, a small enough gesture for the Shopkeeper to miss.

Perhaps the gesture was too small. If Zariel saw, he didn't acknowledge it.

As they approached, however, he bowed. "Welcome, Shopkeep!" he said, grandly. "And this must be the new Apprentice, I assume?"

"Drop the act, Zariel." The Shopkeeper's voice was cold. "I already know about you two."

Everybody surrounding Zariel all simultaneously remembered they had something important to do elsewhere. As they slid away, he glanced from Faythe to the Shopkeeper, visibly recalculating. "Wonderful," he said, after a short pause. "I'm so pleased you're both here."

The Shopkeeper folded her arms. "As I said, you may drop the act."

His eyes glinted with amusement. "Oh, I *may*, may I? How very kind of you! But I assure you, I'm being quite genuine. I'm delighted to welcome you to my Complex."

The Shopkeeper snorted at his emphasis on 'my'.

Faythe interrupted before she could speak again. "Hi, Zariel," she said, smiling shyly.

He ignored her entirely, and addressed the Shopkeeper once more. "May I ask the purpose of your visit?"

The ancient traits clinked as the Shopkeeper emptied the bag onto a table. "I suspect you won't be shocked to learn that I found my Apprentice stealing, and that it turned out she was doing it on your behalf."

Faythe bit her lip, her pride stung. She wanted to shout that she'd acted for herself, too.

Zariel's faint smirk never left his face. He gazed at the traits. "That must have been a terrible surprise for you."

"It was a relief, frankly," said the Shopkeeper, flatly. "If she's going to be a pawn, I'd prefer she be yours."

"I'm not a pawn!" Faythe hated being talked about as if she weren't there.

Zariel's smirk disappeared. "Relieved?! Is that so? You still don't think I matter?" He gestured around at the busy laboratory. "After everything I've achieved?!"

"Perhaps it's better to say I don't fear your games, Zariel."

"You underestimate me."

"I've known you for a long time."

"You've *always* underestimated me."

The Shopkeeper shook her head. "I'm not getting drawn into this, Zariel. We've wasted enough years fighting over your ego." She placed the bag of ancient traits on the lab table. "I brought these for you. Take them."

He looked suspiciously at the bag. "You're *giving* them to me? Why?"

"Because I don't care. You can finish your little experiments."

His eyes flashed with anger. "You don't know what you're talking about!"

"Unfortunately, I know far more than you do. However, there is one condition attached—if you choose to take these traits, you must stop attempting to corrupt my Apprentice."

He laughed. "Corrupt? She didn't require much persuading."

Faythe cringed. That was true . . . sort of. *But should she deny it?* She had no idea what to say, or—more importantly—who she most wanted to impress. Paralysed with indecision, she remained silent.

But to her surprise, the Shopkeeper gave her an affectionate smile. "Perhaps you're right. Some of that is doubtless my fault. But I believe Faythe has always essentially tried her best."

A warm joy spread throughout her chest at the unexpected praise. But it didn't last long.

"Well, she doesn't think so highly of you," sneered Zariel. Her heart lurched in sudden fear as she remembered all the cruel things she'd said about the Shopkeeper in her notes to Zariel. She stared at him imploringly. *Please, stop!* Luckily, he seemed more interested in scoring points in his personal feud. "Your obsessive secrecy has backfired again."

The Shopkeeper snorted. "Again?"

"You can't have forgotten already that Management chose me to be the Supplier, and that nothing you tried could prevent it? Perhaps if you'd been more open with me, they would have seen things differently."

"Is that so?" She looked around at the machines which hummed all around them. "I sincerely doubt that they've been entirely open with you, either. I truly wish I could trust you with the full truth."

"Ha!" He jabbed his finger accusingly. "You're simply bitter. Let me trust you with the truth: they saw in me what you didn't."

"Oh, Zariel." The Shopkeeper sighed. "Are we about to be treated to another one of your rants? Will it be the one about 'hidden greatness' and everyone holding you back? I can probably quote it on your behalf, if you prefer."

He snarled and the Shopkeeper glared back contemptuously. Faythe chewed on her lip. Was the Shopkeeper deliberately goading him? Why?

"You really are too easily riled," said the old lady, after a pause. "I wish you'd put that endless desire for knowledge to use, and ask yourself why they might have placed you, of all people, here. It's clear from what you're doing that you don't—you *can't*—understand their plans, but—"

Zariel didn't let her finish. "Enough!" He clapped. High above on the gantry, guards appeared, a group of tall men, carrying—Faythe couldn't help noticing once more—flaming swords. "I put up with your disrespect for centuries, but it's clear that you haven't accepted how things have changed. I don't need to put up with it anymore."

Faythe looked at him with horror. "Zariel!"

But the Shopkeeper appeared unmoved. "Ah. These must be the infamous 'Zeraph'! I must confess I'm curious as to how you got anybody to sign up to this."

"When you command respect, it's not difficult to gather followers."

She rolled her eyes. "Respect! Really? Another word you've only ever understood at the most superficial level."

"Oh, spare us both your endless lectures. I can quote them word-for-word, too!" He waved his arms like a conductor. "*Sacrifice* and *compassion* and *understanding*. So very tedious."

"Clearly, none of it ever sunk in," muttered the Shopkeeper.

Faythe glanced nervously at the approaching guards. "Zariel, what are you doing?" she hissed.

"Quite," agreed the Shopkeeper, as the Zeraph surrounded her. "What's your plan? Both of us know what you want to know, and we both know you'd kill me before you find out. And I'm sure you know that I'm quite prepared to die if I have to. Again." She looked straight at Faythe. "Still, at least my Apprentice has seen who you truly are now."

His face twisted in another sneer. "And I'm sure you know precisely how much her opinion matters to me."

"I do," said the Shopkeeper. There was sadness in her eyes as she met Faythe's gaze. "Although I'm not sure she realised, until now."

Faythe swallowed. She felt curiously empty and extremely small.

The Zeraph encircled the Shopkeeper. At a nod from Zariel, they grabbed her and thrust her, roughly, inside the enormous glass box. The transparent door slid shut, trapping the old lady inside.

Faythe wanted to move, but her feet were rooted to the ground. A tiny part of her was furious that everybody, guards included, had ignored her this entire time.

Zariel smirked in triumph at the Shopkeeper, who waited silently in the glass prison. "Thank you for the traits, but I'm sure you know I want more. It'd be remiss if I didn't get the very most from your visit. And I want answers."

"I'll never tell you anything which might endanger the Shop," said the Shopkeeper.

"That's neither here nor there. Besides, I believe otherwise."

"You think I'll tell you everything?" She frowned thoughtfully. "You *can't* plan to torture me. Even you know me better than that." Her voice was quiet, but confident, as if he were the one imprisoned.

"I think I'm better than that," he said, pointedly.

"Night shifts don't count as torture, Zariel."

His eyes flashed at the mockery. "Torture isn't only physical. Besides, I can go further."

The Shopkeeper laughed darkly. "What's left after that? Killing me? I'd only be back in the Shop in a day."

Faythe looked on, awed by the Shopkeeper's calm. Her own muscles had turned to pure liquid.

"Yes, the prelife is rather limiting, isn't it?" said Zariel. "I've always admired the system on Earth. Permanent death opens up so many intriguing possibilities."

Faythe couldn't believe how rapidly the situation had unravelled. "Zariel," she said. "I get that you want to learn how the traits work, to make new ones or whatever, so why don't we—"

He spun to face her. "Can you please be quiet while adults are talking?"

Her eyes widened. "Is that how you see me? A child?!"

"Ideally, I wouldn't see you at all."

She quivered, completely lost for words, as he brushed her aside.

He stepped back towards the glass box, reaching into a pocket to withdraw a remote. "You'll be pleased to know, Shopkeeper, that I've been extremely innovative during my relatively short time here. But enough talk. Allow me to demonstrate."

He pressed a button on the remote, and the universe went wrong.

At one end of the glass prison a hole appeared. Except, unlike any hole Faythe had ever seen, it didn't exist in any particular object. It was a hole in everything. An absence. A void. In exactly the way other things *were*, this thing *was not*. Her eyes watered with the strain of the impossible sensation that the void was sucking light out of them as she looked at it.

She tore her gaze away. The Shopkeeper was no longer dignified and calm. She pressed herself close to the glass, as far away from the hole in reality as possible. "What have you done?" she shrieked.

"It works every time!" Zariel barely suppressed a giggle. "As you've probably guessed," he said, adopting an uncomfortably conversational tone, "my attempts to uncover the source of the traits have failed. At least, so far. But I *have* discovered that the machines are connected to these voids. My current belief is that human traits exist in pure form in another part of the universe, and that the voids bring them from there, somehow."

Now that Faythe's eyes had adjusted to the wrongness, she could make out weak coloured wisps of vapour emanating from the emptiness.

"But beyond all those theoretical concerns," continued Zariel, "I discovered a more immediate practical purpose. It turns out that, if you make the holes large enough, you can fit people inside."

Faythe's stomach was tying itself in knots as she looked at the void. She thought she might be sick. Desperately gritting her teeth, she took a step forward to grab at Zariel, fighting to find the right words to stop this. "Please! Whatever you want to know can't be this important!"

He looked at her with naked contempt. "I told you, it's not about mere knowledge. Imagine what can be done!"

"But what do you *want?!*" She held her arms wide. "You already control this whole Complex. Isn't that enough for you?"

He shook his head. "Think! If Management are willing to release the traits—such power! The ability to form individuality itself!—then consider what magic they must be holding back. This goes far beyond normal people shaping their tedious lives."

Faythe recoiled at the venom in his voice. She remembered the playful notes they'd exchanged. "I thought you cared about the Shop! We were going to start one of our own!"

She cringed, suddenly realising what she'd just admitted to in front of the Shopkeeper.

"Oh, I have higher ambitions than a mere Shop." He twirled the remote idly between his hands. "I'm interested in the power that created the Shop in the first place."

"Listen to me," yelled the Shopkeeper, still pressed up against the glass as far away from the void as she could manage. "I know you've spent centuries imagining all this, but it's not real, Zariel."

He shook his head. "That void looks extremely real to me. Now, what was I saying?" He clapped in delight. "Oh yes! I had been admiring the system on Earth. And here's the good news: we don't have to be jealous anymore! I have discovered a method to—isn't kill such an awful word? Personally I prefer *delete*. It seems so much cleaner." He smiled. "I discovered a means of deleting people from the prelife."

Faythe felt suddenly lightheaded. She had never heard anything so monstrous. Weakly, she pulled again at his arm. "Stop!"

The Zeraph stepped closer to intervene, but Zariel waved them away. "You don't like the word delete?" he said, feigning concern. "Would you prefer 'erase'?"

"Not the word!" she screamed. "The idea!"

"I agree. It *is* horrible. And it would be terrible if anything were to happen to the Shopkeeper . . . which is why she's now going to be co-operative and tell me everything I want to know."

The Shopkeeper closed her eyes for a moment. "Very well," she said, fixing Zariel with a determined gaze. "Though I suspect you're not going to like it."

"I doubt that," he said, striding to his table near the glass prison. "I like it a lot already." He picked up a pad. "Let's begin by discussing trait production, and we'll move on from there. Is it really a science? It must be. If machines can do it, it can't be magic. And yet, when I try it myself, they don't work. What's missing?"

The thrum of the void grated against the inside of Faythe's skull while the Shopkeeper considered her response.

"No hurry," said Zariel. "I can wait all day." He sat down, nonchalantly sliding his feet up on the table. "In case you hadn't noticed, you're the one with the time constraint here. When I tire of you, I'll press a button and into the void you'll go. Let's try something different. Is it about how the traits are infused? How does that occur? What does passing through to Earth entail? I want to know *everything*."

Faythe was transfixed, but her eyes were watering from the effort of focusing on the Shopkeeper while the unnatural void twisted and swirled painfully in the background. She blinked and looked away and then gave a double-take as she realised: Zariel was fully absorbed by what was happening in the glass prison.

Which meant *nobody was looking at her*. Or, more importantly, at his remote, which sat beside him on his desk. If she turned off the void, and then, ideally, smashed the cursed thing, then nobody would get hurt—at least, not in any permanent way.

He kept talking while she edged closer. "If you want to keep existing, you'd better answer. What don't I know?"

At that, the Shopkeeper barked a laugh. "What don't you know? I'm not sure we have time for everything."

He stamped both his feet into the desk, sending equipment flying onto the floor. The remote jiggled closer to the edge. "And I'm not sure you understand the seriousness of your situation."

"Oh, I certainly do," said the Shopkeeper. "But what I also know is how you're going to react when—" She stopped as she noticed Faythe, who was now within touching distance of Zariel, and was stretching out to seize the remote.

"Faythe, no!" she shouted.

Zariel followed the Shopkeeper's gaze and acted immediately, scooping up the remote before Faythe could grab it. In the same motion, he leapt towards her, knocking them both to the ground.

Shouts went up from across the lab as the Zeraph scrambled towards them.

"Stop! Both of you! I don't need this!" yelled the Shopkeeper.

Faythe struggled to free herself, rolling from side to side as hard as she could. Zariel had her pinned down, but all her awareness was on the remote—still in his hand, tantalisingly close to her outstretched arm.

Moments later, the Zeraph thundered closer. The instant she felt Zariel relax his grip, she seized her opportunity. As soon as her hand could move she snatched the remote and smashed it down against the rock floor.

"*NO*, Faythe!" screamed the Shopkeeper, from inside the box.

Faythe sat up, holding the damaged remote triumphantly to her chest. "It's okay! I've—"

She trailed off as she saw inside the Shopkeeper's prison. The void hadn't disappeared, as she'd expected.

It was *growing*.

Frantically, Faythe tapped at the buttons on the busted remote, but it had no effect. The Shopkeeper was struggling to hold onto the sheer glass of her prison and then she couldn't grip any longer and then the sound of her screams were silent and then she was elongated and then . . .

As the Shopkeeper was swallowed, her eyes met Faythe's.

And then she was gone.

Some moments are so horrifying that perception of time stretches and distends, turning instants into eternities, searing every detail into our brains for endless replay afterwards.

Even when she had embraced the possibility of death inside the Archives, Faythe had never experienced such a sickening moment.

Until now.

Time stood still, her heart ceased to beat, her lungs stopped drawing in air, and all she could hear was a scream.

Faythe realised she was screaming.

She was sitting, dumbfounded, on the cold, rocky floor, staring at the empty chamber where the Shopkeeper had been. Slowly, she realised that Zariel was laughing hysterically.

"*Hyuk-yuk-yuk*-you really did it." He struggled to speak between giggles. "You deleted the Shopkeeper!"

She still couldn't speak. The void still filled the glass prison, but the Shopkeeper was gone.

Her chest was packed, impossibly, with pure cold.

"I wasn't going to do it, you know," he said, almost conversationally. "And I suppose I should be annoyed that you broke my machine and *erased her*"—another fit of giggles—"as I was about to find out what I need to know. But this is just too funny." He wiped away a tear. "At least I'll discover everything myself soon enough."

"I'm going to be sick," she muttered.

Zariel ignored her. "She deserved it, if anyone did. Although, the more I think about it, it is quite frustrating that you took this opportunity from me."

She stood up. Her nausea was quite powerful now. "From *you*? She's gone, and you're complaining about what *you've* lost!"

But he wasn't really listening. He stared at the empty chamber, talking to himself. "Still, it will be significantly easier to deal with the Shop now. This may be good fortune."

Overwhelmed with disgust, she turned away and stumbled up the steps. Once outside, she ran as fast as she could.

Apparently her subconscious had done a fantastic job of mapping the vast complex, as she went straight to the train platform and clambered into the driver's compartment.

The Foreman looked at her with evident concern. "You alright? Where's the Shopkeeper?" He craned his neck to look along the platform.

She tried to keep her voice from shaking. She still hadn't been sick, but she wanted to be. "The Shopkeeper is staying to talk to Zariel." The lie fell from her lips without a thought. Her internal auto-pilot was tightly gripping the controls and screaming *HOME NOW NOTHING ELSE MATTERS*. "They were arguing after the meeting, and they sent me away. The Shopkeeper said she'd come back later."

He nodded uncertainly. "You look upset. Are you sure you're alri—"

"It was a horrible argument," she replied, firmly. "I'm fine."

The Child didn't attempt another word the entire way home.

Back at the Shop, she fled straight to her room to bury her face in her pillow.

It didn't help. Even with her eyes closed, the image of the Shopkeeper's last look—terrified, yet accepting—was etched into her brain. She wanted desperately to cry but she was too numb.

There was a knock at the door. "Go away!" she yelled, but Omaro entered anyway.

"Are you okay?" he asked, wearing the face of someone who knows the answer is 'absolutely not' but is required by politeness to ask anyway. "What happened? The Foreman told me you came back without the Shopkeeper?"

The tiny part of Faythe's brain that wasn't overwhelmed with shock was calculating fast. The rest was focused on one simple thought. *I erased her from existence.*

"I don't want to talk about it," she said. This had the useful benefit of being entirely true. Her brain, on autopilot, followed up with her earlier lie. "The Shopkeeper stayed to argue with Zariel. They sent me away."

Omaro frowned. She could almost read his thoughts: *that doesn't sound right.* "Sounds upsetting?" he said, doubtfully.

"It was."

Tears welled in her eyes. Apparently killing somebody wasn't enough to make her cry, but lying to her friend was.

"If you want to talk . . ." He opened his arms.

The kindness of the gesture was too much. *She didn't deserve it.* Hot tears began to flow down her cheeks, and the Child hugged her.

She pushed him away. "Please," she said.

Deep concern was etched on Omaro's face. "I'm here if you need."

"I know," she said, trying not to sound dismissive, but wanting to discourage any more questions. "Thank you."

She was grateful that he left her alone, free from any more unbearable kindness.

The pale light from the three mystery jars glinted and shifted, slowly changing the colour of the room as their glows ebbed and flowed.

She cried herself to sleep.

eighteen

DURING PERIODS OF EXTREME DARKNESS, the human brain can cease to function in the normal way. Pain inundates the system, and memories aren't recorded properly. Time becomes strange and bendy—days appear endless, even as they go by all at once.

Sometimes, the pain is so overwhelming it becomes numbness—which might sound better, but guilt at the absence of expected pain can be as difficult as the pain itself.

It's not easy being human.

For a time, Faythe stopped living, and simply existed.

She had no idea how long this time lasted. She worked. She interacted blankly and automatically with customers. She avoided the Children—all of them—as much as possible.

The rest of the time she remained in her room, where the looks and the questions—especially the questions—couldn't reach her.

nineteen

FAYTHE'S MEMORIES of this time were shrouded.

Wallowing in shame and misery, entirely alone. Half-remembered conversations. One with Beris:

"We need an answer. What should we do about this missing delivery?"

Frustration. "Why are you asking me?"

"You're the Acting Shopkeeper now."

Consternation. His, or hers? Perhaps both.

"But why? This is absurd!"

Desperation. "You were the Apprentice. Now you're the Acting Shopkeeper. That's how it's supposed to work."

"I don't know what to do. Sort it out!"

Other conversations with Omaro. Many about the Shopkeeper.

"I'm taking Security over to see Zariel."

They were outside. She didn't deserve beautiful surroundings. "Okay."

"I'll ask about the supply problems, too."

"Uh-huh." That sounded unimportant.

"You really didn't see anything while you were there?"

"I've told you. No."

This answer was reflexive, always the same.

"You understand why I keep asking, right? Both of you went, only you came back, and you're obviously upset."

"Please, Omaro, stop."

"When you're ready."

"There's nothing to be ready for."

A weight crushing her from within, and Omaro leaving her alone, until the next time.

Repetitive thoughts running through her head. How she could have acted differently. Been more careful grabbing the remote. Let Zariel's interrogation play out. Not gone to the Archives. *Never written to Zariel in the first place.*

Most of all, she could have simply trusted the Shopkeeper from the beginning. In all her time at the Shop, they'd only had a handful of real conversations. Each time, Faythe's actions had quickly ruined it.

The thoughts fed her shame, which fed her thoughts, which fed her shame, and that was all she remembered.

All things pass.

Which would be great, except some things are kidney stones, and their passing is the *absolute worst*.

But—and this is very important—they still pass.

Eventually.

Sometimes the final passing of difficulty is itself painful, as the fantasy of dissociation gives way to an unpleasant reality.

Observers might be confused by Faythe's behaviour in this instance. After all, vaporising your boss out of existence is a common fantasy throughout the entire universe. There are tiny intergalactic spores living in the tails of comets which do nothing but dream of ejecting their irritating spore supervisors into the coldness of space.

However, when humans are presented with an opportunity to actually, physically murder their boss, very few of them choose to do so.

'It's just a fantasy', they say. 'Everyone occasionally imagines casually murdering their friends, colleagues, or loved ones. It's normal. But no-one actually does it.'

And observation shows that they are completely right. It seems that if people actually receive what they occasionally wish for, they become unbelievably miserable.

Humans are the best guide to what they themselves want—*and they often haven't got a clue what that is.*

Faythe was working on the checkouts—easy, mindless, and free of Children asking her awkward questions—when a customer rudely shoved to the front of the queue.

"Excuse me," she said, without looking up. "There's a line."

Zariel coughed. "Lovely to see you. And how are you this fine day?" His eyes sparkled with amusement.

She bit down her jaw so hard that it hurt. "Shut up," she said, through gritted teeth. "And get out!"

"I don't think so," he said, with an insouciant smile. He crooked a finger and two tall men stepped forward, flanking him on either side.

"You brought guards?"

"They're called Zeraph. I would think you'd remember them." He brushed dust off the checkout and inspected his finger. "Tsk. Hope this place isn't lowering its standards, now it's under new management."

"I don't care what stupid name you give them. You all have to leave."

"Are you going to force me? Will you call Security over for a fight? Better hope I didn't bring any voids with me. How many Children are you prepared to lose today?"

She hesitated. "You can do that?" He grinned. Behind him, customers were exchanging confused glances. She closed her eyes. "What do you want?"

The Supplier giggled. "Just a word in your office, *Acting Shopkeeper.*"

Cold rage flickered in her stomach, but she nodded. "Fine. Let's go." The three men stepped forward and she held up a hand. "But they're not coming with you."

"They'll be no trouble."

She stood firm despite her anxiety. "You're right. Because they'll be waiting here."

After a moment's consideration, Zariel nodded to his guards, and they entered the administrative area alone. Instinctively, she led him past her own office, which she still used, and into the Shopkeeper's.

"Ohoho." He actually pronounced the sounds rather than genuinely laughing. "Looks like somebody got comfortable quickly. Isn't it wonderful when everything works out for the best?"

She ignored his jibes and took a seat behind the desk, mostly so he wouldn't see her legs trembling. This raw fear was an unfamiliar sensation. She'd grown accustomed to feeling numb, aside from the constant weight of guilt which migrated around her body. She had killed the Shopkeeper; she doubted it would ever go away. Currently it was in her chest.

"Why are you here, Zariel?"

He made a hurt face. "I thought we were friends!"

"No, you didn't." Another emotion was lurking. She prodded at it curiously. *Anger.* "But *I* thought we were."

"Oh, fine, be like that if you must." He crossed his legs, relaxing back on his chair. "I'm here because I heard about the terrible accident. I wanted to pay my respects."

All of her muscles tensed involuntarily. Revulsion multiplied with rage. How had she ever been charmed by this creature?

She kept her voice cool. "I'm not sure who you're performing for. We're alone here."

He tilted his head. "Well, well. Maybe being the Shopkeeper suits you more than I expected. You're certainly no fun anymore."

"I'm not the Shopkeeper."

"Indeed."

A pause.

"Very well." He dropped his pretend warmth. "It seems you're not interested in being friendly, so I'll simply collect what I'm here for, and be on my way."

He stood and crossed to the back of the room behind her desk.

"Wait!" she shouted, spinning on her chair. "You can't steal from here!" Anger was coursing through her, and it felt so good. She'd forgotten what it was like to feel feelings.

But he didn't bother looking around. His attention was on the Shopkeeper's shelves, still piled high with heaps of books, papers, and the occasional jar. "Can't I? We've been over this. Who, exactly, is going to stop me? You?"

She stood and clenched her fists. "I . . ." she began.

But she had no idea how that sentence could end.

"Exactly." Zariel practically oozed raw smugness. "Perhaps Security could stop me. They are surprisingly effective. Perhaps some would get deleted, perhaps none would." He inclined towards her very slightly. "But I wonder about something else . . . who here knows *what you did?*"

The words stung, sharply. In an instant, her righteous fury collapsed inwards, transforming into hot, agonising shame. She was paralysed, punctured by the mere thought of what would happen if everyone knew the truth.

"Precisely," he said, smiling. "I'm sure we both agree it would be awful if everybody at the Shop Before Life knew who had killed their precious Shopkeeper. So I'll take these"—he picked up a small stack of books, which Faythe recognised as the Shopkeeper's diaries—"and I'll pass by Administration on my way out too. There's a little correspondence from my old employer I'd like to catch up on. Thank you." He turned to deliver a final pronouncement before he left. "And, while I'm here, an official warning: as far as the Supplier is concerned, this place no longer serves a purpose."

The door slammed shut, and Faythe slumped onto the desk.

For a moment, she'd been so sure, so certain, so full of rage, but his threat had caused her foundations to crumble under her and she'd collapsed into an inner void—

— just like the Shopkeeper had fallen into a real void. The image was vividly seared into her imagination, impossible to repress.

She sat in the empty office with Zariel's final words echoing over and over in her mind. *No longer serves a purpose.*

Memories surfaced of conversations with Children about missing deliveries, and the pieces clicked together in her head. Zariel was withholding trait supplies from the Shop. That's what he'd meant.

But she couldn't let go of his words. *No longer serves a purpose.* The dismissal of the Shop—so casual!—needled at her.

She glanced outside at the Earth, high in the sky, drifting past the office window. For years, all of her efforts had been directed towards helping people choose who they might become. *That* was a purpose. It might not be Zariel's purpose, but it still mattered.

Although, right now, the idea was remote, abstract. Surely she couldn't be this upset about an abstract concept like 'helping people'?

With a shiver, she realised something. She *was* upset. Her protective stupor was gone. And a fact was crying out for her attention: this *mattered* to her.

The Shop was important, and not only in the obvious way. During the brief eternity since the Shopkeeper's death, this place had been everything to her. At first, she'd had no choice—what else did she have, except for work?

But the more time she'd poured into it, the more it had come to matter. The Shop had given her a reason to live.

Or to pre-live. Whatever.

In theory, giving purpose to just one person was less important than enabling all of humanity to live . . . yet, in practice, it was much more powerful.

Deep inside the emptiness, there was a flicker of emotion. How *dare* Zariel threaten to starve the Shop of traits?! To abandon all of humanity? He couldn't be allowed to do this.

The flicker caught, and burned, and began to rage.

Faythe couldn't bring the Shopkeeper back, but perhaps she could still save the Shop.

Moments later, the office door slammed shut once more, and Faythe was gone.

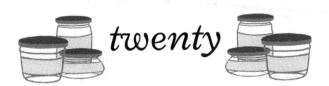# *twenty*

UNFORTUNATELY, being incredibly motivated doesn't actually solve anything.

Faythe wasn't an action hero, like from the stories. What was she going to do—run headlong to the Supplier's Complex to face Zariel in an epic one-on-one confrontation? Only an idiot would try that.

After some thought—well, after some confused charging around, and then some thought—she realised that Zariel had been right about one thing. She was, for better or worse, the Acting Shopkeeper at the Shop Before Life, which meant that the most powerful tool at her disposal was the Committee.

It wasn't clear how they'd be useful—perhaps she could invite Zariel to meetings and bore him into submission?—but she didn't have any other ideas. Perhaps they would have an arcane procedure which would force the Supplier to cooperate.

That evening, there was an unusually frosty atmosphere as she took her seat at an extraordinary meeting to discuss the ongoing supply problems. It seemed the Senior Children were already on edge.

"It's quite unacceptable!" Beris exclaimed, brandishing a paper in the air like it was a weapon. He was red-faced, and as close to shouting as Faythe had ever seen. "We cannot continue like this. Deliveries have been missed on seven of the last eleven days. Already, our emergency supplies are below forty percent. In mere days we will have to think the unthinkable."

This led to an outbreak of concerned muttering, presumably because nobody else could think what the unthinkable might be either.

"I'm still sure it's a simple oversight," said the Foreman. "The Supplier has never let us down before."

"If so, it's a pretty big coincidence," Omaro muttered, darkly.

"ENOUGH!" Beris thumped the table. "We've had ample talk of 'coincidences' already!"

Faythe shifted uncomfortably. It was excruciating to see Beris this upset, particularly since he used the word 'ample' like an assassin would use a dagger. It *sliced*.

She coughed, loudly, and the others turned to her in surprise. She had barely participated in meetings since the Shopkeeper's disappearance, instead sitting vacantly at the head of the table.

The implication of sitting here bothered her—she *wasn't* the Shopkeeper—especially when the Children turned in her direction in search of leadership. But she still preferred this seat. It meant she didn't have to look at the accusatory gap where the Shopkeeper ought to be.

She had no idea what to say. Perhaps tilting their attention towards Zariel would be enough. "Omaro's right," she said, hesitantly. "Zariel is being hostile."

Beris and the Foreman exchanged amazed glances. Too late, she saw where this intervention would inevitably lead.

"Hostile?" said Beris. "What do you know?! I don't think anybody was suggesting—"

"I am," interrupted Omaro, leaning forward with sudden energy. "It's simple. Zariel has spent years causing trouble. Then the Shopkeeper disappeared at the Complex. If that's not hostile, what is?" He glared around the table, daring anybody to disagree.

Incongruously, Faythe wondered how long it had been since she'd last seen him with his yoyo.

Beris' expression was pained. "We agreed that our priority is to keep the Shop open, which means maintaining good relations with the Supplier. I don't see how accusing him of—what? Kidnapping?!—is supposed to help."

"And I still agree," said Omaro. "But I doubt Zariel will even reply to your letters. We should be searching his Complex for her."

The Foreman looked puzzled. "But didn't you visit the Supplier already, and everything was fine?"

"I said it *seemed* fine. They showed us around, all smiles, and Zariel acted surprised when I mentioned the Shopkeeper hadn't made it home. But I'm sure he was lying."

Beris frowned. "Why would he be helpful at all?"

"He was *too* helpful," insisted Omaro. "I hardly saw any of the Complex. If he has her locked up, she could be anywhere."

Faythe grimaced. Everything about this was painful, but it especially hurt to see the Children in distress. Worse, their belief the Shopkeeper was still alive felt like needles in her heart.

Omaro hadn't finished. He banged his fist on the table. "So, I'm not willing to pretend it's a coincidence that he's starting to miss deliveries. And I'm pleased to see that the Appren—the *Acting Shopkeeper*—agrees with me, at last. Please finish what you were saying, Faythe."

As one, the Committee turned towards her. An icy terror spread throughout her chest. In the whole prelife, nearly everybody she could call a friend was sitting at this table. Tapak had gone to Earth, Jahu could be anywhere, and Zariel and the Shopkeeper . . .

The Children could never learn the truth—or she'd lose them too. After all, their natural response would be to ask why she hadn't told them already. And, eventually, her role in what happened would come out. She suppressed a shiver.

"I was just thinking," she said, swallowing nervously. "That, um, maybe it's best if we presumed Zariel was hostile. Then if we discover he isn't, it'll be a pleasant surprise. Meanwhile, is there anything we could do to, I don't know, compel him to send over more traits?"

Omaro was unimpressed. "So, you're sticking to your story, then? What about the Shopkeeper?"

"Story?" She blinked. *Innocent people blink, right? But maybe not quite so much.* To compensate, she held her eyes open wider. *Did that look worse?* She had no idea.

"Your story that everything was fine when you left the Supplier, and you know nothing about the Shopkeeper's disappearance."

She stared at him helplessly. She hated this. Words formed in her mind: *I was there. I killed her.* But instead, her mouth reflexively lied. "I didn't see anything."

Beris toyed anxiously with his glasses, his earlier frustration replaced with an air of awkward desperation. "I don't know about any of this. It all seems so improbable. But perhaps you're right that the lack of supplies is not a coincidence. In which case, we must inform Management before the crisis escalates further. This would normally be the Shopkeeper's duty."

Faythe's stomach plummeted. *Management.* That would be the worst imaginable outcome. Surely Management wouldn't be pleased to hear that their chosen Apprentice had killed the Shopkeeper.

"Let's not rush to any hasty action," she said, quickly.

Too quickly. Omaro narrowed his eyes, but she kept talking before he could interrupt. "Maybe, uh, this *is* a terrible coincidence. Let's take time to think, and we'll revisit everything in the next meeting. In the meantime, Risk and his team can continue searching for the Shopkeeper. And we all very much hope that they are successful." *They won't be, of course.* She had never hated herself more than in that exact moment. "In the meantime, Beris, can you update us on the accounts?"

She waited for an outcry, for somebody to question her authority, to insist that they contact Management. But the protest never came.

Beris launched into his regular report. While he talked, Omaro caught her eye. She held his gaze only briefly before she had to look away.

The next day saw the first fight between customers over the dwindling supplies. In true human tradition, they fought over the final jar of PEACEFUL.

Over the days that followed, such fights became more and more common. After a further fortnight without deliveries, entire aisles of the Shop stood bare. Faythe hated the sight of the towering, empty shelves, so she took to hiding in the Gardens whenever possible.

She watched the Gardener poking intently at a plant. "How do you know what you're doing?"

He didn't look up. "I don't—least, not always. Sometimes what you do is less important than the fact you're doing something. And, if in doubt: water it." He considered this for a moment. "Unless you're doubting whether it's drowning, in which case, probably don't."

She suspected the noble art of gardening was more complex than that, but today wasn't the day to learn. She hugged her knees. From above, the sound of a Security whistle drifted down over the Gardens. They must be breaking up yet another fight.

"I can't believe how quickly everything's falling apart," she said. "A few missed deliveries, and this happens."

"I dunno," muttered the Gardener, engrossed once more in his work. "Ever get annoyed when someone else moves something of yours? Imagine you can't find your trowel. Wrecks your entire day. Now imagine that, but scaled up."

She frowned. "Like a huge trowel?"

"More like thousands of trowels disappearing at once." He gestured around with an outstretched finger. "If I stop work entirely, it's not just me that's missing. It's every little bit of work I do. Every part of the Gardens would eventually overgrow, right?"

"I don't get it. All this fighting is like the Shop overgrowing?"

"Sure. The Shop is just a different kind of garden. Each little part is missing what it needs. All those Children hanging around without any trains to unload get bored. The customers get frustrated they can't have what they want. More and more customers every day, and everybody on edge. Thousands of trowels, all missing."

He was right. It had been many days since a normal amount of customers had managed to pass through, which meant the crowd in the field outside was steadily growing with no release in sight. The air was buzzing with barely repressed anger.

"Now, the trowel in this analogy is especially interesting," continued the Gardener.

But she never got to hear why, as they were interrupted by a harassed-looking Child running into the clearing. "Ma'am—" she said.

Faythe glared at her. She'd told everybody not to call her that.

"Sorry," said the Child. "I meant not-ma'am, ma'am . . . uh . . . Can you come? The Committee is meeting and it's not good."

A meeting? Faythe didn't know what she was talking about. With a quick apologetic wave to the Gardener, she followed the Child up the hill as quickly as she could.

Inside the Shop, many of the Committee were arguing loudly by the checkouts, right in front of the few straggling customers who were picking the last scraps from the Shop.

Once more, Beris was yelling. "This is immoral! We can't allow customers into the Shop if we lack the traits they require. We have to consider closing the Shop."

The Child shook his fist. This crisis was revealing sides of people that Faythe had never imagined existed.

Omaro replied more calmly. "We all know what happens if we don't keep the system flowing. You think *this* is bad? Things will explode if we close."

Risk, who was unconsciously twiddling his Security badge, interrupted. "He's right. The queue is already reaching the Road. I've put an extra team on duty to manage the additional customers, but we're struggling."

"Thanks," said Omaro. "But we can't close, or the queue will reach halfway to Ostholme. Everybody who can pass through, must pass through, or that crowd's going to grow and grow. It'll get nasty."

Beris bit his lip. "But we can't let them pass through without the traits they require! It's *wrong*."

"Nobody disagrees, Beris." The passion suddenly drained from Omaro's voice. He sounded tired. "But I had to break up three fights today. And those were between people who were getting to pass through. Everybody outside is even angrier."

Faythe watched impassively. It was a pity that few customers shared her old desire to hang around in the prelife. Most just came straight here from the Beginning. The human instinct to live was too powerful.

"Zariel still hasn't responded to any letters," said Beris. "And our last train was turned back by his 'Zeraph'."

"We're going to need a plan for what to do if the situation here gets fully out of control," said Omaro.

"I'm on that, sir," said Risk.

Beris fiddled with his cufflinks. "I'm also concerned about the situation on Earth."

Faythe gritted her teeth. She kept forgetting the Earth didn't just look after itself. She barged into the circle. "Aside from helping people to pass through, what can we do about Earth?" she asked.

The Committee turned to her. Strangely, that was starting to feel normal.

"Nothing," said Beris.

Omaro smiled grimly. "At least nobody from Earth ever comes to complain."

His joke was lost on Beris. "That's because they can't. But I wasn't concerned about our complaint statistics. I believe that Earth society would fracture without babies. Wars would start."

"We'll have wars of our own here," said Risk. "We're not far off."

Beris' lower lip quivered. "It's rather more serious on Earth. Here, nobody can truly die."

Except the Shopkeeper. Faythe's heart froze at the unprompted—and unwelcome—thought.

"And if everybody on Earth dies," continued Beris, "nobody can pass through again. The Earth needs us to replenish itself, but we need them to provide a destination for our customers."

There was a sudden uncomfortable silence. "Thanks for the reminder, Beris," quipped Faythe.

Quiet swallowed the group once more.

"Why don't we bring back the lucky dip?" suggested a Child from the administrative team, eventually. A chorus of scoffs went up around the circle, but Faythe held up a hand. "Lucky dip?"

The Child looked embarrassed, so Beris spoke up. "It's an idea we tried a long time ago, to accelerate passing customers through the Shop. Everybody received a selection of traits chosen at random."

Faythe's face twisted in instinctive disgust.

"Exactly." Omaro laughed mirthlessly. "Everybody really hated it. There were constant fights and arguments until we gave in and went back to the system we have now. Imagine trying to tell them"—he jabbed a thumb towards the front door, where the low, irate rumble of the waiting crowd could be heard—"that they don't get to choose anything about their lives."

"It's also immoral," added Beris.

Faythe agreed. Deciding people's lives by lottery was a horrible idea. It would be absurd if the universe relied on pure luck and accidents of birth. Still, it was *an* idea. "Thanks," she said to the blushing Child. "But it's probably not the answer we're looking for."

Silence returned, the silence of a group entirely out of ideas, each hoping that somebody else would be inspired any moment now. Faythe felt the heaviness of responsibility. She was in charge, at least in theory. What would a real wise old Shopkeeper do?

She mentally conjured an image of her old employer. 'What should I do, Shopkeeper?' she asked, inside her mind.

The imaginary Shopkeeper gave her a disparaging look. "I'm just you in your imagination. I don't have thousands of years of experience. I only know what you know." *That made sense. Stupid idea, really.* "But maybe what you already know is enough?"

Yuck. That sounded suspiciously like an attempt to commit wisdom. Still, perhaps it was worth exploring.

She thought hard, and a new—albeit horrible—idea surfaced. "Could we fake new supplies? Or dilute them?" she suggested.

The silence mutated from tense to horrified.

"Fake supplies?" Beris looked as if she had suggested setting fire to her own face. "You surely don't mean that?"

"I meant— relabel some jars? Or mix them in a way that spreads them out a little more." She gulped. "Only until the situation calms down."

The Committee's faces strongly suggested that they liked this idea even less than she did. "Okay, not that," she said. "I was just thinking aloud."

"Faythe?" Beris looked at her over his glasses. "I believe it's time to request aid from Management."

She tried not to panic. She *couldn't* talk to Management. Once she confessed what she'd done to the Shopkeeper—of course, they must know already, but even telling them would be excruciating—exile in the prelife might not be the worst possible fate which awaited her.

"I don't think we need Management yet," she said, her voice dripping with fake confidence. Omaro opened his mouth to object, but she didn't allow him to speak. "I have a plan."

Incredibly, some ideas presented themselves. "First, no public

this in future," she said. "There might only be a few
it, but this is still a professional organisation."
oval from the group. Immediately, the mood lifted.
of action felt like progress. And professional pride
was important. *What had the Gardener said about little things?* Maybe
it worked both ways—tiny positive changes could add up.

Feeling more confident, she continued. "Second, I think Omaro
made an important point. For now, we have to prioritise keeping the
flow moving. We can't allow the crowd to build up, or there'll be riots."

Risk nodded. "The situation is volatile already. Closure, even temporary, would set the whole thing off."

"Exactly." She smiled, grateful for the support—and considerably
more grateful that the group had been steered away from thoughts of
Management.

A quiet voice in the back of her mind suggested that she couldn't
possibly hope to hide her actions from the powers-that-be forever, but
she shushed it.

Short-term thinking only, that was the key.

"So, here's my idea," she said, giddily. The idea was forming even as
she spoke. "How about pre-screening the customers?"

Beris frowned. "How would that work?"

"We take an inventory of remaining jars. We find specific customers
who match those jars, and let them in ahead. This will reduce the pressure, right?"

Risk scratched his head. "Abandoning the queue won't be popular."

"Perhaps. But it'll be more popular than the queue not moving at all.
Alongside this, we could let in small numbers of people from the front
of the queue, like normal. Keep the flow going by any means possible."

*And under no circumstances do we inform Management of anything
whatsoever.*

Beris nodded. "This could work."

She clapped. "Then let's go."

Most of the Committee scattered, leaving her alone with Omaro. "You
did good just now," he said. "You seem better, lately."

"I am. Though I have no idea what I'm doing," she said.

"That," said the Child, "is usually the correct state to be in."

She hoped he was right about that.

"And if you want to talk . . . ?" he said.

She shook her head. "I know where you are."

He smiled at her sadly, and left to work on the pre-screening system.

Somewhere far away, on a planet called Earth, the person who had once been known as Tapak turned to his wife.

"I'm sure the doctors know what they're doing," he said.

She rested her hands on her swollen stomach with a doubtful look. "If even being chemically induced doesn't work, what will?"

The person who had no memory of the name Tapak tapped a few keys on a device. "It says here pineapples might do it?"

"Pineapples?"

"Yeah. Pineapples . . . and spices. And a hot bath."

She didn't look convinced, but he took her by the hand and led her away from the rapidly growing crowd in the maternity ward.

"I'm sure a spicy pineapple will be delicious," he lied, with a smile. "Let's get out of here."

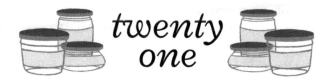

twenty one

THE NEW PRE-SCREENING system was a hastily conceived change, implemented to a tight deadline, under immense pressure, at a large, complex organisation.

Success was surely guaranteed.

At first, everything appeared to proceed smoothly. Questionnaires were swiftly drawn up to distribute among the crowd. Afterwards, while the next wave of questionnaires began to circulate, the administrative team frantically matched customers' answers against the dwindling inventory of remaining traits. The lucky few whose desires could be fulfilled were then invited inside to pass through.

Unfortunately, immense work was required for every single customer, which made the system painfully slow. Each questionnaire must be processed and the relevant traits gathered before the customer themselves could be fetched from the field—which was a tricky task in itself. Not only was it hard to identify a particular individual in such a vast crowd, once people realised what was happening, impostors began to pretend to be whoever the Children were looking for. And, naturally, it wasn't long before fights broke out over the questionnaires themselves.

Faythe couldn't blame them for fighting. The people wanted to live, they were impatient, and they were getting increasingly desperate. She knew the feeling. As time wore on, they were able to find fewer and fewer customers whose needs could be fulfilled with the remaining jars.

She'd put herself in charge of finding acceptable substitutes for customers who could be nearly satisfied by the existing stock. LOQUA-CIOUS could stand in for TALKATIVE, for example. EASY-GOING might just about work when GOOD HUMOURED ran dry. But as the stocks diminished, she struggled to find a combination of jars which could meet any customer's needs.

Her latest customer wanted HARDWORKING, but she was trying to get rid of a surplus of SEES THE GOOD IN EVERYTHING.

"If you see the good in everything," she said, uncertainly, "you'll be more likely to work hard. It's basically the same thing."

The customer gave a doubtful squint at the jar. Inside, a bright yellow gas swirled, sparkling like sunshine. "I guess it does look nice," he said.

She gratefully seized the opportunity. "Exactly! It looks lovely, *and* it does just what you need. Mostly." She thrust it into his basket, and spun him by the shoulder before he could think twice. "The checkouts are right over there. They'll show you where to go next. Best of luck on Earth!"

As soon as the customer was gone, Beris scuttled over. "Acting Shop-keeper," he began. Everybody called her that now. She'd given up trying to dissuade them. "More people have passed through today than on any day in the last two weeks."

"That's good news," she said, rubbing her temples. When had she last taken a break? She couldn't remember. Over Beris' shoulder, the doubt-ful customer was being pointed towards the corridor leading to Earth.

"Ye-es," said Beris. But he didn't look pleased. "There's also bad news. For every person that passed through today, I estimate that two more people arrived from the Road."

She pinched the bridge of her nose, closed her eyes, and sighed. "Really? The questionnaires, the matching, the crowd control, the trait substitutions . . . after all that, everything is worse, not better?"

"I'm afraid so. We simply can't serve enough customers to even main-tain the queue at the existing size, let alone shrink it. And even if we could, our supplies will be exhausted sooner than I estimated. Just now we ran out of ABILITY TO MAKE DO, for example."

She stared at the floor for a moment before looking up. It was clear what must be done, but she didn't like it. "Tell the Committee I'm closing the Shop," she said, eventually. "Start with Risk—he'll need extra bodies

on Security duty, I imagine. And afterwards, I'll . . . I'll fix everything."
She didn't know what that meant—yet.

Beris nodded, though his eyes flashed with worry. "Very well. I think
that's the right decision. Should I tell Risk to announce it publicly too?"

She shook her head. "I'll do that."

He moved as if to speak, but apparently thought better of it. With a
final nod, he skittered away.

As she fetched the megaphone from the office, she became aware of
a growing tightness in her chest. At first, it was indistinguishable from
the constant background guilt she'd long since become accustomed to.
But on closer inspection, her conscience was tingling even more uncomfortably than usual.

Suddenly, she realised why. *She had lied to that last customer.* He was
taking the wrong trait down to Earth.

Quickly, she spun on her heels and sprinted to the passing-through
corridor. She shouted to the guard on duty. "That customer, with the face
and the hair and the jar of SEES THE GOOD IN EVERYTHING—where
is he?"

The Child looked nonplussed. "Him? He's just gone. He passed
through already."

She cursed, feeling sick with shame. She'd selfishly messed with that
man's life. All of this, everything that was happening, it was *her* fault—all
of it! And everything she tried only made things worse.

She clenched her fist and screamed.

A few seconds later, she felt a tug on her arm. "Are you okay?" asked
Omaro.

She shook her head. "I'm closing the Shop. I'm fine, though. Just
needed to vent."

Her friend cocked his head. "You sure?"

"Yes. No. Maybe." She took a deep breath. "I convinced a customer
to pass through with a trait that wasn't even close to what he wanted. I
know we need people to pass through, but . . . not like this."

The Child reached up to put a comforting hand on her shoulder. She
ducked down to hug him.

"Thanks," she said. "I don't know what it'll mean for his life that he
took the wrong traits."

"The Shopkeeper used to say to trust the customers. If he agreed to take it, that was his choice."

"I know." She winced at his use of the past tense. Did he not believe the Shopkeeper would come back? He was right, of course, but . . . it hurt to think that he'd given up. "I remember. 'People grow beyond what they pick here', and all that. Doesn't make me feel better, though."

He shrugged. "You're doing your best."

Automatically, she opened her mouth to deflect the undeserved praise, but she closed it again. He was right. She was trying. "I'm sorry we're closing the Shop," she said, instead. "I know you didn't want to."

He shook his head. "I was wrong. It's worse than I thought—we've near enough run out of everything."

"It'll be okay," she said, with more hope than confidence.

"It will. And I'm happy to see you being yourself again." The Child grinned. "I was thinking . . . if everything falls apart, maybe we could open a toy shop? I know how to make them now."

She smiled back. "You know, as long as we only need one type of toy, and never need to sell more than one a year, that's a great plan."

A short time later, she and Omaro stepped onto the verandah at the front of the Shop, flanked by a small group of Security wearing blue uniforms.

She put her hand to her forehead and stared out over the field. People were packed shoulder-to-shoulder, an ocean of indistinguishable faces bobbing back and forth as they jostled for position. Before the crisis, the queue usually began near to the tangle of old buildings at the end of the Shop, but it now filled the field and snaked all the way along the Road and up the hill, spilling out over the hillside—and presumably beyond, as the Road crested the summit to disappear out of sight. There were odd splashes of colour dotted around where people had built shelters out of whatever they happened to be carrying. One enterprising musician had even constructed an impromptu stage and was entertaining a small gathering.

Closer to the Shop, the crowd was more dense, and it quaked in places as people fought to get closer to the small groups of Children who were handing out pre-screening questionnaires. Just down the stairs from the front door, a thin line of red rope and the linked arms of the Security team was all that held the people back.

Her observation was interrupted by a nudge from Omaro. Together, they moved along the verandah. They would announce the closure near the middle of the main building.

As they walked, Faythe attempted to project an image of confidence and strong leadership. Unfortunately, she wasn't sure exactly how. As soon as she concentrated on her arms and legs she seemingly forgot how to walk. Was she bobbing too much? And did her arms normally swing out this far? Or was that a sign of nerves? Maybe she should swing them less ... or would *that* signify a lack of confidence?

Like an awkward robot octopus, she bumbled to the centre of the platform. She lifted the megaphone to her mouth, and hesitated. Her announcement after the incident with Tapak hadn't exactly been a success. And this time there was no Shopkeeper to step in and save her. She'd better start strongly.

"Er, excuse me," she stammered. Her words drifted, getting lost in the babble of the crowd. "I'm from the Shop Before Life."

The background chatter rose in volume as many people individually made the exact same joke to their neighbours: 'No! You don't say!'

She pressed on. "As you have noticed, we've been having problems." Her amplified voice rang uncomfortably in her ears. Did she normally sound so reedy? "We apologise for the wait. Let me reassure you that we are helping as many people pass through to Earth as we possibly can." She paused for breath. *So far, so good.*

A shout came from the crowd. "When will everything be fixed?"

"I don't know," she said. Frustrated mutters rippled through the assembly, followed by a secondary wave as those who were further away asked one another what she had said. She could virtually see rumours beginning to fly in the bobbles of the crowd. She ought to placate them before delivering the truly bad news. "I'm sorry. I really don't know how long it'll take. But I promise we're doing our best."

The mood was shifting. Some people, sensing an outlet for their frustration, began to boo.

Omaro tugged at her arm. "You can't talk to crowds like they're people," he muttered.

She frowned. "But they *are* people."

"Sure, everyone *in* a crowd is. But the crowd itself isn't. It's more like a wild animal. You have to keep stroking it, or it bites." He looked thoughtful. "Except you probably aren't meant to stroke wild animals, now I think about it. Anyway—"

"I get it," she said. Her heartbeat thumped in her temples as she raised the megaphone again. She tried to remember how the Shopkeeper had calmed the crowd last time. "You're all being very patient, and we thank you for your co-operation."

That was it. Thanking people for co-operation they aren't actually giving is a surprisingly effective means of making them more co-operative.

"Today has been difficult for all of us," she continued. The sun was beginning to sink behind the Shop, turning the sky gently orange. *Stroke the animal. Say soothing words.* "Everybody is working extremely hard to fix the situation."

The nearby crowd were all listening now. A cool breeze was blowing across the verandah, although the people below were still sweltering after the hot afternoon. The boos may have stopped, but the atmosphere still fizzled with repressed frustration.

She swallowed uncomfortably. Having stroked the hungry animal, she now must deny it food. "However, I'm afraid I have unfortunate news. The supply situation is worse than we thought, and, reluctantly, we must close the Shop."

A loud, angry buzz radiated outwards from the verandah as the news spread amongst the crowd.

She tried to keep her voice bright and optimistic. "I know this is difficult," she yelled, fighting to be heard over the crescendo of chatter. "But I promise we are working as hard as we can, and we'll keep you updated. I personally am planning to—"

It was pointless. She couldn't be heard over the shouts and boos raining down. She looked to Omaro for support. He shook his head and gestured towards the front door. She lowered the megaphone and turned to walk back inside.

A man with a loud voice shouted up from below. "What are we supposed to do? I've been here a week! I'm hungry!"

She kept her head down as more questions followed in a flood of unconcealed fury.

"We've been waiting for days too!"

"Why won't you tell us why?"

"We deserve answers!"

"Where's the Shopkeeper? Why haven't we seen her?"

"She's lying!"

"She doesn't want us to live!"

The hubbub rose in intensity. A chant broke out and began to spread. "We. Won't. Stop! Open. The. Shop! We. Won't. Stop! Open. The. Shop!"

The noise had become deafening, impossible to make out individual shouts anymore. The constant jostling beneath the verandah was morphing into pushes and shoves as people fought to get to the front, desperately hoping to make it inside. Yells and boos and hisses followed them as they raced back to the entrance.

Suddenly, a clod of earth flew past, narrowly missing Faythe's head before it thumped into the wall, scattering mud over the wooden verandah.

Omaro's imaginary animal was furious. Then someone, somewhere threw something else. It didn't matter what they'd thrown, who their target was, or why they'd done it. It only mattered that it missed its intended target—if there was one—and hit somebody. Seconds later, a retaliatory object was thrown backwards into the crowd. Within moments, a hail of dirt, stones, shoes, and whatever else people had to hand flew into the air. Pushes and shoves became punches and kicks, and screams of rage and pain mingled with the ongoing chants and shouts and whistles.

A shrill, loud whistle erupted as more Security poured out of the Shop to charge into the crowd, who fell back before surging forward, battling the Children and one another alike.

Faythe watched in horror as the mayhem escalated. Along the platform, a man was scrabbling to climb up onto the verandah. "I just want to live!" he yelled, before getting pulled down by others trying to clamber up around him.

Further along the building, others had already succeeded in getting up. They advanced towards the door, brandishing sticks and other makeshift weapons.

Omaro was tugging at her arm. "Come on!" he said, urgently.

"But, we need to . . ."

"There's nothing we can do!" He grabbed her hand and pulled her towards the door. "Get inside!"

He held the door open. Behind them, Risk whistled a signal, and Security followed them in retreat.

As soon as the last guard made it in, they slammed the thick wooden door shut. Immediately, it bulged in its frame as the people outside threw themselves against it.

They must be getting crushed, thought Faythe, alarmed.

There was a sudden sound of smashing glass. She turned desperately to Risk.

"That's windows being broken all along the verandah, ma'—Faythe," he said.

She looked at him helplessly. "I don't know what to do," she stuttered.

"My team are defending the inner perimeter. And I've sent for the night shift to reinforce. We'll get this under control." Now the windows were broken, the roar of furious rioters echoed throughout the building. "What do you want me to do with those that get inside?"

She could barely understand his words. Everything was spinning. "Do with them?" she repeated.

"Yes. Do you want us to arrest them? Capture them? Put them back outside?"

"Um." She picked at random. "Put them back outside." That sounded humane. But was it the best option? She had no idea.

Risk barked orders as his team swarmed in all directions. Faythe became aware that an alarm was sounding above the cacophony: a gong crashing, over-and-over. Someone had had the sense to activate the mechanism while she had been doing nothing.

"I'm sorry," she gasped to Omaro, as he led her towards the administrative area. "I'm useless."

"You're not useless."

"This is all my fault. I said all the wrong things to the crowd." Behind them, the shouts were getting closer. "Shouldn't we be helping?"

He grunted. "This isn't your fault. This was inevitable as soon as we started running low on supplies. You can't take away people's chance to live and not expect consequences."

Just then, there was a tremendous crashing sound from behind.

"What was that?!" She stopped and looked back in alarm.

"Sounds like they knocked over a whole shelf."

"We should help! They could trash the whole Shop!"

Omaro shook his head. "You and I would not be helpful in this situation. Trust me—Security have trained for this. We need to stay out of the way." He led her into the conference room and sat her at the table.

"Tea?" He waved a mug.

"Seriously?!"

He shrugged. "No sense in going thirsty just because there's a riot."

She rolled her eyes and slumped into a seat. They waited.

Eventually the sounds of distant destruction began to fade. By the time it was quiet, the sun had gone down.

Omaro broke their long silence. "Sounds like it's burned itself out."

"Or they destroyed the whole Shop."

"Nah. They wouldn't have left this wing standing."

That wasn't especially reassuring. Just then, Risk entered the room. "Ma'am. Faythe. Everything's under control," he said. "Luckily, most people wanted to shop, not destroy. A few tried to pass through but they couldn't break the door down. Once we subdued the loudest, everyone surrendered and allowed us to lead them back outside."

"And how is it outside?" asked Omaro.

"Hard to tell, sir." Risk thought for a moment. "Calmer, but unhappy."

"That's an improvement, at least," said Omaro. "The Shop is still standing. Well done, Risk."

"Yes, thank you," Faythe said, filled with sudden gratitude. "You handled this fantastically well. And I'm so sorry about everything."

"It's not your fault, ma'am." Risk saluted and marched out.

Omaro grinned. "He gets all military at times like this. It's quite fun to watch. Or it would be, if the Shop wasn't getting wrecked at the time."

Faythe smiled weakly. Whatever they kept saying, everything *was* her fault. Even if the riot wasn't, the supply problems were.

Not to mention the Shopkeeper's absence. She would have known what to do.

With a heavy heart, she went to survey the damage.

It was after midnight when the frazzled Committee met once more. The damage was extensive, especially in the aisles closest to the field, which had been smashed into a heap of broken glass and fragmented wood. Most worrying were the scorchmarks where a rioter had attempted to set fire to the shelves, in defiance of all rational thinking. Faythe had been amazed and appalled by this, but Risk hadn't been surprised. "There's always a few," he'd said, shaking his head.

Luckily, no fire had caught on, or the meeting—and all future Committee meetings, forever—might have been taking place outdoors.

They were stood in a clear space on the concourse. Already, all but a few of the broken windows had been boarded up, and Risk's team were patrolling inside and along the verandah. High above, the Earth shone brightly through the dome, illuminating the Committee and the nearby aisles in a pale green-blue light.

"At least we didn't have much stock left to smash, right?" said Omaro, brightly, after a long silence.

Faythe gave him a withering look, but Beris stuttered in reply. "I think that was rather the trouble, no?" A pause. "Oh, you were joking."

The group fell back into silence. Through the boarded-up windows, the quiet night-time chatter of the pent-up mass of humanity could still be heard. Faythe shifted uncomfortably. It was eerie knowing the crowd were so close, even if right now they were calm.

"Any ideas?" she asked, desperately trying to distract herself.

The concourse filled with the distinctive sound of people pretending to think. Finally, Beris waved his glasses in the air. "There are no other options. We simply must report this to Management."

Her stomach churned. He was right. Only Management had the power to stop this now. But Management would want to know how the riot came about, and where the Shopkeeper was, and what was Faythe's part in all this, exactly, and . . .

She feared Management's questions even more than she feared another riot.

Just.

She shook her head. "Not yet. We can solve this ourselves. How about . . . um . . ." An idea struck her. It was so obvious. "Everyone just wants to pass through, don't they? Why don't we simply let them?"

Beris narrowed his eyes. "Let them..?"

"Without traits! Everyone could just go directly to Earth. That would reduce the crowd back to a manageable size. Just until we get the supplies restarted, of course."

His face twisted in disgust. "That's abhorrent! Immoral! We would be failing in our duty to prepare our customers for life!"

"Oh." Now he put it like that, it did sound terrible. "Yeah. It was just an idea."

She frowned. There must be something they could do.

But Omaro spoke up next. "I'm afraid I also don't see any other options. We need Management."

An unpleasant claustrophobia gripped her tightly. She desperately scrabbled for more ideas. "I know! Let me try talking to Zariel." The Children exchanged glances. "One final time."

"I suppose I could attempt to arrange another meeting," said Beris, politely. "Again."

Omaro was less diplomatic. "That's ridiculous!" he exclaimed. "He won't even respond to our letters, never mind meet with us."

"He'll meet me," she said. *Even if I have to break in to see him*, she added, mentally. Anything was preferable to facing the wrath of Management.

"And even if he will meet you," replied Omaro, "are you sure it's safe?"

"Safe?" She laughed nervously, pretending not to understand. "How could it possibly be unsafe?"

He was unmoved. "That's exactly what the Shopkeeper said, just before she disappeared."

She swallowed. *How well did she know Zariel, really?* For a time, she'd been convinced they were kindred spirits, but that belief had disappeared into the void along with the Shopkeeper. Even so, she was fairly sure he wouldn't erase her entirely from existence.

He hadn't even intended to delete the Shopkeeper—*she* had done that. Guilt stabbed deeply into her heart. Perhaps being erased from existence wouldn't be so bad.

She shushed herself. She would fix this. She *would*.

"Why would it be unsafe?" Beris looked around in confusion. She envied his innocence. It would never occur to him that anybody might mess with an efficiently working system for merely personal reasons.

"If you go, I'm coming with you," insisted Omaro.

Her heart lurched. She desperately wanted to accept. But she couldn't risk him learning the truth.

"I think it would be better if I went alone," she said, as confidently as she could manage. "I'm sure he'll talk to me." *Mostly, anyway.* "And somebody needs to be in charge here—and that's you."

They stared at one another until he pulled a face. "Fine," he muttered. He looked around at the despondent expressions of the rest of the group. "I wish we could take all those rioters to mess his place up."

She laughed. "If only!" She mouthed a thank-you to Omaro, partly relieved that he'd given in, but mostly grateful that he'd made the other Children smile. "Okay, let's end it there. I'll go see Zariel first thing tomorrow. I promise that if that doesn't work, we'll involve Management afterwards. Thank you all—for everything. Get some sleep."

After the Committee dispersed, Omaro sought her out. "You don't have to keep everything secret, you know."

Oh good, well, in that case, I actually killed the Shopkeeper.

"I don't know what you mean," she said. "Everything's fine."

"Glad to hear it," he replied with a straight face. "And if it turns out it really, honestly isn't fine, you know where I am."

She sat alone for a while and stared out of the window.

In a twisted way, it would be a relief to see Zariel. There would be no secrets, no barriers, no lurking unthinkable confessions which would immediately destroy her last remaining relationships in the universe. Constantly feigning ignorance about the missing Shopkeeper was exhausting.

Plus, now that she was free of any illusions about Zariel himself, she could shout, scream, and cajole until he had no choice but to restart the deliveries. For the first time, they'd meet on *her* terms.

She slumped forward and slept on her arms on the conference room table. She awoke to find that, during the night, somebody had slipped a blanket over her. She went to her bed and slept fitfully.

Around now . . .

. . . whatever *now* means in a complex universe where time runs at different speeds depending on how fast you're going, and who knows how it behaves compared to a prelife which is mysteriously sideways from Earth . . .

. . . at a moment which was somehow related to when Faythe was asleep, anyway . . .

Around *now*, down on Earth, a woman died. She had been seventeen months pregnant.

Another woman reached nine months of pregnancy, only to wake and find her womb empty one morning, as if the pregnancy had never been.

In most countries of the world, fertility clinics were open twenty-four hours a day, except where they'd been forced to close due to riots.

It had been a long time since a baby had been born to anyone, anywhere.

twenty two

FAYTHE DIDN'T QUITE MANAGE to relax enough to actively enjoy her third-ever journey on a train, but she felt deeply relieved once the Shop disappeared from sight. For a brief period, she could let go of her problems—the lying, the guilt, the missing traits, and, most of all, the ever-expanding, seething mass of humanity which waited outside. The Foreman left her alone to appreciate the view, speaking only to offer a choice of equally disappointing refreshments while the beautiful countryside zoomed by. It was almost peaceful enough for her to forget the reason for her trip.

Almost.

It wasn't long before the vast industrial mess of the Supplier's Complex loomed into view; at first, a distant cloud of smoke hovered above the mountains, with tips of belching chimneys resolving slowly as they approached; then the sudden darkness and equally sudden brightness of the tunnel; before, finally, the chaotic, overwhelming sprawl encircled them as they descended to a halt in the station.

As she had half-expected, a group of Zeraph were waiting. They stood on the platform, brandishing their wholly unnecessary—and, frankly, showy—flaming swords.

She grinned and waved as she disembarked. "No need for the weapons. It's only me!"

It was strangely calming to know that if Zariel really wanted to capture and delete her, she wouldn't be able to stop him. Just as in the collapsing tunnel, her complete absence of options was freeing. Maybe she should spend more time in mortal danger.

"I'm the Acting Shopkeeper," she said, with almost genuine cheerfulness. "He'll want to see me."

The Zeraph exchanged glances. One of them, indistinguishable from the others, shrugged. "Follow us," he said.

"What choice do I have?" she asked. They didn't reply.

She followed them through the strange, glassy streets of the Complex. Once more she was unsettled to be invisible amongst the busy froth of human activity. It was an alien sensation—at the Shop, proximity usually led to connection, but that didn't seem to be true here. She got the sense that even if she tripped someone up, they'd still barely acknowledge her existence.

Even those who were guarding her didn't seem to pay much attention. She was slightly perturbed by the disrespect—they could at least pretend she might be a threat. Although, admittedly, each of them was so much larger than her that they might not notice even if she physically leapt on them from behind.

As if reading her thoughts, the backmost Zeraph turned and waved impatiently. "Hurry up!"

"Lucky for you I'm more diplomat than fighter," she muttered—very carefully, so he wouldn't hear.

They found Zariel by the crater inside his laboratory, which was even busier and more filled with ongoing construction than before. He was snapping orders at a swarm of uniformed employees.

"Ah," he said, noticing Faythe. "They told me there was another train. I wondered if it would be you this time. Come to admire my work?" He sounded disinterested, speaking without charm or malice—at least, that she could detect.

She peered down into the crater. At the bottom, several teams of workers clambered over the skeleton of an enormous machine. She couldn't make any sense of it. "It's nice," she said, politely. "But I expect you know why I'm here."

He frowned. "Do I?" An underling handed him a piece of paper, and he peered at it for an instant before handing it back with a nod. He glanced back to Faythe. "If you want the old jars back, you can't have them. They're gone."

Old jars?! He couldn't be serious.

"I'm not here for old jars," she said, biting her lip. The rocky chamber echoed with loud clanging from below. "I need you to restart the deliveries to the Shop."

He was staring into the crater, watching as a minion poked at the machine. It took a moment before he looked up, as if he'd only just realised what she'd said. "What? You came on behalf of the Shop?"

She blinked. "Yes..? Why else would I be here?"

His eyes narrowed. "I don't believe that." He folded his arms. "Why are you really here? What do you want?"

This was unexpected. She'd anticipated mockery, gloating, and maybe even something unpleasant involving fiery swords, but it had never occurred to her that Zariel might simply doubt her intentions.

"I want regular trait deliveries," she said.

"Why?!"

Frustration began to swell in her chest. "People need them!"

He scrunched up his face. "And? Why do you want them?"

"*Because* people need them!"

He paused, before barking a laugh. "Ha! And I used to think we were similar!"

Her frustration had transformed into pure rage. "So did I!" She threw her hands up in the air. "But that's because you lied. I thought we both cared about the same things. You pretended you wanted to open a new Shop!"

Zariel looked at her disdainfully. "I assumed you must be lying too. No wonder I couldn't figure it out."

His workers were waiting awkwardly nearby. Faythe caught one of their eyes and he looked away, embarrassed. For the briefest instant she felt irrationally guilty for keeping him waiting.

"Well now you know. Some people do genuinely care about things other than themselves."

"Ha!" Once again, he made the sound of a laugh without any of the amusement. "Oh, the good-hearted Apprentice *cares*. Isn't that impressive! Sure, she happily stole from the Shop to feed her own selfish curiosity. She consorted with the big bad ex-Apprentice. And she lied to her friends and colleagues, over and over and over. Most of all"—he leaned closer, almost whispering—"she killed the Shopkeeper." He spun around dramatically and addressed an imaginary audience. "But forget all of that, everybody! Because she cares so much for the Shop Before Life that she came all the way here to beg—"

She clenched her fists. "Stop," she said, quietly.

"—to beg on behalf of all humanity! What a grand example she is to us all. All of our hearts are so moved. Why, I—"

"*Stop!*" she cried.

His sneer never moved. "Honestly, I assumed you would have quit by now. Run home to your Rock, perhaps. When you showed up today, I assumed you were planning to ask to work here."

"Work here?!" That was absurd. Although . . . he was right about one thing. She dug her fingernails into her palm. "I did think about running away," she said, quietly.

Zariel's eyes sparkled with interest. "Oh? And why didn't you?"

She looked away. Why hadn't she? In those dark days, why had she stayed? She could have simply left—sought out Jahu, or hidden in Ostholme, or even escaped to Earth. Was it loyalty? Inertia? Fear of breaking a contract signed by Management?

They were interrupted by a loud screeching, as a worker pressed a heavy-looking tool into the machine beneath. The noise was almost intolerable, but Zariel didn't even look around.

Once the noise ceased, she had an answer. "I felt responsible," she said.

"Responsible!" Zariel nearly spat with disgust, as if the word tasted terrible in his mouth. "The Shopkeeper's obsession with responsibility was what killed her in the end. I truly thought you were different."

"I thought you were too."

The pair regarded each other.

Eventually, he nodded. "I suppose I shouldn't be surprised you don't see the bigger picture. Few do."

"I don't care about your bigger picture," she said, hotly. "I just want the deliveries back."

He snorted, and turned to face the crater with his hands behind his back. "Very well. Let me explain about your deliveries." He pointed to the large machine in the centre. "There are the machines which created the raw traits for processing."

She narrowed her eyes, unsure what he was telling her. "Oh?" she said.

"Actually, it used to be several."

The machine was nearly the size of a small house, all pipes and platforms and spiky wheels and glass. Workers shuffled in and out via hatches which were spread along the top and sides.

"Several machines? I don't understand."

"After my experiments on the traits themselves proved fruitless, I began taking the machines apart," said Zariel. "I wanted to understand where the traits came from. It turned out they originate in a single place—you probably remember it." He grinned at the blank look she gave him. "Where the Shopkeeper went."

Her eyelids flickered, and his mouth turned up in amusement—whether at the memory or at her reaction, she couldn't tell.

"Exactly. I knew you'd remember," he said. "The traits are synthesised from the essence which flows out of those voids. But outside of the machines, the essence always dissipates before I can do anything with it. Except put it in one of those accursed jars."

He paused. The sounds of construction reverberated up from the crater.

Despite herself, Faythe was interested. Her own experiments down this path had come to a very early halt. "So you took apart the machines?" she prompted.

"And put them back together, yes. But the voids weren't big enough. I could never capture enough essence."

It was starting to make sense. "So you took more machines apart . . ."

"Precisely!" He beamed with apparent excitement. "Except I didn't know how to make them larger. Thankfully, that's when I discovered correspondence from your Shopkeeper in my predecessor's office. From what she wrote, I deduced that he had shared his designs for larger machines with her."

"That's what you took from the Shop?"

"His half of the correspondence, yes."

"But . . . why didn't he keep his designs here?"

His face darkened. "He destroyed them."

A dozen reasons flew through Faythe's mind. Creative paranoia. Insanity. Selfishness. But one stood out in particular.

"To stop you seeing them..?"

"Yes."

She shivered.

"But not for the reason you're thinking. My predecessor liked to challenge me. He believed I could discover the truth for myself. And I did!"

She couldn't stop herself. "By reading his letters?"

He blinked. "Yes. But regardless of the means, *I* solved the mystery. With that information, I was able to fuse dissembled machines together and design this machine, which will produce the biggest portal to the void yet!"

"That's why the deliveries stopped! You dismantled the machines. I thought..." She trailed off.

"You thought I was being petty?" He laughed. "I don't care enough about the so-called Shop Before Life to bother with revenge. No, I needed these machines for a higher purpose."

The deafening sound from below started up again, but it only lasted a moment before being replaced with a high-pitched whine. Faythe was starting to get a headache.

"Fine," she said. "What's the higher purpose?"

"I've told you before. Once I know how traits are created, I can create my own."

She shook her head. "But what's the use of that?"

"Use?"

"What do you intend to do with them? What's the end goal? Do you want to rule the prelife? Take over Earth? Become a superman and do both? What's the aim of all this power?"

His eyes flashed. "Ask yourself: what do Management do with their power?"

"What have Management got to do with it?"

"Everything! Why should they have unlimited control while I must choose from their useless, restricted jars like everyone else?"

Her scalp tingled as sudden realisation washed over her. "You're jealous... of Management?" The idea was ludicrous. "I'm right, aren't I? You're jealous of gods."

"For now, perhaps. But I won't need to be jealous when I join them."

"*Join them?*"

She froze, mid-word, as the implications sunk in. Zariel's interest in the traits had never been for other people, or for Earth, or even for his own future life. He wanted to become a *god*. No wonder he apparently felt no remorse about the Shopkeeper—what's one human life, on that scale?

The idea was huge, colossal, staggering ... but it was also, still, so ... hollow. Confusingly, amusement bubbled deep inside her. "*Why?*"

"Does it matter?"

She couldn't help laughing. "You're preventing all of humanity from living so you can try to join the gods, so I think you ought to have at least one clear reason."

His cheeks flashed redder. "I have a reason."

Faythe met his gaze. Suddenly, she saw it. "You're scared! You're afraid of being born human."

Zariel's eyes blazed. "Don't pretend you're any different to me. What kept you in the prelife all these years? Admit it! Fear of what awaits you."

She shook her head. "We're not the same, Zariel."

"That's right. Only one of us killed the Shopkeeper."

She laughed in surprise. He had obviously expected that to sting, but it was like being slapped by a breeze. In an instant, her ceaseless guilt seemed absurd. She'd played a part in what had happened, but it wasn't all her. Not even close.

"I did things I'm not proud of," she said. "And I should have done better. But I didn't build a machine which can delete people from existence. I didn't trap the Shopkeeper in a prison. And I'm not the one stopping every single human from living because I'm too scared to live my own life."

Zariel fumed. "You pressed the button that erased the Shopkeeper."

His goading meant nothing anymore. "No. You *built* the button. I was trying to stop you."

He stepped towards her. "You keep pretending you're better than me."

"I'm not pretending. I was never pretending. You really think everyone's the same as you, don't you? That I can't possibly really care. All you see in anyone else is reflections of *you*."

Fury burned brightly behind Zariel's eyes. "Happy?" he spat. "Now you've had that little revelation?"

She was, actually, but she kept her face still. "You're getting boring," she said. "And I'd be happier still if you put the machines back together and restarted the deliveries. There's no actual reason we can't work together. Why don't you build more machines and send the supplies to the Shop? You can do your experiments and figure out how to become a god afterwards, if you like, I really don't care."

But he was still fixated on her mockery. "And I suppose what you see in me isn't just a reflection of you? You're better than me again, I assume?"

She held her breath before answering. "No, I don't think I'm better than you," she said, finally. "Maybe I'm afraid of being alive too. I don't know. But I do know that wanting to become a god to escape my own life is the most cowardly thing I've ever heard. Goodbye, Zariel."

She didn't bother waiting for a response.

As Faythe returned to the train she braced herself to be intercepted by the Zeraph, but apparently she wasn't worth the effort.

An immense weight had evaporated and, for the first time in forever, she felt free. She might have described herself as 'reborn', except *technically* she hadn't even been born once yet.

Yes, this whole mess was partly—only partly, she knew that now—her own creation, and it was still her responsibility to fix. But she no longer believed it was entirely her fault.

Eventually, she might even be able to forgive herself. (Although the Gardener had once said that self-forgiveness was harder than pruning a bush with a foot behind your head, so she wasn't quite sure about that.)

Either way, it was finally clear what she had to do. The Shop Committee *couldn't* fix everything. She'd learned today that the Supplier *wouldn't* fix everything.

And that left only one alternative . . .

twenty
three

MANAGEMENT.

The word was pure poetry, speaking directly to the deepest parts of every human heart.

Beris claimed that on Earth all managers carried the elegant dignity of the gods of the prelife.

In recent months, Faythe's curiosity about Management had faded. All-powerful beings become less compelling when you suspect they might have specific reason to punish you. Instead, questions like "do they take bribes?" suddenly take on a new importance.

Today, Management were very much on her mind. She was standing at the entrance to the long corridor which led, somehow, to Earth. Only a single thick door stood between her and the faraway world.

In a few minutes' time, everything would change. But, in this precise moment, she could still escape, be born on Earth, and forget all this. She would avoid having to see the faces of the Children once she'd confessed the truth, and she would never have to explain her failures to Management.

Then again, perhaps Management's vast power reached as far as Earth, and the possibility of escape was only an illusion. She'd often wondered what form their reach took—could they see her even now? Did they know she was considering running?

She chewed her nails without taking her eye off the door. There was another problem. Nobody had passed through for a long time, and being born as the last baby on a planet undergoing a massive shortage of babies might be a poor idea. Her recent experience of the irrationality of crowds gave her zero desire to see what a planet driven mad by the loss of its children might do to its final child.

With a sigh, she glanced back towards the Shop. Morning sunlight was already streaming through the dome to light the distressingly bare aisles. The Children would be gathering by now.

After one final, longing look at the door to Earth, Faythe went to meet them.

All of the Children were waiting on the concourse, except for a few from Security who were guarding the front from the waiting customers.

Faythe had never seen the whole group together before. Due to the current crisis, most had no work to do, so they wore a hodgepodge of colourful, comfortable clothes—again, except for Security who lined up neatly to one side in their smart blue uniforms. At the back, the Warehouse team hovered awkwardly, always the odd ones out, thanks to working and sleeping in a wholly separate building. And there, lined up at the front, stood the Committee.

As she approached, conversation died down. She coughed to hide her nerves. "Hello, everybody," she began. Her throat was tight. This was going to be difficult. She would be sad to lose all of her remaining friends.

"Thanks for coming at short notice. I have two announcements. But first—a thank you." This bit would be easy; she meant it, deeply. "All of you have been incredible, throughout the recent difficulties, and particularly the riot. You're inspiring. I couldn't have asked for more. You did your jobs, you never despaired, and you carried me when I"—she hesitated—"needed carrying."

She drew breath, heartened by the smiling faces of many of the Children. *They needed this too*, she realised.

"I'm sorry for dodging my responsibility. I want you to know I'm not dodging it anymore. But I know the Shopkeeper will—" She stammered, uncertain what tense to use. "—*would* be proud of you all."

There were many sad faces and watery eyes at the mention of the Shopkeeper. The Children were still hurt and confused by her disappearance, and—for her own reasons—she had entirely failed to engage with them over it.

That was the easy bit finished.

"My first announcement is simple. This situation can't continue as it is. And so I am going to personally petition Management for help."

The Children murmured appreciatively. She caught Omaro's eye, and he nodded. If he was still talking to her after the second announcement, she'd have to physically fight to keep him from coming with her. But that was a problem for later.

She drew a deep breath, struggling to ignore the heavy dread clamping her throat.

"Secondly, I have something to tell you." Her words caught, and she gulped. Omaro closed his eyes, as if he knew what was coming. Moments later, he reopened them and gave her an encouraging smile.

"I should have told you a long time ago, but I couldn't." She spoke quietly, but the crowd listened so intently that her words carried without trouble, even in the vast space of the concourse. "I was too scared. And I'll understand if you think less of me afterwards. Whatever happens, I know it's right that I tell you now."

Another deep breath. "I know where the Shopkeeper is." She pressed on hurriedly over a chorus of hushed gasps. "When we visited Zariel, all that time ago, there was an accident." Her heart was beating impossibly fast. She stumbled on, afraid that if she stopped she'd never be able to restart. "Zariel threatened us. And he imprisoned the Shopkeeper." Angry murmurs rippled amongst the Children. "I tried to fight him, and free the Shopkeeper, but I activated his machine by mistake and . . ." She paused, unsure how, exactly, to say it. "The Shopkeeper was killed. Permanently."

She stopped, stunned into silence along with the whole assembly. She waited for the explosion of rage and violence, but it didn't come. Omaro's eyes were glistening wet, but he mouthed to her to continue.

"I'm so sorry I didn't tell you." She struggled to hold back tears of her own. "I was terrified, and I felt so guilty and I was scared you'd all hate me if you knew what had happened."

A couple of Children were whispering to each other, but almost everyone was still fixated on what she had to say.

"I didn't know what to do. I came back here, afraid, and couldn't tell anyone, and then once I'd hidden it, I couldn't admit it. I thought that if I helped the Shop then I could make up for it, but then Zariel refused to keep supplying us, and this crisis started and—" She drew another breath. "I haven't done a good job. And I lied to you all. Again and again and again."

She stared at the floor, now, unable to meet anybody's eye. "And I'll understand if you don't want me to come back afterwards, but I'm going to Management to make things right. I couldn't leave without being honest." The tears arrived now, hot and quick down her cheeks. "I'm so sorry it took me this long."

There was still no explosion of rage. She heard sobs from the crowd, and then Omaro was next to her. He put a hand on her back—comforting, not angry.

"Thank you," he said, loudly enough for everyone to hear. "I understand why you didn't tell us."

She blinked. "You do?"

"I wish you had told us sooner, but I understand why you didn't. You believed it was your fault." He shook his head. "I'm curious, and I'm sure others want to know. Can you tell us more about this accident?"

Through sobs—part grief, part relief—she did her best to describe how the machine had been accidentally activated. When she finished, Omaro nodded, grimly.

"Thank you," he said, turning to the whole assembly. "I know some of us might be angry this wasn't shared before, but I think Faythe has punished herself enough. Nothing is served by holding onto anger here. Especially since the Shop is in danger."

He looked around the room, meeting the eyes of many of the Children. "I know many of us hoped the Shopkeeper would come back." Somewhere in the crowd, a Child broke down with a loud howl. "But now we know the truth. There'll be grieving to do, but we also have responsibilities. Faythe is facing her own as she travels to Management. So please, grieve as much as you need, but—if you can—do your part too. Thank you."

She wiped away a tear, and swallowed. "Thank you all," she echoed.

The crowd dispersed in strange mix of silence and conversation. Some Children smiled sympathetically as they left—not all, but still more than Faythe had dared to dream. Many cried and comforted one another, while others wore determined expressions—not least the Security team, as they marched to the front door to begin another difficult day of crowd control.

Omaro waited until they were alone, and then he shed a tear himself.

She hugged him. "Thank you," she said, holding him tight. "For what you said. And for understanding." She paused. "I was convinced you'd all blame me, and I'd have nowhere to go."

He shook his head. "Do you think we're idiots? I knew something had happened. And I know you. I knew it wouldn't be your fault."

"I should have trusted you."

The Child waved her comment away. "I understand why you didn't." He wiped his eyes. "No time for wallowing, though. You're serious about going to Management? I'll—"

"—you'll stay here."

That was that interrupting technique she'd seen the Shopkeeper use that day at the Complex. It *was* useful.

"But—"

"I'm serious. This place needs you more than I do. Look at how you spoke to everyone. We need someone to be in charge, and we both know it has to be you."

He grimaced. Faythe gave him a stern look. "You know I'm right."

His tongue stuck out. "I know. I'm just not used to you being right, that's all."

She grinned. She'd never been more grateful to be insulted.

That evening, she slung a couple of changes of clothes into a bag. An impulse prompted her to take the three mystery jars from Omaro, too. If the Shop burned down while she was gone—which, frighteningly, seemed a real possibility—she'd be sad to lose them.

She left quietly, slipping out of the back door and through the Gardens, where she received a pleasant tip of the hat from the Gardener, who was still working even at this late hour. Since the crowd had made the Road virtually inaccessible, she followed the river, which would arc back towards the Road once she got further away from the Shop.

The walk was peaceful. She hadn't been out walking in twilight like this since her years at the Rock, although here, of course, the twilight was brighter, as earthlight added to the radiance from the early evening stars. Even something as simple as a walk was different, these days.

Hours later, the Road appeared once more. She remembered arriving at this part of the Road and gazing down at the water on her first journey to the Shop. The memory felt strange, almost as if it had happened to somebody else.

Arguably, it had.

She stomped up the slope, and her mouth fell open as she gawped around at the scene. Even this far away from the Shop, the Road was full of people. They lounged by the side of the road, sleeping in groups with their heads on their bags. There were even makeshift shelters, like in the field. How long would people patiently camp along the Road without even being in sight of the Shop? And would the Shop survive long enough to find out?

"You been here long?" she asked a woman sitting under a temporary shelter.

"A few days," she replied. "Heard there's problems ahead. Still, at least we're not back there." She thumbed towards the back of the queue, which stretched off into the distance. "If you're joining, you need to get to the back."

Faythe thanked her and moved on. It was lucky her route was against the flow of people—it probably wouldn't be popular to appear to be skipping the queue.

A short way down the Road, a young man called out as she approached. "Hey! What news do you have from the Shop?"

She tensed. *Had she been recognised?* But her brain caught up swiftly. Nobody here would recognise her as the girl with the megaphone and the bad news. On the contrary, perhaps this was an opportunity to spread positive rumours among the crowd. It wouldn't do much, but any antidote to the growing ill-feeling might help. If the situation in the field exploded again, the Shop may not survive.

She smiled. "They're doing their best to fix it, I heard."

"Hmph." The man turned to his companions. "They're useless! Imagine running a Shop for all eternity and still being this bad at it."

She pursed her lips. "I think it might be trickier than you think."

"Oh yeah? What do you know about it?" He jerked his head upwards as he talked, in a weirdly aggressive reverse nod. "Think about this. The Shop runs fine for thousands of years. Then it gets to my turn to live, and they close for the first time *ever!* You think that's a coincidence?"

She was absolutely entirely positively sure it was definitely a coincidence. She tried to appeal to logic. "You think they're causing all this chaos to inconvenience you, specifically?"

He gave her an intense look. "Honestly, you never know what *they* might do, do you?"

It was clear that her attempts to spread goodwill were not landing on fertile soil. She nodded politely, but he shouted after her again as she left. "Anyway, if they're doing such a good job of sorting it out, how come you're going the wrong way?" He laughed, and looked meaningfully at his companions until they laughed with him.

As she walked along the Road, she painted as optimistic a picture as she could whenever anyone asked for news. One little boy charged towards her, flailing melodramatically. "You have given up! It's worse than they say, then? Will I get to have a life?"

"I'm sure it'll be okay," she said, smiling at his earnestness. "I've not given up, I'm just taking a walk. You're going to have a great life!"

"Madam, you have soothed my soul!" he shouted, smiling in return.

She thought of that boy several times over the next few hours. It was fascinating how different people were, even in the prelife.

When she reached the back of the queue she paused to gaze along the Road. She was watching the trickle of fresh arrivals from the Beginning when a familiar voice yelled her name. "Faythe?!"

She whirled around. It couldn't be . . .

"Jahu?!" He was stood just metres away. It *was* him! She yelped in delight. "Oh! I'm so happy to see you!" She stepped towards him with arms wide open.

But he didn't move. "What are you doing here?" he said, with a pained expression. "Shouldn't you be on Earth?"

Oh. Of course.

"Um, I never made it to Earth."

"Why not? Where have you been?"

"I . . . uh . . . I'm the Apprentice at the Shop Before Life."

He looked suddenly angry. "What? Come *on*."

"I'm serious! I really am."

He shook his head slowly. "It's bad enough you lied about leaving for Earth, but why lie *now*? You don't have to escape from me anymore."

Her mouth hung open. "Is that what you think? That I didn't want to live with you anymore?! And that I lied to get away?"

"Why else would you still be in the prelife? You obviously lied about that."

That was . . . fair, actually. "Okay. You're right, I was lying when I left." His face curled up in disgust and he began to turn away. "Wait! But it's because I already had the job as Apprentice. They wouldn't let me tell you."

He frowned. "You're actually serious?"

"Yes. I wanted to tell you both, but—"

"So you've been at the Shop this entire time?"

"Yes! And wait till you hear about—"

"And you could *never* tell me?"

"What?"

"You never thought, in all these years, to get in touch? Send a letter? Come to visit?" He held his arms out, fists clenched. "I thought you were on Earth this entire time. But you were here, and I didn't know, but *you* knew, and you never told me!"

"I, uh . . ." She stammered. "I told you . . . I wasn't allowed to." But as soon as she spoke, her gut twisted. Technically, Aaron and Gabriel's instructions had been to keep quiet until she got to the Shop. Which meant she could have written to him.

She sighed. "Actually, no. You're right. They only said I couldn't tell you at first. But I worried that if we saw each other again it might be harder for both of us, and then . . . so many things happened, and I got drawn in. It's been strange, Jahu, really strange. I missed you so badly, and I kept hoping you'd pass through the Shop. Every day! I wanted to see your face when I surprised you there. But I didn't think . . ."

His face was unreadable. It suddenly hit her how much she'd missed him.

"And . . ." She stepped closer. "I wanted to see your face in general. You're right—I should have written to you. All my reasons not to get in touch were bad, and I was cowardly, and scared of hurting you, and I thought maybe you were better off without me, but I was stupid and I should have reached out to you. I'm sorry."

Her gut had untwisted and her head felt light. Being honest was becoming a habit, apparently. Perhaps it wasn't the worst habit she could have developed.

Silence. And then a slow, growing smile, and a question. "You *honestly* got a job at the *Shop*?!"

"You really aren't going to believe this . . ."

twenty four

THEY TALKED by the side of the Road until the sun rose. Around them, people slowly awoke into another day of waiting.

Faythe had hesitated when she reached the part of the story when the Shopkeeper died. Even with her newfound appreciation of honesty, it was difficult to admit to killing the most famous person in the entire prelife. But she didn't hold back.

Jahu listened in increasing astonishment. "And now you're going to see Management for help?"

He had the widest eyes she had ever seen. She couldn't help enjoying it a little. "I thought I might," she said, nonchalantly.

"I always said you'd do something great," he said, shaking his head. "I just assumed it would happen on Earth."

She instinctively glanced to the sky, but the Earth wasn't visible. After so long at the Shop, it felt as if something important had been stolen from her. "Wait until you see it," she said softly. "Anyway! Enough about me. What are you doing here? Were you going to the Shop?"

He nodded. "Tapak went a while ago. Wait—did you see him?"

"I did! It was so good." She smiled at the memory. "Although, we caused trouble—no, don't ask. But what happened with Tapak?"

"After you'd gone, everything felt weird. So I sulked. A lot. Like, champion levels of sulking."

"I did the same after the thing with the Shopkeeper."

He blinked. "I can't really compete with that."

"Sorry. Carry on with your story!"

"I think I sulked so much Tapak decided to leave," said Jahu. "I don't blame him. I stayed alone for a bit, but it was so boring. Then I went to Ostholme, but I never really settled."

"What's it like?" She'd only ever heard stories of the prelife's biggest city.

"It's incredible. I knew it was inside a mountain, so I'd pictured a bigger Rock, but it's so much more."

She remembered the Supplier's Complex with a slight shudder. "People have made pretty incredible things in the prelife."

"Yeah. But I didn't feel at home there. Eventually I realised I was hanging around for nothing. So I decided to go to Earth." He laughed. "Looks like I picked a good time for it."

"I'm sorry."

"You should be!" He cocked his head. "But seriously, this isn't your fault, right? It's Zariel's."

She bit her lip. "I guess. But it's partly my fault too—what are you laughing at?" He had let out a sudden giggle. She punched him, incredulous. "What?! How is this funny?"

Apparently her reaction was funnier still, as he doubled up, unable to speak. Eventually he managed to stammer between howls of laughter. "It's just . . . I just realised . . . you broke . . . the Shop . . . Before . . . Life . . ."

Despite her annoyance, she laughed too. "It isn't funny, Jahu! It's . . . stop laughing . . . ! It's serious."

The pair collapsed into fits of giggles, completely ignoring the confused looks from people nearby.

"Oh, I needed that," Faythe said, minutes later as she wiped her eyes. "I can't believe you made me laugh at this. It's so bad."

"It's just—of course you left for Earth but accidentally got a job at the Shop Before Life and then shut the whole place down and now the whole Earth is in danger. It's so you. I'm not sure why I'm even surprised."

She punched him on the shoulder again. "Tapak said the same," she said. "I missed you."

"I missed you too. I'm glad you didn't forget me."

"Never."

A nearby traveller was building a rain shelter out of clothes and sticks. The pair watched for a minute before Jahu turned to her. "You've changed," he said.

She considered this for a minute. "Well, I'm definitely a lot more stressed," she offered. "Honestly, I probably wouldn't have gone into retail if I'd known all human life would depend on me afterwards."

He snorted. "Not only that, though." She shifted, a little embarrassed, as he studied her. "You're more you."

She looked at him blankly. "I don't know what that means."

"Maybe it's just that you've done more now. I've not done anything since you left—since before that, really. Everything always stayed the same."

"I know what you mean," she said. "All those years, and they're kind of a blur."

He looked sad, and she reached for his arm. "They're a happy blur!" she clarified. "But two hundred years in the same place, and we never changed at all. Even after all that time, we were children—no, these days I know plenty of Children who know more than we did."

He nodded. "And I never did anything to change it. Until you forced me to."

"But you have now! So that's something."

"I guess." He paused. "I think the Shop has been good for you."

She looked at him in disbelief. "Good for me? Half of humanity are rioting, and Management might erase me from existence when they find out how badly I've screwed everything up."

"Yeah, but you seem happier." He saw her face and hurried to clarify. "Deep down, I mean."

She shook her head. "You're right, you've not changed. You're still an idiot."

"That's fair," he said, affably. "So. When are we going to see Management?"

"We?!"

"Yeah. You don't think I'm going to wait here on the Road, do you? Especially not now I know this queue won't be moving."

She frowned. She'd been stringing out the encounter as long as possible before saying goodbye. But did that have to happen?

"I don't know," she said, scratching idly at the dirt with her finger. "I haven't been great company lately."

"I'm enjoying myself."

"Yeah, but it hasn't gone well for people around me. The Shopkeeper's dead. Most of the prelife is stuck in a queue that might never move. The Shop was literally on fire this week. Maybe I'm bad luck."

"I survived two hundred years with you and only got hit by a few eggs."

"This honestly could be worse than eggs. Anything could happen."

"That's even more reason I should join you."

She was rapidly running out of excuses. "Beris told me not to share where Management can be found."

"I won't tell anyone."

There was one reason left, a worry which hadn't been far from her mind for months. "Management might be angry about what I've done. I don't know what they'll do to me when I tell them. Or to you."

"Maybe they'll hit *you* with an egg."

"I'm serious, Jahu."

"So am I." His eyes shone as he looked at her. "I'm coming with you, you know."

Fine. She nodded. That was that, then.

"We'd better go. I don't know how much time we have before it'll all kick off at the Shop again."

Without another word Jahu stood up. "Lead on."

They resumed following the Road. Beyond the Beginning, there was a turn that would lead towards the edge of the prelife. The queue and the Shop and the slowly simmering pot of people disappeared gradually behind them.

Faythe hoped it wouldn't boil over before she got back.

The storytellers who had visited the Rock were obsessed with epic journeys. In stories, people were always travelling to petition the gods for one thing or another, perhaps even with an old friend as a companion. But everyone knew that the real prelife wasn't like the stories.

Unless you counted the magical shop, or this exceptional trip to Management, that is.

Still, it didn't feel very epic. Since passing the Beginning, nothing much had changed. There were fewer people, but the landscape looked similar to the rest of the prelife. Rolling hills, trees, fields, mountains in the distance.

Faythe wasn't sure what she'd expected, but she'd pictured it being a little less . . . normal.

She glanced over at Jahu. "Do you think stories are true?" she asked.

He looked up from his feet. He'd been playing a game while they walked, landing his boots in a certain pattern on the path. Faythe didn't understand the rules. "What?" he said.

"Stories. You know—the things storytellers say. Do you think they're all real?"

He shrugged. "I think they're real, but they probably never happened."

"I can't tell if you're being very clever or very stupid," she replied.

"Me neither. But what's real, anyway?" He scuffed his step dramatically and then gave a little hop. "We're going to the 'edge' of the prelife, right? Well, what's that? Does the world actually have an edge, or is it just a name?"

She scrunched up her face. "I don't know. I can't picture it physically ending. But I can't picture it going on forever either."

"Exactly. Neither option makes sense, but one of them has to be real. So if what's actually real doesn't make sense, why can't stories be true?"

It wasn't obvious how to argue with that. "I'm almost convinced," she said slowly. "Maybe the whole world is impossible."

She couldn't help smiling. Now that the ice had melted between them, this felt like their old conversations at the Rock. Neither really knew what they were talking about, but it didn't matter at all.

They walked on.

"Have you ever thought that maybe we don't exist?" he asked, a few minutes later.

"I wish! Then I wouldn't have to listen to your stupid theories."

By now, the sun was lowering. Jahu halted to stare towards the horizon, where the path disappeared into a clump of trees. She followed his gaze. "From what Beris said, it'll take a day or so from there," she said.

He nodded. "Maybe let's take a break here?"

"Good idea."

Minutes later, they were leaning against a tree, arms touching, and staring at nothing in particular when suddenly everything flickered. There was a huge rumble, and the ground shook.

Jahu ducked as a branch fell from above, narrowly missing his head. "What was that?" he yelped.

"No idea," she replied, dumbfounded. "Did everything . . . blink . . . for you?"

"Blink? Yeah, sort of. Everything went black, but it came back right away."

They waited, but it didn't happen again. The landscape around them was calm.

Eventually, they relaxed back against the tree, and returned to a comfortable silence.

In stories, it's customary for epic journeys to be packed with trials and tribulations.

Adventurers usually meet at least one talking tree, or narrowly survive attacks by bandits, or become stuck in an unseasonal snowstorm.

Faythe wondered whether the person responsible for adventure at Management had the week off, because—aside from that strange flicker—nothing much happened.

And on the following day they emerged from the forest to find a narrow gap between tall cliffs, at the top of which they would meet the Management of the entire universe.

twenty five

JAHU CURSED. The sound echoed off the overhang high above, bouncing in the tight space between the cliffs.

It was apparently so satisfying that he did it again.

"Shut up!" hissed Faythe.

Neither of them had much patience left. The path—if you could still call it that—had become steep and unstable, and littered with spiky rocks. The cliff walls on either side were so tall, and the space between so narrow, that they had to battle their way upwards in near-darkness. As a result, they kept blundering into the virtually invisible sharp rocks which jutted upwards from the floor, scraping their shins painfully in the process.

Jahu cursed again as he crashed into yet another unseen obstacle. "I don't get it! If you built the entire universe, why would you choose to live here?"

She didn't disagree, but she was tired of his complaining. "I know. But look—that's light up ahead. We're nearly there."

He rubbed his leg, and then, because he was *very* human, he kicked the rock he'd just walked into, hurting himself once more in the process. "I'm beginning to question Management's judgement," he said. "This place is terrible."

Despite her irritation, she grinned. In a weird way, she was grateful for the unpleasantness of the journey. Even the sharp pain in her leg was a helpful distraction from where they were going—and why. Part of her was excited to arrive, of course. It wasn't every day you got to communicate with the gods, and learn how that worked. Were they like a talking fire? A mystical voice in her mind? Or maybe they spoke only through particular priests.

But then, she was intensely aware that how they spoke was less important than whatever they said. Satisfying her curiosity about Management would be no comfort if they ordered her immediate destruction for killing the Shopkeeper.

She swallowed a sudden lump in her throat. *This* was why she had been avoiding thinking about it.

Thankfully, conversation could be a useful distraction too. "Where would you live then, if you were Management?" she asked.

"Underwater, obviously," replied Jahu, without hesitation.

"*Underwater?* That's even stupider than up a path covered in—ow!—rocks."

"Is it though? This path is very, very stupid."

"Yeah, but at least we can breathe here."

"I'd make it so we could breathe underwater, *obviously*. I'm not an idiot." A thought struck him. "Is there a jar in the Shop that does that?"

She frowned. "I don't think so. That sounds like the sort of trait Zariel wants to make, though."

"Really? He has good ideas, that Zariel. Maybe I should join his side."

She kicked out in the direction of her friend, but misjudged the distance in the gloom. "Go join him if you want!" She thought of the maniacal intensity in Zariel's eyes when he'd revealed his desire to join Management. "You and your stupid ideas would fit right in with his, honestly. Hey—look!"

The light had seemed to be faraway, but it turned out to be higher up and much closer. They were nearing a wall made from off-white brick, which blocked the narrow path at the top of the passage. An arch was set in the wall, about three times taller than Faythe, inset with a normal-sized door. A bell hung nearby, and underneath it, a single flowerpot.

None of this was what she'd expected. "Is this it?" she said. She stared at the door. Incongruously, it reminded her of the one which had led to her bedroom in the Rock. "Why are these doors always so boring?!"

Even in the darkness, she could feel the funny look Jahu was giving her. He gestured at the bell. "Go on."

This was it. After a momentary hesitation, she reached out and rang the bell. The sound echoed eerily in the pass.

After a brief anxious wait, the lock clicked and the door opened a fraction. Light flooded onto the opposite wall, and the silhouette of a head appeared in the gap.

His eyes are made of fire! Faythe yelped and leapt in terror. Moments later, her own eyes adjusted to the sudden brightness, and the terrifying silhouette resolved into a stocky man wearing reflective glasses. "I'm sorry," she said. "It looked like your eyes were on fire."

"What?" said the man, warily.

"Forget it," she said. "We're here to see Management."

The man frowned. "Nope," he said. "Management won't be seeing nobody."

Jahu pointed triumphantly at him. "So they *will* be seeing somebody?"

"What?"

"Look, if they *won't* see nobo—"

Faythe interrupted this unhelpful lesson in logic as fast as she could. "Never mind! Can you let us in, please? We really need to see Management."

The man laughed. "You don't just 'see' Management. What do you think this is? How did you even find this place?" He peered suspiciously behind them.

"We're from the Shop Before Life," she said. "I'm the Appren— the Acting Shopkeeper there."

"The Shopkeeper?!" The man removed his glasses and squinted at her.

"The Acting Shopkeeper," she corrected.

He frowned. "Can you prove it?"

Faythe and Jahu exchanged glances. *Could* she prove it? The Shop didn't exactly hand out badges. That was a good idea, though. She'd have to talk to Beris after—

No. Now was not a good time to mentally reorganise the staffing system.

"Don't you have anything from the Shop?" asked Jahu.

"Yes! Good thinking!" She rummaged in her bag and pulled out one of the mystery jars Omaro had given her all those years ago. It cast a pale yellow glow all around, illuminating the dark rocky walls where the light from the barely open door didn't reach. "As you can see, we are indeed from the Shop. Can we come in now?"

The guard scratched his chin thoughtfully, then nodded. "Looks like you'll have to," he said. "Wait here."

The door slammed shut. To Faythe's surprise, Jahu rounded on her furiously. "You've been carrying that light the *whole time*," he said, gesturing wildly at the jar. "And you let me slice myself open on a hundred rocks?"

She calmly slid the jar back into her bag. "I'm sorry, I forgot! It's not like I—"

Suddenly the door opened, blinding them again with a flood of sunlight.

"Take them inside!" yelled the guard. A group of men surrounded the pair, grabbing them roughly by the arms. "They've stolen jars from the Shop, and are telling tales about being the Shopkeeper."

"Stop!" Faythe struggled, but the men were too strong. "I *am* the Acting Shopkeeper! Let me go!"

Her protests fell on uncaring ears, and they were dragged up the path. As they emerged from between the cliffs, their destination came into view. Despite the situation, her jaw fell open. It was both simpler and more magnificent than she'd imagined.

Before them stood a castle. An actual castle, made of the same off-white stone as the entrance wall at the top of the path. The towers soared high in the sky, but low enough to remain hidden from the outside world by the circle of hills which surrounded them. From outside, these hills appeared grey and featureless, but the inner hillsides were green and laden with colourful flowers. On one side, the circle was broken by a tremendous waterfall, crashing down with a pleasing roar.

"This looks more like it," Jahu muttered to Faythe. One of the men gave him a warning poke to the shoulder—not roughly, but hard enough to encourage him to be quiet.

They were led along the path and over a bridge. The waterfall thundered past, not quite close enough to touch. Faythe stole a glance over the side to see it land in a lake, far beneath. The group passed through a neat garden, past a maze of hedgerows, before finally climbing stone steps which led to the castle entrance.

The front door opened as they approached, and a figure dressed in white gestured for the group to come inside. Once they crossed into the hall, the air was warmer. Faint music drifted from deeper within the castle.

Faythe's eyes roved around the huge chamber. She'd never had a reason before to use the word 'opulent', but she now understood why it existed. Wide passages led away in many directions, each painted with colourful murals and intricate patterns. Even here in the entrance hall, the carpet was so thick she could feel it through her boots. Sunlight was streaming through the windows, reflecting off an intricate chandelier high above into a thousand bright spots dotted around the floor and walls. The chandelier itself was packed with candles, an almost intimidatingly wasteful extravagance at this time of day.

She gulped. The cosiness of the Shop suddenly seemed backward and ramshackle.

After a quick whispered conversation with their escorts, the person in white turned to the pair. "Follow me," they said, sternly. They carried themselves with an air of importance. A priest, perhaps.

"Are we—" began Faythe.

The person in white shushed her immediately. This was a very strange welcome. She hoped Management would be more receptive.

Obediently, she followed as the person in white led them deeper into the castle. She quickly lost track of the twists and turns they took—although the passages were distinctive enough that she was confident she'd be able to find her way back. Every wall—every surface, almost—was covered in art. Statues of figures lined the corridors, each around eight feet tall. She felt a glimmer of recognition she couldn't quite place.

A few minutes later, they were ushered down steps and into an empty, windowless room, painted all in white. "Stay here," said the person in white.

Faythe looked around desperately. "Wait! We need to talk to Management. Quickly. It's urgent!"

The person in white remained completely impassive. "We need to decide what to do with you. Impersonating the Shopkeeper is a serious offence."

"What?! I'm not imp—"

The door was closing. She ran to block it, but it was too late. They were trapped.

She slumped onto the floor and shut her eyes.

"Great," said Jahu. "I'm not sure they like us."

"I don't get it. What were we supposed to do?" She spoke flatly, without opening her eyes. "We told them we were from the Shop, but they never believed us."

Jahu didn't reply. After a few minutes of pacing around the room, he turned to Faythe. "What do we do now?"

"Do?" She had flopped her arm over her eyes and hadn't moved since. It was a strangely comfortable position. "I don't know. But we need to get out of here fast."

"Do you think they'll hurt us?"

"I'm not worried about us." To her surprise, that was true. She swallowed. Her chest was a glacier. "If they don't help quickly then everything is lost. The Shop, everybody's lives, the Earth, the whole universe. And it'll be my fault."

He laughed. "You've got a pretty big opinion of yourself these days."

She moved her arm to glare at him. "It's true!"

"I think Zariel has a *little* to do with it," he said, shrugging.

Her glare intensified. Annoyingly, he was right. "*Fine,*" she said. "I get it. There's no point being self-pitying." She exhaled. "You know, I expected I'd get punished here, but I assumed it'd be for something I'd actually done."

Her friend snorted. "You shouldn't have impersonated the Shopkeeper then, should you?" He winked as he sat next to her, and leaned back against the wall.

She closed her eyes.

"Everything's going to be fine, though," he said, a minute later.

"What makes you say that?"

"Nothing. Except that I believe in you."

She snapped her eyes open. Was he joking? He was staring at her with an innocent, trusting expression.

He meant it, the idiot.

"I have absolutely no idea what I'm doing." She remembered saying the same thing to Omaro, back when the supply crisis had started. Already, that felt like a different prelifetime. "That ought to be my catchphrase."

"Catchy. But I do believe in you. You always—"

Suddenly everything flashed dark and the room shook violently. Jahu's bag skittered away, and a crack went up one of the walls, breaking the smooth emptiness of the paintwork.

Then, just as suddenly, everything stopped and silence returned.

"What was that?" Jahu said, quivering.

She bit her lip. "It's like what happened yesterday by the tree. It must be because we're near to Management."

"Maybe."

They both looked at each other. "We have to get out of here," she said, standing up. She stretched her arms, and began to pound on the door. "LET US OUT!" she yelled.

Jahu followed her lead. "HELLO! WE'RE FROM THE SHOP!" He thumped the door. "This is fun," he added to Faythe.

She stuck out her tongue. "You're not technically from the Shop, you know."

He gave her a disparaging look, and they resumed pounding and shouting and yelling.

Minutes later, they heard a click. The door was being unlocked.

They looked at each other. She took a step back, her shoulders tensing and her heart accelerating. This was their chance. She needed to convince the person in white to let them talk to Management. And the prospect of failure scared her even more than success.

Just.

The door swung open. To her amazement, a familiar face appeared.

"Oh. Hello, Faythe."

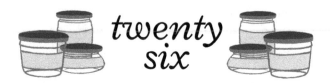

twenty six

MOST PEOPLE pass through each other's lives without making a lasting impression. But they do say you never forget the people who signed you up to work at a magical shop for a thousand years.

Aaron and Gabriel looked exactly as they had on that fateful day near the Rock. They wore the same clothes, and even the same expressions: a bright, toothy grin from Aaron, and an air of long-suffering, resentful irritation from Gabriel.

Faythe's scalp tingled with relief. "I'm so glad to see you! The people here didn't believe I was the Acting Shopkeeper."

Gabriel sniffed. He looked around the cell disdainfully as they stepped inside. "And that justifies making all that noise and banging on our door like that, does it? You're lucky it was us that found you."

"Wait," said Aaron, looking puzzled. "Did you say 'Acting Shopkeeper'?"

"Yes, I did! It's a long story. And I need to tell Management about it as soon as possible."

"Procedures exist for a reason," snapped Gabriel. "Did you file for an appointment?"

"No," said Faythe urgently. "We left it too late to send a letter, so I'm reporting it personally. Can you at least take me to a higher priest?"

The pair exchanged bemused glances. After a short hesitation, Gabriel shook his head. "I'm afraid you'll have to return to the Shop," he said. "And tell the Shopkeeper to send messages through the proper channels next time."

"That's the problem." She took a deep breath. "I can't tell the Shopkeeper anything."

But Gabriel was already holding the door open. "Come on, get out! You should be grateful we aren't keeping you here. And, remember in future: we don't care if your relationship with the Shopkeeper isn't going well"—he caught Aaron's look of surprise—"yes, I *do* read the reports. Sometimes, anyway." He wagged a finger at Faythe. "That's between the pair of you, and has nothing to do with us, and even less to do with Management."

He sounded stern but his eyes betrayed a nervousness that Faythe didn't understand.

"It's not about our relationship," she said, in a small voice. It hurt to hear the Shopkeeper had sent reports on how poorly their relationship had been going. "I can't tell her anything. Nobody can. Because she's *dead*. Permanently."

After all this buildup it felt . . . strangely empty to have said it out loud.

The reaction from Aaron and Gabriel was slightly more dramatic. Aaron's eyes couldn't have boggled further out of his head if she had vomited on the floor and married the puddle.

"Dead?!" spluttered Gabriel. "Don't talk nonsense!"

"I realise how that sounds, but I promise—she's dead. And that's not even the worst news."

"That's not the worst news?" He wrinkled his face in disbelief. "What else? Did you trip over and break the *Earth?*"

Her insides lurched. "Funny you should mention that. There is a problem with the Earth, too."

The two men exchanged looks. Faythe stared intensely, trying her best to interpret what they might be thinking. *Scepticism? Horror? Disbelief?*

Finally, Gabriel threw his arms in the air. "This is *your* fault," he barked. She sighed inwardly. *Or they might just fight over who's to blame.*

Aaron held up his hands. "Whoa, what did I do?"

"I told you to be careful when we first met her. But you were so sure, weren't you? Or, let's be honest: desperate to get home. Well, it's not going to be me explaining why your hastily-chosen Apprentice has abandoned her post and turned up here telling stories. If he hears about this, I'm going to tell him everything."

Aaron laughed. "You honestly think he cares?"

"Even if not, he isn't going to appreciate any hassle. We had one job, and we—*you*—screwed it up."

Aaron's confident smile wavered, and he looked thoughtfully at Faythe. "Let's say you're right. What if this is an opportunity to accelerate the plan?"

The shorter priest folded his arms. "You want to make that call now? Without speaking to the others? I'd like to see you explain *that*."

"Good point." Aaron sighed. "Then . . . how hard would it be to dispose of her and find another new Apprentice? It's only been a few years. They might never notice."

Her stomach plummeted in shock. "What do you mean 'dispose'?"

Gabriel ignored her. "Pretty risky. He'd need to hear nothing at all."

Aaron clicked his fingers. "So what if we kept her here . . ."

". . . feeding her so she doesn't starve . . ."

". . . yes, don't want her escaping that way. And meanwhile, we find a replacement . . ."

". . . lose the reports from the Shopkeeper . . ."

". . . and he never needs to know a thing!"

She watched this exchange in increasing astonishment. The escalation was so unbelievable that the horror of what was being discussed hardly registered. It just didn't seem real.

Across the cell, Jahu coughed. "Listen," he said, trying to stand as heroically as possible. "This is important. You have to let her speak to Management."

Aaron glanced over in astonishment, as if noticing him for the first time. "Who are you?!"

"I'm her friend."

"Oh, well that changes everything," said Gabriel, sarcastically. "As long as her friend says so!" He turned to Aaron. "I think a one-way trip to the blue place might be in order for that one."

258

Faythe stepped forward. She needed to get past these idiots and get her story to Management as quickly as possible. "Listen! Whatever you do won't change the fact that *everything I'm telling you is true*. Zariel built a machine which sucked the Shopkeeper into a void, and now the Shop has run out of supplies so nobody is getting to Earth. There's been a riot, and the entire Road is full of people, so there's going to be a bigger riot really soon, and we need help *now* because it's getting worse."

"It's true," supplied Jahu, with a sheepish glance at Faythe. She smiled encouragingly, and he brightened.

Meanwhile, Aaron's grin sunk into his face and disappeared entirely. He looked strange without it. "Uh," he said. "Really?"

One final push. She decided to appeal to their desire for self-preservation. "I don't know who this 'he' is that you keep referring to, but I promise he's going to hear about the whole prelife falling apart. Better he hears it from you than wonders why you hid it from him."

Her spine tingled as she stopped talking. Jahu was watching her proudly.

Aaron sighed. "Fine. We'll take you to Pluton."

They were led upstairs along yet more art-laden hallways. White-clad people paced along the corridors with their heads held low, looking up only to hold open doors for the group.

"Who are those people?" asked Faythe, after passing the third door in awkward silence.

"What people?" Aaron looked around in confusion. He was being uncharacteristically quiet.

"The people in white. Are they training to be priests?"

"Oh, them," he said. "Um, sure."

She wanted to ask more, but they had stopped in front of a grand door. "Welcome to the Hall," said one of the white-clad acolytes, bowing low as the four passed through.

The Hall turned out to be more opulent still. Tapestries of red, gold and purple—and other colours which aren't as officially impressive—hung on the walls, beneath timbers carved with ornate decorations. In the centre of the room was a large table, easily big enough to seat fifty people. Off to one side, a lone musician was playing a jaunty tune on a flute, while on the other side, a group of acolytes in white were building a tremendous display of flowers, twice as tall as Faythe.

At the far end of the table, three people were sat having a meal. The closest person was a massive hulking figure, seemingly made wholly of muscle, except for a blond beard tied up in braids. The furthest away was a woman, older-looking than Faythe, but seemingly younger than the Shopkeeper, whose long white hair cascaded all the way down her back. And in the middle was an old, thin man wearing a colourful robe and hat. He looked up in displeasure at the interruption.

"What are you two doing here? And who is this?"

Faythe frowned. *Who were these people?* Nothing in this whole castle made any sense.

She looked over at Gabriel, who nudged Aaron. The taller man gamely attempted his most confident grin. "So sorry to interrupt, Pluton, Kaine, Eva." He nodded at each as he named them.

"We know who we are, idiot," barked the thin man in the middle. "Make this quick."

Pluton's voice was deeper than Faythe would have guessed. It had the exact right frequency to reverberate loudly off the stone floor of the room. It was clear from everyone's body language that he was important. Perhaps he was the intermediary to Management that she needed.

She seized her chance. "Hello! I need to speak to Management about problems at the Shop."

He scowled. "I can't imagine why you're bothering us with that. Who are you, and how did you get in?"

"I'm the Apprentice," she said. Jahu nudged her. *Oh, right.* "Technically I'm now the Acting Shopkeeper."

The woman next to him—Eva, wasn't it?—raised an eyebrow. She tapped at her wine glass and a person in white appeared to refill it. "The Shopkeeper never informed us about a holiday," she muttered to Pluton, darkly.

Next to her, Kaine was eagerly spreading butter on a tremendous hunk of bread. He'd barely looked up at all.

"I remember hearing about a new Apprentice," mused Pluton. "I thought it was a boy, though."

"That was the last one, sir," said Gabriel, helpfully.

"Oh. Right. I remember now. And you two selected the replacement, correct?"

Aaron and Gabriel exuded the impression of cowering whilst standing up straight. It was extraordinary to see.

"That's right," confirmed Aaron, hurriedly. "And this is her. She was very impressive. Passed all the tests, no problem."

Tests? Faythe opened her mouth, but Aaron carried on. "And all the reports indicate she's been doing a fantastic job. A great choice."

A sudden light flickered in Gabriel's eyes, the light of somebody having a last-minute idea that might just save them. He looked meaningfully at Aaron. "But we're sorry to announce that there's a problem with those reports."

"Oh yes," said Aaron, uncertainly. "That's what we're here to tell you about. Um. The problems with the excellent reports."

Eva extended a finger to toy with her wine glass. "So, these reports, which you just said are evidence that you did a fantastic job and made the right choice of Apprentice . . . there's a problem with them?"

Aaron clearly saw the trap. Unfortunately, he wasn't quite deft enough to figure out how to avoid it. "Um," he said. "Maybe?"

Eva smirked.

"That was cruel," said Kaine, through a mouth full of bread.

Faythe's mouth hung open. Why were these people just sitting there eating, drinking, and joking? She had to get to Management *now.* "Please!" she said. "I don't know anything about any reports. But there are truly problems at the Shop I need to tell Management about. It's *urgent.*"

"Very well," said Pluton. "Speak."

She hesitated. She would much rather talk directly to Management. But was this the best chance she'd get?

Behind her, Aaron and Gabriel were having a frantic, whispered conversation, presumably about who was to blame for all this.

"Silence, idiots!" commanded Pluton.

Next to him, Kaine laughed, without looking up from his food.

Faythe shuffled her feet. "It's just . . . can I talk to Management directly?"

Glances were exchanged around the table. "Perhaps later," said Pluton, not unkindly.

She sighed. *Fine.* But she'd do this quickly. She drew a deep breath. "The Shopkeeper is dead. Zariel killed her with a machine he made by deconstructing half of the Supplier's Complex. The Shop is running out of supplies, so nobody can pass through to Earth. People are angry, and I'm not sure if the Shop is even still standing—there was a riot before I left."

Pluton's face was stony. "I see . . ." he said. Bizarrely, next to him, Eva was smirking with apparent . . . glee?

Faythe made her final plea. "Can you please ask Management for help now? We're desperate."

Another round of glances passed between the seated group. "Oh, I can't stand it any longer," said Eva, impatiently. "Child, who do you think you're talking to?"

"I have absolutely no idea," admitted Faythe. She glanced at the enormous piles of meat in the middle of the table. "None of this is what I expected."

"Tell her," boomed Kaine, waving a chicken leg. Sauce dribbled over his chin.

"Agreed," said Eva. "If even part of her story is true, then the scheme needs to be brought forward. Regardless, the old plan is dead."

"That's what my idea was!" exclaimed Aaron, with a triumphant look at Gabriel.

"Silence!" said Pluton. Aaron shrank back, and the old man turned to Faythe. "Child. *This* is Management."

She did a double take. "This..?" Comprehension dawned like a rotten sun. "All of you?" The group nodded. Jahu stood open-mouthed. Next to him, Aaron and Gabriel nodded along. "And *them too?!*"

Gabriel glowered. "Why wouldn't we be?"

"You told me you weren't!"

"Technically," said Aaron, "we said we were representing Management."

Gabriel shrugged. "It's not our fault what you believed."

"In their particular case, however," said Eva. "I can quite understand your scepticism."

"Indeed," agreed Pluton. "After all this is resolved, I think you two will have to explain your actions."

Aaron gulped, and Gabriel looked like he was about to be sick.

Faythe was still struggling to absorb this. "Management are *people?*"

Kaine laughed. "What else would we be?"

Eva took a gulp of wine. "We've found it useful over the centuries to keep the true nature of Management mysterious."

"I always thought . . ." She trailed off, and started again. "I always visualised Management as more of a force. Like, a big shining orb with a personality. Or something."

Pluton smiled. "Oh my! Looks like our stories really evolved out there." He sounded almost nostalgic. "Still, you thought what you were supposed to think."

Eva gestured for a refill from one of the people in white. Suddenly another mystery clicked into place. These weren't trainee priests, or acolytes. *They were servants.*

None of this could be real. All of this must be an elaborate joke. Any moment they would laugh at her gullibility, and show her into a holy temple filled with the unconstrained power of Management.

Surely.

An uncomfortable thought surfaced. "Did the Shopkeeper know?"

Pluton looked at her blankly. "Of course. She was one of us, after all."

Faythe reeled. "What?!" She slumped into a seat, feeling dazed. "Why didn't she tell me any of this?"

Eva swirled her glass around. "The Shopkeeper had as much reason as we do to maintain the illusion. More, perhaps. Though she did go a bit strange after years of living at that damned Shop."

Faythe put her head in her hands. She felt Jahu pull up a chair next to her and put a comforting hand on her arm.

The gods aren't gods, they're people. And not even impressive people. They had chicken juice in their beards and silly colourful robes, and two of them were complete idiots who would lie to save their own skins without a second thought.

And the Shopkeeper had been one of them.

She looked over the table at the trio in desperation. "If the gods aren't here, then where are they? Who are your Management?!"

Pluton met her eye with apparently genuine compassion. "I'm afraid there's only us humans."

"But the Shop needs help!"

All of her hope had rested on this. She'd believed that Management, the beings who created the Shop, could save it in its hour of need.

"You'd better put your hope in humans, then," said Eva. Kaine snorted again, breadcrumbs flying everywhere.

Pluton turned to Aaron and Gabriel with a clap. "Time for you two to make yourselves useful," he said. "Summon the others for an immediate meeting. I think it's time we addressed the problem of the Shop Before Life."

They say you should never meet your heroes, but perhaps you should never meet your gods, either.

Especially if you're still going to need their help afterwards.

twenty seven

IN THE VERY BEST traditions of management meetings, they began roasting the hogs immediately.

An army of servants placed elaborate decorations on every available surface. Very soon, a fire was roaring in the enormous fireplace at the end of the Hall, and the servants scattered to light dozens of intricately carved candles and lay complex arrangements of polished silver cutlery at each seat.

Faythe watched idly while they worked. One thought echoed repeatedly in her mind: this vulgar display of wealth and extravagance *was* Management.

A foundation she'd been standing on for her entire prelife had only ever existed in her imagination. Management were the very first thing she'd been told about after appearing at the Beginning, closely followed by how to reach the Shop. It was strange to witness the reality behind the story.

So many questions suddenly made sense, yet it felt as if she'd been hollowed out.

In a very practical way, the revelation was a relief. The much-dreaded retribution from Management seemed unlikely now. Hardly any of them had even seemed interested in the news about the Shopkeeper at all.

Her fingers drummed on the table. She suddenly grinned at the thought of Zariel. His grand plan to join Management seemed considerably less impressive now. She hoped she'd be present if he ever found out.

Next to her, Jahu watched the musicians, apparently fascinated by their tuning up. She tapped her foot impatiently, and counted the members of Management around the table. Twenty-three, plus her and Jahu. Only Pluton appeared to be missing.

When was this meeting going to start? It couldn't be long. Already, the stacks of meat and vegetables were piled worryingly high on the table.

Beneath the impatience, she felt oddly relaxed, lulled by the warmth and delicious smells into forgetting the chaos of the outside world. Back at the Shop, there were no decorations, musicians, fancy clothes or obscene amounts of food. Just the threat of collapse and . . . not death, exactly, but potentially worse. Never getting to live at all.

She looked up to see Pluton striding purposely back towards the table. It appeared the meeting—or feast—was ready to begin.

The musicians struck up in a hurry, but he held up a hand to silence them. "I'm afraid we have business to discuss first," he announced.

There was a chorus of groans from around the table. "But we still eat?" asked Kaine. Without waiting for an answer, he reached out for a thick slice of beef, carefully scraping a cooked egg off the top with a look of distaste.

"Certainly," said Pluton. He gestured to Faythe, who was sitting at the bottom end of the table. "This is the Acting Shopkeeper from the Shop Before Life." She shrank away as the assembly turned to her with a mixture of boredom and hostility on their faces. "She has information which we will need to discuss."

Her legs trembled as she stood up. Around the table, most of the gathering had followed Kaine's example and were helping themselves to food. The big man was already ripping apart ribs on the huge plate in front of him.

Over the noise of chewing and sloshing and occasional rude whispering, Faythe told the story of the crisis at the Shop—the death of the Shopkeeper, the loss of supplies, the riots, and the continual buildup of frustrated people desperate to get to Earth. She stressed the fragile state the Shop was in, and the scale of the possible destruction that awaited.

"—and so, I've come to seek the help of Management," she finished, attempting to make eye contact with anybody who would look up.

She sat down, relieved to have unburdened herself by telling the story. The problem was shared now. She couldn't wait to hear Management's ideas for restraining Zariel. Perhaps their mere reputation would be enough, but if not, their army of servants would certainly help.

"So, there we have it." Pluton stood and dabbed at his mouth with a napkin. "I have a proposal to make, but before we discuss a joint response, I'm curious. Why is Zariel doing this? If I remember rightly, we expected a long period of stability from the Supplier." He pointed to the big man next to him. "Isn't this your business, Kaine?"

Faythe frowned, confused. "Why him?" she whispered to Aaron, who was sitting on her right.

"Kaine used to be the Supplier," he whispered back.

"*Him?!*" She looked again at the hulk who had done nothing but eat since she'd arrived.

Aaron noticed her scepticism. "He's the cleverest person I've ever met," he murmured.

Kaine was still chewing. Even on a day of revelations, it was hard to believe that he had been the Supplier before Zariel.

Finally, Kaine swallowed. "I've retired," he declared. "Not my problem any longer."

Pluton narrowed his eyes. "Perhaps so, but you still know him best. What's Zariel's goal?"

Faythe knew this one. She stood again. "He wants to figure out how the traits work," she announced. *Should she explain his greater ambition—that he wanted to become one of them?*

But she didn't have time to decide, as the gathering were already murmuring amongst themselves.

The old man sighed at Kaine. "You never told the replacement Supplier about the traits?"

"Why would I?" Kaine grinned. "All that tinkering was keeping him busy. Didn't want to take his hobby away from him."

Pluton rubbed his temples. "But even when you retired to live here full-time . . . you didn't think it was prudent to explain the details to the new Supplier?"

Kaine grinned wider. "Nah. I told him I was using the knowledge to become a god, and that if he figured it out he'd be able to follow me."

He took another bite of his rib. Many around the table laughed, but Faythe's jaw dropped open. She stared at the ex-Supplier in horror. "But he believed you!" she shouted.

He laughed. "I know! Funny, isn't it? Such a smart kid, but so easily fooled."

Righteous anger raced through her. "But don't you realise? All this chaos is happening because you lied to your apprentice! He thinks he can actually become a god!"

Kaine roared with laughter, thumping the table with his enormous fists. "Incredible!" He radiated pride. "And not a word of it was a lie. I told him the absolute truth, and he fooled himself. In a way, he must have wanted to be fooled."

Pluton looked troubled. "I appreciate that you've entertained yourself with this game, Kaine, but it does seem irresponsible that the Supplier has been operating without this knowledge. This was always destined to cause trouble."

The huge man broke off another rib and chewed on the end. "Look, I needed to keep Zariel interested so I could retire. He would never have stuck around for the real job. Maybe none of you remember how tiring it is to work every day. Prelife isn't meant for it." He put the bone down. "But Zariel was interested in playing with the traits. So it was a choice between this, or training a new Apprentice Supplier. Why should I ruin the mystery for him and retirement for me?"

Pluton sighed. "It sounds like our mistake was hiring Zariel in the first place."

"Let's not rehash that argument." Eva's voice was scathing, acidic. "Although it is such a shame the Shopkeeper isn't here to lose it once more."

Faythe glanced to Jahu on her left. He was frowning as he attempted to follow the conversation. She gave him a sympathetic smile.

"I stand by the decision," Kaine said, shrugging. "He had experience at the Shop. Best available candidate."

"And it helped you to retire as quickly as possible," interjected Gabriel, from the far end of the table. The whole room turned to look at him. He trembled, seemingly surprised that he'd spoken.

"That's what I said." Kaine spoke with an even menace. "And perhaps you'd like to discuss hasty hiring decisions of your own?" His eyes flicked to Faythe.

She wished they'd all be quiet for a moment so she could think. Everything about Zariel was crystallising in her mind. He was precisely arrogant enough to imagine he'd been chosen by Management because he was special, rather than because of Kaine's laziness and, apparently, Eva's desire to spite the Shopkeeper. And then a combination of his own ambition, bitterness and Kaine's misdirection would so easily have led him down the toxic path he took. For a moment, she almost pitied him.

Aaron leaned forward to deflect Kaine's barb. "Now, now. If we'd been told the full plan when we hired Faythe, then of course we'd have—"

Gabriel whirled around to face him. "Leave me out of this. I warned you the full truth would come out. You were the one who insisted on doing the quickest, shoddiest job imaginable."

"Do you think it's fun travelling around the prelife while you sulk? Have you—"

At the far end of the table, Pluton clicked his tongue. Presumably he'd spent centuries practising, because it echoed loudly enough to silence the argument. "Enough!" he said. "I said we'll deal with you two later. Now, this explains the happenings at the Supplier. If we can move on to consider the Shop—"

"I don't see how we can talk about this freely with her still here," interrupted Eva. She pointed a fork to indicate Faythe, and then pointed to Jahu. "Or him."

Jahu looked up in surprise. He'd given up on following the conversation, and was instead building a huge sandwich filled with everything he could physically reach.

"I know we planned to induct the girl Apprentice eventually," continued the old woman, "but it's obvious that our initial plan is as dead as the Shopkeeper." Faythe blanched. There was a slight gasp around the table, but nobody objected. "Perhaps we need time alone to formulate a new idea?"

Pluton shook his head. "If she's going to co-operate with us, she might as well be here while we make the plan."

"Agreed," mumbled Kaine.

The noise of eating was subsiding as most of Management were finishing their first course. Faythe leaned forward. "Um, can I ask what plan you're all referring to?"

Gabriel held up a hand to answer, and Pluton indicated for him to speak. "She means our long-term plan for the Shop," he said. "We have a particular vision for the future which the Shopkeeper doesn't—"

"*Didn't*," corrected Eva.

"Sorry. A vision which the Shopkeeper didn't share. In order to influence the situation, we decided to place somebody in the Shop who would argue things from our perspective."

Faythe frowned. "Me?"

"That's right."

"But I don't know your perspective. How could I argue it?"

Eva smiled. "You would have come to know it eventually, child. We were playing a long game."

"In fact, it was important that you didn't know, at first," said Gabriel, almost apologetically. "That's why we had to have no contact with you at all. The Shopkeeper would have been suspicious, otherwise."

Faythe blinked. "But the Shopkeeper *was* suspicious!"

"Quite right too," said Pluton. "She was a very smart woman. I'm sure she had an inkling of our intentions."

It would take time to digest this, but for the second time today Faythe's conception of reality was being threatened. "I don't understand," she said, weakly.

"This isn't complex, child," said Eva. "Once the Shopkeeper no longer had reason to be suspicious of her new Apprentice, perhaps centuries from now, we would have contacted you. We would convince you of the importance of sharing our viewpoint, after which you would have done what needed to be done."

She screwed up her face. "But how would you have convinced me of anything?"

"Child," said Eva, placing her wine glass down carefully so her hands were free to point for emphasis. "Until a few hours ago, you believed we were literally gods." Faythe flushed as titters echoed around the room. "We have means of persuasion."

A long-forgotten conversation with Omaro surfaced as Faythe's mind made connections. "So I *was* part of a plot, and I didn't even know it?"

Pluton shrugged. "We prefer the term 'strategic plan'."

A deep sadness settled in her stomach.

Jahu stirred from his seat. "But what was this plan? What did you want her to do?"

Faythe was barely listening. Her mind was recontextualising everything that had happened since she arrived at the Shop. Right now, she was recalling the Shopkeeper's relief after discovering she had 'only' been conspiring with Zariel. That relief had led to complacency, which had killed her. *But she'd been correct to be suspicious.*

Faythe wanted to cry.

Eva looked at Pluton. "Regardless of how we decide to proceed, I don't think we should share our long-term aims today."

A white-clad servant leaned over the old man's shoulder to remove his plate. He mumbled a thank you, and then steepled his hands and rested his elbows on the table. "Actually, I think we will," he said.

But just then, there was a *BOOM* and the universe blinked. The candles all extinguished in an instant, and even the starlight stopped shining through the huge windows of the Hall. Moments went by, long enough for Faythe to panic that she'd gone blind, before light reappeared.

She looked around the table. Everybody else appeared similarly petrified—except Kaine, who was merrily building a fresh plate of food for his second round.

"What *is* that?" she asked. "It keeps happening. Is it you?"

Even as she said it, she realised it couldn't be. *Management aren't gods.*

Pluton looked nauseous. He waved a servant offering a drink away.

At the far end of the table, Kaine spoke up. "It's Zariel." He sounded unconcerned.

The old man scowled. "His machine? Is it going to affect us?"

"Can't say for sure," said Kaine, "but I doubt it. He could make a huge void though."

"Big enough to destroy us?"

"No." Everyone visibly relaxed. "Big enough to ruin his Complex, certainly, and possibly even the Shop. This far away, we'll be fine."

Eva signalled to a servant to refill her wine.

Faythe couldn't believe how calm everyone was. "I'm sorry," she said. "Did you say it might destroy the Shop?"

"Quite possibly," said Kaine. "Unless he stops his machine or fills the void up."

"Then can I request we move on urgently? How are we going to stop him?"

Pluton rubbed his chin. "Zariel is summoning ancient and powerful forces he can't understand or control. And there's an important principle which goes: *don't do that.* But the fact that he is continuing rather suggests he won't be open to reason."

Eva took a sip from her wine glass. "Well, I'll say it, then. I can't be the only one thinking that this problem solves itself? And that it may even solve our other problems in the same instant?"

There were nods around the table. "That's what I was thinking," said Pluton.

Faythe was now lost. She looked around wildly. "I'm sorry . . . how does this solve the supply crisis at the Shop?"

Kaine held up a mug and a servant ran forward to fill it. "Zariel creates a huge void, he gets sucked into it, so does the Shop. End of problem," he said.

"The only issue I see," said Pluton, slowly, "is that if the Shop survives but the Complex doesn't, it may present short-term difficulties, similar to those described by the Acting Shopkeeper here." He looked around the table. "But I think we're all on the same page about that eventual transition, too?"

More nods of assent, except from Faythe. "I'm sorry, again . . . what page are we all on?"

Pluton looked directly at her. "The Shop has more or less served its purpose. Our plan was to slowly wind it down over the next several centuries. But if everything happens considerably faster, then it might be easier for all concerned."

"*What?!* That's what you planned for me? To convince the Shopkeeper to close the Shop? Why would you do that?"

"It's become more trouble than it's worth," said Eva.

The group mumbled agreement. Faythe was numb with shock. She'd assumed that beneath all this gluttony and laziness Management must still care about the Shop they'd created. "But what would happen without the Shop? What replaces it?"

"The Shop was a means to an end, child," said Eva. "And we reached that end a long time ago. We did inform the Shopkeeper of these plans."

Another memory resurfaced. The Shopkeeper replying anxiously to a letter, late at night. "The Shop was a means to an end? What end?"

"It's all around you. Look at everything we have. None of this would have been possible without the Shop."

"But the purpose of the Shop isn't for you to have comfortable prelives." She was yelling now, which was probably a gross breach of meeting decorum, but she didn't care. "It's so all of humanity can experience their *real* lives! Nothing *changes* here!" She looked around the table for support, but there only appeared to be a faint sense of embarrassment at her earnestness. "And if we don't act fast, everyone on Earth will suffer, too. And humanity will die out entirely!"

"Yes, and . . . ?" Eva looked perplexed. They stared at each other in mutual incomprehension.

"I don't know how to explain this to you. If everybody on Earth dies then that's it. The end of humans on Earth. This is worse than killing the whole planet—you're talking about preventing the possibility of life for everybody, for all eternity."

"What I think you're not understanding," said Eva, with a smile which never reached her eyes, "is that absolutely none of that affects us."

"It might affect you!" Jahu spoke up suddenly. "If people can't get to Earth, the prelife will fill up. Stands to reason."

Kaine laughed. "Nice try, but that wouldn't happen. We have ways of getting rid of excess people."

Jahu hung his head. Faythe wanted to hug him for trying. She turned to Kaine. "Well, what if you're wrong about the void?" she countered. "What if it is big enough to destroy here?"

The big man shrugged.

Astonishingly, none of the others appeared to be concerned, either. Surely Management weren't *so* decadent that they couldn't even rouse themselves to prevent their own possible destruction?

Eva sniffed. "Kaine is rarely wrong. Besides, why do you care? What's Earth to you? Or the Shop? You might as well stay here, too."

"Stay here?"

"Why not?"

She opened her mouth and closed it again. Could she justify caring about the fate of humanity? Either you care, or you don't, right? A quiet voice in the back of her mind whispered: *Maybe she has a point. Why NOT stay? Incredible food. Beautiful music. Admittedly, awful company. But maybe they'd turn out to be okay?*

Would a comfortable—no, luxurious—eternity be so bad?

But that train of thought never reached its destination. "I can't stay here," she said. "The Shop is important. Whatever you believe doesn't change the reality that it matters."

"To *you*," said Eva.

She glared at the old woman. "Yes. To me." The others watched with open amusement as they ate. Gabriel, alone, shifted uncomfortably as her gaze swept around, although he said nothing. "I really had the wrong idea about Management."

"Which was all part of the plan." Eva smirked. "After all, who do you think started the rumours about us?"

Faythe closed her eyes. Perhaps one final route of persuasion remained. "Okay. Even if you're right, and Zariel's actions won't affect you, *and* you don't care that it's going to affect countless others, can you help me *anyway*? Let's keep the Shop running. A well-run Shop, with a friendly Acting Shopkeeper, just like you wanted. There's no need to close it down. Let's not spoil your well-planned eternity with unpredictable chaos."

You horrible parasites, she thought. But because she had learned a lot about diplomacy in recent years, she kept that bit quiet.

"That would be a desirable outcome, if it were possible," said Pluton. "But I believe every possible action would require immense effort on our part. It's easier to allow Zariel's events to run their course, and then either clean up the mess, or not."

By this point, most of the table had seemingly lost interest in the conversation. They whispered to one another as they sipped wine on their plump cushions.

"What's a little effort weighed against the fate of humanity, forever?" she countered.

Someone opposite her yawned.

Eva tutted. "Didn't we hire you to fix problems at the Shop? Fix this, if you care so much."

There was a quiet rumble of agreement from those who were still listening. Faythe's eyes opened wide. "Me? But I don't know what to do! That's why I'm here."

"Then I suppose the Shop deserves to fail."

Pluton stood up. "Perhaps it's time for music?"

The group cheered.

"Wait!" she shouted, desperately. *The answer was so obvious.* "There is one thing we have that Zariel doesn't. Maybe we can still save the Shop."

Eva glowered. "Aren't you listening? We don't care."

Gabriel leaned forward. "But maybe we should listen to her?" he said, trembling quietly. "As she said, a well-functioning Shop would lead to a quieter prelife."

"Very well," sighed Pluton. He held up a finger. "But let this be the final word. This meeting has gone on long enough."

"Here's my idea," said Faythe, excitedly. "What about the traits? Zariel doesn't know how they work. We could use their powers to fix this."

Pluton frowned.

"You won't have to do anything," she pleaded. "Just tell me. I can use the secret to bargain with Zariel. Or maybe even stop him." The old man nodded uncertainly. "Hasn't enough harm come from Kaine keeping the secret? Tell *me*."

Kaine snorted, but Pluton held up a hand. "Very well. I shall tell you." A wave of relief flooded through Faythe. "Afterwards, you may do as you wish. If you stop Zariel and his machine, all the better. If not, so be it." He pointed towards the door of the Hall. "Follow me," he said.

Jahu squeezed her hand as she got up. "You did great," he whispered.

"So did you," she replied, before scampering after Pluton, her heart racing.

Even before she reached the door, the Hall was filled with conversation and music, the meeting already forgotten. Management were not hesitant to begin the real work of enjoying themselves.

She followed the old man through the castle. *At last, she would learn the secrets of the Shop.* She hoped they would be enough to save it.

twenty eight

FAYTHE LIKED TO THINK that the naive girl who had left the Rock all those years ago had grown up. After learning dramatic lessons in the buried Archives of the Shop, the laboratory deep under the Supplier's Complex and the Grand Hall of Management's castle, she surely couldn't be surprised by anything.

And yet she was mildly confounded when Pluton led her to the bottom of a winding staircase. "*Up*stairs?" She frowned. "Don't people normally discuss ancient secrets in basements?"

He looked at her with apparent concern. "Would you prefer that? It's just that it's easier to demonstrate up there."

She shrugged. "If you say so."

After they'd climbed several floors, she leaned over the banister to look up. The stairs spiralled above them with no end in sight.

"As you can imagine," said Pluton, "we don't come up here very often." The old man rested against the wall, puffing slightly from the exertion. Despite missing the feast, he seemed in a relatively good mood.

"How come you're in charge here?" she asked, as they resumed the climb.

"It's ... that's ..." His face creased with effort. "It's always been this way."

Apparently that was all the answer he had. As they ascended, she fantasised about what she was soon to discover. Even before she'd accepted the role of Apprentice, she'd imagined learning about the traits. The possibilities of this knowledge were endless. Perhaps she could stop Zariel with temporary traits, like SUPER STRENGTH, BRAVERY or GENIUS, or maybe even a legendary trait which only existed in rumour, like ACTUAL MAGICAL POWERS.

For now, though, she'd be content with MILDLY STRONG THIGHS. These stairs were murdering her.

Eventually they reached the top, where they entered a circular room without walls. An ornate conical roof was held up by several pillars dotted around the edge of the tower, but her attention was immediately captivated by the spectacular view beyond. The hills surrounding them were covered with a low cloud. Ahead, the waterfall gushed out from the mist, passing the bridge far below and crashing into the lake, which glittered in the starlight. A strong wind blew steadily between the pillars, so she had to lean very slightly to keep her balance.

The stars illuminated the only item inside the room: a tall statue of a person—faceless, featureless and smooth—standing with their arms by their sides.

"Your answer is in there," said Pluton, walking to the statue.

She peered closer. "I don't see anything."

"Patience." He fiddled with the statue's chest, and it slid open with a satisfying click. She leaned over his shoulder.

The statue's chest was empty. "Oh," she said, underwhelmed.

He lit a candle. The flame flickered violently in the wind as he shielded it with his hand and brought it closer. The compartment remained dark.

No . . . the light was simply absorbed.

Suddenly, Faythe understood what was inside the statue.

"It's a void." Her pulse quickened. None of her memories involving voids were particularly positive.

"More than that," whispered Pluton. "This is the first one we ever discovered."

"When?" she murmured. Hushed tones seemed fitting in this open chamber.

"I don't know," he admitted. "I lost count a long, long time ago."

The sorrow in his voice caught her by surprise. His tone had softened once they left the Hall, like an actor no longer playing a role.

She studied his face—lined, just like the Shopkeeper's. "You're like me, aren't you?" she said.

He frowned, not understanding.

"I mean . . . I know now you're not gods. And that you never were. But you discovered the traits and created the Shop, so I thought you must be special." Her eyes met his. "But you're all only human."

He nodded, slowly. He hadn't changed at all, but he looked so different now. Frail and vulnerable. The intimidating, confident leader of Management was just a person. And he was *old*.

Pluton stared into the distance. "We were the first to remain in the prelife." He spoke hesitatingly. "In those days, everybody left straightaway for Earth. There was no Ostholme, no cities anywhere at all. And, of course, no Shop."

She nodded slowly. Logically, there must have been a time before anybody built those places, but it was still tough to imagine a prelife without them.

"We stayed here, and we played. They were happy days. We built homes, and we fashioned them. Some grew into large settlements, while others faded away. And we experimented, always learning more about the prelife. Earth would come, eventually." His words came with great effort, as if it physically hurt to dredge up the memories. "And then, one day, we found the voids."

"How?" she murmured, agog. Tiny colourful wisps were drifting from the statue, infinitesimal tendrils of colourful smoke which disappeared almost as soon as they materialised.

"Kaine found them. He was always tinkering with things, machines, whatever. One day he discovered he could make little holes in space. They emitted such beautiful colours. Everybody came to stare." He smiled, wistfully. "Eventually, he managed to capture those colours in jars."

How long would her trio of friends have had to stay at the Rock before discovering this sort of technology? After two centuries, she had barely mastered the seesaw.

"People started hearing rumours of our little jars," he continued. "They visited, and they all wanted to take one as a souvenir. They were the most beautiful art in the whole prelife. After a while . . . I don't remember how long . . . we started naming each jar."

The wind whistled louder. She tensed against it, entirely focused on the story.

"It was a joke, at first. Swapping HOPE for a favour, or a story, or a meal. It made trading more interesting. And it excited the people. They knew the truth. Everyone knew. But then . . ."

"No." A creeping dread was beginning to slither down her spine.

"We started trading our jars near the entrance to Earth, where the gap is so small that Earth is visible. It was good business sense—everybody was guaranteed to go there eventually. And nobody wanted to miss out on taking our jars with them. Like a kind of good luck charm."

"No."

"Customers started doing favours for us. Work in return for a jar. That's how we built the first Shop"—he laughed softly to himself, lost in memory—"it wasn't much, but it was ours. A room. Tiny. It might still be there, somewhere, buried."

"Please . . ."

"The people wanted more, so we made more. New colours. New varieties. Kaine found he could turn those colours into all kinds of things: powders, liquids, gases. He was a real wizard with them."

She was frozen to the spot.

"And the traits the people wanted! HOPE wasn't enough anymore. Everyone wanted to be different! Unique. They demanded every element of human existence, carefully labelled in our beautiful jars. And gradually, the people who were in on the joke disappeared—they tired of the prelife and went to Earth. And the legends began. Our traits stopped being good luck charms, and they became the real thing . . . in everybody's minds."

Faythe realised that she hadn't been breathing. Her grateful lungs began to move again.

"People didn't want to know the truth, so we stopped telling them. They wanted to believe they were getting the real thing. It was good for everyone, you understand? We got to trade for our art, they got to buy a dream. And as you can see"—he gestured at the grand castle which surrounded them—"we did very well out of it, over the years. All that labour. Through the Shop, we began to own the passage which led to Earth; and with that, we could own everything we ever wanted."

He paused.

"So, that's the magical secret of the Shop, Faythe." Another pause. "There IS no magical secret."

There was a sudden, loud whoosh of wind, as if the universe let out a breath of its own.

Emotions fought for control within Faythe. She refused to believe this. She couldn't. "But what about the Shopkeeper?" she said, desperately. "She always said the Shop was important! Didn't she know?!"

Pluton shrugged. "Like I told you, she was one of us. She knew. Then again . . ." He chuckled ruefully. "She did really believe, I think. But, make no mistake, she knew exactly what the Shop had to offer, even if her staff don't."

The Children don't know, then. That was somehow worse. A painful angry despair reached up inside Faythe's throat to close it.

"Now you understand," he said. "This is why we planned to close the Shop eventually. We got what we needed from it centuries ago. I can't even remember the last time we made a customer work for their traits. And each day it remains open is a liability. The people today couldn't cope with the truth. They're too invested. Even though we began by promising nothing, they want more. None of us are willing to lose what we've built. So we planned to manage the transition, gradually, carefully, so all will remain well."

She felt a curious sensation, as if her insides were falling while her outsides leapt away. *The traits aren't real.* Yet another cast-iron certainty had turned out to be nothing at all and the vertigo felt as real as if she were plunging off the top of the tower.

She swayed slightly as the implications rebounded back and forth in her mind, crystallising as realisation after realisation struck her. Her hopes of using the traits against Zariel—gone. The Shop was doomed to crumble as the mass of angry humanity built up and eventually overwhelmed it.

But, then, did that even matter now? What was the point of a Shop which sold nothing?

Another realisation. The vast multitude gathered outside the Shop were rioting over empty jars.

Her mind flicked over to Zariel's grand machine. All that was for nothing, too. Just colourful gas, with no prospect of new traits, and *certainly* not of becoming a god. After centuries of endless, determined effort to investigate and understand the traits . . .

She erupted into laughter.

Pluton looked at her, worriedly. "Are you alright?" he asked.

She leaned against the statue, still laughing. "No wonder the traits only ever disappeared when we touched them!" She wiped away tears. "No wonder we couldn't figure out how they worked, no matter what we did! We thought we weren't doing it right, but, oh . . ." She remembered her disgust and shame when she'd suggested they might survive the crisis by relabelling jars. "That's what the Shop already did!" she said, between giggles. "Jars of nothing!"

She doubled into more laughter—manic and painful, but it felt so good. *Better than crying, anyway.*

He watched her for a moment. "So. Now you know," he mumbled.

She didn't reply.

Moments later, he left her alone in the tower with the smooth, featureless statue, and the void where its heart ought to be.

twenty nine

FAYTHE HUGGED her knees to her chest and stared at the hills. The grass billowed in the wind beneath the thin mist.

She hadn't moved since Pluton had left. Thought required effort, so she'd simply sat, vacant. After the nervous energy and the fits of laughter had subsided she was left with an uncomfortable emotional hangover, a slight headache, free-floating despair, and a confusing craving for roast chicken—which was probably just hunger, now that she thought about it.

Her last hope to save the Shop had vanished. But, then, so had her reasons for saving it in the first place.

Nothing had ever truly mattered.

She wandered down the stairs. Sickened by the sound of music and feasting from the Hall, she made for the front of the castle. Nobody gave her a second glance as she stalked through the plush hallways and outside to the bridge.

A stone lay nearby. She threw it, hard, into the chasm. It skittered loudly as it clattered down the rocky cliff and into the pool below.

This wasn't even despondence. It was emptiness.

Another stone rattled down the cliffside. Countless afternoons at the Rock had been spent throwing stones—sometimes for sport, occasionally to annoy Jahu. Two hundred years, and she'd barely changed at all. A handful of years at the Shop, and her old self had disappeared. She'd grown comfortable with her new self, but today's events had shattered everything she'd ever believed in.

Another stone. Pluton must have lived here for thousands and thousands of years. Had he changed at all during that time?

It might be her imagination, but the sound of the feast was just audible over the roar of the waterfall. Maybe she should take Management up on the offer to stay, and enjoy wealth and power of her own. Let the Shop rot, along with the millions of souls gathering there. It was all lies.

Anger flared within the emptiness, and she threw the next stone harder.

Who was she even angry with? Management? Sure, they were selfish. Unbelievably, almost impressively, selfish. But . . . in their place, would she have acted any differently? They'd tried to tell humanity the truth, but nobody wanted to hear it.

Being angry with the universe seemed pointless. It lacked the magic she'd believed in all her prelife. But whose fault was that?!

There was no sense even blaming Zariel. He'd never been trusted with the truth. His actions were inexcusable, but she understood why he saw it differently, given what he'd been told.

Anger ebbed away, and sadness washed in to fill the space. The Shop would close, either due to riots or an exploding void. *But a Shop that sold nothing was surely no loss* . . . although the Shopkeeper would likely have disagreed.

A tear came to her eye. The old lady had been right to suspect her. She wished she could say sorry.

She suddenly felt very tired. She picked up a final stone and heaved it towards the castle, in an extremely human act of pointless defiance.

"OW!"

Her eyes widened. "Jahu?!"

He emerged from the darkness, rubbing his shoulder and muttering. "Yeah, thanks. I spent hours looking for you, so of course you hit me with a stone."

"I'm so sorry!" She put her hand to her mouth. "I've had a bad night."

"Yeah? Well, maybe I did too! I was at that party for hours after you left." He cocked his head and smiled at the memory. "Actually, that bit was good. They really know how to have an excellent time." Suddenly he remembered he was supposed to be annoyed. "Anyway! Then you never came back. And I got worried and looked for you everywhere. And now you've hit me with a rock."

"Just like old times . . . ?" she offered, before reconsidering. "I'm sorry. It was an accident."

He sat down. "It's fine. What happened to you?"

"I don't even know where to start. Sit with me?"

He did, and she told him about her conversation with Pluton. When she finished, he pulled her in for a hug.

She breathed out against his chest and smiled as they sat back up. Discovering that your whole existence had been built on lies shouldn't feel less empty after a single hug, but it did.

Jahu looked thoughtful, and then let out a soft whistle. "Unbelievable. I mean, it was one thing meeting Management like this . . . but the traits?! That's just . . ." He shook his head.

"I know!" She suddenly felt light and free. "Maybe we should go hide somewhere?"

"Hide?" His face contorted with bewilderment. "Like, in the castle?"

"No! In Ostholme, or somewhere like that? Let's go live a nice prelife."

"But what about the Shop?" He stared at her. "You're basically the Shopkeeper."

"I'm not!"

"Aren't they expecting you back?"

She hesitated. Omaro and the Children would be waiting for her. "I suppose," she admitted, finally. The heavy weight of responsibility rushed back in an instant.

"So we have to go fix this."

"But how? Even if the Shop is still standing, Management are frauds. Meanwhile, Zariel has an army with flaming swords and a huge machine that could suck the whole prelife into a void." She drew breath. "And even if I could magically do something about all that—or even *any* of it!—even then, why would I? The traits aren't real! The whole Shop, the whole prelife, *everything* was built on a lie."

Jahu looked at her for a long moment. "On the plus side, if Zariel blows up half the prelife, it'll save us a long walk back."

She laughed bitterly. "That's something, at least. But seriously, what can we do?"

"Why not tell everybody the truth?"

She considered this, and then shook her head. "It wouldn't work. Even Management planned to close the Shop gradually. If we just announced it, many wouldn't believe us. And those that did would be angry that they'd been lied to."

Jahu frowned. "Why wouldn't people believe us?"

"They'd say we were lying so we could keep the power of the traits for ourselves. Or trying to keep the best ones secret. Or that we just hate people and don't want them to live."

"You really think people would say that?"

She thought of Zariel, and of the man on the Road who'd been convinced the Shop was closing just to personally spite him. "Some would. When people are invested in an idea, I don't think they like hearing that it isn't true. Telling the truth might be right but it wouldn't help. It has to come out slowly, I think."

Jahu looked impressed. "I told you the Shop had changed you."

She sighed. "Maybe. But I'm tired."

"Me too."

Already the sky was lightening. Had they been up all night? Soon, Management and their servants would wake and begin a long, hard day of feasting, or whatever other nonsense they spent their days on.

She stood up. "Come on. Let's get out of here."

"Okay!" Jahu sprang up.

She couldn't help smiling at his unquestioning readiness. "You really still think I can fix this, don't you?"

He grinned back. "I don't think so. I *know* you can."

She shook her head. "Idiot."

They crossed the bridge and started down the dark, rocky path leading under the hills and, eventually, back to the Road.

 *thirty*

THE WHOLE PRELIFE was open to them, but there was only one destination in Faythe's heart. She needed to know what had happened at the Shop.

It was a relief when the building came into view and it wasn't on fire. Her brain had spent so long exploring worst case scenarios that she'd almost forgotten they weren't guaranteed to actually have happened.

"Whoa," breathed Jahu. Before them, a thick, winding snake of people filled the Road for miles and miles. From here, they could see the heaving mass of humanity which still occupied the field. There was no hint of order—the queue had long since broken down—but the familiar dome of the Shop still glinted in the sunshine, seemingly untouched.

Most strikingly for Jahu, as he drank in his first sight of all of this, was the Earth hovering high above, majestic and beautiful.

Faythe smiled as he admired the view. It felt good to be back.

Soon after, they resumed their wide, looping route behind the Road to the back of the Shop. Inside, they found a group of the Children talking anxiously by the checkouts.

Omaro saw them first. He yelped with delight and leapt into Faythe's arms. "You're back!"

She gripped him tight. "How's everything here? What's happened since I left?!"

"Nothing we couldn't handle," he replied, confidently.

Risk was standing nearby. He coughed and saluted. "Ma'am. Yesterday the main building nearly burned down after we spent twelve hours physically fending off rioters. Currently, there's a strong chance of more violence beginning at any moment. People are getting very impatient out there." He dropped the salute smartly to his side. "Ma'am, I'm sorry to report that I'm not sure there will be a Shop in another few days."

Omaro waved his hand with an airy confidence. "Like I said, it's been nothing we couldn't handle. How was Management?" He was smiling, but she could see the desperation behind his eyes.

She hesitated. It was a relief to see that the Shop was still standing—and that the Children were okay, most of all—but she still had no idea what to do. She couldn't tell the Children that the Shop served no purpose. Even if they believed her, it would break her heart.

"It was complicated," she said, instead. Suddenly, she became aware that Jahu was lurking awkwardly nearby. "Oh! This is an old friend. Jahu, meet Omaro."

They shook hands. "Welcome," said Omaro, grinning widely. "Technically you jumped a record-breaking queue to get in here, you know."

Jahu laughed. He glanced towards the front door, through which the crowd were clearly audible. "I noticed. Can I do anything to help?"

"Oh, I'm sure you can be useful somehow," said Omaro.

Risk coughed again. "I know you're both joking, but we could genuinely use help if you're willing." He sized Jahu up. "Can you stand still and get in the way of anyone trying to pass? There's usually more to the job, but for today that's all we need."

Faythe stepped forward with a worried expression, but Jahu waved her away. "I'm pretty sure I can handle that." He gave a mock salute and disappeared with Risk.

Omaro turned to Faythe. "Shall I summon the Committee?"

She shook her head. "I don't know what use that would be."

He sighed. "Not good news? I suppose I shouldn't be surprised. The Shopkeeper wasn't a fan of Management, either."

"So I discovered."

"Hey! Look at what I learned while you were gone, though!" He sent his yoyo spinning to the floor, up his leg, over his shoulder, down one arm, back to the floor and up into his hand again.

"Wonderful!" She smiled. "I missed you."

"We missed you too."

There was sadness in his eyes. He knew she was out of ideas.

She sighed. "I need a minute. Can I tell you everything after?"

He nodded. Instinctively, she headed for the Gardens. It was too pain-ful to remain indoors—the aisles felt ghostly and unnatural with bare shelves and no glowing traits.

The Viewing Platform was similarly desolate. Someone had stacked up all the empty tables and chairs so the wooden deck was barren. Even down the steps, the Gardens themselves felt eerie without customers strolling around and admiring the flowers.

She went to her favourite spot, and was surprised to find it occupied.

"Beris!" The Child was gazing mournfully at the sky, the green of his suit contrasting with the slightly darker green of the grass. "Are you okay?"

He leapt to his feet, hurriedly offering an officious handshake.

Faythe hugged him instead.

"Yes, I am fine," he said, brushing dirt off his suit. "But . . ." He pointed up at the Earth. It was currently in darkness, so only the spots where humans lived were lit up. "See that bit there? Where the land goes like this?" He made a swooshing motion.

She followed where he pointed. "Yeah, I see it." She squinted. "But what am I looking at? There's nothing there."

"That's right," he said, forlornly. "There used to be lights there. One of Earth's great cities has gone."

Her mouth fell open. "Cities can't just disappear!"

"We can be certain that they're not taking the current crisis very well down on Earth."

She closed her eyes in horror at the scale of what was happening. Nobody on Earth would even understand why. No wonder they were tearing themselves apart.

"I'm sorry," she said, looking up at the faraway planet.

"It's not your fault." Beris smiled sadly. "I should get back upstairs."

"Maybe it isn't my fault," she said, as he left her alone in the clearing. "But I am responsible."

Her idle fantasies of escaping to Ostholme had long dissipated. She couldn't ignore this. Or even forgive herself if she tried.

"I have to fix this," she muttered. The familiar burden of responsibility settled like an old, comfortable coat. It felt surprisingly good to have one thing she could count on. She said it again, louder. "I have to fix this!"

A voice came from the bushes. "No, it's alright! I'll do it."

She scrambled in terror as the Gardener appeared from within the thicket, brandishing a bamboo cane and a piece of twine.

"Looks like someone stood on it," he said, conversationally, bending over and strapping the cane to a broken plant. He straightened up and took off his hat. "Good to see you back."

"Thanks," she said, distantly, staring at the plant.

"Best I can do, but I think it'll be alright now."

"That's good," she said. "But you might have noticed we have other problems. That big crowd is still waiting outside. And Zariel's still not sending any supplies."

The Gardener scratched his head. "Sounds like we ought to do something."

"Believe me, I've tried."

"You tried everything?"

"Pretty much."

"Well." He put his hat back on. "If in doubt, water it and hope for the best."

She raised both eyebrows. "What am I going to do—water Zariel?"

The Gardener shrugged. "Why not?"

She inhaled, unsure where to begin. "For a start, he has guards with flaming swords, voids which can wipe people from existence, and he lives in a massive, well-guarded complex."

"Have you tried watering the swords, at least?"

She snorted. "I'll think about it. Thanks." She'd missed the Gardener. He was excellent at listening to problems, even if his solutions tended to be completely impractical.

"It'll be alright," he said.

She wished she had a fraction of his confidence. Her current best idea was to open the corridor to Earth and encourage the crowd to pass through without traits, and hope that nobody asked awkward questions about what was happening. Unfortunately, her past experience with crowds suggested that this plan might last for five minutes before someone demanded they be given traits *anyway* and the whole thing collapsed in another riot.

Suddenly, she was grateful for the listening ear. "The problem is," she said, as the Gardener wandered over to inspect a flowerbed near the path, "even if we solve the crowd issue, I discovered things while I was away which change everything."

"Interesting! What things are these?"

"I can't tell you."

"Ah, secrets. I know some too. Did you know—"

". . . is this going to be about worms?"

"Maybe." The Gardener's eyes sparkled. "Let me ask you something. These things you learnt—were they already true?"

She frowned. "What do you mean?"

"You said that learning them changes everything. But were they already true? Or did they *become* true when you learned them?"

She blinked. "I guess they were already true."

"So nothing has actually changed then?"

"No. Well, yes! But . . ." His logic was undeniable. All those thousands of years of history at the Shop had taken place in a universe where the traits were already not real. Only her knowledge had changed. But surely that must matter?

The Gardener appeared to read her mind. "Maybe it matters. But perhaps not in the way you assumed."

She nodded. She felt on the cusp of understanding something important.

A connection formed in her mind. The memory surfaced, unbidden, of the Shopkeeper closing the Shop after Tapak's mix-up with the jars. She frowned. Why would the Shopkeeper do that? She *knew* the traits weren't real . . .

The Shopkeeper had battled Management on behalf of the Shop, and even, in the end, been prepared to die for it. But why would she also believe in the *traits*?

Faythe flickered on the verge of a realisation. It was an uncomfortable, frustrating sensation, like her whole brain wanted to sneeze.

"Thanks Gard—" she began, but the word wasn't out before the sky flashed black and the entire universe blinked in a painful spasm. Her body juddered, as if every atom leapt several metres sideways in an instant. After a momentary deafening sensation which she could only describe as *screaming silence*, her vision returned.

In the distance, the sky was wrong—red, but too red, like a fire had itself been set on fire. Above the mountains, near the Supplier's Complex, there was a hole in the sky.

Faythe grimaced. She turned to the Gardener. "Tell the others I had to go."

She grabbed her bag and ran for the Warehouse, where she boarded a train. After pulling a few levers, she was on her way to the Supplier once again.

thirty one

THIS WAS THE WORST journey to the Supplier's Complex yet. As usual, the train rattled rapidly through stunning countryside, but the scenic moment was marred—not unreasonably—by a spiralling vortex shooting up from the mountains which was turning all colour in the world *wrong*.

Just like the void which had killed the Shopkeeper, it hurt to look at. Nevertheless, Faythe made herself stare until her eyes watered and her brain could—nearly—make sense of what she was seeing.

It seemed more spread out than the first void, as if it wasn't quite *there-but-not* in the same way. It was neither moving nor still, but somehow both, like an optical illusion which shifted as she tried to focus. If she looked out of the corner of her eye, a huge coil of smoke seemed to rise from somewhere within the valley, widening into a tremendous spinning disc in the sky. But as soon as she gazed directly at it, everything shifted and the image disappeared.

Her bag clinked at her feet. Inside, the jars Omaro had given her so long ago rattled with the movement of the train. On impulse, she took them out. As ever, they lit the driver's compartment with a pleasing, colourful sparkle.

She smiled sadly at the blank labels covering the real ones underneath. *Even those 'real' labels were lies.*

Suddenly, she wanted to know what these jars were pretending to be. It only took a little tug at the corner to peel the first label away.

Underneath, in beautiful calligraphy, the original label read: ALWAYS KNOWS WHAT TO DO.

She laughed aloud. What wouldn't she have sacrificed to have had this trait during the last few years? The universe clearly had a cruel sense of humour. If there was such a thing as Management's Management, she planned to make several serious complaints when she met them.

The label on the next read BRAVERY. She laughed again. A counterfeit copy of everything she needed—exactly right and completely useless, all at once.

And then the final jar: IRREGULAR BOWEL FUNCTION. It was perhaps less obvious what ironic point the universe might be making in this instance.

She slid the jars back into her bag and stared out of the window, biting her lip. It wouldn't be long before she arrived, and she still had no idea what her plan was.

The Gardener had talked a lot of nonsense, but he had been basically correct about her lack of options. She had to find Zariel, and hope she'd know what to do when the time came.

But how? The station would surely be swarming with Zeraph. Not that their numbers mattered—even a single Zeraph was a one-person swarm, as far as her ability to fight them went. It would be better, then, to get off the train before it reached the station, without being seen.

Aha! Her thoughts crashed together in her mind to form an idea: she could stop the train in the tunnel before it ever emerged into the valley.

Unfortunately, by the time she had this idea, the train was already in the tunnel, and moving fast.

Without pausing to think, she pulled hard on the lever. The train began to brake, but too slowly. The wall of light grew and grew. It was clear that the train was going to limp out to a halt on the mountainside, exposed and far from the station. The worst of all worlds.

Her only other option was truly stupid. She could jump off now while the train was still moving.

Naturally, this was exactly what she did. She yanked the door handle and leapt out immediately.

It turned out that jumping face-first into darkness from a moving train isn't easy. She landed on her bag, which crunched and absorbed most of the blow. Immediately, she curled up with her hands over her ears to soften the deafening screech of the braking train as it echoed in the cramped tunnel.

She ached, and would be covered in bruises tomorrow—if there was one—but she was otherwise alright. When the noise eventually subsided, she crept, painfully, to the exit.

The Complex stretched out in the valley beneath. It was impossible to ignore the void jutting into the sky like an anti-matter helter-skelter. Everything else looked amiss, as if the universe had been washed too many times, and all the colours and textures had bled into one another.

Despite this wrongness, the view was familiar. The tremendous stone wheel still turned, and the chimneys still belched. Something was missing, though, and a moment later she realised what it was. The people. The long lines of workers which usually snaked around the complex had disappeared.

A nearby movement caught her eye. A group of Zeraph were walking along the tracks to intercept the train, which had come to a stop halfway down the hill. She'd better move quickly.

Her bag tinkled as she stood up. She opened it to see the smashed remains of the jar of BRAVERY glaring up at her.

She cursed and tipped the bag up, feeling an odd sense of loss as she dumped the shattered glass just inside the tunnel. At least the other two jars had survived her idiotic jump. Pity about the fake BRAVERY, though.

She followed the track briefly down the hillside before darting off to the side, cutting between two of the low buildings which were dotted across the hillside. She took an empty-looking alleyway between two warehouses, keeping her gaze down as much as possible so the huge rip in reality wouldn't hurt her eyes. Luckily, the spiralling pillar helped with navigation, as it made her destination obvious. At the base of that column was Zariel's lab.

She crept through eerily quiet streets of increasingly tall metallic buildings, taking whichever road led her closer to the base of the void. As she got nearer, it became more and more difficult to breathe. The oppressive, tight air took on an unpleasant, almost tangy, flavour. And she *itched*. Her scalp crawled with an uneasy swelling sensation, like invisible sparks were gathering all around her. Her bones prickled and her heart pounded as she edged ever closer to the column of unreality.

She was only a couple of blocks away when a shout from across the street startled her. "What are you doing here, miss?"

Her breath caught in her throat. A Zeraph was standing in a doorway. Like all Zeraph, she was tall and imposing. In the unusual voidlight, her uniform was oddly discoloured, but—unfortunately—her sword remained aflame. She shouted back inside the building. "She's here! The girl from the train!"

Faythe reached deep inside her brain for a plan, praying that her subconscious had prepared for this exact moment without her realising. "Um . . ." she said.

The Zeraph covered the distance between them in seconds and grabbed her arm.

She squirmed uselessly as the Zeraph dragged her along the street. "Where are you taking me?"

"We've got orders to lock you up."

She gritted her teeth. It was unlikely she would succeed even if she got to see Zariel, but her odds were zero if she didn't. She attempted to wriggle away again, but the guard was too strong. "Can't you take me to see Zariel instead?"

"Why would I do that?"

"I don't know. What do you want? I can help you!"

"I doubt—"

Just then, there was an almighty crashing noise everywhere at once, another noise so loud that Faythe could barely hear it. Every colour in the complex suddenly multiplied, blinding her with a darkness which left bizarre afterimages on her retinas.

The Zeraph's grip on her arm slipped.

An endless instant later, everything snapped back to normal—aside from the huge spinning void disc in the sky, of course.

"What was that?" muttered the Zeraph.

"It's Zariel. Management told me his machine might destroy everything. So I'm trying to stop him."

She looked at the Apprentice sceptically. "You . . . ?"

Faythe drew herself up to full height, which was about level with the woman's armpits. "I'm from the Shop Before Life." She had an idea. "Have you ever been there?" The woman shook her head. "But you want to go sometime, right? I've got a gift for you. May I?"

She reached into her bag, and pulled out the first jar her hand found. It was ALWAYS KNOWS WHAT TO DO. Even in the bizarre reddish air of the complex, it sparkled like sunshine.

The Zeraph gazed in awe as Faythe handed it over. "It'll come in handy on Earth. Tell the Children at the Shop that you're happy just to take this jar. I promise it's enough."

More than enough, really.

The woman smiled. "I will. Thanks!"

Above them, the sky flickered again, much more briefly, and there was a sucking sound, as if all the air disappeared and rushed back into the universe at once.

The Zeraph gave her a frightened glance and ran for the train.

Faythe didn't wait either. She slipped the final jar into her pocket and ran as fast as she could in the opposite direction.

thirty two

THE HUMAN MEMORY is fickle. It isn't a vast bank of moments, painstakingly catalogued for perfect retrieval.

Recollections are often tied to specific perceptions, like the smell of a perfume, the sound of a voice, or the sight of an object. Any of these can bring a bygone moment crashing back with the force of a tidal wave.

As a result, memory plays tricks. Revisiting a place where important memories were formed can be disconcerting, as if everything since the last visit was nothing but a dream.

Alternatively, it can feel as if aeons have passed, and that a whole new person is standing in a familiar old place.

It all depends on how much you've grown in between.

Faythe prickled with dread as she descended into the cavern where Zariel's machine stood. Her previous visits had been terribly brief, yet every detail was seared so vividly into her mind that everything from the deep reddish colour of the rocky walls to the clanging of the metal gantry brought memories rushing back.

One difference was immediately apparent, and, admittedly, it was a big one: there was now an enormous hole in reality twisting up and out of the centre of the cavern.

She leaned over the gantry and gazed into the pit, sniffing at the musty underground air. The construction beneath was several times larger than last time. It now nearly filled the crater with pipes and whistles and belts and gears. Here, above the machine, light bent awkwardly around the base of the void column, twisting the top half of the room nauseatingly as she looked around.

The air felt simultaneously too thick to move through and too light to breathe. Merely existing this close to the void was making her tired.

Luckily, this oppressive atmosphere seemed to affect everybody the same way, as none of the Zeraph even looked up as she entered. Tired-looking underlings stood around the rim of the crater below, whispering to one another nervously.

And there was Zariel, still bounding with energy. He was shouting into the crater at a man who was fiddling inside a hatch on the giant contraption.

She couldn't hear what was being said, as the whole universe had been humming loudly since she'd entered the lab. The noise covered her descent on the metal steps to the rocky surface near the crater. Ahead, a pair of Zeraph stared, rapt, as the hapless man fiddled with the machine. Occasionally he paused to glance up, terrified, at the huge thrumming void high above.

After a threatening gesture from Zariel, the man lifted a wrench and did something inside the hatch.

Suddenly, the thrumming halted and once more, the entire universe blinked. Everything was black and bright and empty and full all at once.

Even if she could become accustomed to these blips in reality, this one would have been disturbing. No matter in which direction she looked she could see the outline of the unlucky man, his body contorted unnaturally, neon bright against the blackest black. The glowing outline stretched before snapping back down like a rubber band and then melting apart with a scream . . .

. . . and then light and sound returned to the universe with the now-familiar sucking sound of air rushing back to fill a vacuum.

Everyone blinked, disorientated. Zariel folded his arms and regarded the now-empty hatch on top of the machine with a furious, impatient expression.

Faythe ignored the Zeraph and made straight for him. As she approached he looked up, and his frustration morphed into a smirk.

"Aha! Welcome back." He sounded almost bored, as if she had only gone to fetch fresh milk, and as if he weren't creating an apocalyptic hellscape of pure nothingness for literally zero reason.

"No time for pleasantries, Zariel. I'm here to say"—wait, what *was* her plan, exactly?—"um, you need to stop this."

He laughed. "You don't know what you're talking about."

"Oh, I do," she said. It made a nice change to be more informed than Zariel for once. "This machine is dangerous! It could swallow everything in the prelife."

"I believe not. But even if it did, that doesn't sound important."

She blinked. "Does your existence not matter? It would swallow you too."

"And what happens if it does?" His eyes flashed. "Two possibilities: either I cease to exist—a prospect which I won't be around to regret— or I am right, and I become one with Management. Either outcome is acceptable to me."

She spoke as patiently as she could. "But I'm here to tell you that I know that won't happen, Zariel. I spoke to Management."

"Management!" He giggled. "As if they'd speak to you. Do you think I'm a fool?"

"No." She hesitated. "Well, yes." His eyes narrowed. *Bad time for honesty.* "But look at what you're doing! It's unbelievably foolish. At least wait till you hear what I learned from Management!"

"You're lying. But even if you weren't, nothing I could learn from you would compare to the merest possibility of becoming Management."

"Come on, Zariel, I know you've invested a lot in this, but let me—"

He gestured. Within seconds, a Zeraph was beside her, holding a flaming sword uncomfortably close to her face. Her cheeks reddened, and she flinched away.

"Throw her in," said Zariel.

"*Wait!*" she screamed. "You have to listen!"

The Zeraph ignored her screams and flung her effortlessly into the pit.

She landed on top of the machine. It wasn't a long drop, but her shoulder throbbed anew as she stood up.

"I don't care for your lies about Management, little Apprentice," yelled Zariel. "But you can still be useful! You're going to make the final adjustment to my machine."

Images of screaming neon silhouettes danced unpleasantly through her mind. "I don't know how!"

"Don't worry!" He sneered down over the crater's edge. "It's simple. All you have to do is tighten the final connection. And there's good news— we've thrown enough people at the problem that we must be extremely close by now."

She looked around. There was a ladder leading back up. However, the Zeraph was standing menacingly at the top, brandishing his sword. *No escape there.*

"How do you know I won't break the machine?" she shouted back, defiantly.

Zariel fixed her with an intense stare. "One volunteer tried that already. Instead of the quick experience you just witnessed, he appeared to spend a long time regretting his decision. Even now, we still hear his screams in the darkness."

She gulped. Being turned into a neon shadow and stretched to the size of the universe was one thing, but . . . "He's trapped, but still alive?"

Zariel shrugged. "Not 'alive', exactly. But still aware, we think. Fascinating, isn't it?"

She shuddered.

"Hurry!" yelled Zariel. "Or I'll send my friend down to persuade you."

She glanced at the Zeraph. Perhaps there was an escape route left. "He's gambling with your life too!" she shouted. "You should stop him!"

The man didn't even blink.

It appeared she had no choice. She walked gingerly over the top of the machine towards the hatch. Her teeth began to tingle and her eyes felt like they were being squeezed out of her skull. The throbbing noise scraped against her brain like sandpaper through her ears. No wonder the last 'volunteer' had appeared so distressed. It was amazing he'd been able to function at all.

As she bent down to the hatch, the jar in her pocket dug into her thigh.

She placed it inside the panel, next to the wrench left by the previous unlucky worker. IRREGULAR BOWEL FUNCTION, proclaimed the label, in lovely, neat writing. She stared at it for a moment. It was fitting that she would be left with that particular jar, rather than BRAVERY, or ALWAYS KNOWS WHAT TO DO. It seemed a better metaphor for her entire prelife.

Which was apparently about to end.

Suddenly afraid, she hugged the jar to her chest with one arm, like the world's least comforting teddy bear. With her other hand, she picked up the wrench. She could almost feel the loose valve whistling, a high-pitched screech made of touch rather than sound.

Zariel shouted down triumphantly, and she could just about make it out. "I always thought you'd make an excellent Apprentice, Faythe. Now you get to learn a new trade!"

She drew a deep breath. There were two options: break the valve, or tighten the valve. Either might destroy the machine. And either could destroy vast swathes of the prelife.

There was no way of knowing which option led to which outcome, but she didn't like her own chances either way.

Her legs trembled as she fumbled the wrench into place around the valve. After a momentary hesitation, she made a decision.

She twisted the wrench. The screech in her brain intensified and a tiny void escaped from the valve, releasing a wisp of colourful sparks which dissipated in the air around her hand. She gritted her uncomfortably tingling teeth and twisted harder still.

The screech peaked and then stopped, as the valve clicked into place with an admittedly satisfying pop.

Absolutely nothing happened.

The sudden silence was blissful. The light from the jar of IRREGULAR BOWEL FUNCTION reflected around the inside of the hatch.

She hugged the jar tighter.

Nothing continued to happen.

She exhaled slowly, with great relief.

"I think I did it," she shouted upwards, jubilantly. "It's—"

The machine, and the universe, exploded.

thirty three

FAYTHE WAS FLUNG UPWARDS and out of the crater, narrowly missing the top of the ladder before colliding with something soft—*a person, probably?*—and then smashing into something hard. *A wall, definitely.*

Seconds passed before she opened her eyes. Amazingly, she was alive.

Even more miraculously, her jar of IRREGULAR BOWEL FUNCTION was unbroken. She slid it back into her pocket and scrambled to her feet.

The crater in the centre of the room was empty. *Really, extremely empty.*

The tall column of unreality had collapsed down into the cave, and the crater where the machine had been was now filled with a spinning sphere of nothingness, which whirled around like a drunken tornado.

All of her senses were overwhelmed. Her skin appeared to be telling her the room was so hot that everything must be on fire, but also so cold that she was freezing to death.

Across the chamber the few remaining Zeraph were fleeing to the outside world. Blearily, still shaking off the impact of the explosion, she began to follow, but someone gripped her arm from behind.

She whirled around. Zariel stood before her, smiling in manic triumph.

"Let me go!" she cried, struggling to prise her arm from his grasp.

His attention was elsewhere. He stared reverentially at the dizzying sphere. "We did it!" he yelled.

Already, the void had grown so large that it nearly touched the rocky, narrow ends of the cavern. Her heart stopped as she realised they were about to be trapped on this side of the crater.

"We can still escape, Zariel," she said, as calmly as she could manage.

"Escape from what?" He took her hand, tightly, and gestured towards the rotating emptiness. "*This* is what I wanted. A proper void."

He sounded uncertain, almost like he was trying to convince himself. She tried, unsuccessfully, to pull away.

"Why would you want this?! What's different about it?"

"I figured it all out." It was becoming harder to hear him over the gathering wind. The void was rotating faster and faster as it expanded, dragging the air in the cavern around with it. "The key to becoming Management must be where the traits are! I found notes from the old Supplier, about how he experimented with the bigger voids, and I realised *they* must be the way in, the real way."

She closed her eyes. "Oh, Zariel, no."

"It was so obvious." His face softened. "In a way, I'm grateful that you're trapped with me. I don't mind sharing this opportunity with you. Infinity halved is still infinity."

With that, he dragged her towards the edge of the crater.

"*No!*" She attempted to pull away again, but his grip was too strong. "Listen! I wasn't lying earlier about meeting Management. None of this is real!"

He snorted. "It looks extremely real to me."

She babbled, her words escaping with maximum urgency. "Please, you have to listen! I'm not lying. I went to where Management live, to their castle." She sucked in a breath. Even a whole lungful of this thinning, whirling air wasn't enough. "They're not gods, Zariel. They *aren't*. They're just people. You can't become like them, because you *already are* like them. I promise!"

He laughed, shaking his head. "It's ridiculous how scared you are." He held her hand tighter, and she leaned back with all her weight, slowing him from the edge as much as she could.

"*Kaine* told me!" she cried. "The ex-Supplier. He lied to you when he said he was becoming a god. It was all a joke to him!"

Zariel frowned, perturbed.

Sensing she'd finally found a way in, she continued, desperately.

"That does sound like him, doesn't it? And how else would I know what he said? Or about his stupid blond beard!"

He looked suspicious. "You could have seen pictures."

"Maybe. But have I ever lied to you? These notes you found, they might have helped you build a bigger void, but they have *nothing* to do with becoming a god. I promise."

She waited desperately while he considered this. Blood pounded through her veins. She felt fragile, as if each heartbeat might be powerful enough to shatter her entirely. She was acutely aware of the edge of the crater, mere inches away, and of the pulsating vortex just below.

"Maybe you did meet Kaine," said Zariel, slowly. "But the answer lies inside this portal, I'm sure of it."

"What makes you so sure?"

"Think about it. Management discovered the traits and set up the Shop. And that must be how they became Management in the first place! Kaine told me I was close to figuring out his puzzle, that I was on the right path. *This* must be where he went. The answer must be inside these voids."

She sucked air through her teeth. "You're so close, Zariel," she said, softly enough for him to hear over the whooshing of the wind. "The answer *is* in this void." *This was going to be difficult.* He was already in a fragile, volatile state. She didn't want to push him over the edge—figuratively or literally. *But these truths needed to be shared.* "The void is empty. And so are the traits. They're not real."

He narrowed his eyes. "What are you saying?"

"I didn't believe it either. I didn't want to believe it. But Management confessed to me. The traits . . . they're beautiful trinkets, nothing more. That's why you can't get them to work."

For a moment, the screech of the swelling void was the only sound in the chamber.

She spoke as gently as she could. "I'm sure it hurts, but, all this time, you've been investigating nothing, Zariel."

More silence.

"NO," he howled, finally. "I don't believe it." He glared at her. "This is all lies. You don't want me to ascend. Or you're trying to trick me."

"I'm telling the truth, I promise." She attempted to wriggle backwards as he pulled them both towards the edge once more.

"The traits can't be nothing!" he shouted. "*Everything*—the whole of the prelife!—is built on them. You believe humans arrive on Earth *unprepared*? That's impossible! You must be lying! You're just scared."

"I'm not the one who's scared, Zariel."

It was true, she realised. She wasn't afraid. But Zariel preferred the certainty of death over the uncertainty of life. It was only natural that he'd latch onto the traits, with their promise of power, safety and, above all, *control*.

Over the last few years, she had survived the loss of every certainty she'd ever had: her friends, her home, her belief in herself, her faith in Management and then, most devastatingly, her faith in the traits. After the pain of accepting her part in the death of the Shopkeeper, merely 'going to Earth unprepared' seemed like a walk in the Gardens.

Anyway, it wasn't as if people went to Earth totally unprepared. Even without the magic of the traits, they'd always had the Shopkeeper talking them through it, and the experience of visiting the Shop . . .

. . . incongruously, the image of the Gardener popped into her head. *What had he said?*

These secrets she'd learned had *always* been true. The traits had *always* been nothing.

Suddenly, everything clicked into place.

The traits weren't magic. *But they didn't HAVE to be magic to work.*

At last, Faythe KNEW WHAT TO DO.

Using her free hand, she reached into her pocket for the jar of IRREGULAR BOWEL FUNCTION, carefully covering the label with her fingers.

"I can demonstrate the secret, Zariel," she said. "I know it now."

He glanced down at the jar. "What secret?"

"The traits aren't magic. I told you that. But that's not the whole secret." She loosened the lid as she talked. "There's a secret to the secret, and I'm pretty sure even Management don't know it. They stumbled onto a deeper truth without realising. But the Shopkeeper figured it out."

He watched her suspiciously. *This was her final chance.* She held up the jar, and he leaned closer to see.

For the second time in a minute, she gave thanks for the accidental wisdom of the Gardener. She *would* water Zariel. Sort of.

She flicked her wrist to dislodge the jar lid, and launched the smudgy brown powder of IRREGULAR BOWEL FUNCTION straight into Zariel's face.

It dissipated—of course—but he staggered in surprise, loosening his grip on her. She shook herself free.

For an instant, he teetered on the edge before falling. Instinctively, he scrabbled, halting his fall with his forearms on the rocky edge of the crater.

She crouched and grabbed his hand, digging her feet into the floor as hard as she could. He dangled above the spinning void, his feet barely scraping the surface. He kicked out, trying to get her to let go.

"Everything I've said is true," she shouted, gritting her teeth. The void was shrieking now, and her bones itched with the buildup of energy in the chamber. "You just experienced the secret for yourself."

Even suspended precariously above a deathly gap in reality, Zariel still managed to sneer. "A trick?"

"Precisely," she said softly. "It's all a trick. And it always was. But is a trick that *works* still a trick?"

"What are you talking about? Let me fall!" He dug his nails into her hand, wriggling to escape, but she refused to relax her grip.

"Nice try, but I'm not letting go." She probably *should* let go—and run!—but she didn't want to kill him.

Not if there was a chance he could understand.

"Fine! Explain!" he cried.

"Like I said, the first secret is that there is no secret. The traits aren't magic." Zariel was silent. He kicked his feet back and forth, vainly. "But the second secret is that *that doesn't matter*. The power of the traits was never magical, but it did exist. It came from the *choices* people made. People took WISDOM because they already wanted to become WISE. And what could be wiser than that?!"

Her arm hurt, but she barely felt tired at all.

Suddenly, another realisation flamed into life in her mind. "Choosing is just pursuing what we already want! That's why the Shopkeeper always said nobody was ever defined by what they picked in the Shop! They had the power to grow *already*."

Zariel shook his head, dumbfounded. "This can't all have been for nothing."

"It *wasn't* for nothing. That's the point."

The void screeched. At any moment, it would burst and kill them both. And maybe destroy half the prelife, but that seemed oddly less important in this exact moment.

If they were ever going to escape, it had to be now.

"Zariel, it's decision time. I've told you the truth, and you can accept it or not. Either way, I'm going to run for the door. I can either bring you with me, or let you fall. What should I do?"

His expression was unreadable.

"I'm serious. Choose!"

He gazed up at her. "Kill me if you want."

"I don't want to kill you."

"Then help me up."

She closed her eyes for an instant, then nodded and pulled him out of the pit.

"Okay," she said, turning for the exit at the back of the cavern. "Let's get out of here. Maybe we can outrun the sphere, and—"

But as soon as she turned her back, he leapt for her with a murderous snarl. "You liar!" He twisted and shoved her towards the crater, a few steps away. "It *can't* be nothing!"

She screamed and instinctively grabbed at him for support as she fell backwards.

But instead of standing steady—he *could have*, he could have chosen differently—he wrapped his arms around her and sprang forward.

In that instant, the void beneath them contracted down to a tiny point and the screech became unbearable. Zariel gazed triumphantly into her eyes as they plummeted inside.

The last thing she saw was his smile.

thirty four

ALL WAS empty.

Not black, not white, not any colour at all.

Just empty.

But within the emptiness—part of the emptiness, the thing that emptiness was made of, really—was everything.

It was all there. Existing, and not existing, all at once, except . . .

With no sensation of time, Faythe simply was.

Motionless, moving through everything, which wasn't there.

All time was a single instant, and that instant lasted forever and no time at all.

Until, finally, instantaneously, everything felt like a question.

She answered immediately.

thirty five

FAYTHE HAD NO MEMORY of what had happened, or, indeed, who she was.

This wasn't as bad as it sounds. Many humans spend much of their lives aspiring to this forgetful state. Unfortunately, once achieved, it is all too fragile, and—

Memories rushed back like distant family members after a lottery win. She jerked and sat up, blinking, as she attempted to make sense of her senses.

First, she hurt. A deep, dull pain, like a headache throbbing through her whole body, and—

It was bright. And blurry. Everything was brown—no, grey, maybe?— but the blurs moved and—

It was noisy. Her brain became aware of her ears and she was overwhelmed by a cacophony of sound and—

She really, really hurt. She closed her eyes until the pain ebbed away, and, slowly, the incomprehensible noise resolved into intelligible sounds. Snippets of conversation. Yelling. Hurried footsteps. A rhythmic clicking sound, a not-quite-constant beat which slowed even as she listened.

She opened her eyes and grimaced as her brain revolted away from the devastating onslaught of information. Patiently, she waited for the blurs to gradually resolve into a picture she could understand.

This was Zariel's laboratory. Which made sense. Although, a memory of falling into the void nudged at her. *Maybe it didn't make sense?*

Somehow, she still existed. And so did the laboratory. But the scene was different. In the base of the pit, instead of a spinning void of unreality, the remains of the machine were collapsing slowly, clicking irregularly as they cooled.

"Ahgnf," she said. Her voice cracked, sounding strange to her ears. Raspy, perhaps. She tried again. "Eeaaaaanggg." Making sounds, simply to see if she could, had never been so pleasurable.

She didn't seem to be dead. That was something.

The sound of conversation was becoming more urgent. She concentrated. Someone was talking to her.

"...you okay?" said the voice. It sounded concerned.

It wasn't clear how to answer. She'd established she was pleased not to be dead—at least, *probably* pleased and *probably* not dead—but she hurt a lot and she had no idea what was happening. Did all of that add up to 'okay'?

She realised she was thinking. Which meant her brain was beginning to work properly again. *Maybe she was okay after all.* She nodded.

"Can you tell us where you came from?" asked the voice, still sounding concerned. "Nobody saw you in the chamber before the incident."

That was weird. She attempted to stand, waving away an outstretched hand. "I can do it. I'm alright."

"You don't look alright, ma'am." She stared at the speaker. A Zeraph. Not one she recognised. "You weren't moving, ma'am," he continued. "Neither of you were."

Neither of you? She followed the Zeraph's gaze.

On the ground behind her, Zariel lay completely still.

To her surprise—and slight irritation—her heart lurched at the sight of her former friend and, now, former adversary.

She grunted in pain as she bent down to touch his forehead, and—

That was not her hand.

Her breath stopped at the alien sight. Her hand—her hands, really— were not her own. They were wrinkled.

Wrinkled, dry and foreign shapes attached to equally wrinkled, dry and foreign arms. *She literally didn't know the backs of her own hands.*

"Ma'am? Are you okay?" asked the Zeraph.

She looked up. "Don't you have anything more important to do?"

He shook his head. "We're prioritising survivors. And you were closest to the accident, so you're the highest priority I have." He took her arm. "Let me take you upstairs so you can recover."

She was too weak to shake him off. "I'd like—" The rasp in her voice distracted her. She coughed, but the croak remained. "I'd like to stay here. Just for a moment."

"If you insist, ma'am."

Across the crater, a group of Zeraph were gingerly clambering down towards the machine. Everywhere she looked, people were running around without any clear purpose. There was, however, plenty of shouting.

She rubbed at her temple. It felt wrinkled, too. She glanced down at Zariel, who looked exactly the same as he had when they . . .

What had happened, exactly?

They'd fallen, and . . .

. . . she recalled the void, that brief eternal instant of everything and nothing all at once. Her brain recoiled at the effort of comprehending such an impossible experience. Already, it was fading like a dream, leaving only confused echoes behind.

She walked towards the ladder and began climbing down into the pit. Even after only a few minutes, her muscles were stronger, though they ached.

"Where are you going?" shouted another Zeraph.

She ignored him and walked over to the remains of the machine. It felt empty, lifeless, calm, a far cry from the energetic monstrosity it had been.

Her reflection was visible in the cooling metal. She leaned in to examine herself, and shivered. Her hair was white, and her face wrinkled. She moved back and forth slowly to get a better view.

It was certainly her face. But she was *old*.

In her entire prelife she had seen only one other woman who'd looked *this* old: The Shopkeeper.

She climbed back up and found the first Zeraph waiting by Zariel's body.

"He's gone," she said, flatly. She knew it to be true. He wouldn't be coming back.

The former Supplier looked peaceful. All that frenzied energy had faded into the void along with him.

"Good riddance," spat the Zeraph. "He sent my friends into that thing. Best news I've heard all day."

She smiled sadly. The Zeraph was right: Zariel's demise was good news. But she felt no triumph.

How much had Zariel shared of her experience in the void? Had he, too, witnessed the entire universe all at once?

... had she? The memory was fading.

But enough remained.

"Right!" She clapped, and turned to the Zeraph. "Who's in charge here?"

He blinked, taken aback by her sudden change of mood.

"Come on!" She snapped her fingers. "We don't have all day."

The Zeraph gestured helplessly around at the chaotic scene surrounding them. Zeraph and lab workers ran around aimlessly, performing the traditional human ritual for when nobody has a clue what they're supposed to be doing but they all want to look busy.

Faythe nodded, understanding. "Alright then," she said. "You're in charge now. See to the injured first. Then put him"—she pointed at Zariel—"somewhere safe. A nice quiet room will do for now. Then, we're going on a journey."

"Me?" The guard looked terrified.

"Consider it a promotion. What's your name, Zeraph?"

She was beginning to enjoy herself.

"Lazarus," he said. He looked around helplessly. "But what if nobody listens to me?"

She leaned over the gantry rail and clapped until she had the room's attention. "Everybody, this is Lazarus. He's in charge, and he knows what to do, so listen to him." She turned to Lazarus and winked. "I'll be upstairs—find me when you've got this place in order."

The stairs provided her with a disappointingly large amount of painful argument from her knees. Nevertheless, she was satisfied. Nobody had questioned her authority to give orders. Doubtless, her new appearance had helped. After all, everybody in the prelife knew the legend of the wise old lady who assisted humanity at the Shop.

But perhaps it was just that she'd known what to do—and then done it.

Shortly afterwards, she was sitting with her eyes closed, enjoying the warm sunshine on her face, when Lazarus found her.

He coughed politely. "Ma'am? Everything's under control downstairs."

She snapped her eyes open and grinned. "Excellent work," she said. "I knew you could do it. Next, I have two more tasks for you."

"Very good, ma'am. But first . . ." He hesitated. "Do you mind if I ask who you are?"

She smiled at him. "How about you call me . . . the Acting Shopkeeper."

He nodded to himself, as if that's the answer he'd been expecting. "What can I do for you?"

"First, is there anybody here who knows how those damnable machines work?"

Lazarus frowned. "The technicians will know. The Suppl— *Zariel* wouldn't let them leave the valley."

"Perfect. Tell them Zariel's gone, and they're free, but that the Shop would appreciate it if they set everything up how it used to be."

"They'll be happy with that." He thought for a moment. "We all will. It got quite nasty."

Above them the sky was bright, blue, and cloudless; a stark contrast to the red roiling chaos it had been last time she had seen it.

"It did," she agreed. "Next question! Do you happen to know if there are any extra traits stocked up around here?"

He grinned. "Oh, definitely. If the old boss was keen on anything, it was plentiful stocks of traits. Shall I get a group together to load up the train?"

She looked at the Zeraph with pride. "You know, Lazarus? I think you and I are going to work together very well indeed."

It wasn't long before the train was packed full of the finest human personality traits the Supplier had to offer.

This was technically true—even if the traits weren't what they purported to be, they *were* the finest the Supplier had to offer. Either way, it was a grand sight. The open crates sparkled as the traits danced in their jars, promising the full range of human experience to any who wished.

Faythe shook hands with Lazarus. "I'll send help, but, trust me, you're doing a great job. A train full of supplies, and zero massive holes in reality—if you carry on like this, you'll be the greatest Supplier of all time!"

He chuckled, albeit nervously. She didn't blame him—she remembered the terror of being unexpectedly thrust into leadership. He had surely never *dreamed* of replacing the Supplier. But if he could keep things stable for a few weeks, she would be forever grateful.

As the train sped back to the Shop, she relaxed for the first time in a long, long while. Zariel was gone—and, along with him, all of her problems, forever.

She laughed wryly. She wasn't naive enough to believe anything was so simple. But as long as she kept replacing her current problems with new problems, she'd be alright.

And, ideally, her new problems would be more along the lines of "Can you help me find POETIC SOUL?" and less like "I am creating a void to destroy the prelife in an ill-thought attempt to become a god."

She closed her eyes until the train slowed to a stop, and she awoke in the familiar surroundings of the Warehouse.

The Children must have seen the train approach, as nearly all of them were gathered around.

She opened the cabin door and the crowd gasped.

"Welcome," called the Foreman. "Um, may I ask who you are, ma'am?"

Before she could reply, Omaro pushed his way to the front of the group. "Faythe! It's you!"

Astonished whispers echoed around the Warehouse as the Children craned on tiptoes to get a better look.

Omaro ran up the steps to hug her.

"I *am* me!" she said, grinning. "As you can see, I had an eventful trip." She couldn't remember the last time she'd felt this truly unburdened. "And I have good news. Open the wagons, please, Foreman!"

The Children hooted eagerly as the Foreman obliged and the colourful glow of the traits sparkled onto the faces of the crowd.

Omaro gazed at the full wagons, and then back at her in awe. "What happened?"

"It's a long story," she said, stepping off the train and amongst the Children as they surged forward to pick up crates. "First—how are things here?"

The Child looked grim. "Security are fighting to hold the front door."

She nodded, unfazed. "Let's get this train unloaded, then, and I'll tell you the plan." She grabbed a crate from a passing worker. "I'll carry this one."

He pretended to be shocked. "Oh no you won't!" He reached out to take the crate from her. "A lady of your age needs to get her rest."

She kicked his shin and he let go of the crate.

Minutes later, she leaned on the checkout and watched as the Children charged back and forth across the concourse, rapidly restocking the nearest shelves.

Her thoughts were interrupted by a polite tap on her shoulder.

"You're back," said Jahu. He gazed at her. "It's good to see you."

"They told you I'd ... changed?"

He shook his head.

"You just recognised me?" A tear came to her eye. "Really?"

He nodded. "Of course."

They hugged until it felt too long, which turned out to be for about twenty-five seconds, and then a little longer, just because.

"There's one more big thing we've got to do," she said. "Will you help me?"

"Obviously. What is it?"

She drew a deep breath.

"Someone once told me the end of everything is in its beginning. He didn't know what he was talking about, but he was right." Jahu smiled at the memory. "This isn't quite the end yet. We need to go back to where everything started and fix it properly."

Faythe thrust open the front door of the Shop Before Life.

The verandah was filled with a tremendous brawl. Everywhere she looked, people were attacking Security, each other, and even the walls of the Shop. A burly man charged straight for the door, but he stopped at the sight of Faythe.

"Hello," she said, pleasantly.

He turned to the crowd and yelled. "It's the Shopkeeper! The Shopkeeper is back!"

To Faythe, he spoke shyly. "Are you back?"

"Yes. And I have an announcement to make. Can you help me encourage people to listen?"

He nodded, and separated a pair of smaller brawlers, before recruiting them to break up fights too.

She strolled out along the verandah as a growing army of Security and volunteers quashed the hostility around her.

For a few minutes, she stood and watched calm flowing across the field, the rumours of the legendary lady's return visibly spreading. So *this* was how Management had relied on mere rumours of their own power for so long.

Eventually, she held up the megaphone, and began to speak. "I'm sorry," she said. "I'm truly sorry for everything that's been happening. I know it's been difficult. But I have good news."

Everyone's attention was focused on her. But the part of her brain which would normally anxiously imagine how this might go wrong was quiet.

"The problems with the Supplier have been resolved, and we will shortly reopen the Shop."

At this, deafening cheers filled the field—loud, raucous, and thrilled. She waited before waving the megaphone for silence once more.

"But there is one thing we must do first. And I need to ask for your help—from all of you."

The burly man shouted from behind her on the verandah. "Whatever you want, Shopkeeper!" Others cried out in agreement.

"Thank you," she said. "It's a big job, and we have to all do it together. We're making a trip to see Management."

Next to her, Omaro's jaw dropped. She hadn't told him this part of her plan.

"I will lead the way, but I need you to join and support me. And by the time we get back, I promise the Shop will be ready to open. Even now a fresh train of supplies will be on its way."

"Are you sure about this?" muttered Omaro.

She nodded. "I'm sure." She took up the megaphone one final time. "Are you with me?"

The burly man, and many others, cried out together. "We are!"

Enough talk. It was time for action.

She climbed down from the verandah. Immediately, people thronged around her. She began to walk towards the Road, expecting those in front to part to let her through.

Quickly, a guard formed around her, walking just ahead to make a path.

And so, the slow charge of humanity to Management's castle began. Faythe spent the journey walking at the front of the crowd, happily chatting with the many who came, filled with curiosity, to talk to the Shopkeeper. She listened to the stories of their prelives, affirmed their dreams of life on Earth, and spread her instructions for what to do when they arrived at Management's castle.

Even the narrow path under the hills to the castle turned out to not be a problem. They easily filled it with lights, moving the boulders down and out of the way, and overpowering the bored guard before he knew what was happening.

Within hours of arriving at the narrow passageway, the castle was filled with tens, hundreds, thousands of people.

As Faythe had requested, they rounded up the pretenders of 'Management', and gathered them together on the grass outside. A circle of people surrounded them with their arms locked together.

Eva was the last to be found. She cursed and spat as she was dragged out of the castle, and shivered as the people thrust her onto the grass. "You're forcing me to make contact with the ground, like an animal," she hissed, twisting awkwardly and trying to keep her fine dress from touching the dirt.

Faythe ignored her disgusted glares and inspected the twenty-four people who called themselves Management. "Management. Perhaps you recognise me."

"You're the girl Apprentice," said Pluton, sounding resigned.

Aaron and Gabriel exchanged looks of open-eyed astonishment.

"That's correct," said Faythe. "And currently, I'm also the Acting Shopkeeper. You might have guessed from my presence that Zariel is no longer a threat."

"Couldn't you have told us this inside?" whined Eva.

"Eva," said Pluton. "Can't you see it's over?"

Faythe smiled. "Indeed it is. All of you are responsible for what happened. You pulled Zariel's strings for your own laziness and entertainment. And you sat back when he threatened to destroy everything. Your only concern was for your own benefit, so you could live indulgent prelives on the backs of the rest of humanity. But, as Pluton says, those times are over."

"Get it over with, then," said Pluton. "Are you going to kill us? Throw us into Zariel's machine?"

He almost sounded eager. Faythe pitied him. "Kill you? No, I don't think killing you is the answer."

"Then what is?"

"It's time you learned what it means to be human. In particular, how it feels to grow and change." She took a deep breath, and then smiled. "You're all going to come work at the Shop."

thirty six

HAPPINESS IS infuriatingly unpredictable. Deep, true happiness can suddenly spring from unexpected sources, and long-awaited joys can be strangely empty once they finally arrive.

Luckily for the vast, frustrated throng of people, the reopening of the Shop lived up to their hopes. They poured inside, eager and thrilled to grasp onto their chance to live—at long, long last.

But perhaps nobody was happier than Beris, who nearly cried with joy on discovering he had twenty-four unexpected students to train in the ways of retail. His delight peaked moments later, when Faythe asked him to calculate how long it would take for the queue to reduce to normal levels. He muttered intently about flow differentials and extra shift variations until she gave up and went away.

For a time, relief and delight were everywhere. The Children smiled constantly, grinning wider whenever they saw Faythe. They were happier than she'd seen them since . . . well, since the Shopkeeper had gone.

She tried not to think about what that meant, exactly.

Faythe herself was content, but exhausted. She felt obliged to remain as visible as possible, greeting customers at the door, reassuring them that the Shop's troubles were over, and helping on the checkouts whenever more hands were needed—which was essentially all the time.

As evening came on the third day, Jahu came to find her. "You need a break. Sit with me in the Gardens?" he asked.

"I'd like that."

They sat in her favourite spot, beneath the Viewing Platform, surrounded by colour all the way down to the glittering river. As always, the Earth meandered gently across the sky above.

Jahu glanced over. "Have you decided what to do about the traits yet?"

"Do?" She frowned.

"About them not being real."

She hadn't talked to anyone about this yet. But she had a simple answer. "I realised—while I was with Zariel—that they *are* real. They're just not magical."

"Fair enough."

She felt a rush of gratitude that her friend didn't push for more. A gentle breeze whistled through the flowers around them.

Everything was right, in that moment.

Eventually, after a comfortable silence, Jahu shifted again, this time nervously. "Can I ask you a question? That void . . . what happened in there?"

"You can ask, but I'm not sure I can tell you." She smiled affectionately as he wrinkled his face. "Don't look like that. I don't understand it myself."

"Understand what, though?"

"It's all memories I can't even describe." She paused, trying to recall sensations which didn't fit into the dimensions she currently existed in. "Except for one thing . . ."

He was staring, fascinated. "What was it?"

"It was like the whole universe asked me a question. And I knew I had to answer the right way."

"What was the question?" He looked thoughtful. "No, wait—it's impossible to say, right?" She nodded. "Then what was your answer?"

She looked him right in the eye. "I said this: 'No, but I'm okay with that'." Her old friend nodded. *He'd figure it out.* "Now you know all of my secrets."

Just then, the Gardener emerged from a nearby bush. "More secrets in my Garden?"

He looked from Faythe to Jahu and back again. With a sudden jolt, she realised she hadn't re-introduced herself to him. He was probably wondering who she was.

"It's me," she said. "Faythe."

The Gardener looked confused. "I know that! Who else would you be?"

She smiled. *Of course.*

The old man scratched his head. A butterfly landed on his hand and he smiled at it affectionately. "Want to let an old man in on these secrets?"

"It's something I learned about the Shop while I was travelling." She gave him a look of warning. "You can't tell anyone this."

He nodded. "Don't tell anyone you went travelling. Got it."

"Not that!" She threw up her hands. "I meant not to tell anyone what I'm about to say."

He winked.

She rolled her eyes. "I'll take that as a yes." She hesitated. But if anyone deserved to know, it was the Gardener. "It turns out the traits here don't actually do anything. There's no magic."

"Oh, *that.*" The Gardener looked disappointed. "I thought you'd learned something new."

"You knew?!" Her mouth was agape.

"Obviously," he said. "You can't be here as long as I have without learning a few things. Honestly, you could have asked me ages ago." He almost looked hurt. "Nobody ever asks me anything that isn't about gardens."

Faythe wasn't sure she'd ever be able to close her mouth again. "This could have saved a lot of trouble," she said.

"Could it?" The old man's eyes glinted mischievously.

Her brow wrinkled. What if she *had* known about the traits earlier? Would she have believed it, or would she have preferred the comfortable lie, like Zariel?

And even if she had known, what would she have done differently?

"I have no idea," she said with a shrug.

"Me neither," said the Gardener. "You'd think predicting the past would be easier than predicting the future, but it isn't."

Jahu held up a finger. "Okay, I could tell that you didn't want me to ask earlier, but now we're talking about it, I have to. If the traits aren't magic, how do they actually work?"

The Gardener looked at her expectantly.

Faythe turned to her friend. "My theory is that it's all about choice," she said. "Someone picks HAPPY-GO-LUCKY because that's the kind of person they want to be."

"Or that they already *are*," added the Gardener.

The sun was sinking, and turning the sky a deep red. The trio gazed down at the river below.

"I get it," said Jahu, after some thought. "Choosing SMART doesn't bring you knowledge, but it encourages you in that direction."

The Gardener smiled. "Funny that it took you so long to figure out."

"Hey!" said Jahu, affronted.

"Not you," said the Gardener.

"You're saying this should have been obvious?" said Faythe, with a frown.

"Didn't you ever wonder why people had personalities in the prelife already?"

"I . . . suppose I didn't."

"You thought people only got a personality when they chose it at the Shop? What made them choose, if not their personality?"

"I figured they just wanted to choose things."

The Gardener shrugged. "Way I see it, wanting to choose something is much the same as having already chosen it. Anyway . . . good talking." He tipped his hat towards Faythe. "Glad things are getting back to normal around here . . . *Shopkeeper*."

After he left, there was a long silence.

"So," Jahu began.

"Don't."

"I have to."

"You don't."

Silence again. She glanced at Jahu, who was doing a terrible impression of keeping a straight face. "I'm *not* the Shopkeeper."

He held up his hands in protest. "I never said you were!"

"You were thinking it."

He stuck out his lip. "I was thinking, someone's got to be here. And everyone knows the legend of the wise old Shopkeeper. And, well . . ." He trailed off.

"Maybe the Gardener should be in charge."

"Do you think he'd want to be?" asked Jahu.

"Obviously not."

She sighed. "I *know*. I was the Apprentice. And I grew old, somehow. But I don't know what that means. Or what to do."

"Are you sure? You really don't know what to do?"

She thought about it. The answer was obvious.

"No. But I suppose I'm okay with that."

Weeks later, Faythe was walking to the Gardens once more.

She passed Pluton and Eva as they worked on the checkouts. Pluton scowled as he saw her, but she got the impression his heart wasn't really in it. As soon as he thought she wasn't looking, he resumed chatting to a customer with a broad smile across his face.

She grinned. Meeting other humans seemed to be good for Management.

The last of the people in white had left yesterday. After working at Management's castle for so many centuries they had mostly forgotten there was a world outside. They'd needed to relearn that they had the ability to make choices. Many had chosen to pass through to Earth, but a few had decided to explore the prelife first.

She dodged around a little girl who was standing in her way. She gave Faythe a look of recognition, and Faythe returned her smile and moved on, stealing an automatic glance into the girl's basket as she passed. SELF-SACRIFICIAL, COMPASSIONATE, and SEEKS TO UNDERSTAND PEOPLE. All good choices.

The reports from Lazarus at the Supplier were excellent. They were nearly back to full production, and morale had never been higher. They'd even planted a tree in the Complex, although the residents didn't much like it.

Her brand-new Shop Before Life ID badge reflected brightly in the evening sunlight as she stepped outside. Beris had been thrilled when she'd suggested the idea, and had consulted widely on the design. A vast number of Children had expressed no particular preference, and the result was a simple badge. But—and this was surprisingly important—if any staff member ever found themselves having to prove their identity to a suspicious security guard at a possible god's house, their prelives would be considerably easier.

As she crossed the Viewing Platform she passed a plaque they'd put up: *In Memory of The Shopkeeper*. Customers were confused by it—after all, the Shopkeeper was right there—but every day Faythe and many of the Children took a moment there to remember.

The rest of the Viewing Platform was quiet. Lately there had been fewer customers in the early evening. A rumour had spread through the field and around the prelife that the earlier in the day you passed through, the earlier in the day you'd be born on Earth. People figured it would give them more time to adjust before their first night's sleep. Faythe suspected it didn't *quite* work like that, but she appreciated that it made her evenings more relaxed.

Most days she spent this time giving personal attention to the few remaining customers, but today she was taking time for herself.

She'd gathered a pile of stones, and was happily toying with them, stacking them up in a neat pyramid. It occupied her hands while her mind wandered. And it liked to wander. There had been a lot to fill it lately, and it needed moments like this to empty itself.

A short time later, Jahu approached. "Can I sit?"

She nodded. They sat in silence for a time.

"How was your day?" she asked, finally.

"Good," he said.

"And you're getting on well with the rest of Security?"

He nodded.

"Good," she said.

They drifted into silence. She waited patiently until Jahu spoke again. "There's something I have to ask."

He sounded apprehensive.

"Please." She put the stone down and folded her hands in her lap. All of a sudden, she felt nervous.

"I don't have a place here, not really. I think it's time for me to go. To Earth." He choked slightly. "Will you come with me?"

He awaited the inevitable answer with obvious sadness. She reached out and rested her hand on top of his. "Thanks for asking, but I'm going to stay."

He nodded. "I knew you would."

"The Shopkeeper used to talk about sacrifice a lot. I get it now."

"You think the Shop's important enough? Even knowing what you know now?"

"More so."

A little boy walked past on the platform, swinging his arms happily. He saw Faythe and stopped, startled. She waved, and he shyly returned the wave before continuing on his way.

"You don't have to go to Earth, you know," she said.

"What would I do here?"

She looked right at him. "Anything you like." She gave him a sly smile. "Unless it turns out you're totally useless, which is possible, now I think about it . . ."

He pushed her hand away, but his eyes shone.

"Stay," she said.

"I'll think about it," he replied.

Above them, the Earth spun slowly in the sky, calling out to anybody who wished to listen: come, if you like, and live.

You can be whatever you want.

acknowledgements

I'm lucky to have many incredible people in my life, and while I'd love to individually introduce each of them to the entire world and shout things like "this person is FANTASTIC, and you should know and love them too", I would like to highlight just a few who helped me to share the world of the prelife with you.

Chief among these excellent people is Sienna Tristen, whose boundless energy, encouragement, enthusiasm and skills—as both a writer and type-setter—played a crucial role in getting me through the endless mire that is creating a novel. (She writes amazing books, too: see siennatristen.com for more.)

Huge appreciation also goes to the talented Tom Humberstone, who did such a tremendous job extracting the prelife straight from my imagination and onto the cover. Please admire his work and send him appreciation (and commissions!) at tomhumberstone.com.

Thanks to Salomé Jones for her assistance with editing. Without her help this book would have been considerably more annoying to read, I promise.

I can't express enough gratitude to my wonderful beta readers who gave up their time, energy and talents to help hone my ramblings into a much better story. Thank you to Gemma Scott, Anna Fruen, Tina Hannemann, Claire Nyles Suer, Nat Smith, Rick Brewin, Kimberley Owen, Sarah Topping and Valerie Wernet.

There are literally dozens more people I would love to parade around in gratitude, but I must mention Simone Grace Seol, Karolina Frydrych, Avi Silver, and particularly Ellen Schwaller, who put up with my endless sighing at my past self's abysmal writing in every coffee shop in the city.

Many thanks to the delightful Emilie Wapnick, Erica Buist, Harriet Allner, Rosemary & Nick Lees, the Quizmasters, all at the Puttytribe, and to John, John, Albert, Tom and Smita. Your friendship and encouragement means the world to me.

Love to Ian, Jo and Jill.

And all the remaining love in the world goes to my mum, who is so supportive and wonderful that I cry whenever I take it in.

Lastly—and most importantly—thanks to you. I've lived with this story for a long time, and it means the world that you've joined me on this journey. Do stay in touch.

Love, Neil

Join the *Occasional Email Experience* at

walkingoncustard.com/mailing

to receive irregular stories, thoughts
and updates from Neil Hughes.

Or contact: neil@walkingoncustard.com

(Neil likes it when people say hello.)
(He reads every email, and replies to as many
as possible.)

Walking on Custard & the Meaning of Life: A Guide for Anxious Humans

Neil Hughes lived with anxiety for years. And now he's written a book about it. Unfortunately, his Inner Critic isn't best pleased with this decision.

This rollercoaster ride of hilarious real-life stories, inventive fantasy fiction, and badly-drawn graphs has helped many people to be less anxious and more happy.

Part-self-help, part-autobiography, part-fantasy-fiction, this unique and useful book also features the very first appearance of the Shop Before Life.

From practical advice for emotional management to laugh-out-loud stories, *Walking on Custard & the Meaning of Life* has something for everybody.

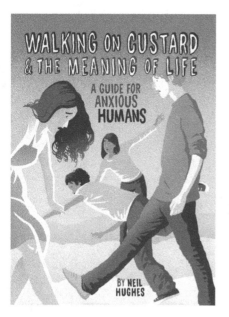

"A brave book and a noble one because, really, what better thing can a person do with their own suffering than to use it to try and help others. It's on my read-this-again shelf."
Nathan Filer, author of *The Shock of the Fall*

"A humor-filled and useful guide for anxiety . . . disarmingly relatable."
Publishers Weekly

"Must read for anyone suffering from anxiety—minor or major, it doesn't matter. It's helpful, funny, and insightful."
Tragically Dull Adventures of an Almost Librarian

Neil Hughes finds it difficult to describe himself, especially in the third person. He's spent time as a comedian, writer, computer programmer, travelling speaker, physicist and mental health campaigner, and now he's generally pretty tired and trying not to worry too much about everything.

After many years living all over the place, he has returned to the north-west of England where—between answering questions about mental health & custard and attending pub quizzes—he does various other things that help people to be happy. He wishes there was a way to say this without sounding so painfully cheesy.

CPSIA information can be obtained
at www.ICGtesting.com
Printed in the USA
LVHW020250260423
745382LV00022B/185

9 780993 166846